I0788179

Glowing
Heart

This is a work of fiction. Names, characters, places, and incidents either are the product of the author's imagination or are used fictitiously. Any resemblance to actual persons, living or dead, events, or locales is entirely coincidental.

Copyright © 2022 Whitney Morris

First paperback edition April 2022

Published by WRLMorris Publishing
Book design by Whitney Morris

ISBN 978-1-916935-02-0 (paperback)
ISBN 978-1-916935-03-7 (hardback)

www.wrlmorris.com

For Melody

My lovely little bookworm,
you are the reason I kept going

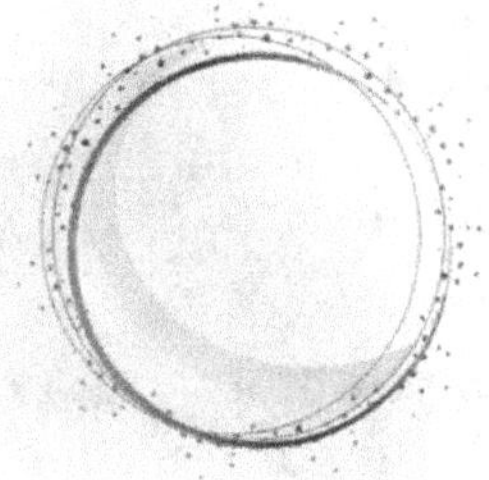

Prologue

Laxus

eaves crunched under Laxus' feet as he ran clutching his injured wing. He weaved his way through the forest, the tightly knit clusters of trees making it difficult to see where he was going. All he knew was that he needed to get as far away from his village as possible. He was the target, and he didn't want to put anyone else in danger. Pushing past branches he tried to take flight, only to tumble to the floor. There was no way he could fly like this – his wing was too badly damaged. A twig snapped behind him. He flinched. She'd found him.

"There's no point in running, boy," said a soft, melodic voice. "There's nowhere for you to go." A tall bird-like woman stepped out from behind a tree. Her yellow, hawkish eyes peered at him. She stepped forward opening her black wings, revealing their magnificent span. It wouldn't matter if he could fly. His delicate pixie wings could not out-flap those gigantic eagle ones.

"I will never stop running." He shouted shuffling backwards, "I won't let you take what I protect."

She lifted her talon as the yellow stone around her neck glowed. "There is no one that can stand up to my power."

Laxus knew that wasn't true. There were three beings capable of opposing her and he knew where one of them was – he just needed to make it out alive.

She fired a shadow ball at him. He dove to the side, and as she ran at him, he twisted around, throwing a bag of pixie dust at her. She screeched, flapping her wings as the bag burst in her face.

Laxus took the opportunity to scramble to his feet and run. Frantically scanning his surroundings, he pushed his way through the wilderness. His legs were sore and his throat dry. It wouldn't be long until she caught up with him again. He needed to find a way to lose her.

A screech echoed through the forest. Laxus looked up. The shadow of a giant bird loomed over the forest. Another approached it. This one was too large to be a normal bird – it must be her. Could she control other feathered-fowl? He was at a major disadvantage if this was true. He needed to divert her attention, so she looked for him elsewhere. The right kind of pixie dust could transport you anywhere. He didn't have any on him, but she didn't know that. A squawk sounded above him. He'd been spotted. Running towards a bush he threw some pixie dust over himself and shrank to the size of a moth. He flew into the bush and burrowed down to the bottom, camouflaged by the leaves.

The ground shook as she landed. A huge arm brushed over the bush. Laxus held his breath. He hated how vast everything was when he was this size. The arm disappeared and he could hear was the rustle of leaves blowing in the breeze.

"My Queen. I can no longer see the boy running through the forest," announced another female. This voice was gentler.

Another loud screech filled the forest. "Damn pixie dust. He used it to escape."

"Don't worry, my Queen, we will find him again."

"You better hope we find him. Get back in the skies and search for him."

"Yes, my Queen."

There was a loud whoosh, and everything became quiet

again. Laxus didn't dare move. There was no way of knowing for sure if she was gone. She also had help. Perhaps, another being like herself. With all his extensive reading, he'd never come across a creature quite like her.

Laxus listened to the sounds of the forest for hours. After the sun set, he finally emerged from his hiding spot. Growing back to full size, he sprinkled some healing pixie dust on his wing. With a bit more time he should be able to fly again. He walked towards the veil. Help could be found on the other side. His next obstacle would be getting past the queen's stone guards.

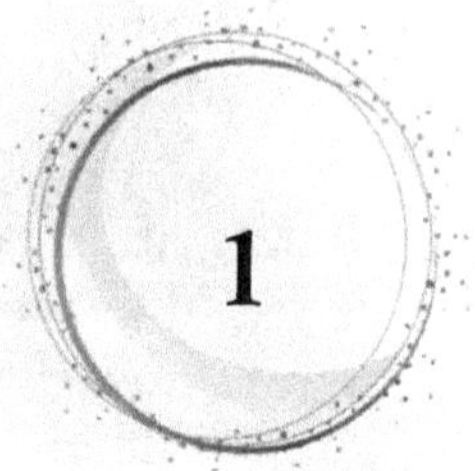

The Pixie Protector

Mellissa

I stood by the door watching the clock. Victoria sure knew how to waste my time. The school day had ended twenty minutes ago but she was flirting with some guy and I had to wait for her. This happened a lot. Victoria was tall and slim like a model with gorgeous long blonde hair and she knew how to act all girly and sweet when it suited her. Everybody loved her. They didn't know how harsh and brutal she could be. Nobody here knew Victoria the way I did. She was currently batting her eyelashes at the latest guy attempting to chat her up. I rolled my eyes. There was always a new dude asking her out. It was likely she would say yes, but quickly get bored. Then a new chap would try his luck. It was a vicious cycle that she loved to repeat.

My phone buzzed and I groaned as I read a text from Harkura.

You're late for combat training.

I wished my guardians would coordinate better. Harkura should be sending these texts to Victoria, not me. It wasn't my fault I was late. They were the ones that didn't allow me to walk home alone. My phone buzzed again.

Remember you have a council meeting tomorrow and dance lessons with Daniel.

I should never have got him a phone, then he'd only be

able to tell me these things in person. I sighed as I typed my reply.

I haven't forgotten. It's Victoria holding me up.

Three months had passed since I'd handed the moon crystal over to the sea king and everything had returned to normal – well as normal as it could be having discovered there was an entire magical world hidden behind a veil. I was also heir to the elf throne with no idea how to be regal. That was where Daniel came in. He'd been leading the elves long before I'd been discovered and was now my chief of staff. We'd set up a new settlement in the magical world: Urbem Folium, the city of leaves. Apart from that, I was your average eighteen-year-old trying to get through the last few months of school.

"Hey, Mellissa," yelled Victoria. "Stop daydreaming, we're running late." She had her hands on her hips and was looking at me as if I was the one holding her up. What a nerve! I'd just spent half an hour bored out of my mind waiting for her. I grabbed my bag off the floor and shuffled over to her in a sulk.

"Stop dragging your feet," she said as we walked to her car, "and you shouldn't slouch. It's not becoming of a queen."

I slouched even more. "On this side of the veil, I'm a nobody, so I can do what I want."

"It doesn't matter what side of the veil we're on, you are Queen of the Elves and you should act accordingly."

"Technically I'm not queen yet."

She rolled her eyes. "The date of your coronation has been set. Come summer you will officially be crowned queen. You may as well get used to it."

I looked down at my hands. She had a point. The idea of me as a queen seemed crazy but in a couple of months, it would be a reality. We got in the car and Victoria drove me home. It seemed pointless to drive to my house from school as it was only a five-minute walk, but Victoria was insistent. According to her, it was safer, and I was less likely to be ambushed. The leprechauns had signed a peace treaty and were integrating their society to align with the rest of the magic world. They no longer wished to harm me, so I wasn't sure who'd attack me. However, it was pointless to argue as it was two against one. Both my guardians were obsessive about my safety. Victoria pulled up outside my house and watched as I walked up to the door. She drove off once I'd gone inside. As I turned to close the door, I almost jumped out of my skin as a young boy appeared on my doorstep.

I knew he wasn't human just by looking at him. He had curly cerulean hair and pink eyes, and his olive skin shimmered in the light – but it was the translucent wings on his back that caught my eye with luminous hues of every colour, a little like mother-of-pearl. It was like nothing I'd ever seen before. I gazed at him in awe wondering why a fairy was on my doorstep. He staggered forwards, clutching his side. I quickly put my arm out to steady him and realised he was bleeding. I bent down to assess the wound. "Are you all right?" It didn't look good and healing magic was not my forte.

"I'm okay, thanks, Your Majesty," he said, "My wounds are insignificant. Nothing a little pixie dust won't fix."

How could he say that while he was bleeding? Then again magical healing did make serious wounds seem like nothing. "Who are you and what are you doing here?" I asked, "Are you one of the Fay?"

"My name is Laxus," he replied, bowing to me, "I'm a Pixie and I need your help."

"What do you need my help with?"

"A great darkness has awoken and if you don't heed my warning everything could be destroyed."

I stepped back, wide-eyed. That was unexpected. It was clear something bad had happened to him. And where was this boy's parents? Someone this young shouldn't be crossing the veil on his own.

"What do you mean everything could be destroyed?" I asked, "I thought with Kadon gone, the world was at peace."

"I'm sorry to inform you there's a much greater evil out there than Kadon." Laxus looked around the hallway as if checking for something. He leant towards me. "You are the only one who can protect me from her."

I rubbed my forehead. "You're not making any sense.

Where are your parents and how did you get here?" I didn't know what to make of him. I also wanted to know the difference between the Fay and the Pixies, but I didn't think now was the time for such an enquiry. I rubbed my chin. He'd clearly travelled to the human world to find me. Surely there was someone back in the magical world that could have assisted him. If the world really was in danger, the council would surely have informed me about it. This boy couldn't possibly know something they didn't.

"I forgot how new you are to this. It's obvious that you're not very knowledgeable about pixies."

My mouth fell open at his remark. He was right but I didn't need a kid pointing this out to me. I'd tried to learn as much as I could but there was so much to cover. I was still learning about the elves and I was meant to be their leader.

"Your Majesty is that you?" Harkura's voice came from the kitchen.

Laxus shrank to the size of a butterfly and flew around leaving a trail of shiny dust. I blinked a few times unable to see what the difference was between a pixie and a fairy. He appeared to have the same abilities as all the fairies I had met. "We'll talk later," he whispered in my ear as he flew past my head.

I didn't get a chance to reply as he'd vanished just as Harkura came into the hallway to greet me.

Harkura inquired how my day was and then rushed me off to get changed so we could start our session. Harkura had taken over my training since Greg returned home to become the new elder after his father's death. I missed being coached by Greg. He was never as harsh on me as Harkura. Now, I had a very strict schedule: Harkura made me run every morning, pushing me to my limits. It was hard but I couldn't deny that this exhausting training worked. My skills had improved massively thanks to him.

As I got changed out of my school uniform and into my joggers and t-shirt, I thought about the pixie boy. He hadn't seemed like a threat. He'd asked for my protection. Perhaps, I should tell Harkura about the encounter. He'd grown up in the magic world so he should know about pixies.

Once changed, I wandered towards the back garden where Harkura was waiting for me but as I walked out of the back door, balls of fire flew at me. I screamed, quickly putting up a barrier, deflecting them.

As Harkura came running at me, I spun around releasing a pulse of light. Harkura absorbed the attack in a wall of fire, twirling the flames around his arm, and then throwing them at me. I squealed and quickly teleported myself out of firing range, and then slammed my hands on the ground as rapidly growing vines sprung up. I wrapped them around Harkura lifting him off the ground.

"Harkura what the hell? A little warning next time!"

"An attacker is not going to warn you before they kill you," he yelled, "You need to be prepared for any surprise attacks. Expect the unexpected." He always had to go to extremes. Why did my theoretical attacker always want to kill me? Maybe they just wanted to steal a piece of my hair as a trophy.

"That doesn't make sense. How can I expect the unexpected?"

I was answered by Harkura blasting his way out of the vines and throwing a spiral of fire at me. Rolling out the way, I spun my legs around, throwing rays of light his way. Unfortunately, Harkura was a brilliant acrobat and simply flipped over my attack while shooting a row of fireballs at me. I put a protection bubble around myself which absorbed the fire.

Harkura had me now. I was trapped inside my own bubble, the moment I took it down, he'd have me beat. I smiled to myself. The earth was my element. And this fight wasn't over yet. I put my hand to the ground again and focused. Sending a pulse of magic through the earth, everything shook and the ground opened up below Harkura as he fell into a massive hole. I lowered my bubble. Now, I had him beat.

In retaliation, Harkura launched himself in the air using his fire and sent a flaming kick at me, knocking me to the ground. He attempted to punch me, his hand engulfed in flames, stopping short of my face.

"You did very well, my Queen," he said, putting his fire out and helping me up. "Your manipulation of the earth is getting better, and you didn't overly rely on teleportation."

I dusted the dirt off myself. "I may be improving but I still can't beat you."

"The day will come eventually. I was thinking we could have a five-minute break and then work on your flying"

We walked back to the kitchen and I sat down at the table. "Harkura, you know I can only hover half a foot off the ground. I haven't been able to fly since I fought Kadon."

"You'll never get any better if you don't practice," he said handing me a glass of water.

I rolled my eyes. I don't know how many times he'd told me that. Now that he wasn't attacking me, I could talk to him about my odd encounter with the pixie boy. "I know this might sound a bit random, but what do you know about pixies?"

"They are rare creatures," he said, "much like the Fay but they tend to have a longer life span. I'm afraid, I don't know much more. Maybe you should ask Lord Ainsworth next time you see him. Why do you ask?"

"Oh, no reason, and seriously, just call him Greg." I slumped into my chair pouting. Why was that always his response when I wanted to learn something that wasn't combat related? I didn't like being told to consult Greg. He'd been busy with elder things and I felt like I was in the way whenever I asked him about stuff. I also needed to prove I could get by without always running to Greg for help. As Victoria had pointed out, I was going to be queen soon, so I had to figure stuff out on my own.

"Shall we get back to training then?" Harkura stood by the back door.

We spent the next thirty minutes training. Harkura kept trying to get me to fly but I just couldn't pull it off. It was frustrating that I still didn't fully understand my powers, but I seemed to be getting there slowly. I had much better control of my abilities. I could grow any plant I wanted from nothing and could shape the earth to suit my needs. Harkura had also taught me hand to hand combat. His fighting style suited me well. We were around the same size and he was experienced with taking on opponents more athletic than he was. However, I wasn't an acrobat like him, so I couldn't pull off his flips and high jumps, but I was a lot stronger than before.

We ended training with a meditation session. Just as I was feeling relaxed, Harkura handed me a file of papers. "You need to go over these before tomorrow's council meeting."

Great more homework to be added to the pile. I skulked off upstairs to bore myself to death reading.

I sat at my desk looking over my English homework. Sometimes I wondered why I bothered keeping up a normal human existence. There was enough work for me as it was without adding schoolwork on top. Things would be a lot easier if I simply embraced being an elf, but that idea scared me. A part of me wanted to hold on to my old life just in case it turned out they'd made a mistake and I wasn't really heir to the elf throne. I knew it was silly thinking like that. The fact I could use the crystal was proof enough I was the right person.

I was trying to think of a suitable rhyme when the boy from earlier appeared beside me. I jumped out of my chair almost tripping over my own feet. "Where did you come from?" I finally understood why everyone was startled whenever I teleported in.

"I flew in through the window. You're not very observant are you?"

I looked over at my window. It was only slightly ajar. "My window isn't wide enough for you to fit through."

"I came in before growing to full size. I wanted to go unnoticed."

First, he tells me I'm unobservant and then tells me that he'd shrunk to go unnoticed. Instead of dwelling on this contradiction, I decided to let it go and find out what he wanted. "Why don't you want to be noticed?" I asked.

"There's an evil bird woman after me, and thus, I'd like to request sanctuary from the elf queen. I'm lead to believe that's you."

"I'm not officially queen, yet, but yes, that's me. So, why is there a bird-woman after you? To be honest I didn't know there were bird people."

Laxus flicked his head back, brushing his blue curls aside. "I don't believe they're actually called 'bird people'. I couldn't find her race in the books I own. What I do know is that she has giant black feathered wings and is extremely dangerous."

I put my hand on my forehead as I tried to make sense of what he'd said. He was asking me to protect him from a creature I didn't even know existed. I hadn't realised people could request sanctuary from me. What could this boy have possibly done to need my protection and why was he alone? "I'm not sure what's happened to you but maybe if I get Harkura, he can help." I walked towards the door.

"No, you can't." he cried jumping up and grabbing my arm. "You're the only one who can be trusted." His big eyes filled with worry.

What could be so terrible to make him mistrust others so much? I took his hands and knelt down to his height. "Okay, but you need to tell me exactly what's going on. You said your name was Laxus right?"

He nodded.

"So, who exactly is this person you're running from and why is she after you?"

He looked around the room as if to check we were really alone. "I guess I should start at the beginning."

He sat in the chair at my desk as I sat on the end of my bed across from him.

"You already know the story of how the life crystals came into existence?"

I nodded.

"Well, there's another part of the story that's not widely known. The life crystals embody an enormous amount of light energy designed to bring harmony to the world. In order for the life crystals to do their job, they themselves need to be balanced, so, an equal amount of dark energy was needed.

Three dark stones were then formed: air, sea and land stones."

I leaned forward. "Wait, so there are three stones full of dark energy as strong as the life crystals. Why have I never heard about this?" Surely what he was saying couldn't be true? There's no way that I wouldn't have been informed about theses stones during my training.

"It was the wish of the gods that they be kept secret. The dark stones weren't designed to ever be used …they are pure evil. No matter the intention of the user they could never be used for good. They were solely created as a balance to the life crystals."

I tried to open my mouth to speak but no words came out. How could the gods make something so powerful and expect no one to use them? They were asking for trouble. I knew there were tons of people that would love to steal my power, they just didn't dare try.

"Each stone was given to a creature as its protector," Laxus continued. "These entities protected the stones and ensured they were never used. As each protector has such a long life span, the stones haven't passed through as many hands as the crystals. This helped keep them a secret. Also, they're encased in special boxes to shield their magic presence, so their power cannot be sensed."

I pressed my finger to the side of my forehead. I was having flashbacks about the discovery of the heart crystal and a headache was forming. The idea that there was a stone full of dark magic equivalent to the heart crystal worried me, but considering what had happened over the last few months, I'd learnt that anything was possible. "Even if this is all true, what's it got to do with this bird woman that's after you? Surely you can't be a protector, you're only a child?"

Laxus sat up straight and crossed his arms. "I am not a child. I will have you know that I'm much older than you, my dear. I'm two hundred and four years old."

"You're how old?"

"Pixies have extremely long lives and don't reach adulthood until the age of three hundred. The only other creatures that I know of with a similar life span to us live in the ocean."

I shook my head. This boy was a walking contradiction. He may be over two hundred but from what he just said in pixie terms he was a child. I ran my fingers through my hair trying to focus on the danger in claimed to be in. "So, what you're telling me is that you're one of these protectors, and this bird woman wants the stone you have?"

"That's exactly what I'm saying. There's another thing. This woman is also a protector of a dark stone like me. The pendant she wears around her neck is the air stone. I don't know why but she's abused her position and taken the stone for herself."

"How do I know what you're saying is true and you don't have some alternative reason to get close to me?" Part of me hoped what he said wasn't true. He did, however, seem genuine, but I had to be careful. Things weren't always what they seemed when it came to magic.

"Your Majesty, please, you must believe me. If this woman gets the stone I protect, it will destroy the balance of the universe, and cause absolute chaos."

"Prove to me that the dark stones exist, and I will help you protect it from this woman." I figured, if he really had a dark stone, he'd surely be able to show me. It would be a lot easier to believe if I could see it. After all, I didn't know anything about him, so I couldn't just blindly take his word.

"Very well." He put his hands together and they started to glow. When he pulled them apart, he produced a box. Taking a deep breath, he opened it. Inside the box was a green stone surrounded by shadows and I instantly felt the darkness being emitted. The power within it was the complete opposite to the energising power I felt from the heart crystal. I stepped closer to look at it. The heart crystal glowed violently. It was reacting to the stone and didn't like its presence. Laxus quickly shut the box. And as he swished his wrist, the box magically went back to wherever he kept it.

"Do you believe me now?" He asked

"I've never felt so much dark energy concentrated in one spot. I didn't expect the heart crystal to react so strongly."

"The stone I protect is the land stone. It's the dark stone that balances the heart crystal. They should definitely be kept apart from one another."

"Yes, we won't let them get close again." I shook my head, story curls falling into my eyes. "I still don't know what to do about this."

Suddenly my bedroom door flew open. Harkura rushed in, his sapphire eyes intense. He pushed me away from Laxus and I toppled backwards onto my bed. "Who are you and what do you want with the queen?" demanded Harkura with fireballs in hand, aimed at Laxus.

I jumped up and grabbed Harkura's arm. "Don't hurt him, he's just a kid."

"He's a pixie, they're much older than they look." Harkura's eyes were ablaze with magic. He pushed closer to Laxus who was pressed up against the back of my desk chair, his pink eyes wide with terror.

I stepped in front of Harkura putting up my hands. "Calm down. He came to me for help. He isn't a threat."

Harkura glared at Laxus over my shoulder. "I sensed a dark presence moments ago."

I turned to the pixie. "Tell him what you told me."

Laxus looked at me with pleading eyes.

I placed my hand gently on his shoulder. "He's my guardian. The heart crystal wouldn't have chosen him if he couldn't be trusted."

I forced Harkura to extinguish his flames and we both sat on the end of my bed as Laxus retold his tale of the dark stones.

Harkura brushed his hand through his black hair. "This is troubling."

"That's an understatement." I said, "When you sensed the power of the dark stone, you came hurtling in here ready to attack a twelve-year-old."

"He's hardly a twelve-year-old. He's probably well over a hundred."

"I'm two hundred and four," said Laxus puffing out his chest.

"How did you know he was a pixie?" I asked, "I thought he was a fairy when I first saw him."

"His aura is different to a fairy," replied Harkura.

I rubbed my chin. "If we're going to hide him, his aura is going to be a problem." Just because I couldn't accurately differentiate auras by species, the majority of other magic users could.

"We should consult the council before making any decisions," said Harkura

Laxus jumped up, throwing his arms out. "No one else can know about me. Promise me, you won't tell anyone on the council about this."

"Why not?" I asked. "These dark stones are a big deal. Surely the more help we have, the better."

Laxus shook his head. "You're the only person I can trust with this information. As keeper of a life crystal, you are pure of heart and not easily corrupted." He looked Harkura over. "And I guess your guardians can be trusted too, but that's it."

"The council are meant to protect their people. They will help," I said.

Laxus locked eyes with me, his stare intense. "I'm not saying they're bad people, but they're more susceptible to the temptations of the air stone. They may think they can use its power to help people. But as I previously said, no matter their intent, the dark stones will only create chaos."

Annoyingly what he said made sense, but I didn't feel qualified to make such an important decision by myself.

Harkura stood up. "The boy is right. We must hide him, even from the council." He tilted his head to the side while staring at Laxus. "But we'll have to do something about his aura."

"Wait." I held my hands up in front of Harkura. "A moment ago you wanted to roast him alive and now you're agreeing to hide him?"

"That was before I had all the facts. As keeper of the heart crystal you must protect him, and if that means deceiving the council," Harkura said with a shrug, "so be it."

I sighed. "You're right. If anyone asks, we'll say he's my cousin." I gestured towards Laxus. "However, you're going to have to blend in better." He might be able to get away with the blue hair, but his shimmering skin and wings would definitely draw people's attention.

"A simple glamour spell should do the trick." He clicked his fingers and his appearance transformed. "Now we look like we could be related."

He'd turned his blue hair, dark brown like mine, and changed his eye colour to match; his skin no longer glowed, and his wings were now hidden. He looked like a normal human boy.

"I suggest that you project your energy field onto Laxus," said Harkura, "Your aura is strong enough for it not to be suspicious when he's in your company."

"Good idea, anyone magical won't sense that he's really a pixie. So how do I do it?"

Harkura instructed me on what to do and I cloaked Laxus with my atmospheric field. They both said it worked but I couldn't sense anything different. I was going to have to get better at this aura business. My senses were only heightened when I detected a strong dark presence.

There was a knock at the front door and Harkura went to answer.

Once he'd left the room, Laxus clasped my hands in his. "Thank you, Your Majesty."

"You will have to stop calling me, your majesty." I said, "I'm just Mellissa in this world."

"As you wish," he replied, bowing to me.

"You don't need to bow to me either. I'm going to have to tell my dad something. He wasn't happy the last time I asked to have a boy stay over. At least this time, it's a sweet little boy. He now knows about magic, so at least I can tell him most of the truth."

"I'm sorry to cause you such inconvenience."

I put my hand on his shoulder. "It's all right. It's not your fault, you're in danger."

Harkura returned with Victoria. She strutted across the

room striking a pose. "I came to show off my new dress." She twirled on the spot, flicking her long blonde hair over her shoulder. "So, what do you think?"

It was dark blue with lace sleeves and the skirt skimmed the middle of her thigh, showing off her long legs.

"Very nice," I said.

"You could be a little more enthusiastic. I was going to take you out." Victoria's eyes narrowed as she took in Laxus. "What's with the kid?"

I put my arm around his shoulders. "This is my cousin, Laxus."

Her body tensed as she looked Laxus over. She spun around, punching my arm. "You don't have any cousins."

I rubbed my arm. "Harsh much." Of course, she knew I didn't have any cousins. We may not have been friends until recently, but we'd known each other for years. We went downstairs for snacks and Laxus told his story for a third time.

When my dad finally got home from work, I explained the situation to him. I left out the part about the dark stones. I just told him that Laxus needed my help. He was happy to know that the pixie was a two-hundred-year-old that looked twelve and not a nineteen-year-old boy.

I'd already set Laxus up in the spare room. I checked in on him to find him fast asleep. It must have tired him out travelling all this way. He looked so sweet and innocent, it was hard to believe how old he really was. Then, I went to bed myself. I had a council meeting to attend in the morning where I wasn't going to say a word.

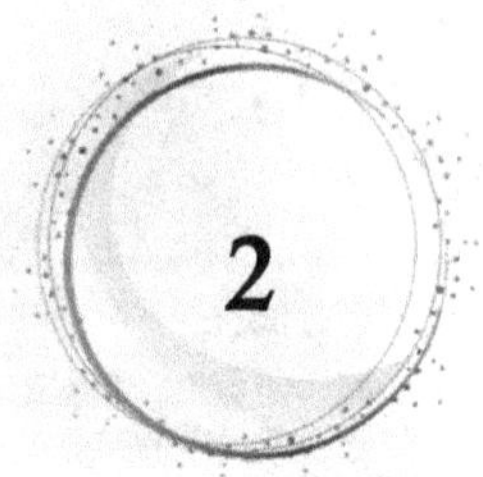

Under Pressure

Gregory

Greg slouched in his seat. This meeting was going on forever. It was meant to be a bog-standard council meeting. A couple of hours of his time, yet, Lee somehow managed to drag this meeting out, trying to get the council to pay for yet another project for his city. The witches were one of the richest nations, yet according to Lee, they couldn't afford to rejuvenate certain areas. The truth was Lee could afford it, he just wanted to see if the council would pay out first.

Greg looked at the clock on the wall. He didn't have time for this; the last few weeks had been chaotic. He was short-staffed with a lot of his father's staff retiring. His chief of staff had also quit to join the circus and his long-term assistant Anna was leaving at the end of next week. He needed to find replacements fast. It was hard enough living up to his father's reputation, but it was going to be near impossible without two key members of his staff. Anna had worked for his father from day one and she'd got Greg through the first few months of the job. He'd had lots of applications but not one had Anna's experience. Lee was wasting valuable time with his demands.

"Gregory."

Greg shot forward at the sound of his name. Beatrice stared at him across the table, her fingers steepled together.

"What do you think? Our cities are doing well. The changelings could spare some finance for the witches."

Of course, she would think that. Did she assume he didn't know about her relationship with Lee? She really shouldn't be letting him influence her decisions. The changelings could spare the money, but Lee didn't need it. He was being greedy. If someone came along that genuinely needed their help, there'd be no more funds simply because Beatrice had the hots for him.

"I think Lee should pay for it himself," Greg said.

Beatrice raised her eyebrows, so they looked as if they'd shoot off her head. "You what?"

"The witches are just as wealthy as us, Beatrice. They just have a problem with how they distribute their wealth. Sort that out and Lee's problem is solved."

Beatrice's mouth fell open. Lee stuttered as if to say something, but no clear words came out.

"I second that idea. Lee should pay for it himself," Mellissa said to his right. This was the first time she'd looked up from her notebook, having spent the entire meeting doodling.

Lee snorted. "Since when were you an expert in city rejuvenation, Lady Mellissa?" He said her name with disdain. It was no secret he wasn't fond of her.

"I never said I was an expert." Mellissa's eyes flashed an emerald green but quickly returned to their usual dark brown. Her skin shimmered with magic. Greg knew it meant she was annoyed. She stretched her arm across the table and her complexion returned to its normal tawny brown. "My people have built a city from scratch with barely any funds. Surely, you should be able to renovate with the millions or is it billions you rake in."

Lee's nostrils flared and he looked as if he'd tasted something sour.

Lady Gabrielle stood up giving him a stern look. "Shall we vote on it? Those in favour of Lee funding his own project, raise your hand.

Mellissa's hand shot up and Greg followed suit. Lady

Gabrielle looked around the room before also raising her hand. Slowly most of the others also raised theirs. "As you can see the vote is not in your favour, Lee. Anything else?"

Greg looked up at the ceiling. Please, nobody say anything.

Lady Gabrielle closed her notebook. "Very well, meeting adjourned."

Mellissa grabbed her things and shot out of the room. He'd never seen her move so fast. He needed to hurry up if he wanted to catch her. Her teleporting ban only applied to this room.

Emerson stepped in front of him just as he made it to the door. "We need to talk about the expansion of the library in Novosvillas."

"What's there to talk about? It's still in the planning stage."

"Beatrice and I need to approve it before you go ahead."

"Yes, I know. Once the plans are finalised, I'll send you both copies. Just make sure, Beatrice doesn't give all our funds to Lee."

Emerson curled his top lip. "Yes, her relationship with him is a nuisance, but then again, so is yours with Lady Mellissa."

Greg narrowed his eyes. "What's that supposed to mean?"

"I think you know. Don't forget to send those plans. I can take over the job if you can't manage it."

"I can manage just fine." Greg marched around him and walked out of the door. Emerson had some nerve. He'd never questioned his father anywhere near as much as he constantly questioned him. And Mellissa was probably long gone by now.

He went out to the tree of time just in case she was attempting to free Matt again. She was obsessed with trying to free her best friend after Kadon had tricked her into getting him sealed away. She'd made countless attempts but without any luck. She wasn't there. It wasn't important anyway, he just felt bad about the lack of time he'd spent with her recently.

He made his way to the tea rooms. There was another

hour until the next train home. Thanks to Lee he'd missed the earlier one. He bought a slice of cake and sat at a table flicking through job applications. It was a good thing he'd brought them with him.

"Oh, cake." He jumped on hearing Mellissa's voice beside him. An arm reached across him towards his plate. He pulled it out of her reach.

"How do you do that?"

"You know I teleport."

"No, I mean, how do you sniff out cake like that? I thought you'd gone home."

"I had, but apparently, my notes on the meeting weren't good enough so my bossy staff sent me back to get official copies." She disappeared and reappeared in the chair on his other side, swiping his fork.

"Don't eat my cake," he said.

She looked up at him all wide-eyed. "Sharing is caring."

Sure, it was when it was something of his. It wouldn't kill him to lose a slice of cake, so he didn't argue. "You're not going to find the official notes here."

"I know, but I left Harkura behind so I can eat cake without him moaning at me. "She tilted her head to look at the papers in his hand. "Still not found a new assistant then?"

"No. I'm starting to think it's impossible. To top things off, Duncan just quit to join the circus."

"Duncan. Which one was that?"

"My chief of staff."

She almost choked on cake as she burst into laughter. "Your chief of staff is joining the circus. That's a bit of a career change."

"Apparently it's always been a dream of his." Greg pushed his red hair from his face. "So, now I need to find a replacement for him, too. As if replacing Anna wasn't hard enough."

"Maybe you need to lower your expectations. Anna had years of experience. You need to find someone with the potential to become as good as her."

He sat up straight and frowned. She was right. Searching

for a duplicate of Anna was impossible but someone who could learn to be as good was more plausible. If he really needed to, he could always hire two assistants. His chief of staff problem may be easier to solve. He already had an idea of who he wanted to hire … assuming Samson wanted the job. And he couldn't see why he wouldn't take it. It was a step up from the position he held with the council.

"Here, you can have the rest." Mellissa pushed the remaining crumbs towards him. She stood up, her dark brown curls tumbling down her back.. "Well, I have notes to get. I guess I'll see you tomorrow."

"You will?"

"You're the worst." She put her hands on her hips. "The last time we had plans, you were late, and now you're just forgetting about me. I don't care … I don't need you. Besides, I'm sure someone else in the city will help me out. Your people love me."

A smile spread across his face. "That they do, but I said I'd go with you, so I will."

Mellissa had been so excited when she'd heard about the festival celebrations in the city. It was the last week of the month-long event celebrating the beginning of spring. Hatching chicken eggs was one of the many attractions. It was mainly for kids. Greg had gone plenty of times with his father, however, he'd quickly learned that the incubators were full of eggs close to hatching – there wasn't much actual magic in it. Of course, this was all new to Mellissa, so it was still exciting for her.

"Don't inconvenience yourself for me. I finally have a day to myself so I'll have fun on my own."

He knew she was being dramatic. She also wouldn't be alone. Her guardians wouldn't let her go anywhere without one of them. They'd probably have returned with her if they'd known she was going to be more than a few minutes.

"It's not an inconvenience. I've just been distracted by all these job applications. I will be there."

She narrowed her eyes. "Fine."

He watched her march off. He needed to ensure he turned up on time the next day, otherwise, she might kill him.

Actually, no, she'd have one of her guardians kill him, which was worse as they were lethal.

He got up to buy another slice of cake and then went back to flicking through the applications.

"Greg." Samson waved at him from across the room. He raced over to him and sat in the chair opposite. "You'll never guess who I just ran into?"

"Mellissa."

Samson frowned and then nodded. "Well, you'll never guess what she wanted."

Greg placed the paperwork onto the table. It didn't look like he was going to get much work done. "Enlighten me."

"She offered me a job."

Greg leant forward. "She what?"

"She wants me to move to the elf city when she does and become her adviser."

"What did you say?"

"I said, yes, of course. It's the sort of job I've always wanted. I thought you'd be happy for me."

"I am." Greg forced a smile. He was happy for him; he was just unhappy for himself. Samson was the perfect candidate for his chief of staff, but now he'd lost out to Mellissa. There was no way he could ask him to pick between the two roles. It would be unfair. And he'd never know if he picked the job with him because they were family or if he actually wanted it. "I'll just miss you when you're gone. Wouldn't you prefer to remain in Novosvillas and not have the hassle of moving?"

"Yes, but there are no jobs at this level in Novosvillas. Besides, I think the move will be good. The elves are just starting out, so I think I can make a bigger impact there. And it will be interesting working with Queen Mellissa."

"Are you sure it has nothing to do with a certain guardian?"

Samson's face turned bright red. "You know I'd never make a career move based on something like that. It's just an added bonus that my office will be opposite Victoria's."

"Why does Victoria need an office? I didn't think she did any work."

"She assists the keeper in many ways."

Greg raised an eyebrow. He wasn't sure Mellissa would agree with that statement. "You haven't seen them together much, have you?"

"It's her job to protect the keeper. There's nothing more fragile than a person's heart. In Victoria's view, you're a threat."

"What's that supposed to mean?"

"You know exactly what I mean. Anyway, I assume you aren't any happier as you still haven't found a new assistant."

"Yes and no. Duncan just handed in his notice. I was going to offer the role to you."

"I'm sorry, I didn't know."

"It's fine. I think working for Mellissa might actually be better for you."

Samson picked up some of the applications from the table. "Well, I can assist you for now. I won't be moving for a few weeks yet. Queen Mellissa is going to have a cottage built for me."

Greg really was happy for him. In fact, he was slightly jealous. He wished he could be excited about a new job in a new location. As an elder, it was likely he'd never be able to move away from Novosvillas. He may have a high status that most people envied but it came with a price. A price he wasn't sure he liked.

Greg grabbed his jacket and ran out of city hall. He'd lost track of time and was running late. Mellissa was going to be mad. If he flew, he could be there in five minutes. Before he could shift, someone shouted his name. He turned to see Emerson marching towards him.

"What are you doing here?" Greg asked, "I didn't think we had a meeting."

"I was in the area and thought I'd take the time to meet up. Shall we go to your office?" He pointed to the door.

"I was just on my way out."

"I won't take up much of your time."

"Very well." Greg walked back through city hall towards

his office as Emerson followed.

When they arrived, Emerson walked around the room, carelessly browsing the books on the shelves that lined the wall. He tapped Greg's desk before taking a seat , looking at Greg with his grey eyes expectantly.

Greg sank into his office chair, with a sigh. He rolled his shoulders back and forced a smile onto his face. "So, what can I help you with?"

Emerson interlaced his fingers as he crossed one leg over the other. "It's come to my attention that you're short-staffed."

"Well, I'm in the process of sorting it out. It's nothing to be concerned about."

"I'm just worried it may be affecting your ability to lead. I'm willing to take over some of your responsibilities if needed."

"Thank you for your concern but that isn't necessary."

"Very well, but don't think Beatrice and I haven't noticed you're struggling. It makes one wonder why so many of your employees have left at the same time."

Greg clenched his jaw. "A big chunk of my father's former workforce are of retirement age. Don't worry, if I feel it's too much, I'll let you know. Now, I have somewhere I need to be."

Emerson lifted his chin, his lips drawn into a tight line. "Very well. We just want to ensure that you're taking care of your father's city." He gave Greg a steely look, stood up, straightened his jacket and left.

Greg clenched his fists. How dare Emerson bring up his father like that. There was no way he'd ever ask him for help, even if he needed it. Emersons solution for reduced staff was to move in on his role. A good partner would have offered to loan some of his workers temporarily, not try and take over.

Greg looked at his watch. Now he really was late. Hopefully, Melissa wouldn't have given up on him yet. He walked around his desk and noticed a letter he hadn't seen earlier. Maybe he'd missed it when he'd gone through his mail. He picked it up and stuffed it into his jacket pocket to look at later.

Leaving his office, he ran through city hall again. As

soon as he was outside, he shapeshifted into a bird and was at the chick hatching stand within five minutes. He walked around for thirty minutes but Mellissa was nowhere to be seen. Of course, he was over an hour late, she could be anywhere now. He put his hands in his pockets and started walking home.

"Greg," shouted a male voice.

Greg turned to see a man waving frantically at him. He squinted. "Steve is that you?"

"Yeah, long time no see. How've you been Greg or is it Lord Ainsworth now?"

"Greg is fine. I thought you'd moved to the capital."

"I moved back recently. Anyway, you'll never guess who I just met. I lived in the capital for years and never met anyone famous … been back here a few months and I meet the elf queen."

Greg's ears twitched at the mention of Mellissa. "You saw her?"

"Yeah. She's so small and cute. Nothing like I imagined."

"Where? I was just looking for her."

"Just round the corner. She was putting on a light and ice show with her guardian."

Great, she was with Victoria. Why couldn't Harkura have been on guard duty? He would have kept Mellissa calm. Victoria would only add fuel to the fire, making Mellissa even angrier with him.

Steve patted his back. "I can see that running into the elf queen doesn't impress you. Rumour is you two are pretty close."

"We're friends. I do need to talk to her about something. Council stuff."

"Good luck with that. I don't think she'll be wanting to talk work."

"Can't hurt to try. Which way?"

Steve pointed south. "We should meet up sometime and catch up."

"Sounds good. Call my office to arrange something."

Greg ran in the direction Steve had pointed and turned

into the first corner. A crowd had gathered, clapping and cheering by a nearby fountain as flickers of light shot into the air. Mellissa had been so close, yet he hadn't sensed her magic till now. Thinking back, her aura hadn't been as strong the last few times he'd seen her. Harkura must have taught her how to dampen her magical presence. He made his way through the crowd until someone grabbed his arm yanking him away.

"Stay away from her, " snapped Victoria, "I've finally got her in a good mood and I'm letting you ruin it."

"I know I'm late." Greg looked back at Mellissa. He could just about glimpse her through the crowd. "Emerson showed up unexpectedly. I'll just go apologise and explain. I'm sure she'll understand."

He turned to walk away but Victoria had a tight hold of his jacket. "No. This is not the first time you've left her waiting. Every time she tells you it's all right, she's lying.

Greg looked down at his feet. "You think I don't know that. I can tell when she's not being truthful."

"Then why do you keep doing it? You don't have to deal with her afterwards, but I do." There was a slight growl in her voice as if she was trying not to shout.

"It wasn't intentional which is why I need to apologise."

He yanked his jacket out of her grip. As he stepped forward an icy blast just missed his feet. He narrowed his eyes at her. "Don't you think you're overstepping your duties?"

"It's my job to protect her and right now you're the biggest threat."

"That's not true."

"She doesn't want to see you."

"Did she actually say that?"

Victoria waved her arm in Mellissa's general direction. "Look at her. She's happy. Do you really want to ruin that?"

That was a no then, but she had a point. When he looked at Mellissa her brown eyes sparkled as she laughed at whatever someone had just said to her. If he went over there now, they would argue. Naturally, she'd forgive him, she always did, but the light in her eyes would go out. He hated to admit it, but Victoria was right. In the long run, Mellissa might be better off without him. It was for purely selfish reasons that he wanted to see her – to rid himself of his guilt. He'd already upset her. Just because he hadn't meant to, didn't mean he should add to the hurt.

"Fine. I'll go." Greg shoved his hands in his pockets and walked home.

How had things ended up like this? It hadn't been his intention. Nothing seemed to go his way recently. As he rummaged through his pockets for his keys, he found the letter he'd picked up earlier. There was no address just his name. Once inside his house, he walked into the living room and opened it. It was handwritten with a quill.

> *Dear Gregory,*
>
> *I hope this letter reaches you. It has been far too many years since I've seen you. I want you to know, I'm sorry for everything. Your father and I lied to you. I hope you can find it in your heart to forgive my deceit and that I'll be able to see you again soon.*
>
> *Love G.A.*

What did that mean? His father had lied to him but about what? And who exactly was this G.A.? No one in his father's circle had those initials – except himself, of course. Maybe that was the lie, not telling him who this was. It was clear the letter hadn't been posted. Someone must have dropped it off in person. He could check security and ask his staff if they'd seen an unfamiliar face around.

He slumped into the sofa and looked up at the ceiling. The last few weeks had been hell – he'd lost a large chunk of staff, upset Mellissa, and had Emerson sniffing around. He barely had time to think and now there was this letter. His father made the job look so easy. He wished he was here now; he'd know what to do. Sadly, he was completely alone.

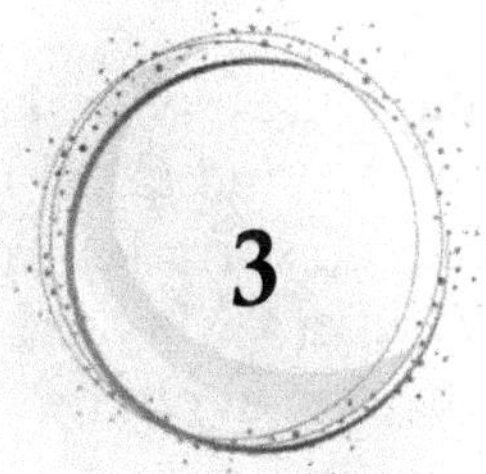

3

Out of Control

Mellissa

The sun shone brightly through the cracks in my curtains, my head was pounding and my throat sore. I pulled the covers over my head. That was the last time I'd go out on a night with Victoria. She kept handing me drink after drink and like an idiot, I accepted them. I couldn't even remember coming home but my teleporting was the only way we'd have got back here. Greg didn't show in the end. At one point I had thought I had seen his red hair in the crowd, but it had just been wishful thinking. He probably got stuck at work again. As usual, I was expendable. My current headache was also his fault. I never would have been left to Victoria's juvenile antics had he shown up. By now I should know, he always made promises he couldn't keep. I wrapped myself even tighter in my duvet.

There was a knock at the door. Hopefully, if I stayed quiet, they'd go away. I wanted to remain curled up in bed feeling sorry for myself. I heard the click of the door opening and footsteps across the floor of my room.

"Rise and shine, sleepyhead," said Harkura. I heard the swoosh of my curtains opening. "It's time for your morning run."

"I'm not going," I croaked, my voice hoarse. "I'm taking the day off."

"I gave you yesterday off. And I've already let you sleep in an hour late. Now get up or we won't fit in a run before school."

Yeah, he let me have the day off and I got stood up. Why couldn't Harkura understand that I wanted to spend the morning lying around, feeling sorry for myself? I popped my head out from under my duvet. "Maybe I don't want to go to school. I thought I was the one in charge. So, shouldn't I decide when to have time off?"

"I am your guardian and sometimes I have to protect you from your own laziness. If you don't go to school, then that just means more magic training." Harkura took hold of my duvet. With a strong tug, he pulled it off, rolling me out of it.

I yelped as I just managed not to fall off the bed.

He dropped my duvet onto the floor. "I expect you to be ready to run in ten minutes or I'll be back with a fireball." Harkura marched out the room shutting the door behind him.

I dragged myself up and put on my running gear. I'd learnt that if Harkura made a threat, he'd follow through. I hurried downstairs. Harkura was waiting at the front door with Laxus watching the clock on the wall. I grabbed my trainers off the shoe rack and sat on the stairs to put them on.

"Cutting it close there, Your Majesty," Harkura said. Perhaps he wanted to set fire to my bedroom. I'd been told demons didn't exist but I was sure the heart crystal managed to locate two. They may protect me, but they did it in their own evil way.

Laxus raised an eyebrow. "You look rough."

"Gee, thanks. Why are you up so early? You were out with us last night. Aren't you tired?"

"A run is a great way to start the day." He shrugged. "Besides, I only drank juice. I am playing the role of a twelve-year-old, after all. "

"You don't have to come with us."

"Wherever you go, I go. Except for the council. They can't be trusted."

"Why is that again?"

"Only a crystal keeper can be trusted." His face darkened

fleetingly until he quickly returned to his bright and cheery self.

He came across as seriously paranoid, but I couldn't turn him away, not after he showed me that stone. If it fell into the wrong hands, it would be disastrous.

Harkura jabbed me in the side. "Let's get going lazy." He pulled me up from the stairs and shoved me out the front door.

Laxus followed with a big toothy grin on his face. He was a weird combo of a grumpy old man and a sweet child. Maybe it was a good thing Greg hadn't shown up yesterday, I'd have needed to explain who Laxus was, and I wasn't good at lying to Greg. The pixie probably wouldn't have been too pleased if he knew Greg was part of the council as well.

We did our usual circuit of the village, the fresh air revitalising me. When we got back to the house, I kicked my trainers off and ran to the kitchen. I was starving. Hopefully, Harkura would go straight upstairs, and I could make my own breakfast. I was out of luck. He'd somehow got ahead of me and was already waiting by the stove. "I'll make omelettes for breakfast," he said with a smile.

"Sounds good," I answered. It sounded much better than the weird seaweed wraps he'd forced on me the day before. Harkura was a health freak which I had no problem with. He ate fish and eggs, but no white or red meat. The problem was he forced his eating habits onto me, claiming it was better for my wellbeing. He might have been telling the truth, but all sweet things were off-limits, and I was missing cake the most. He was such a control freak.

"Oh, I forgot to mention, you have four missed calls from Lord Ainsworth."

"Well if he calls again, tell him I'm not talking to him."

Harkura walked over to the fridge and pulled out a carton of eggs. "Have you fallen out?"

I went to reply but forgot what I was about to say, distracted by the pile of stuff dumped on the table. "Um, Dad, what's with all the stuff?"

Dad was sat reading a newspaper with a cup of coffee. He peered over the top of the print. "It all appeared about thirty minutes ago. There's a card with it." He pointed to the end of the table closest to me.

I picked up the envelope with my name on. It was from Greg. I recognised the super neat handwriting straight away. He was also one of the few that knew enough about my interests to send such appropriate gifts. There was a stack of multi-coloured paper, a sketchbook, chalks and pastels, a quill and a bottle of ink. Hmm, he was clearly trying to buy my forgiveness. I turned the envelope over in my hands. Did I really want to read yet another excuse for why he'd ditched me? If Victoria and Laxus hadn't been around, I'd have looked like an idiot. It was one instance of many times and I was the fool who kept forgiving him. Well not anymore.

"Aren't you going to open it?" Dad asked, "I assume it's from Greg."

"No, I'm not. It's my turn to ignore him," I cleared some space at the table and sat down in a chair, pouting. I tapped impatiently on the table as Harkura cooked.

Dad glanced over his paper at me. "Want to talk about it?"

"There's nothing to say."

"Well I'm sure you'll make up, you always do."

I lay my head on the table. He was trying to comfort me, but his words made me feel worse. I thought I'd grown stronger, but I was just the same pushover I always was. Not this time. I really was going to stand my ground. Greg couldn't buy my forgiveness with material things.

"Head up, please," Harkura said. I sat up as he placed a large omelette in front of me.

"Thanks," I said tucking in.

"If you want, just say the word, and I'll bestow all sorts of hell on Lord Ainsworth. My allegiance is to you, and you, alone."

I almost choked on my eggs. "Um, I'll let you know if I need your help, but for now I'll deal with it myself."

As nice as the image was of Harkura burning down Greg's house or blasting fireballs at him, it was a bit extreme. He might even get arrested for arson and Greg was an elder which would make the penalties worse for any crime.

Once we finished eating, Harkura gathered up our plates and started washing up. He might boss me about, but at least my chores had halved since he'd moved into a tent in our backyard. For some reason he refused to sleep in the house. I jumped, almost falling off my chair as bright lights swished around the table. Dad didn't bat an eyelid as the lights dispersed revealing a slice of strawberry gateaux, just like the one they served in the tea rooms at the council. I stood up, clenching my fists. "Oh, I hate him."

My dad glanced at me over his paper again. I went to walk out but stopped myself. Biting my lip, I picked up the cake with a fork and stormed to my bedroom. I may be mad at Greg but there was no reason to waste a good dessert. Harkura would only have thrown it away.

Water slammed into me, throwing me to the ground. I gasped for air. A stream rose upwards and swirled around the tree of time.

"You failed me, Mellissa," Matt screamed.

I pushed myself up onto all fours. "I'm sorry," I yelled.

A torrent crashed onto me, knocking me off my feet. I was engulfed. I tried to swim through it, but the current was too strong. My lungs burned as I struggled for air. A wave threw me up and then slammed me onto the ground again. Water formed into a tower above me, taking the shape of a huge bird. I slammed my hand onto the ground, but it shifted beneath me. Sand! I tried to haul the sand upwards to protect myself like a shield, but I couldn't manipulate it like I could normal earth.

The water bird screeched and took a nosedive towards me. I screamed covering my face.

I woke up screaming, throwing my blanket off. It was a dream. Everything was fine. Except it wasn't. A cool breeze sent shivers down my spine, and I took a deep breath. The smell of salt-water filled the air as waves crashed onto the shore. I lifted my hand and sand fell through my fingers. I had somehow teleported to the beach in my sleep.

I jumped up and ran in the opposite direction of the sea with my blanket trailing behind me. I tripped as I got to the edge of the shore, my heart pounding in my ears as I struggled to breathe. I needed to calm down; I was nowhere near the water. I pushed myself up and brushed the sand off. It was no good, it was everywhere. There was no way I could hide this from Harkura. Sleep teleporting was a dangerous side effect of my powers. It happened whenever I had a nightmare. Harkura had worked really hard to keep me grounded while asleep, and I hadn't done this in ages, but clearly, my subconscious had a weird sense of humour bringing me to the ocean. If I could just get rid of the sand, no one would ever know. I had enough on at the moment without people thinking I couldn't control my powers. I bundled up my blanket and teleported home.

Luckily not too much sand came back with me. I chucked my blanket in my wash basket and vacuumed my room. Suddenly, my bedroom door flew open. Victoria marched in followed by Harkura. Neither looked happy.

"Where on earth have you been?" Victoria yelled.

"Nowhere," I stuttered.

"You weren't here when I came to get you for your morning run," replied Harkura.

I looked up at the clock. It was only 7.30 and he'd already called Victoria. "I- er- snuck out for ice cream."

"Seriously" shouted Victoria, "You and your ridiculous sweet tooth."

"I'm bitterly disappointed," Harkura said shaking his head. "You know we have a busy day. You will have to miss your morning run as we have a meeting with Daniel and then you have a dance lesson."

I hung my head. "I really do apologise." I was genuinely sorry to have worried them but so happy they'd believed me.

Harkura put a hand on my shoulder. "If you wanted ice cream you should have said. I have a great recipe for seaweed gelato. Now get dressed. There's a new ball gown in your wardrobe.

"What do I need a ball gown for?" I asked.

"Daniel wants you to learn how to move in a dress," he replied. "Don't worry, it's nothing too fancy."

"You should be grateful you get all these nice dresses." Victoria glared at me. "Be downstairs in ten minutes." She stormed out of my room. I was going to have to find a way to make it up to her. Thankfully, Harkura gave me a gentle smile as he left.

I had a quick shower and found a pale blue dress in my wardrobe. It fitted snugly around the top half with lace sleeves and a puffy skirt with layers upon layers of fabric. It was beautiful and I hated it. The long skirt kept swishing around and getting in the way as I walked. I had no idea how I was meant to dance in it. Lifting the bottom of the skirt up with my hands to avoid tripping, I made my way downstairs.

"You look lovely." Harkura handed me a pair of strappy heels that matched the dress.

"Is this really all necessary?"

"You're a queen so you can't go to events in leggings and trainers," said Victoria. "You'll be in a gown and heels for your coronation, so you need to get used to moving about in this sort of thing."

I slumped onto a chair to put the shoes on as I felt I had less and less control over my life. Holding on to Harkura, I stood up. The shoes where majorly uncomfortable. "Where's Laxus?"

A small hand tugged on my arm. "I'm right here," he replied. "You look like proper royalty now."

I felt my cheeks heat up. He was sweet but a dress shouldn't be what made me regal. I wasn't sure what did, but I knew it wasn't clothes. With a frown, I teleported us to Urbem Folium.

The meeting with Daniel about the running of Urbem Folium was the easy part of my day. Everything in the city seemed to be running smoothly except for the pesky fairies getting in the way of us building a train line as it had to go through their land. The construction of the castle was going well. They only had the top floor to complete which was where I'd be living. My move here was getting closer. I was scared and still feeling out of my depth, but I was glad to have Daniel guiding me through it all. He made my job a lot easier.

It was just a shame his knowledge on the council and the other nations was so out of date. This was where Samson came in. It was Daniels idea to hire an adviser for that aspect of the business and Samson was the first person that sprang to mind. I was so happy when he said yes on the spot. But now was the horrible part of my day – dance lessons.

I sat in the ballroom with my guardians and Laxus waiting for Daniel to come back with my latest partner. The dancers kept quitting for some reason, probably because I was terrible at moving my body to music and they didn't want their good name tarnished by association.

"What's taking him so long?" I asked no one in particular.

Victoria shrugged. "Maybe he stopped for ice cream."

I glared at her. "I said, I was sorry."

"You did, but what for exactly? Worrying us or lying?"

"Wait, what?"

"Victoria," snapped Harkura, "I thought we agreed to discuss this with her later."

"Yeah, well, I changed my mind," she said through gritted teeth. "Did you really think we believed that stupid lie?"

I hung my head. "I didn't want to worry you."

Victoria slammed her hand on the table. "Worry us about what?"

The doors to the ballroom swung open and Daniel strolled in, his dark curls bouncing with every step. As usual, he was wearing a suit, looking very professional. His light brown skin was flawless making him look thirty instead of mid-fifties. He clapped his hands together. "Well, shall we begin this lesson?"

Victoria glared at me mouthing, 'this isn't over'

I stood up. "Where's my dance partner?"

Daniel rubbed his chin. "Um, well, I couldn't find anyone willing to dance with you, after your last partner broke his leg when you tripped him."

I gasped. "I thought it was just bruised."

"Not exactly, but it's all right. For now, I shall dance with you until we find you a partner for your coronation dance on the big day." He smiled and held his hand out to me. With a sigh, I took it. I couldn't believe that not one person was willing to take a chance on me.

I spent the next ninety minutes spinning around in circles. Daniel claimed it was a traditional elfish jig, but it was more a case of not stepping on his toes or falling over my own feet. The dress I'd been forced to wear made things harder. The fabric kept bunching up and getting in the way. Daniel was also taller than me and I kept bumping my head on his shoulder.

Laxus burst out laughing. "You really are bad at this."

I rubbed my forehead and pouted. "Do you think I don't already know that."

Daniel put his hand on my shoulder. "It's all right, Your Majesty. We still have time until your coronation to get this right. How about a quick break for lunch, then we can practice some more before you meet with the fairies?"

A break sounded good. My feet were killing me. And I didn't think they'd be much improvement in the hour before my meeting. We could spend all month on this, and I still wouldn't get it. Ballroom dancing just wasn't my thing.

"Lunch would be nice," I said. Harkura was upstairs inspecting the progress of the offices, so I could break the crazy diet he had me on. "A cheeseburger would be great and is there any cake?"

"I'll see what there is." Daniel strode out of the ballroom.

I sat at the table with Laxus and Victoria. They already had drinks and popcorn, like they'd been watching a show. The rest of the room was empty. There was another table with a stereo on but that was it. Laxus stuffed a handful of popcorn in his mouth. "You really are a terrible dancer."

"I actually think you're getting worse," said Victoria.

I folded my arms. "Well, you don't have to watch me fail at this."

"I prefer to stay close to you," replied Laxus, "Besides your lesson is extremely entertaining. Like a comedy."

"You're not funny."

Laxus nodded at me. "But you are."

I put my head in my hands and they both laughed. I'd walked right into that one.

Daniel returned with two drinks placing them on the table. "I've asked the chef to make you something. While we wait, shall we go over the steps again?"

He held his hand out to me and I stood up and took it. We took a few steps away from the table as I placed my other hand on his shoulder. Biting my lip, I tried to remember the right stance to take.

"Shoulders back," Daniel said. "Head held high and no looking at your feet. Remember, I lead not you, and right foot first."

I nodded as I attempted to stand tall. Daniel pushed forward and I stepped back. We were in sync for about ten seconds until I stepped on his toes and as he tried to adjust to my pace, I fell backwards pulling him over with me.

I quickly got to my feet and helped Daniel up. "I'm so sorry."

Daniel adjusted his crumpled shirt. "It's quite all right. You just need more practice."

"Really? I don't think it matters how much I practice. I'm hopeless."

"Everyone can learn to dance. Some just take longer than others."

"I don't see why this ball has to be so formal. Why does there even have to be a ball? Can't I just get my crown, then go to bed?"

Daniel's hand shot to his chest as if he'd received some shocking news. "Your Majesty, your coronation is an important event. It's tradition to mark it with a ball. Your first dance as queen is extremely important."

I had to stop myself from rolling my eyes. Daniel was always going on about tradition. We were a new settlement. How on earth did we already have traditions?

"How about we have a nineties themed party instead. You know when it was the era of the boy band?"

"The people of this world don't know about boy bands. They're expecting a traditional ball."

"We may be elves but the majority of us are also part human. You're half-human like me. We can show the magic world what it means to be a human elf. Also, I'm pretty good at the chicken dance." I did some of the dance moves to illustrate my point which earned a laugh from my audience of two.

Daniel took a sharp intake of breath and fiddled with his collar. "The chicken dance won't be featured at your coronation." His eyebrows rose as he shook his head. Perhaps he was finally realising what a lost cause I was. "How about we stick with formal for this one, and you can do what you want for your birthday ball."

"Since when am I having a birthday ball?"

"It is tradition."

"Of course, it is"

A man walked in with a tray. I almost jumped for joy. I skipped over to the table and sat down. He placed the tray on the table and removed the lid revealing carrot and celery sticks with a dip in the middle. Daniel had an odd way of interpreting what I'd asked for.

Daniel frowned. "Dean, this isn't what I ordered."

Dean rubbed the back of his head. "I know it's just …"

"I made him change it," Harkura said marching across the ballroom. "And it's a good thing I did. How could you order something so full of fat and sugar for the queen?" He wagged his finger at Daniel.

"It's what she requested. Dean, take this back to the kitchen and get what I originally ordered."

Dean went to pick up the tray but Harkura slammed his hand down onto it. "If the queen requested you get her poison to eat, would you?"

Daniel's mouth fell open. "How is that the same thing?"

"The only difference is the sugar will kill her more slowly."

I gritted my teeth. He was being unreasonable. Poor Daniel had just done as I'd asked and now had to suffer the wrath of Harkura.

Harkura got right into Daniel's face. He may have been almost a foot shorter than Daniel, but he was very intimidating. "I am the queen's guardian. I know what is better for her than you do."

"Harkura stop," I shouted. "Daniel just did as I requested. If you want to have a go at someone, have a go at me."

Harkura glared at Daniel before sitting down opposite me. "You heard what I said. Don't let it happen again."

I turned to Dean. "The carrots and celery are fine. Thank you."

He nodded. With a bow, he mouthed, "Sorry" before leaving.

Daniel sat beside me scowling at Harkura. I crunched on a carrot stick. It confirmed that I definitely wasn't the one in charge. It appeared Harkura was fighting for that position, and it looked like he was winning. No wonder Greg thought it was okay to let me down when I couldn't even take control of my staff and guardians. Being royal wasn't all it was cracked up to be. I pushed the celery towards Laxus. He turned his nose up at it and munched on the last of his popcorn. I had to make a stand. Harkura placed his hands on the table. "We need to talk."

He'd beaten me to it. "Yes, we do. You can't go biting people's heads off because I asked for a burger."

He shook his head. "That's not what I meant. It's time you thought about finding yourself a partner."

"Why do I need to find a partner?" I shook my head. Somehow, I'd already lost control of the conversation. "Daniel keeps everything going when I'm not around. Samson advises me on all the political stuff, and I have you to nag me about my bad life choices."

"Again, that's not what I meant. You need a life partner.

It doesn't need to be an equal partnership but as queen, you'll need an heir at some point."

"What?"

Laxus leant towards me and whispered. "He's trying to marry you off."

I jumped up slamming my hands on the table. "What! That's not happening. You've gone too far with controlling my life."

"Be reasonable," replied Harkura, "This cannot come as a surprise. Surely you knew you'd be expected to have children."

"No, I didn't. It isn't something I've ever thought about."

Victoria stood up, sliding between the two of us. "Harkura, I already told you this was a bad idea."

Harkura folded his arms. "We also agreed not to confront the queen's lie from this morning."

"That's hardly the same thing," said Victoria.

My entire body stiffened. I took slow breaths as my mind began to spin. They'd been making decisions about me behind my back. Making plans for my future. At least Victoria didn't agree with this craziness, but it was still too much. My life wasn't mine anymore. "I will do my best for the elves, and well, the whole world, but they don't get to decide if or when I'll have children."

"As keeper of the heart crystal, your responsibilities go beyond yourself," said Harkura.

I clenched my fists. How dare he. I knew exactly what my responsibilities were. It was the reason I put up with so much of his bossiness. He was overstepping the line. What had happened to the super polite water nymph that first showed up to save me. This was my fault. I'd left him to take control and created a monster.

Daniel clapped his hands together. "Shall we get back to dancing then?"

"No," I said, "I have a meeting to prepare for."

"The fairies aren't even here yet."

"Well, I wouldn't want anyone thinking I don't take my responsibilities seriously." Before anyone could say anything else, I teleported away.

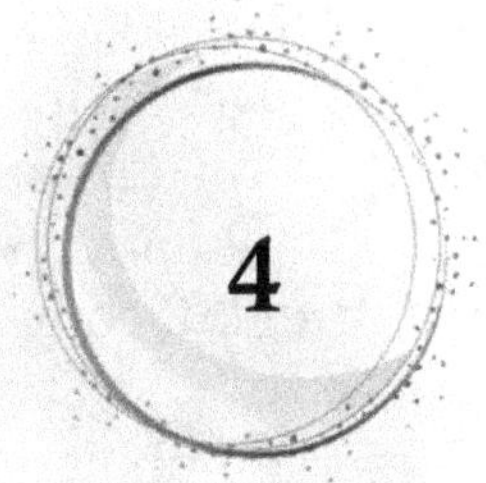

Nightmare

Mellissa

White clouds drifted across the sunlit sky as a light breeze made my wild curls fly around. I pushed my hair out of my face to get a better view of the skyline. Everything was so much calmer up on the roof of the palace – my secret place, hidden from everyone. All my problems seemed minuscule as I looked out at the vastness of Novos forest that surrounded our city. Our settlement was designed to blend in with its surroundings, utilising materials native to the forest, so many houses were designed to look like trees. The building I was sat on stood out the most, but as breath-taking as this view was, it emphasised just how secluded the elves were from the rest of the magic world.

The middle of the forest was the only space large enough for a new settlement. I'm sure the council purposely did it to make my job harder, so I had to constantly teleport in supplies. Luckily, as the elves are experts in plant magic, we're never short of food. But we so needed this train line to make the rest of the magic world more accessible. That's why the meeting with the fairies was so important, but they were being deliberately awkward. It seemed almost pointless for the elves to return to the magic world just to be stuck in the forest.

Our settlement was the closest to the only tear left in the veil. When I reconstructed the veil, all the tears were sealed up, so I purposely created one in the forest that led back to my village in Yorkshire. I then created two stone guards to protect it. I still didn't know how Laxus got past them. Maybe, the council planned to force us all back to the human world. I pulled at my hair as I yelled in frustration. I came up here to clear my mind but ended up thinking myself into more of a mess. I spun around at the sound of someone clearing their voice.

"I was hoping I'd find you up here," said Daniel. "May I join you?"

I shrugged. "If you want."

He sat down beside me, looking out across the forest. "It's so peaceful up here. I suppose that's why you like it."

"Everything is quieter here. I used to soak in the bath when I wanted to think, but it isn't as relaxing as it used to be."

"It's understandable that you no longer trust the water."

My eyes widened. "It's not that … it's just …" I sighed as I pulled my legs up to my chest, wrapping my arms around them. "Who am I kidding? Being submerged in water reminds me of him. Kadon almost drowned me twice. What sort of queen will I make if I can't even get in the bath without freaking out? Then there's all this tradition stuff and Harkura taking over my life. I just feel so …" The words escaped me. I had so many feelings swirling around inside me, I couldn't think of the right way to describe what I felt.

"You've been through something traumatic and it's left scars. You can't always see those scars, but it doesn't mean they aren't there, and sometimes their effects are delayed." Daniel laid a hand on my shoulder. "Your guardians also went through something traumatic – they almost lost you. Trying to control every aspect of your life is their way of coping. Show them you're strong and capable as I know you are."

I hung my head, letting my curls fall over my face. "Sometimes I think I've gotten stronger, but other times, everything feels like it's falling apart."

"It's okay not to have it all together. What matters is that you do your best. When I first took over as elf leader, I had no idea what I was doing."

I snickered. "I find that hard to believe. You're so good at this stuff."

"That's because I've had years of practice. I'm also very good a faking it. Re-joining the magic world is all new territory to me, too. Why do you think I suggested a political adviser?"

"Because Samson has knowledge we don't."

"Exactly. It's okay not to have all the answers as long as you find a way to get them." He put his finger under my chin, lifting my head as he looked me straight in the eyes. "Now, this is important. I would never have stepped down as leader if I didn't think you could handle it. It's not just that you're Freya's heir, but I see your potential. I know you'll grow into something magnificent."

"How can you be so sure?"

"Because you have a good heart and I'll be here to guide you along the way."

I could feel my eyes welling with tears and squeezed them shut to stop them falling. When I opened them again, I smiled. "Thank you, Daniel."

Daniel stood, and held his hand out. "The fay will be here soon. Hopefully, we can convince them to stop being so stubborn." I took his hand and he pulled me to my feet as he led the way off the roof. I knew I'd be completely lost without Daniels guidance.

I teleported to the corridor outside the main hall with Victoria. A while ago, Lee had somehow managed to ban me from teleporting into meetings. It was a silly rule. Victoria also wasn't allowed to accompany me – all guards had to remain outside – although I knew she wouldn't stand around with the other leader's guards. She'd probably go window shopping and be back just in time, but pace up and down mad as hell if the meeting ran late. Unfortunately, it was an afternoon meeting, and they always ran late. I quickly made my way into the hall as I saw Greg and his guard approaching. I was still actively ignoring his calls.

Once again Lee droned on and on, trying to get more

money out of the council for yet another project. He was one of the wealthiest people in the room, yet seemingly couldn't afford anything. I looked around, recalling when I first met the council. A lot had changed since then. Nearly half the members were new faces and I was the least experienced and the youngest. I knew I wasn't what they'd expected. Greg was the only other member close to my age, but he'd been raised for a leadership role. I felt completely out of my element, although, I was slowly getting the hang of things and managed to get most of them onside. I was proud to say I'd now learnt all their names and titles.

There were six senior council members – seven, including me. I was the only elf on the council, representing the elves sole authority figure. However, other nations had different hierarchy systems. The changelings had three major cities with three elders overseeing them. There was my so-called friend, Lord Gregory, Lady Beatrice and Lord Emerson. Greg was the elder of Novosvillas. This was the biggest changeling city, making him a senior councilman. The warlocks had two major settlements run in a similar way to the changelings. Lady Gabrielle was the senior council member and there was also Sir Cole representing the warlocks. There were also three water nymphs, but they only had one central city with a bunch of small villages following the river's path. They were ruled by the high priestess, Yoko, alongside priestesses, Akito and Kai. Even though they were all priestesses, They were not all females. Gender was more of a fluid thing for nymphs.

The dwarves had two councillors: Caleb of the hillside was a senior member along with Hogan of the caves. The fairies lived in the same forest where Urbem Foilom was located. They were governed by Lord Ping and Chancellor Den. Sir Brandon was the newest member of the council and the first leprechaun. The leprechauns had previously been denied representation on the council, but things had changed for the better. Then, of course, there were the witches who only had one big city, but it was magnificent. They were ruled by Lee and Lady Kate. Lee had the senior membership and he let everyone know it.

The changelings, witches and water nymphs were all born into their position, much like I'd been. All the others were elected officials. Lady Gabrielle had been on the council longer than anyone else, which meant all these years later, there hadn't been another warlock beating her in an election.

Once Lee finally stopped talking, I hoped the meeting would be over. I intended to get myself some cake before heading back to Urbem Folium to argue with Harkura. Once again, I was out of luck as nearly everyone in the room objected to Lee's comment and debates commenced. I sighed. It seemed I'd be stuck here for a long time. I felt my eyes glaze over as I zoned out, imagining I was somewhere more interesting.

Waves crashed along the shore like thunder. My first instinct was to run, but my body wouldn't move. I tried to lift my legs, but I was sinking, the sand swallowing me up. I attempted to latch on with my magic and force my way out – but it was no use, I kept being sucked down. Water bubbled up from the sand, the waves smashing onto the shore as the water rose higher. An enormous wave rolled towards me. I screamed as it crashed down, submerging me in its icy cocoon.

I was shocked awake as I fell into a large pool. I tried to scream but water filled my mouth. Throwing my arms out, I rapidly kicked my legs and forced my head to break the surface, gasping for air. My heart was pounding as I tried to swim, my arms and legs trembling. The water pulled me back under. Again, I frantically kicked, throwing my arms out. It was no use. Shutting my eyes, I teleported.

I hit the table with a thud, and as water splashed down on me, I slid off the end. Yells of displeasure sounded around me as I screamed trying to pull myself up. I needed to get away from the water. A pair of hands were under my arms lifting me to my feet. I pulled away, trying to run, but I'm held in place.

"Mellissa," said Greg, bending down to look me in the eye. "It's okay. You're back at the council."

I threw my arms around him and he held me tight as I burrowed my face into his chest. "I was going to drown," I whispered.

"What is the meaning of this?" yelled Lee making me jump. The urge to run filled me again but Greg wrapped his arm around me as I tried to slip away. "There is a ban on teleporting in this room." said Lee, "You broke the rules and should be punished."

"Seriously, Lee, it was obviously an accident." I heard Yuko's melodic voice from behind us.

Hogan snickered. "I wish I could teleport away from your boring speeches."

Lee glared at Hogan. "Rules are rules. She isn't allowed to teleport. It's not my fault she can't control her powers."

"That's enough, Lee," boomed Lady Gabrielle above everyone else. "It was not a deliberate rule break. Gregory if you could see Mellissa to her guardian, then we can continue this meeting"

Greg led me out of the hall and I could hear the rest of the council bickering as we left.

As the reality of what happened sunk in, I thought I might die from embarrassment. I'd completely freaked out in front of the whole council and now they all assumed I couldn't control my powers. The good impression I'd worked so hard to give had been destroyed in minutes.

"Where's Victoria?" Greg asked looking up and down the corridor filled with all the other guards.

I wrapped my arms around myself. "She's shopping."

"Luke," Greg waved his guard over. "Can you go find Victoria and tell her Mellissa needs her urgently. She's probably in the fashion district."

Luke bowed before running off to follow Greg's orders.

Greg led me to a small room down the corridor. He pulled out some towels, handing me two and using the other to dry himself.

"I'm sorry I got you wet," I said draping one of the towels over my shoulder.

"It's okay. Do you want to talk about it?"

"There's nothing to say. I took an accidental trip to the sea." I shrugged trying to make out it was no big deal. "You need to get back to the meeting. No need for us both to be absent."

"I'll wait with you until Victoria arrives."

"Greg, really, I'm okay, and I kinda wanna get out of these wet clothes."

Suddenly he didn't know where to look. "Okay, but can we talk later?"

I nodded. "Sure."

Once he'd gone, I slumped down into a big armchair and covered my wet hair with a towel. I needed help. Teleporting in my sleep was becoming dangerous, but it wasn't just that – I needed help to sort my head out. Bizarrely, I'm a really good swimmer. It's the only sport I was ever good at. So, I shouldn't have sunk like that.

The door banged open as Victoria came running in. "What happened?" she asked. "Are you okay?" She looked me up and down, her azule eyes full of worry, her face flushed. It looked like she'd run all the way here.

I put my hands up in front of me. "I'm okay. Physically anyway."

She sat on the sofa across from me, letting out a long breath. "What is going on with you?"

I twiddled my thumbs. "I sleep teleported."

"I thought you and Harkura had sorted that out."

"We had, but then it started again."

Victoria lent forward, leaning on her knees. "It's the nightmares. They've gotten worse since Laxus rocked up."

"How do you know?"

"It makes sense. If what he told us is true, we could be facing something really bad. I can see how this could be a trigger for you."

I hung my head. "I'm sorry I didn't tell you before. I didn't want you guys to worry."

"Mellissa, we're always going to worry about you. It's what we do." She sighed and then sat back on the sofa. "Look, I'll talk to Harkura about being less controlling if you promise to tell us immediately something like this happens."

"Deal," I bit my bottom lip. "There's something else. I think I need to learn how to manipulate sand."

She frowned. "Um …okay."

Victoria left to get me a fresh outfit as I dried off. I pulled my hair out of the plaits Harkura had put it in that morning and wrapped a towel around my head. Victoria quickly returned with a dress and some snacks and I pulled on a pink, knee-length, lacy thing with a frilly skirt. "Did it have to be so fancy?"

She rolled her eyes. "How many times do I have to tell you to enjoy the pretty outfits?"

There was a knock at the door. Victoria turned to open it. "What do you want?"

"To check Mellissa is okay," replied Greg.

"She's fine."

Victoria went to close the door but Greg slid into the room before she could shut it. "There's something else … council stuff."

Victoria narrowed her eyes at him.

I put my hand up in front of her. "It's fine. Would you like to join us for some tea? Victoria just got us a pot."

Everyone sat down as I poured out three cups of tea. Victoria glared at Greg in silence, and typically, he took no notice of her as I got comfy with my cup. "So, what's this council business?" I asked.

He sat up straight flicking his fringe to the side. "I thought you might want to know that the sea king is coming to land and wishes to see you."

I put my tea down on the table, almost dropping it. "He wants to see me?"

Greg nodded.

"Why?"

He shrugged. "The message didn't say, but Lady Gabrielle has arranged for you to meet him at the edge of

Purlvues on Saturday in two weeks. She said it would fit with your schedule."

If Lady Gabrielle said it would fit with my schedule, then it surely would. She knew it better than I did – more evidence that I wasn't really in control of anything. King Radius may as well meet with Lady Gabrielle. She knew what she was doing more than I did and would most likely make the final decision anyway. My shoulders dropped. "Lee wouldn't happen to be accompanying me?" There was no way he would let me do this on my own. He always had to have his piece of the action so he could take some credit for whatever went on.

Greg cringed. "Actually, it has turned into an entire council outing."

"What?"

"As expected, Lee objected but Lady Gabrielle defended you. Beatrice also objected and it also came out that the water nymphs are big fans of King Radius. Then Caleb and Hogan decided they were going if the nymphs were, and Brandon didn't want the leprechauns to be left out of the first major political meeting."

I put my head in my hands. This meeting with the sea king was going to be worse than I'd originally thought. "So, they all acted like children?"

"Pretty much. The only two not attending are Lady Gabrielle and Lord Cole."

I pointed at him. "What about you?"

"What about me?"

"What's your reason for coming? Don't you trust me to do a good job?"

"Of course, I trust you. But Emerson backed me into a corner. It wouldn't look good if all the elders didn't turn up."

Yeah right. He trusted me to meet with King Radius as much as Lee did. The only difference was he wasn't as rude about my lack of formal upbringing.

"Don't give me that look," he said.

"What look?" I asked.

"That look of disbelief. How many times do I need to say, I'm sorry?"

"You didn't exactly say it, you wrote it down."

"You did get my note. A response would have been nice."

I turned away from him. "I've been far too busy. You're not the only one with an important job."

Greg sighed, his red hair falling into his eyes as he did. "I know. I'm sorry."

Victoria shot to her feet, making us both jump. "Well, it seems the council stuff is sorted. Mellissa has a very busy schedule, so we better be leaving."

I could always count on Victoria to have an exit strategy. I bit down on my thumb nail as I followed her to the door.

Greg grabbed my wrist, his emerald eyes serious. "You know sleep teleporting is extremely dangerous." His words sent shivers down my spine.

"What?" I said in pretend shock. "I would never fall asleep in a council meeting."

Greg raised his eyebrow.

"Okay, I was totally asleep, but they were boring, and I was tired."

"I thought Harkura had taught you how to control your powers even while asleep."

Victoria swiftly removed his hand from my wrist. "We have this covered. This is not your concern."

Greg clenched his fists. "Very well."

I forced Victoria behind me. "I'm okay, really, but we have to go." My heart ached at the look of sadness in his eyes. I took Victoria's hand and teleported home.

The sand crunched under my feet as I walked hand in hand along the beach with Greg. The waves gently lapped across the sand, the water touching my toes. I tensed but I didn't feel the need to run. Greg pointed to the ocean. A mermaid was swimming towards us. No, a merman. I jumped as King Radius appeared in front of us.

"Mellissa you have failed as keeper of the heart. I have come to take it to a new keeper."

I grasped the crystal around my neck. "No," I shouted.

Radius moved his arm and the water shifted with it. I hurled my arms out wide, calling out to the sand, and this time it responded.

I awoke to a gentle breeze on my face. I run my hand across the grainy sand beside me and quickly sit up. My breath catches. I'm back at the beach again. My first instinct is to run. I jump to my feet and make it to the edge of the shore when I pause … I turn back to the ocean. Curling my toes, the sand rubs against my feet. Taking a wide stance, I lift my arms. Nothing happens. I close my eyes, slowing my breathing. I gently swipe my foot across the sand, feeling every grain on my skin. I open my eyes as I lift my arms. The sand rises, and as I push my arms out, it sweeps out towards the water.

I smile to myself. My training with Harkura was paying off.

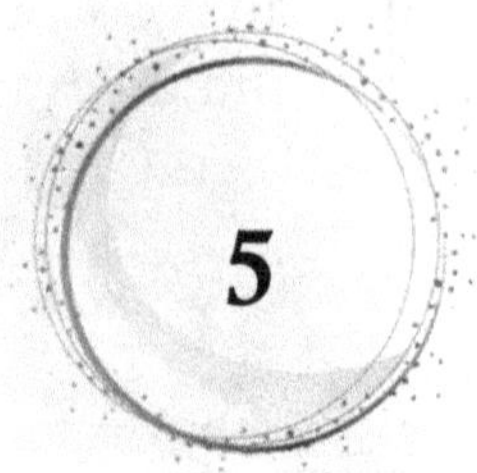

The Sea King

Gregory

Greg was at his desk, killing time as he flicked through another pile of applications. He'd arrived the night before ready for the upcoming trip to Perluves. It would have been quicker for him to travel direct from Novosvillas but Lee insisted they journeyed together, probably to ensure no one arrived before him. He would have hated the fact that Yuko and the other water nymphs were hosting the meeting and would be greeting King Radius first.

All members had an office in the council building for when their work brought them to the capital. Although, it didn't feel like Greg's office. It was still full of his father's things, yet another reminder he wasn't an established elder like he was, but at the same time, he couldn't bring himself to get rid of them. The only reason he'd managed to rearrange everything at city hall was thanks to Anna but now she'd left. Maybe he should consider Steve's suggestion. He'd turned up at city hall unannounced and made himself very comfortable in Greg's office. Steve's visit had been annoying but he'd mentioned a cousin who'd just finished college and needed a job. All the applicants he'd scrolled through were also fresh out of college. Steve may not be super smart, but he was a hard worker. If his cousin was anything like him, he'd be able to learn on the job. It wouldn't hurt to give him a trial run. He could pick another candidate from the list and do the same. Having two assistants would help while searching for a new chief of staff. He hadn't received many applications for that position yet. It would be harder to fill that role as he needed someone highly skilled.

Greg's ears twitched at the sound of knocking. He looked up to see Lady Gabrielle stood in the doorway. She was dressed in a smart black dress and blazer with her ash brown hair in its usual tight bun. It was good to see someone else was up and working. The last time he saw Hogan, he was running around in his pants and Caleb was nursing a hangover in the tearoom. Everyone else appeared to be still asleep.

"May I come in?" Lady Gabrielle asked.

"Of course," Greg replied.

Lady Gabrielle strode across the room and sat in the chair opposite him. The way she held herself always made you sit to attention. She had an air of authority about her. She placed some papers on his desk. "You need to fill these out."

Greg took the papers, frowning as he read the title. *Notice of Relationship Status*. "Why are you giving me these?"

"I thought you wouldn't disappear on me, leaving the forms on the floor like Mellissa. She isn't an easy person to pin down."

He put the forms back on his desk. There hadn't been a change in his relationship with Mellissa. Well, maybe a step backwards in their friendship but not the sort of change this form suggested. Emerson had mentioned something about not liking his relationship with Mellissa a few weeks ago. Surely, he wouldn't have complained to Lady Gabrielle. If that was the case, he'd have also complained about Beatrice. Even if Emerson went behind his back. there was nothing to report.

"I don't see why I have to fill out these forms." Greg handed the form back to Lady Gabrielle. She put her hand up, pushing them back towards him.

"Don't you? It is the rules of the council that if two members become more intimate they must inform the council chairman. I have not been informed so I thought I'd bring the forms to you."

"Mellissa and I are just friends."

Lady Gabrielle shook her head. "Kids these days don't even know when they're in a relationship."

"I think I would know, and I'm not. Why would I lie to you?"

"Not consciously, perhaps. But it's possible the two of you may be lying to yourselves. You cannot deny the two of you are close."

"We practically lived inside each other pockets when I was training her."

"Call your relationship what you like but I want these forms filled out. It won't be long until Lee tries to use your relationship against you."

Greg lent forward. "How could Lee use something like that against us?"

She jabbed the papers with her finger. "He can't if you fill in those forms. I'm only looking out for you. It's no secret that Lee wants my position as chair. He'll do whatever it takes to gain power, including picking apart your relationship with Mellissa."

"Lee could never take your place."

"That way of thinking is exactly why you're a target."

Greg rubbed his chin. "It isn't going to be easy getting Mellissa to sign these. She's just as likely to disappear on me."

"No one said you had to tell her what she was signing."

"You're bad."

"No, I'm extremely good at what I do."

That she was. If Greg could be half the leader she was, he'd be happy.

Lady Gabrielle stood. "Now I need to hurry everyone else along. You leave in thirty minutes and Hogan needs to get some clothes on. I swear, it sometimes feels like I work with children." She marched out of his office like a woman on a mission.

He knew what she meant about working with children. Most of his childhood was spent looking up to members of the council. Now that he was a member, he couldn't remember what he'd found so impressive about them. He looked down at the forms Lady Gabrielle had left. There was no doubt how he felt about Mellissa. Lady Gabrielle had obviously picked up on it, Emerson too. But he had no idea what was going on in Mellissa's head. Once upon a time, he thought he knew where they stood. That was before she'd kissed him. Then she acted like it never happened. Bringing this up could go terribly wrong.

Greg looked out the window as the scenery rushed by, the train chugging along at high speed. They were heading directly to Perluves. Unfortunately, they'd then have to get a carriage down to the beach as the train line ended too far inland to walk. That meant he'd be in even closer quarters with his travel companions.

"Why so glum?" Samson asked.

"I'm not glum" he replied. "I'm just thinking."

"About?"

"What King Radius wants."

Samson raised an eyebrow. He was here in his new role as advisor – Queen Mellissa's go-to guy for political stuff. It was a good thing she'd brought him along, otherwise, Greg would have been stuck with Lee, Lady Kate, Beatrice and Emerson. It was nice having someone to talk to without an agenda. Lady Gabrielle had confirmed Lee's dislike for him, and Kate followed Lee's lead no matter what. Beatrice and Emerson were also elders, but always poking their noses in. He couldn't blame them. He was the youngest elder there'd ever been. Although good partners should offer assistance and advice not just constantly look down on him, waiting for him to make mistakes.

Fortunately, Mellissa could spare Samson for the journey as she had her guardians and the boy she claimed was her cousin. Something was definitely going on that she wasn't telling him about. He needed to work his way out of her bad books if he had any hopes of finding out what she was hiding.

"You think too much," Samson said, "Just relax and enjoy the journey."

"I can't help it. I don't like not knowing."

"The queen is an over-thinker as well. I never realised how similar you two are."

Greg's brow rose. "Are we? he seems pretty impulsive to me, though, never stopping to think of the danger she might run into."

Samson laughed. "She does that too. She second-guesses herself a lot, and doesn't see how powerful she really is."

That he did know. It wasn't always easy to see yourself as others did. Greg lent back. "How are you liking your new role then?"

"It's great. Working for Queen Mellissa is nothing like working for the council. She's so bubbly and kind. She actually listens when you talk. The cottage she's having built for me will be finished soon so I'll be able to move permanently."

"I'm happy for you." Greg smirked. "I'm surprised you didn't want to sit with Victoria for the journey."

Samson turned the colour of a tomato but then a smirk crept onto his face. "I'm surprised you didn't want to sit with Queen Mellissa."

"I wanted to remain with the other elders."

Samson raised an eyebrow. "That's why you're sat in the furthest corner away from them with me."

Greg elbowed Samson in the side. "I bet you don't talk back to Mellissa like this."

"Of course not." Samson put his arm around Greg's neck and ruffled his red hair. "She is the elf queen, you're just my little cousin."

Greg pushed him away and patted his hair down. "This whole train journey is ridiculous. It would have been easier to travel straight from home."

"Yes, but it sends a message; you all arriving together."

Greg lowered his voice "Exactly Samson. Attack this train and you wipe out a big chunk of our world leaders"

Samson gasped. "How did Lady Gabrielle let this happen? Is that why she stayed behind to look after the capital?"

Greg shrugged. "Maybe she just wanted some peace and quiet."

Samson looked around the carriage. "It's all right, we have lots of guards."

Greg hung his head. He hadn't meant to freak Samson out. This whole pretence of togetherness just annoyed him. The council weren't united, they were split down the middle on everything.

The train screeched, it's speed decreasing as it neared its destination. Greg looked out of the window. In the distance, the sea glistened in the sunlight and there wasn't a cloud in the sky.

They finally arrived with Priestess Kai waiting for them as they got off the train. He led them out of the crowded station and ushered them into carriages flanked with guards. If the people of Perluves didn't know they were here, they would now.

Greg sat across from Emerson and Beatrice with a guard posted on the front and back of the carriage. Samson had left him to return to Mellissa. Greg reflected on the day ahead as the other two elders chatted amongst themselves. The main part of the city was built on a clifftop giving the water nymphs a wonderful view of the ocean. However, that wasn't where they were going. They passed the main road into the city and headed straight down towards the bay. Kai had explained that King Radius had arrived early and Yuko and Akito were giving him a tour of Perluves.

The water nymphs had gone all out with beautifying the bay. Flower petals formed a path over to a couple of big marquees with seashells and lilies hung from the sides. They'd arranged seating for everyone and each chair had a large bow tied around it in blue ribbon. It looked as if they were preparing for a beach wedding than a meeting with a crystal keeper.

Kai directed everyone where to sit. Of course, Greg was sat with the other two elders. As nice as everything looked, Greg still didn't see why they all had to be here. Mellissa could have simply teleported and spoken to the king herself. This all seemed like overkill. He could have arranged a day of interviews instead. Emerson tapped his arm. "I told you it was better we came. Just think how bad it looks that the warlocks didn't attend."

"Don't you think it's a bit much with us all here?" Greg asked.

Emerson straightened his back and held his head high. "Maybe, but appearance is everything. We want to put forward a united front."

Greg shivered at his words. Emerson sounded just like his father. Keeping up appearances had always been important to him. It turned out he hadn't been the only elder to think this way. Akito came running across the beach. His pale blue face tense. "Good, you're all here. Yuko will be here shortly."

Just as she finished her sentence, High Priestess Yuko appeared from behind two large rocks. She had a beaming grin on her face and her deep blue eyes shined. Greg had never seen her so excited before. She was followed by King Radius, his wife and two other people. Greg squinted. They didn't seem to be merfolk. They must be the King's new guardians. There was a female probably a little older than him and judging by her pink skin and webbed fingers she was an oarfish. The male was a stargazer. His tough orange skin and large bulging eyes were a giveaway.

Once they reached the marquee, Yuko clapped her hands. "Now we are all here, we can get started."

King Radius gazed at everyone. "I didn't realise the entire Queens council would be here."

Greg took a deep breath to hold back a laugh. He'd said they didn't all need to be here.

"We are not her council, " snapped Lee.

Yuko shot Lee a warning look. He crossed his arms and stuck his nose in the air. Yuko turned to the king. "We wanted to show you how seriously we take your visit."

"I appreciate that. Where is Queen Mellissa?"

"Right there." Yuko pointed at the second row. Mellissa quickly stood up and rubbed her eyes, looking as if she'd been about to fall asleep on Harkura's shoulder. She smoothed out the ruffles in her dress.

"You wanted to speak to me?" She sounded surprised. Greg told her the king had requested to meet her. Everyone else had just jumped on the bandwagon.

"Of course." The king marched over to Mellissa closely followed by his people. Those sat near her quickly moved out the way. Why had they not placed her at the front? "Keeper to keeper." The king gave her a gentle smile, but his eyes said it all. He was worried. His chestnut hair was flecked with more grey then the last time Greg had seen him. His tanned skin crinkled as continued talking. "You remember my wife, Harmony?" The slender woman with firefly red locks curtsied. Mellissa nodded in acknowledgment to her, giving her a sweet smile. The king pointed to the other two members of his party. "These are my guardians, El and Torq, they came to me after I activated the moon crystal, just like you said."

"It's nice to meet you." She shook both of their hands, smiling brightly. Pointing over her shoulder, she said, "It would probably take too long to name everyone here so how about we focus on what you want to discuss."

"I like the way you think." Radius patted her on the back causing her to stumble. The king took her arm and gestured for her to sit as he sat next to her. "The sea kingdom is currently experiencing a problem."

Mellissa bit her lip and quickly glanced at Laxus. "What sort of problem?"

"It's hard to explain." Radius looked at his wife.

Queen Harmony put her hand on her husband's shoulder. "Our people have been experiencing temporary fits of madness. They forget themselves and do terrible things. It's almost as if they're possessed."

"Could it be some sort of virus?" Mellissa asked.

Harmony shrugged. "We've been unable to find any links between the people that have been affected. We were wondering if you land folk had experienced anything like this."

"No, we haven't. Have we?" Mellissa turned to Yuko who shook her head. "But we'll assist you in any way we can."

Greg scratched his head. Only a life crystal would be strong enough to affect someone's mind like that and there was no way any true keeper would do something so sinister. No other living being could harness magic like it. Unless they weren't a living being. "You could be dealing with a spirit creature," he said.

All eyes were suddenly on him. Beatrice nudged him. "Don't be silly. Spirit creatures are practically unheard of."

Greg scowled. "They are extremely rare but that doesn't mean they don't exist. A year ago, human elves were unheard of, now we have a city full."

Beatrice gritted her teeth and curled her top lip. Queen Harmony walked towards him. "They are so rare we didn't consider the possibility, but you could be on to something. Do you know anything about protecting us from the spirit creatures?"

"I'm sorry, I'm not an expert on the subject. If I'm right at least you know what you're dealing with." Greg jumped out of his seat as Mellissa appeared beside him. It had been a while since she'd surprised him like that.

She poked his arm. "Why didn't you tell me spirit creatures were a thing?"

"You never asked."

"I never know what to ask."

"It's Harkura's job to teach you all this stuff."

"Harkura mainly ensures I can fight off theoretical assassins."

King Radius laughed. "I forgot you're still learning about this keeper stuff. You seem to have a better grip on it than I do, though."

"I do?" she asked her cheeks turning red.

Greg nudged her.

"I mean …" She put her hand over her mouth, turned to Greg and whispered, "What do I mean?"

Greg placed his hand on his forehead. A few of the others tutted and the row behind him muttered something. Emerson cleared his throat and pursed his lips. This was not the sort of image he'd discussed earlier. It didn't matter what they all thought, though. What mattered was the conversation with King Radius. Greg touched Mellissa's shoulder. "Mellissa, I mean The Queen hasn't had any experience with spirits. None of us have, but as she said, we'll assist any way we can."

"Yes." Mellissa nodded. "The Sea may not be my domain but all you have to do is ask and I will assist."

"Thank you, Queen Mellissa." King Radius stood and bowed. His wife and guardians copied him. "We now know what we're dealing with and can search for a solution."

A strong gust suddenly blew through the marquee. The once clear sky had quickly filled with dark, grey clouds. The wind grew stronger, blowing sand around. The marquee shook as the decorations on it crashed to the ground.

"Mellissa," screamed Laxus. Gusts of wind surrounded him, lifting him from the ground. Victoria grabbed his arm and Mellissa ran in his direction. Thunder roared above and the marquee collapsed. Shouts and screams surrounded Greg as he pulled himself out from under the collapsed marquee.

The sapphire-blue sky was now dark and ominous. Thunder rumbled and rain burst forth from the clouds. The force of the wind made it hard to stand as Greg searched the area for Mellissa. She was nowhere to be seen but Laxus was caught up in a ball of air being dragged towards the sea. Greg ran towards him. Then, placing his hands together, he focused his magical energy, pushing it outward, and cut through the ball with a carefully placed barrier.

Laxus hit the sand with a thud. "Gregory?" The boy sounded shocked.

The air began to swirl around the boy again. With a flick of his wrist, Greg put a protection bubble around Laxus. "This weather sure is weird."

Laxus put his hands on the bubble, his eyes wide. "Why are you helping me?"

Greg looked down at the boy. "You were in trouble."

"Look out," yelled Laxus. Greg ducked, narrowly being hit by a glass hand. The creature pulled its arm back and went to strike again. Before he could form any magic, the creature was shattered by a beam of light.

"Laxus," Mellissa shouted, running towards them. Behind her, the remains of the marquee were on fire. That must have been Harkura's doing. A bit over the top but everyone was now free.

The torrential rain lightened but Greg winced as he was hit by hailstones, his arm cut. He soon realised, it wasn't hail but shards of glass. Glass creatures began popping up all over the bay. Both pairs of guardians were quick to engage in battle, along with the council guards. As quickly as the creatures were smashed, more were created. Some council members joined the fight while others like Lee hid behind rocks.

Greg had never seen magic like this before, but he deflected any creature that came his way. He knew it took someone powerful to manipulate the weather. He saw a group of creatures try to break through the protection bubble around Laxus. There was something about that boy that Mellissa was keeping to herself. A gust of wind took Greg's feet out from under him and the creatures surrounded him. He was now the target. If he was taken out, the bubble around Laxus would burst.

Pushing both hands out Greg created two barriers slicing the creatures in two, but it wasn't enough. Another group surrounded him, pushing him down. A bolt of lightning shot over him and shards of glass shattered over his head. Mellissa jumped over him her foot engulfed in light energy as she kicked a creature. It shattered on impact. She dove to the ground, cartwheeling whilst releasing light energy from her feet, taking the rest of the group out. Whatever Harkura was doing in her training, he was doing an impeccable job. Her fighting ability had developed fast in the last few months.

The hail of glass stopped. The sound of the waves hitting the shore was all that could be heard. The sky rumbled and the hail started again but this time concentrated over Laxus. The power behind the spell had grown dramatically. Greg ran towards him. "Mellissa, you need to reinforce the protection bubble. My magic won't hold under that."

Running beside him, Mellissa lifted her arm, but they were blown over. Greg covered his face as the barrier burst, and Laxus screamed as a ball of wind picked him up again. Mellissa's teleport was deflected, sending her crashing to the ground. Her magic wasn't working on it. How could that be? She was quickly back on her feet running after Laxus, and then froze on the spot as Laxus was dragged out to sea.

"Mellissa," Greg shouted. The colour had drained from her face and she didn't move. Water still freaked her out. Greg ran past her towards the edge of the ocean as the ball of wind turned into a funnel, whirling round and round. He couldn't get any closer. A cold blast flew past him and Victoria skidded to a halt beside him throwing icy blasts at the vortex. The ball of wind was now a full-blown tornado with Laxus at its centre. Yet, their magic couldn't touch it.

"How can we stop that thing?" Victoria asked.

The only person strong enough to fight something like this was frozen in fear. If Mellissa could release enough energy, she could disrupt it. But wait. She wasn't the only superpower here. Greg swivelled round. "King Radius."

Everyone's attention was on the tornado. The king's ears twitched. "Yes?"

"Can you manipulate all forms of water including moisture in the air?"

Radius nodded. "Yes, but how does that help?"

"If you pull the moist air from the tornado it may disperse it."

"It's worth a try." The king ran as close as he could towards the vortex. He pulled at the air as if pulling on a rope. After a few seconds, the whirling of the tornado began to slow down. It was working, but it wasn't enough – they needed something more to disrupt the storm.

A flash of lightning shot through the middle of the tornado and the ground shook violently. Mellissa had come to life and was pulling the sand towards her. It swirled around her in heaps. A roar echoed over the bay as she sent the sand crashing into the vortex. A shadowy figure appeared above the clouds. It looked like a bird. Both Radius and Mellissa blasted the vortex with a ball of light. Greg threw his arm over his face as the bright light blinded him.

"Victoria," Harkura cried running past Greg into the sea. Mellissa and Laxus were falling at speed towards the water. She had teleported to catch Laxus. Why wasn't she teleporting back? Greg blinked twice as a set of ice stairs appeared mid-air.

Harkura ran towards them and then jumping off the end, he reached out and caught Mellissa and Laxus. An ice slide appeared under his feet and he gracefully slid back to shore. Victoria ran to Harkura's side.

Harkura laid Mellissa on the sand. She still had tight hold of Laxus. Victoria pulled Laxus away and blasted Mellissa. Mellissa screamed as she shot up to a seated position. "What are you doing?"

"Shocking you back to reality. Why didn't you teleport back?" Victoria yelled.

Harkura put a hand on Victoria's shoulder. "Maybe we should have Lord Ainsworth check her for any injuries."

Greg's ears twitched at his name and looked down at his hands. He suddenly realised he was the only one that knew healing magic. Why hadn't anyone thought to bring a team of healers? They had loads of guards. Lee should never be allowed to plan these things again. He walked over to them and knelt in front of Mellissa. Apart from a cut on her hand, she looked in good form. The real issue was her head. He took her hand and healed it.

Mellissa pouted. "And you said my guardians weren't demons."

"Victoria isn't a demon, just a special kind of crazy," he replied.

Mellissa laughed.

Victoria flicked his ear. "What are you saying about me?"

"Nothing." Greg sighed. "Listen, Mellissa, I think you need to talk to someone about your fear of the water.

She looked at the sand. "I know."

Greg forgot what he'd planned to say. He thought she'd come up with an excuse and deny the issue, not agree. This was good though. Admitting it was a problem meant she could deal with it and find a way to recover.

"Gregory," said Emerson snapping Greg back to reality, "If you don't mind a few others require your healing expertise."

Greg looked over Emerson's shoulder. A queue of injured council members had formed. He groaned. "Very well.

I'll check the boy and be over momentarily."

Mellissa grabbed his arm. "No." She pulled her hand back and bit her thumb. "I mean, they need your help more."

Victoria slapped his back. "Laxus is fine. Harkura is warming him up with his fire." She pushed Laxus over to Harkura. "Just need to get Mellissa and Laxus some fresh clothes. The idiot destroyed the pretty dress I picked out for her with that energy blast." She pulled Mellissa to her feet.

Greg stood up, looking down at them. They were all acting weird. Did they not realise they couldn't fool him? However, now was not the time to question them.

Kai walked over to them and put his arm around Mellissa. "I'll take you into the city to get fresh outfits."

As Kai lead them away, Greg went with Emerson to heal the injured. No one was badly hurt. In his opinion the majority of the group's injuries were so minor they could have waited. Once he was done, High priestess Yuko wandered over to him. "Next time, I'll bring a medical team from the city. It was an oversight on my part. It will save you healing every tiny scratch that occurs."

Greg stuffed his hands in his pockets and leant against a boulder. "Next time, I'm not coming."

"Don't say that; you were probably the most useful out of everyone here."

A heavy hand patted his back. "Aren't you a clever one," smiled King Radius, "I can see why the queen keeps you around."

Yuko beamed at the king, her pale blue skin shimmered with glee. "Yes, Gregory is a valued member of the queen's council."

"I remember you from last time," said Radius. "You were practically holding the queen's hand through the whole crystal handover."

Yuko's eyebrows rose. "Was he now?"

"What no!" snapped Greg.

Yuko tilted her head.

Greg pointed at her. "It's not like that."

"Lady Gabrielle wants those forms on her desk first

thing tomorrow."

"How do you know about that?"

She smiled knowingly. "I know more than you realise, Gregory." She bowed to King Radius and sashayed across the sand, her long robes trailing behind her. As she spoke with Queen Harmony, she glanced back at Greg and winked.

Greg placed his hand on his forehead. There was no way he could get Mellissa's signature on those papers in that time frame. In fact, he wasn't sure if she'd ever sign them.

"It's all good," King Radius said, "My wife and I met when she was one of my advisers. I fell for her brains as well as her beauty. I'd be lost without her."

"Really, you have the wrong idea."

"Do I? You're the only one other than her guardians that referred to Queen Mellissa without her title. Also, you and her ice guardian were probably the most concerned for her safety."

"Am I that obvious?"

King Radius shrugged. "I don't see why it's a problem. Although, I think Queen Mellissa should rethink a few of her council members."

"If only it was that simple, but I'll let her know. Oh, I have something for you." Greg pulled a card out his pocket and handed it to the king. "Direct contact details for Mellissa. Will save you all this fuss next time you wish to talk with her."

"Thank you. What about you?"

"What about me?"

"It's my understanding you are a changeling. You're not limited to shift into only land animals?"

Greg shook his head. "I am not limited to the land."

"Someone with your smarts would make a useful contact."

"Very well." Greg rummaged through his jacket pockets and produced a pen. He took the card back and added his contact details to the back.

"What are you two talking about?" snapped Lee. Greg hadn't noticed him approach.

Greg pushed his fringe to the side. "Oh, just how bizarre the weather is."

"Yes, it was rather odd," agreed Lee, "Luckily the king was here to save us."

King Radius gave Lee a nod. "I will always assist when I see someone in need."

Lee bowed to the king and then glared at Greg before walking off.

King radius pointed at Lee. "There's one that definitely needs to be reconsidered."

King Radius had no idea. If only it was that simple, but Mellissa didn't have the same sort of authority on land as he appeared to have in the sea.

"Will you be at Mellissa's coronation?" Greg asked.

"As much as I would like to, with the strange occurrences in my kingdom, I don't think I'll be able to attend. It's a much longer journey and I couldn't leave my people while they are in need."

"I'm sure Mellissa will understand."

"Yes, that queen of yours is a truly good-hearted person. She will be a great ruler. What am I saying, she already is!" Radius patted his shoulder.

Greg raised an eyebrow. Even with what had just happened the King was still enthusiastic. Being slightly eccentric must be a crystal keeper thing.

A woodpecker chirped and flew out to sea. It was weird to see a forest bird this far out. But then, this whole day had been weird. And he now had more questions than ever, but he wasn't sure he'd get answers any time soon.

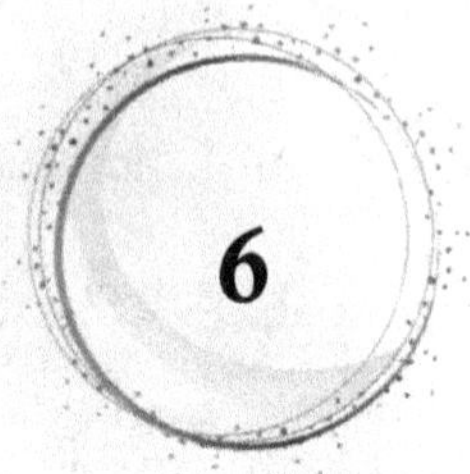

6

Break

Mellissa

"Well, what happened?" Harkura asked.

I handed him my notes from the recent meeting. After the strange weather and attack of the glass creatures, an emergency council meeting had been called. It was pointless. No one had any idea what had caused the strange event, and I couldn't tell them about Laxus. I'd spent most of it trying to stay awake. No one seemed to get how tired I was.

Harkura flicked through my notebook. "You call these notes?"

"Let me see?" said Samson taking my scribbled words from Harkura. He frowned as he flicked through the pages. "Is that character meant to be Lady Gabrielle and who is she stepping on?"

"That's Lee," I said

"And how does the drawing relate to what happened in the meeting?"

"It's how I wish the meeting had gone."

Samson and Harkura looked at me with blank faces.

I snatched back my book. "Everyone was going on about what happened at the bay. Emerson volunteered to look into it."

"So, no mention of the item," Harkura asked.

I shook my head. "No." Luckily no one had questioned why Laxus had been the one thrown up in the air by the gust. They all believed he'd just been unlucky.

"What item?" Samson asked

"Queen Mellissa lost a gemstone on the beach. I thought, maybe, someone might have picked it up."

"Next time we won't bring precious things to a meeting like that," I said.

"You have a point. It is something to discuss later," said Harkura.

Samson looked at us like we were crazy and then shook his head as he handed me back my notebook. "Is there anything else I need to know about the meeting?"

"Not really, the council were completely clueless." I rubbed the sides of my head. "Can we just get out of here? I'm tired and I have an exam in the morning."

Harkura took my hand. "Don't forget you have a therapy session with Daniel."

My shoulders sagged. I'd forgotten about that.

"Don't look so deflated. Even I'll admit these sessions with Daniel have helped you."

"I just have so much to do."

Samson smiled at me as he took my other hand. "If there's anything I can help with let me know."

"Thanks," I replied.

Holding onto them both tightly I teleported back to Urbem Folium leaving them both in my office in the castle. Samson was more than happy to do my paperwork for me and go over council procedures with Harkura.

I arrived in Daniel's office where we just sat and talked. They couldn't really be called therapy sessions as Daniel wasn't qualified as a psychotherapist. But he was a good listener and never judged me.

Daniel lent forward. "Apart from feeling you have too much to juggle, is there anything else bothering you?"

I shrugged. "I don't think so. I'm sure I'll feel better once my exams are over."

"You know there's no need for you to finish school.

Your human education won't mean anything here."

I twiddled my thumbs. "I don't know if I'm completely ready to let go of being human." It felt liberating that I'd soon be done with school but at the same time I was scared of how life would be without the safety net of being a student. Daniel already had my coronation all planned out for next month. My position as elf queen would be made official. It was a terrifying thought.

"You'll never stop being human. As you said, we are a settlement of human elves." A smile spread across his face. "We'll show the magic world what that truly means."

I nodded feeling like a weight had been lifted from my shoulders. "So, can a boy band make an appearance at my coronation?"

He rubbed his chin. "I'll consider it for your birthday ball."

I chuckled. "Fine."

I screamed as a dark shadow threw me off a cliff. I tried to teleport, but it wouldn't work. Just as I was about to hit the floor, I was shocked awake. I found myself screaming for real as I fell from a great height. Waving my arms around, a giant vine shot up to catch me … then something snapped as I hit the vine, sliding down it to the ground. This was insane. I thought my sleep teleporting was getting better. Since I'd started regular therapy sessions with Daniel, I'd managed to go two weeks straight without rematerializing somewhere random.

Where had I beamed into this time? This was so going to end up in the newspaper. It wasn't a common occurrence for giant vines to grow overnight in the human world. Luckily there didn't seem to be anybody around. If I got out of here fast, at least this incident wouldn't be associated with me.

I tried to move but a sharp pain shot through my body. Attempting to stand, putting weight on my left leg, I groaned, hearing a cracking sound. I slumped back down, my eyes watering. This wasn't good. Even if I managed to get myself to the magic world, healing bones still took hours. This was definitely going to ruin my schedule for the day. Should I teleport straight to a healer or go home first? Victoria would be mad if I didn't tell her what happened.

"Are you all right?" shouted a woman running over to me.

"I'm fine," I replied. Had she witnessed what happened? I shuffled about on the floor. There was no way I could get up on my own. My leg was definitely broken.

"You just fell out of the sky!" she exclaimed. "That plant thing was a good trick, but I can tell you're injured. Let me take you to the infirmary, it's not too far away. It just so happens that I'm on my way there as I work as a healer." She smiled at me, helping me up and supporting me as we walked. "You can be my first patient for the day."

Hmm, she'd referred to herself as a healer which meant we were in the magic world. That was good. Giant plants appearing out of nowhere was more common, so it wouldn't be such a big deal. Although it depended on which city I was in. Plant magic wasn't as commonly used as it was amongst the elves.

As we walked, I recognised a few buildings. I sighed. "We wouldn't happen to be in Novosvillas would we?"

"Yes, we are. Now come this way."

Leading me through the infirmary, she took me straight to a treatment room. She asked a receptionist to call her cousin on the way in and let him know who she'd arrived with – which meant she recognised me. No doubt she wanted to name drop to her cousin. What a story it would make when she got home. This was becoming ever more common. Wherever I went in the magic world someone recognised me as the keeper of the heart crystal. I hated it. It made keeping a low profile impossible. I hoped she wasn't the gossiping type. If this got back to Greg, I was sure he'd have something to say, and I didn't need one of his lectures on top of the one Harkura was going to give me – both of them so quick to judge but didn't stop to look at their own faults. The healer helped me up onto the tiny hospital bed.

"My name's Cynthia by the way." She said with a smile.

I looked at her properly now that I was sat down. Her mouse brown hair was tied up in a messy bun and her round cheeks where rosy. Her brown eyes creased at the side as she examined my leg. "Is there anyone you want me to call, so I can let them know where you are?" she asked.

"Not really. I'm hoping to be healed and out of here before anyone notices I'm missing."

"I'm afraid you're going to be stuck here a while. Your leg is broken so it will take a few hours to mend." She got out some healing stones and placed them around my leg.

This was great, Harkura was going to freak and I was losing valuable study time. Luckily, I didn't have an exam today. My first few assessments had gone well but that didn't mean I had time to slack off now. I sighed, looking up at the ceiling. If I hadn't panicked, I would have easily teleported myself to the ground. Hindsight is a great thing.

There was a knock on the door. Cynthia opened it and spoke to whoever it was and then said she'd leave the two of us alone for a bit. As she walked out, in walked Greg.

I shot forward. "How did you know I was here?"

"Cynthia had the receptionist call me," he replied.

I slumped back, putting my arm over my forehead. "You're her cousin. Is there anyone in this city that isn't related to you?"

"My dad had five younger sisters and a brother, so I have a lot of cousins. You're lucky Cynthia found you. What exactly were you doing falling out of the sky?"

"It's the latest craze free-falling from extreme heights. You should try it sometime. It's a real rush."

"Really, that's what you're going with? Saying it was a training accident would have been more convincing. You sleep teleported again, didn't you?"

Why hadn't I thought of that? It would have been much simpler and easier to believe. "Okay, I did, but it was a one-off. I've been getting better. I even started talking to someone."

He lent on the side of the bed. "That's good to hear. I'm glad you're working through it. There wouldn't be anything else going on?"

I shrugged. "I'm just stressed with exams and my impending move, so I've taken a back step in my recovery."

"Are you also stressed because your cousin is visiting?" Greg looked at me suspiciously. He knew something was off about Laxus, but I wasn't going to say anything. Laxus would be mad if I revealed who he was to another person. I couldn't betray his trust. If he stopped confiding in me, it would be a huge problem.

"He doesn't stress me. I'm just concerned about him being around all this magic stuff. I mean he is only twelve."

"He seems pretty well adjusted for twelve."

I bit my thumb nail. "What's with all the questions about my cousin?"

"So, you're sticking with this cousin thing then?"

I glared at him.

He shrugged. "Fine if that's what you want."

Cynthia came back to check on me, and Greg was about to leave, so asked her not to discharge me until he got back. I told her not to listen to him. She laughed stating I was just as Greg described. I wasn't sure if that was a good thing or not. Greg knew too many of my bad habits to give anyone a good impression of me. Unfortunately, he returned just before Cynthia gave me the all-clear so I couldn't escape him. I didn't need him asking me any more questions. He was really hard to lie to.

"Shouldn't you be working?" I knew if I asked questions first, it would stop him from questioning me.

"You are hard work," he replied.

"Hey, I resent that remark" I answered with a glare.

"Why? because you know it's true." He chuckled to himself. "I wouldn't be doing my job properly if I didn't ensure the heir to the elf thrown wasn't looked after well when she visited the city."

I looked down at my hands. "You know this is probably the longest I've seen you since the meeting with Radius. You always have something important to do."

"That's not true. I saw you last week at the council meeting."

"Council meetings don't count. Especially since I'm not always fully present. I mean, Lee starts talking and my consciousness leaves the room."

Greg laughed.

I don't know why I'd bothered to point this out. I shouldn't have expected to get any other sort of response from him. It was probably more convenient for him to only see me at council meetings.

Greg pushed his fringe to the side. "You're right."

"I am? I mean, yeah I am."

"I've been a terrible friend. You know what, I'll make it up to you today. I've already been pulled away from work because of you."

"Hey, I didn't make you do anything and Harkura is going to wonder where I am. What time is it?"

He looked at his watch. "Nearly ten."

I gasped. So late already. Harkura would have woken me hours ago. He was going to be so mad when I got home. He'd have called Victoria too so, I was going to have two angry guardians on my return home. I should have had Cynthia contact them as well.

"I assume you haven't eaten." Greg said, "I'll buy you breakfast. We can go to the bakery you like."

"The one with the flaky pastries?" I asked.

He nodded.

I jumped down off the bed. "Let's go."

Greg grabbed my arm as I went to walk out the door. "Don't you have shoes?"

I looked down at my bare feet. "I teleported in my sleep remember. I'm wearing my pyjamas."

"We'll have to buy you some on the way then."

"I could just teleport home and get some" I paused, unsure sure why I'd said it. If I went back now, I'd be ambushed by my guardians. "Never mind what I just said. Let's go. Can you get a message to Harkura so he knows I'm all right?"

"Sure."

I went to walk out but he stopped me.

"Wait a minute. Put this on." He took off his jacket and draped it around my shoulders.

I smiled at him and then shifted my arms into the sleeves and put the hood up. "You know what this is missing? Cat ears on the hood," I said putting my fingers above my head.

He shook his head at me and grabbed my hand leading me out the infirmary.

I sat on the edge of Greg's desk swinging my feet as I admired my new boots. They were similar to a pair I had that mysteriously vanished and replaced by a pair of ridiculously high heels that I couldn't walk in.

"Must you sit on my desk? You're getting crumbs everywhere," Greg moaned as he dusted off his desk.

I tore a pastry in two. "I can't help it; the pastry is so flaky"

"We could have sat in the bakery."

"I may now have boots but I'm still wearing pyjamas remember and I thought you had work to do."

Greg handed me a napkin. "At least use a napkin and stop picking your food apart."

"Jeez, you're starting to sound like Harkura." I stuck my tongue out at him.

"Harkura wouldn't let you eat that pastry."

"So, you do remember things I tell you."

"Of course, I do. Now will you move, your butt is in the way."

He sat at his desk and looked at me with his emerald eyes expectantly, gesturing to the folder he couldn't open due to me being in the way. I let out a long exaggerated breath as I laid across the desk with my arm over my face. "This is so boring. Is this what you do every day?"

"So sorry my job bores you. Some of us don't have loads of staff to do things for us so we can lay around getting in other people's way."

I sat up. "Hey, I do plenty of work and it's just as boring. Why do think I haven't gone home? I'm avoiding my job."

"Is that why you made me contact Harkura instead of doing it yourself?"

"I'm avoiding the inevitable lecture he's going to give me."

"You know that you're the one in charge."

I swung my legs around and jumped off the desk. "Yeah I am the one in charge and you know what? You are too. We should avoid our jobs together."

Greg lent on his desk. "And what do you suggest we do while avoiding our work."

"We could free fall from extreme heights. It's the latest craze." I winked.

Greg laughed. "You're crazy." He got up and walked over to a filing cabinet with a pile of papers. "It's not easy for either of us to walk away from our responsibilities."

I dug my nails into my palms and looked down at the floor. "Harkura accused me of not taking my responsibilities seriously."

"I didn't mean …"

"I know you didn't, but maybe, I should get back." As much as I wanted to avoid the tasks Harkura had for me, I had a responsibility to take care of Laxus. If something happened to him, the whole world could be at risk. "It's just hard adjusting to everything. You met my dad. He's so laid back, I used to be able to do whatever I wanted. Now, I'm told how to act, what to eat, where to go, and I swear Victoria is binning my clothes."

"You know what even crystal keepers should get a break." He came over and took my hand. "Where do you want to go?"

"What?"

"Well, it's impossible to avoid my job here. We should probably also avoid Urbem Folium, the capital and your house."

I looked at my hand in Greg's. Laxus was safe with Harkura. He looked after him when I was at school and in council meetings. I deserved a proper day off. "I know where we can go." I pulled Greg towards me and teleported.

I threw myself down on my bed exhausted from my day out at my favourite theme park. A break from my busy schedule had been exactly what I needed; it was also exactly what Greg had needed, but since magic had been part of my life, I hadn't been back. Going on all the rides and playing different games had almost made me feel normal again.

Victoria burst in my room bring a gust of icy air with her, followed by Harkura and Laxus. I'd expected them sooner.

"What time do you call this?" Victoria shouted. "We thought something had happened to you. Then we get a call from Greg's office to say you're in Novosvillas."

I sat up. "I'm sorry, I just, well …" I still hadn't come up with an excuse to tell them. Although, I didn't need to come up with an excuse – Greg was right. I was the one in charge. Now was the time to take Daniel's advice and show them I was capable. "I needed a break."

"No, you sleep teleported," yelled Victoria.

"Yes, but that's not it," I shouted.

"Isn't it obvious why she disappeared?" Laxus said. "She was in Novosvillas. She was with Greg."

Victoria slapped my arm. "Seriously, you ditched us to go hang out with that idiot changeling."

I rubbed my reddened skin. "So, what if I did? You guys were stressing me out."

"You should have come back for one of us," said Harkura.

"You are why I needed a break. I need more freedom. I shouldn't have to make up excuses for why I want to hang out with a friend."

Victoria gritted her teeth. "She's right, Harkura, you need to back off.

Harkura sighed. "I'll try, but all I want is to protect you, although I realise, I may have smothered you in the process."

I tugged at my ear, shocked at what I'd just heard. "Thank you."

Victoria placed her hand on my shoulder. "Seriously, though, he doesn't deserve your time. You're too good for him."

She took Harkura's hand and led him out of my room whilst I stared at the spot where they'd just stood. That had been almost too easy. However, Laxus remained, sat at the end of my bed staring at me with his big round eyes.

"Okay, what's up?" I asked.

"I'm sorry if my arrival in your life has caused you stress. It was unintentional but I think I can help you remain grounded."

"It's not your fault. I was having nightmares long before you showed up." My nightmares were a result of trapping my best friend in the tree of time and my battle with Kadon. My paralysing fear of water came from almost drowning twice.

"Unfortunately, I can't make the nightmares go away but this should help you stay grounded." He smiled, showing me a small bag of what looked like green sand.

"What is it?" I asked.

"Pixie dust." He sprinkled a handful of the green stuff over me and chanted: "For the wandering spirit stay bound to this earth until the host demands you fly."

I felt warm lights surround my body and a rush of magic swept over me.

"I didn't mean to worry you about the safety of this world. I wouldn't have come if I didn't believe you could keep it safe." He bowed and left.

When I awoke the next day, I was still in my bed. And the pixie dust seemed to have done its job. I couldn't turn my worry off overnight, but Laxus was right. So many people believed in my power, it was about time I started to. Whatever happened next, I was going to keep Laxus safe along with the rest of the world. My new-found resolve didn't last long, though. I screamed as fire rained down on me. Throwing my arms up I created a barrier. This must be what Harkura meant when he said, expect the unexpected. I was never going to get a proper break.

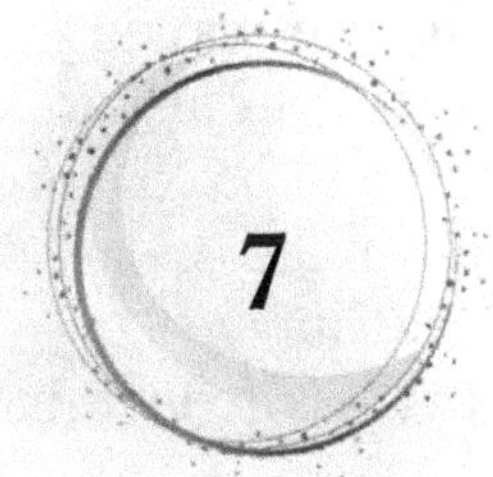

7

Pens and paper

Gregory

Greg let himself into city hall. As usual, he was the first one there, his desk overflowing with papers and a few notes from his staff. Considering he'd disappeared the day before without telling anybody, no one questioned where he'd been. But a day off was just what he needed to destress.

He studied his new assistant's CV, scanning her employment experience as he prepared to meet her. After showing her around, filing his messy pile of paperwork would be her first job. If she couldn't sort through that in a couple of hours, there's no way she could handle more complex tasks. But he shouldn't think negatively. She may be Steve's cousin, but she'd seemed pretty capable in her interview.

He continued to rifle through the morning mail: bills, request forms, and a few applications. He picked one letter from the stack and put the rest down. It seemed different from the others with no postmark or address, just his name. And the handwriting seemed familiar like the weird letter he'd received before. He opened the envelope. Inside was a picture of the lake on the western edge of the city. On the other side it read:

Meet me here at six and I'll explain everything about your father.

G.A.

Why was this G.A. sending such cryptic messages?

There wasn't anything he didn't know about his father. And he wasn't about to meet someone who didn't sign with a full name. He'd have no idea what he was walking into – it could be a con to get him somewhere isolated or just an idiot playing a practical joke. He turned the photo over in his hand.

There was a knock on the door. "Come in," he yelled as he dropped the photo in the bin.

In walked a tall, dark-haired woman. "I was told to report directly to you, sir."

Ah yes, his new assistant. He got up and shook her hand. "Good morning, Julia."

She straightened her glasses. "It's Julie."

"Julie, sorry. Well, as it's your first day we'll start with a tour of the building. Has anyone shown you your desk yet?"

"No, sir."

"No problem, I'll do that as well.' He held the door open for her.

"You're doing the tour?"

"Yes." It's what he did with all his new staff. He felt it made them more at ease and willing to approach him; he finally had an office full of fresh-faced employees and he wanted it to remain that way.

"Okay then." She looked down at the floor as she followed him out of the room.

Greg took her on the usual tour of the building making it clear which areas the general public had access to and which ones were staff only. She talked a lot just like Steve but at least she seemed enthusiastic. After showing her to her desk, they ended back at his office. "Organising this mess will be your first task," he added as he handed her the huge pile of paperwork. As she stood there holding it with both hands, he realised he'd need to go over the complex filing system. This induction was going to take longer than he thought.

After getting Julie set up, Greg was back at his desk, trying to focus on work, but his mind kept wandering back to the photo. He didn't like the idea that there was something he mightn't know about his father. Greg looked at the clock on his desk. It was now 5.30.. If he left now, he'd have plenty of time to get to the lake and unravel this mystery. He grabbed his jacket and left.

Shifting into a bird he flew to the lake and circled it a few times. It was a fairly open area. Pebbles lined the edge of the lake, the rest was grass with a few trees dotted around the area. A group of kids were playing near the water so he landed on the higher side of the lake where he had a good view. Whoever this person was, they'd have to fly or use the only path that came that way – which meant, no one could take him by surprise.

He sat under a tree and got comfortable. The sun was low in the sky and a gentle breeze rustled some cherry blossom's as pink and white petals fell onto his head. Frogs croaked nearby as he watched seagulls circle the water. He glanced at his watch. An hour had gone by, and nothing. Why would someone send him that note and not turn up? But what if the note arrived yesterday? That would mean he was a day late. He sighed. It looked like he'd wasted the last two hours and was left again without answers.

"I hear you have a new assistant," Samson said taking a seat at his table in the tea rooms.

"You heard right," Greg replied.

"Anyone I know?"

"Do you remember Steve?"

Samson's eyebrows rose as he leant forward. "You hired Steve?"

Greg shook his head. "No, his cousin. She just finished college. It's only on a trial basis but she seems all right so far."

Samson leant back in his seat. "That's a relief. I can now move away knowing you're getting organized."

"You don't need to bother about me. It's Mellissa you're meant to be worrying about. Where is she anyway?"

"She and Victoria are trying to break the seal on the tree of time again. I was sent to get an official copy of the meeting minutes. As she stated, she's the one in charge and if I don't like the notes she took, I'll have to sort it myself."

Greg chuckled. It was good to hear Mellissa was finally taking control. "Well she is the boss, but I understand why you might have a problem with her account. As good as her drawings are, they don't usually relate to the meeting."

"This is what she drew today. I assume you were talking a lot." Samson handed him a piece of paper.

"Is that me with bunny ears?"

Samson nodded. "It's a good likeness. Yours is better than the one of Emerson. I assume he also spoke a lot."

"I was merely questioning his investigation into the glass creatures and that weird weather we experienced. He's made next to no progress. Someone else should be given the job, it's been weeks. He should have found something out by now."

Samson rubbed his chin. "That is concerning. If you want, I can look into it, but I'll need access to your library. Urbem folium doesn't have a fully equipped one yet."

"Just because you're moving to another city doesn't mean I'm going to ban you from the library. Besides I'm pretty sure Mellissa is already stealing books from me."

"I did see a few books in her office with your initials on. She said she borrowed them."

Greg put his hand on the table. "I loaned her two books. If she has more than she's stealing."

"I prefer the term secret-borrowing," Mellissa said appearing in the chair next to Samson, causing them both to flinch.

"I see that you're still alive then. I guess your guardians aren't as demonic as you keep saying," Greg said.

"Hey, I woke up to flames licking my skin, then an ice blizzard swept through my room – all in the name of training. They completely destroyed my bedroom."

Greg was starting to see why she called them demons, even as a training exercise that seemed like overkill. Samson opened his mouth to say something but paused. This was a side of Victoria the poor boy hadn't seen. He'd learn so much more about his crush once he moved and it would either put him off her for good or make him like her even more. But if Samson dated Victoria it would be weird. Greg shook his head; he didn't want to think about it. The odds of romance flourishing between those two would be low, much like his own odds with Mellissa. It must be a family thing to fall for the infuriatingly stubborn sort.

"You!" shouted Victoria pointing at Mellissa from the opposite side of the room. Her blue eyes shimmered with anger.

Mellissa hid behind Samson.

Victoria marched across the room as most of the room stopped eating and stared at her. She slammed her hands on the table. "I can't believe you ran off and left me like that."

"Sorry, I panicked. I thought I had hold of you when I teleported," Mellissa answered, still hovering behind Samson's shoulder. She looked up at Victoria with her big brown eyes, pouting.

"I assume the attempt to break the seal didn't go well," Greg said.

"No, it didn't. I'm starting to think nothing will work."

A troubled expression flashed across both of the girl's faces.

Victoria threw herself into a chair. "Anyway, that idiot." She pointed at Mellissa. "Set the courtyard on fire, squealed and then disappeared. I kept my cool, but stuck up, Lee had a go at me."

Greg looked at Mellissa. She hadn't run because of the fire. She'd know that Victoria would extinguish it. "You ran away because you saw Lee coming?"

Mellissa sat back in her chair, fiddling with her fingers. "Yes."

Victoria clenched her fist. "You little …"

Samson cleared his throat. "Ladies don't we have a cake tasting to attend."

Mellissa jumped up clapping her hands. Her face lit up as she smiled. "Yes, we do. One of the few duties I have that's fun."

"I guess with the council's recess, I won't be seeing you till your coronation then?" Greg said. He knew there would be no more council meetings over the summer unless there was an emergency.

"That's right." Mellissa put her finger on her lip. "Unless …"

Victoria smacked her around the back of her head. "Unless nothing. You have a very strict schedule over the next few weeks."

Mellissa rubbed the back of her head. "Harsh much."

Victoria jabbed her finger at Greg. "If I find out she has gone off gallivanting with you again, I'll break your legs."

"Victoria!" exclaimed Samson

Mellissa tugged Victoria's arm. "I think we should be going." She grabbed Samson with her other hand and then tilted her head to the side. "I guess I'll see you whenever." The three of them then disappeared in a flurry of light.

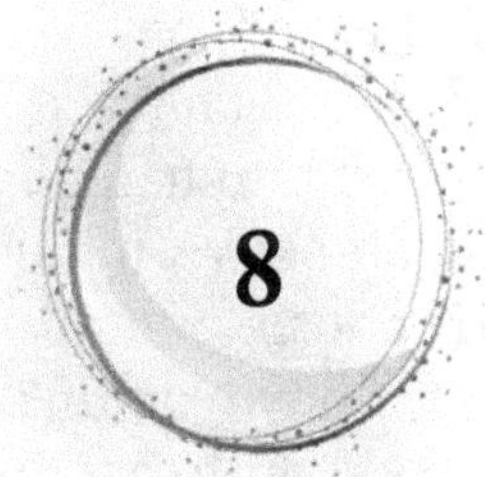

Moving Day

Mellissa

Today was the day! It was my final exam and I would be done with school and living in the human world, forever, and moving to Urbem Folium that coming weekend. Everything seemed to have come round so swiftly.

I had used finishing school as a reason to put off this move. At the time it had seemed ages away but now it was becoming reality. I took a deep breath as I entered the exam hall unsure what I was more nervous about, this exam or the end of my human life here. There had been ups and downs, but overall, I couldn't complain. Life had been good. I found my seat and placed my stationery on the desk. I needed to focus on the task at hand.

After spending three hours solving maths problems, I left the exam hall feeling confident I'd passed. But I still felt nervous. It was the fact that this was the end of a way of life, rather than the actual exam that bothered me. I searched for Harkura. He was on guard duty for me today as Victoria had her own exams to complete. Someone shouted my name and I quickly turned around. Ashley and Heather, two girls from my class approached me. What did they want? They were both popular and my existence was only fleetingly acknowledged by them.

"Hey, is that guy over there your boyfriend?" Ashley

asked pointing at Harkura sat on a bench. So that's where he was.

"What, Harkura?" I asked.

"Is that his name?" Heather asked biting her lip. "It sounds so exotic. We've seen him hanging around you a lot recently. So, what's going on between the two of you?"

"Nothing. He's my cousin." I told them the first thing that popped into my head. They wouldn't understand if I told them the truth. In fact, they'd probably think I'd lost my mind if I did.

"You have a Korean cousin?" asked Ashley.

"Yep." Better they think he was Korean then know he was really a water nymph wearing a glamour charm to hide his blue skin.

Heather was practically drooling over Harkura now. "I can't believe you have such a cute cousin. He looks like he works out."

"Well, I have to go." I didn't like the way they were drooling over Harkura. He was my guardian and trainer, not eye candy.

Ashley grabbed my arm, "Wait. I'm having a party this weekend to celebrate our finals. Come along and bring your cousin."

"Okay," I replied

"So, you'll come?" Heather asked.

"I'll have to see if we're free." I felt pressured to say yes even though it was the last thing I wanted to.

"We'll see you there then," they said in unison waving at Harkura. He looked confused but waved back. And they both giggled, flicking their hair.

"Don't forget to bring your cousin," Ashley reminded me. She blew a kiss at Harkura. He waved at her awkwardly.

I stood there staring at them as they walked away whispering to one another. So, this was the reason I didn't have a big group of friends growing up, not because I was socially awkward, but because I didn't have any cousins girls wanted to flirt with. They'd be gutted to learn that Harkura wasn't a human boy but a genderless water nymph. The only reason I referred to Harkura as male was because that's how I'd perceived him when we first met and he could care less about gender labelling.

I walked over to Harkura and told him what happened. He informed me that he was flattered but wasn't interested in going to a party and reminded me we were moving that weekend. I grimaced at the mention of my move. I was excited but scared at the same time.

We spent the next few days sorting out what I'd need to take with me to the magic world. Apparently, I wouldn't need a lot as my living quarters were already furnished to the highest standard. I hadn't seen them yet but if they were as wonderfully designed as the rest of the rooms, I'd be more than comfortable. And equally, I didn't need any clothes as Daniel had ordered the royal seamstress to make all my fancy garments. I hadn't realised there was a royal seamstress, but it seems I had a royal everything now. When my measurements were taken, I figured it was just for my coronation gown but that wasn't the case – Daniel had ordered an entire new wardrobe for me. I wasn't sure what my outfits would look like but I hoped it wasn't just about glitz and glamour and that they were comfy.

Now the castle was finished, it looked stunning. The design showed off the elves love of nature, all built from natural materials and the exterior draped in vines and vibrantly coloured flowers. Inside the floral theme continued in the decor and furniture. The ground floor was designed for meetings and formal events, and the large ballroom had the most high-tech kitchen I'd ever seen attached to it along with two smaller function rooms. On the first floor were the offices of everyone that worked there.

My living quarters were on the second floor. Using my powers, I'd designed the castle gardens myself. It had been part of a training exercise. Harkura had demanded I dedicate a section to an outdoor meditation area. He may be bossy, but it was a brilliant idea if I needed to destress during my queenly duties, just because Harkura was stressing me out.

By Saturday, I was all packed and ready to move. I spent the day teleporting back and forth with my stuff. Dad came with to help but after the day ended I felt tearful when I finally teleported him home. My chest tightened as I hugged him. "You know there's plenty of room for you in the castle too."

Dad placed his hands on my shoulders. "As nice as it would be to live in a castle, this is something you need to do yourself." He hugged me again and sniffled. "It seemed like only yesterday you were a baby. Now you're going off to be a queen."

"All that time you were married to royalty and didn't know."

"I don't think your mother knew she was of regal bloodline." He put his arm around my shoulders. "You never know, Urbem Folium, the city of leaves, sounds like a nice place to retire in a few years."

I grinned, my eyes wet with tears. "That makes me so happy, Dad. I'll make sure a cosy cottage will be waiting for you."

He let go of me. "Now off with you. You're going to make an old man cry."

I hugged him one more time before teleporting back to my new home. It felt weird. I'd spent most of my life in that 3-bed semi-detached house. It had been just me and my dad for years, and it felt wrong moving without him, but he was right, this was something I needed to do for myself.

Once I'd arrived, I went upstairs to my new enormous bed-chamber to finish unpacking. It felt weird, my old room would fit into it three times over. The walls were green with what looked like hand-painted flowers on them. I had an elegant four-poster bed with a sofa at the end of it. Two double doors lead out onto a balcony, that over looked the forest. To the right of my bed was a small coffee table with two armchairs with high backs either side of it. There was a spacious dressing room that led to a giant en suite bathroom which had the largest bath I'd ever seen right in the middle. I was pretty sure I could swim in it. I'd have to try it out once I was finished with everything. My fear of water would finally be mastered.

I was lost in thought when Victoria burst into my room

unannounced.

"Damn, Mellissa, I thought my room was fancy," she exclaimed. Both her and Harkura had their own living space in the west wing.

"It's amazing isn't it?" I replied, "I don't know what to do with all the space."

"You'll have no problem filling up that dressing room with all the fancy outfits Daniel has arranged for you." She walked into the dressing room. "Jeez, I swear this is the same size as my old bedroom and that mirror is colossal."

It was true, the mirror was magnificent with its gold flourishes that curled around the edge.

Victoria threw herself down on the sofa at the end of my bed. "By the way, you have a fitting tomorrow. We can make it like a mini fashion show. I'm also having a ball gown made for your coronation. I'm going to look amazing."

"I'm sure you will Victoria. I saw Daniel earlier, but he didn't tell me about a fitting."

"He gave me a copy of your schedule for the week. Surely you got one too."

"He gave me this folder with it in but I thought it wouldn't start till Monday, so I haven't looked at it." I picked up the folder I'd been given and flicked through it to see what he'd planned for my week. Victoria grabbed it out my hand before I had a chance to read anything. She opened it up and pointed to the second page. "It's right here. Dress fitting at ten tomorrow morning. You should know by now that you don't get the weekends off." She continued flicking through the folder. "Boring, boring. Oh, you have another cake tasting Tuesday afternoon. You are taking me with you to that."

"I assume Harkura will be coming with me to all the things you labelled as boring."

"Too right. I have better things to do than accompany you to budget meetings, train line proposals and dance lessons. Although watching you try to learn to dance is hilarious. I might rethink that one."

"Gee thanks. Well now that I'm all unpacked, I'm going to check on Laxus."

Victoria gave me a dismissive wave. "Oh, he's fine. I looked in on him on the way here and he was already in bed. Not sure if it's 'cause, he's still a kid or he's a grumpy old man."

"I think Laxus has the right idea. Not everyone likes to stay up partying like you. I'm going to bed."

"I don't think so." She jumped up and grabbed my arm. "We're celebrating this move tonight. Even if it's just me and you dancing around this castle."

She dragged me out of my room. We spent the rest of the night exploring the castle while Victoria downed shots like they were nothing. I stayed clear of the drinks as I knew I couldn't handle my alcohol the way she could. Victoria didn't make it back to her room. I spent my first night in my new home with Victoria sleeping at my feet. Truthfully, I was grateful. Her presence made me feel less uneasy in my new life as queen.

The next day, I was in and out of meetings. Now that I was here full time, Daniel wanted to confirm the plans for my coronation. He'd had me meet with decorators and musicians, and I had my dress fitting with Tamara, the royal seamstress. Victoria was right when she said my dressing room would be full once Daniel was done. I hoped I wasn't expected to wear this sort of thing all the time. As breath-taking as all the dresses were, they weren't practical for everyday life.

After a long day of decision making, I decided to try out my giant bath. Soaking in the bath used to be my way of relaxing, by suddenly my heart raced and I struggled to breathe. I shut my eyes, trying to feel safe. Images of Kadon trapping me in a sphere of water plagued my mind. Clenching my fists, I yelled. There was a loud bang and I slid out the bath as it cracked in two. I screamed releasing a pulse of light and crawled along the floor looking for a towel. And then I felt a robe being draped over me.

"Hey, it's okay," Victoria said rubbing my shoulders.

"I thought I could do it but …"

"It's fine. We'll get this cleaned up and then I'll have

them install a shower." I pulled the robe around me tightly and nodded. My stomach tightened as I looked at the mess I'd made of the bathroom. I still wasn't strong enough to face the water.

Harkura stood in the doorway, worry written all over his face. "Don't worry I'll sort this." He marched off with his fists clenched.

Victoria led me out of the bathroom. I put on the fancy pyjamas I'd been given by Tamara and Victoria spent the night at the end of my bed.

The next two weeks flew by. When I wasn't training with Harkura, Daniel was attempting to teach me to dance. I had a few meetings with the fairies to discuss the train line. We were the only settlement this far south of the capital, and I thought it a brilliant idea to expand the transport through the forest, except the fairies didn't agree. Luckily, I had Samson helping me with all the official forms and proposals. It was annoying that I couldn't get a simple train track built. Even more frustrating, I still couldn't get through basic dance routines without tripping. With my coronation only a day away I knew there was no hope, yet, Daniel insisted I had to have at least one dance.

We had two rehearsals of the actual ceremony and I got through that fine. I didn't see why we couldn't leave it at that. Why did we have to have this ball as well? But somehow, Daniel cleared my day so we could spend it dancing.

When I went to the ballroom for rehearsals, it was already decorated. Banners and balloons hung from the walls in dark green and gold and bags of confetti were stacked by the door along with ribbons and bows which were draped over the tables.

Daniel paced around the edge of the dance floor, looking as if he was about to pull his hair out. I walked over to him, tugging on his shirt. Daniel pasted a smile on his face. "Your Majesty, I have great news, Harkura has agreed to be your dance partner tomorrow."

What he actually meant was, it was the day before my

coronation, and he was still unable to find a dancer willing to risk. I'd never seen Harkura dance. Naturally, he'd be fantastic like he was at everything else.

Harkura extended his hand to me. "Shall we get started?"

"Are you sure about this?" I asked.

"If I can teach you to fight, I think I can improve your dancing."

At least he was realistic. Harkura's approach to this might just be what I needed. I took his hand as Daniel turned on some music and led me around the dance floor. After five hours of rehearsals, I was finally getting it. I still tripped occasionally and stepped on Harkura's toes but nowhere near as much as before. Harkura seemed to adjust to my clumsiness.

An hour later, Daniel stopped the music and walked over putting his hands on each of our shoulders. "Your Majesty, I think this is the best we're going to get from you. You only have to do one dance, then sit the rest of the evening out if you wish."

"I like the idea of sitting the entire evening out," I said.

"Unfortunately, you must dance at least once. I don't wish to insult you, but you really are a terrible dancer, but Harkura seems able to make suitable adjustments."

"I've become accustomed to her clumsiness in the time I spent living with her in the human world," said Harkura.

I couldn't even be insulted by what they were saying as they were both right.

"I did tell you I couldn't dance." I said, "You were convinced you could teach me. I will happily have one dance with Harkura and then sit down and enjoy the evening."

Harkura bowed, pressing his lips to my hand. "It would be an honour to help you get through your first dance as queen."

"Once your social obligations are over." Daniel put his hand on his heart. "I promise you can relax."

I felt better knowing I didn't have to worry about social obligations or traditions. I could get through one aerobic exercise around the dance floor with Harkura. Hopefully, the procession line would take so long that by the time it got to me, everyone would have drunk just enough wine to be gyrating just as badly as me. I went to bed that night feeling optimistic, confident I could handle what the next day had in store.

Ghosts of the past

Gregory

Today was not going as planned. Greg headed back to his house. He should have left city hall hours ago but Beatrice and Emerson had turned up unannounced stopping him from leaving on time. Why they felt the need to come such a long way simply to get plans for the library expansion was beyond him. It wasn't exactly a big project, yet they still felt the need to constantly undermine whatever input he gave.

He went to unlock his front door but found it ajar. Pushing it open as quietly as he could, he crept inside. He was unsure what to expect but he hoped to catch a thief in action.

Tiptoeing through the hallway, he threw open the kitchen door ready for an attack. The light was already on. He froze on the spot, his blood running cold. This must be a hallucination. How could she be here? "Mum," he said with a lump in his throat.

A woman that resembled his dead mother stumbled, knocking over a pile of saucepans in the draining board. She picked them up and then pushing a stray red hair behind her ear, she walked past the counter towards him. "I'm sorry to barge in like this. It's just that I waited at the lake, but you never came."

So, it was his mother who'd sent him the notes? Of

course, her initials were the same as his – G.A. – which stood for Gwendolyn Ainsworth. But the note couldn't be from her. She'd died when he was seven. Yet here she was. How? Greg clutched the worktop beside him, his head spinning. "I don't understand."

"I know it's confusing. I can explain." She paused, her green eyes watering. They were the same emerald as his. "It's just so good to see you. My, how you've grown." She reached out to touch him, but he backed away. She spoke as if she were back from a long trip, not back from the dead.

"There was a funeral," Greg stuttered. "We mourned your death. Father was never the same." He shook his head as a pit of sadness, that he pushed deep down, opened up inside him. It had all been a lie. Was being his mother so bad she had to fake her death?

She wrapped her arms around herself. "It's not what you think. I had to disappear. I wanted to come back. It's just …"

"Just what?" he shouted. "Why leave in the first place?"

"It's been so long, maybe, I should have stayed away."

"Maybe you should have. What do you expect to achieve revealing yourself now?"

Did he really want to know the answer to that question? What sort of person up and left their family? Leaving a seven-year-old to believe their mother was dead. He may have been young, but he remembered it all so clearly. His brilliant memory was just as much a curse as a gift. She'd left him at his father's office with Anna saying she had a few errands to run. Hours had passed but she never returned. That evening his father had called him into the living room with tears in his eyes informing him that there had been an accident. Apparently, she'd been too badly injured to be healed. That was the reason he'd become a healer – so that he could save others from the pain of losing a loved one. But it had all been a lie! The misery and grief she'd caused just so she could run away.

Gwendolyn interlaced her fingers and looked down at her hands. "I know you probably think I'm a terrible person, but I didn't have a choice. Your father made me leave."

"Liar. My father wasn't perfect, but he'd never do

something like that."

"I don't wish to tarnish your memory of Steffen, but you must know how important image was to him."

Greg tightened his fists and looked away from her. Yes, he knew that all too well.

She stepped forward and gazed directly at him. "Your father cared more about us appearing as a happy couple than actually being one. All the rules and regulations were too much for me. I couldn't keep up with the expectations of being an elder's wife. I needed to be free."

He glared at her, anger bubbling inside him. "Just because you didn't want to be married anymore didn't mean you had to stop being a mother. Why fake your own death?"

She put her hand on his arm. "I wanted to take you with me, but your father wouldn't allow it. Faking my death was all Steffen's idea and he forced me to go along with his plan. A broken relationship was bad for his image but a death in the family tugged on people's heartstrings."

Greg pulled away from her. "I don't believe you." His knew his father could be cold at times, but surely, he'd never have gone that far, to put him through so much pain. He clutched his head in his hands, his mind racing as he tried to assimilate what she'd said. There was no way this could be true. His father loved him and wouldn't have deliberately taken his mother away.

"It's true," she cried, "I never wanted to leave you. I could either remain here, trapped in this house and marriage or go into exile and be free. I knew Steffen would take care of you. You were his only son and heir."

Greg lowered himself into a chair at the table. This couldn't be true. He remembered how broken his father had been. There was no way she was telling the truth, only her tailored version of it. Sadly, his father wasn't around anymore to give his side of things.

Gwendolyn sat on a chair beside him and grabbed one of his hands. "I know this is a lot to take in and you have no reason to believe me. But I've missed so much of your life and I want to make up for it now. That is, if you allow me to?"

Greg snatched his hand away. "I think you should leave."

She stood up. "What?"

"You're not welcome here."

"Gregory, please."

"I don't have time to deal with this right now, I have to be somewhere." He stood up and walked to the back door and held it open for her. "Just go."

"Will you think about what I've said. I don't want to lose you again."

"Maybe, but not now."

"Very well, but I'm not going to give up on you, son." She put her hand on her heart and sniffled as if she might cry but walked out of the door with her head held high.

Greg closed the door behind her and leant his head on the back of it. How was he meant to stop thinking about that? As usual, he was alone with no one to confide in. Moments like this made his house feel even bigger and emptier. He could call Samson. Maybe he could offer some advice. He squeezed his eyes shut. No, Samson would be too busy to speak. He was a key member of Mellissa's staff now, preparing for her coronation the next day. Crap … he looked at his watch. It was late and he should have already left, but he hadn't even packed yet.

Greg ran through the house gathering clothes and toiletries. Mellissa would never forgive him for being late. They were finally back in a good place and he couldn't ruin things now. But surely, she'd understand if he was. It wasn't every day you found out your dead mother had come round to visit. He couldn't tell her that though. She didn't need to be burdened with his problems when she had enough challenges of her own. He just had to hope he'd made it to Urbem Folium on time.

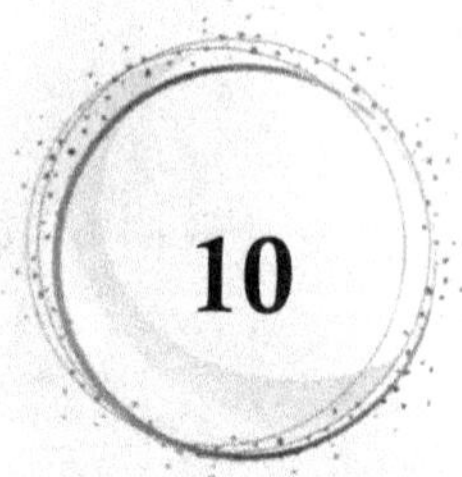

Coronation Day

Mellissa

A group of hairstylists were weaving flowers in my hair. I sat on my hands trying not to bite my beautifully manicured nails. Harkura was sat beside me going over breathing exercises. But that only helped so much when today was my coronation. People had travelled thousands of miles to get here, already arriving the previous night. There'd be no need to set off so early if the fairies had approved the train line, but today was not the time to focus on that.

I hadn't realised how many people Daniel had invited. He'd not only sent invites to the many leaders of each nation, but he'd also included all their staff. Celebrations were going on throughout the magic world. It was being supernaturally transmitted via energy frequencies on a virtual hologram so non-attendees could watch my coronation live. It was bad enough having to go through all this stuff with a room full of people, and even worse knowing the entire magical world would be watching.

Time was ticking by and I still had to have my makeup and hair done. There was no way I would be ready in time.

Victoria came into the room with Laxus following behind. She looked stunning in the black gown Tamara had made for her. There was a slit in the black fabric revealing an emerald-green underskirt. Her dress matched Harkura's suit, distinguishing them as my guardians. Laxus looked adorably cute in a grey suit with long coattails and a green tie.

"Aren't you done with her hair yet?" Victoria demanded, "We have a schedule to keep."

"Sorry, Miss Victoria. We're nearly finished," my hairstylist replied.

It had only been a few weeks since we moved but Victoria already had a 'don't mess with me' reputation. She was lovely and sweet until someone annoyed her, and then everybody would know about it.

"You look amazing Victoria," I said, "and you look extremely cute in that suit, Laxus."

Laxus frowned whilst smoothing down his jacket. "Someone my age should not be called cute."

"So twelve is too old to be called cute?" Victoria asked with a smirk.

The hair stylist turned me towards the mirror. "All done your majesty."

I gasped. My wild mass of dark hair had been pulled up into a bun with flowers threaded into it. Carefully placed curls hung loose round my face. "It looks great." I said with a smile. With my hair finished, the makeup artist worked his magic with lightning speed, and Victoria rushed Tamara in with my dress. Harkura and Laxus then kindly left so Tamara could help me into my gown. The colour was the traditional dark green worn by all the elf royalty since time began. It fitted flawlessly with a lace bodice and sparkling diamond beads, and there was a sash of skilfully sewn roses, along with a layered skirt that swept across the floor as I walked. The strapless style showcased the beauty of the heart crystal around my neck, and I felt truly regal wearing it, yet terrified it might get ruined.

"You look great, Mellissa,' said Victoria, her eyes widening. "I wish you could have sewn some diamonds onto my dress, Tamara."

"I reserved the diamond beading for the queen, Victoria." Tamara looked up at me. "You do look truly stunning. I'll let Daniel know you're ready." She handed me a pair of elbow-length lace gloves that complemented the dress perfectly.

"Thank you", I replied.

She bowed, and as Tamara left the room, Harkura and Laxus returned.

I pulled the gloves on and then interlocked my fingers to stop my hands from shaking. It wasn't long until the ceremony began and all eyes would be on me.

Harkura took my hands in his. "You can do this. Just breathe."

He was right, of course. I focused on my breathing, calming my mind as I squeezed Harkura's hands. "Now we're fully in the magic world, you don't have to wear your glamour charm anymore."

He tilted his head, his dark hair falling over his eyes. "I just thought you'd prefer me like this as it's how I looked when we first met."

"I want you by my side in your true form."

Harkura swept his arms over his body producing a shimmer effect. He looked exactly the same, except his skin was now pale blue.

I kissed his cheek. "Beautiful."

His indigo eyes sparkled as he smiled and then he held his arm out to me. "Are you ready?"

I nodded, linking arms with him.

Victoria let out of a moan of disgust as she stood beside me. "You two are sickly sweet." She grabbed my other arm. "Right, let's get this over with."

The door creaked open and my dad gasped as he entered. "Words can't describe how stunning you look."

I rushed towards him, hugging him tightly. "Dad, what are you doing here? You should have already taken a seat."

"I wanted to see you before you got swept away with all your queenly business."

"I'll always have time for you, Dad. I had Daniel add you to the greeting line so you'd see me in all my formal business glory."

He straightened his back and threw his shoulders back as a beaming smile spread across his face. I'd never seen him look so proud. "If it means, I get to spend more time with my daughter, it would be my pleasure."

Daniel burst into the room, interrupting our moment as he frantically exclaimed that we all had to be ready to proceed as the ceremony was about to start.

"Just remember, head held high," Harkura said as he led me out of the room.

We followed Daniel down the corridor while Victoria led Laxus and my father in the other direction. I let out a long breath. Being crowned queen should be easy in comparison to my other responsibilities.

There was no need for me to be anxious. The ceremony went exactly as planned. I didn't trip or fall, and I remembered all the things I had to recite and where to stand. And now, I had a long line of guests to greet. I knew the script off by heart: Daniel would announce who they were, and then I'd formally greet them and welcome them to the ball. Then they'd swan off and do as they wished, while I was stuck repeating the same greeting over and over. It seemed silly having to formally greet people I already knew, but as Daniel kept reminding me, it was tradition. I zoned into autopilot after a while, although my hand ached from all the endless shaking.

This all seemed to be going well until Daniel announced Lord Gregory Ainsworth, elder knight of Novosvillas. A wave of anger washed over me. "Daniel, next person please." Greg wasn't going to get the satisfaction of a greeting. I mean, I knew he wouldn't be early, but he could, at least, have been on time. I almost wished the guards had refused him entry. It would have served him right.

"But my queen you must abide by tradition," Daniel said with a frown.

I folded my arms and turned my head away. "Yeah, well, I already know who he is and he's not getting an official greeting."

Daniel placed his hand on his forehead as if exasperated and then stepped towards me. He opened his mouth to speak and then closed it again.

"Mellissa, you don't have to greet me, but at least let me apologise," Greg said, stepping towards me from the line of people. "A meeting with the other elders ran late and I was delayed."

I threw my arms down by my side in temper. "You always seem to have some sort of excuse. I've had enough."

"What can I do to make it up to you?" he asked as he extended a hand.

"How about you move along. I have other guests to greet." I pointed to the right, showing him a seated area with tables, but he didn't budge.

"Can we talk about this later then?"

"I don't think so, Gregory."

"Don't call me Gregory."

I shrugged. "Why not? It is your name after all."

"Yes, but you only call me by my full name when you're annoyed and trying not to scream."

"I do not!"

"You're doing it now."

"Well, constantly apologising for being late is getting tedious. Clearly, you have a memory issue or you don't mean what you say."

"Things happened that were beyond my control."

"Like what?"

He ran his fingers through his hair "That doesn't matter right now, but I do mean it when I say I'm sorry. I really wanted to be here."

"Then you should have been on time. You had plenty of notice. It's not as Daniel planned this all overnight." I folded my arms again. "Now move along, you're holding everyone up."

Daniel stood with his hand mid-air as if bewildered, glancing at Greg and then back at me.

Thankfully, Samson slid through the line of people and tapped me on the arm. "Excuse me, Queen Mellissa and Lord Gregory, I don't think this is the best time for a discussion. There are still many other guests to greet."

"You heard him, I have important royal duties," I snapped. "Samson, escort Lord Ainsworth away, please."

Victoria pushed passed Samson. I had no idea where she came from, but her eyes were pinned on Greg. "Out the way Samson, I've got this." She grabbed Greg's arm. "How about a tour of the castle, Lord Ainsworth," she said, enunciating his name with venom. Victoria didn't wait for a response as she dug her nails into his arm and pulled him away.

As Daniel announced the next guest, I could see Victoria from the corner of my eye, jabbing Greg in the chest as she sneered at him. I couldn't help but smirk. I knew Victoria would have some choice words. She wasn't shy about expressing herself.

Once the greetings were over, I walked towards the royal stage. It was a raised area where only an exclusive list of VIP's were allowed, such as Laxus, Samson, my dad, Daniel, and my guardians. I kept the list short, mainly because I wanted to be left alone. I slouched in my chair. I wasn't good at social events with crowds of strangers. Although I had to admit, the ballroom looked wonderful. Daniel had outdone himself with the lavish decorations and the vast display of food, all in the colour scheme of royal green and gold. Looking at all my guest's mingling, I felt strangely out of place, even though, this was my ball. Victoria was gyrating on the dancefloor as she always loved a good party. Daniel had worked so hard on this so someone may as well enjoy it. I just prayed that no one would ask me to dance. I didn't want to showcase my terrible dancing skills any more than I had to.

Laxus walked over and leant against my chair. "I know he needs to sort out his priorities and get on top of his workload, but he clearly cares about you."

"Who exactly are we talking about?" I asked

"Gregory of course. I've seen the way he looks at you. He hates it when you're mad at him."

"Well, it's his own fault. It's as if he goes out of his way to annoy me. Anyway, what exactly does a twelve-year-old know about relationships?"

"We both know I only look twelve."

I leant on my hand. "You know if I ever live to be over two hundred, I hope I look as good as you."

"Don't change the subject." Laxus subtly nodded towards the crowd. "Don't look, but he's heading over here."

"Who's coming?"

Laxus rolled his eyes at me.

It was a silly question. Unfortunately, this stage left me nowhere to hide.

"Can we talk?" Greg asked as he appeared in front of me. "Samson said your royal obligations were over."

"I'm sorry, Gregory, but I'm extremely busy looking after my cousin right now."

"No, she isn't. Her plan is to hide up here for the rest of the evening." Laxus tapped my shoulder. " I will happily go and hang out with your dad and Harkura".

I clapped my hand over my mouth. "Laxus, you're meant to be on my side," I whispered.

"I am on your side," he whispered in response. "In fact, the queen would like to dance."

"No, I don't," I said, "I'm a terrible dancer."

"You still have to have your first dance as queen."

"I was going to dance with Harkura for that. We practised and everything."

Laxus turned towards Harkura. "Harkura would you mind if Mellissa had her first royal dance with Gregory instead?"

I rubbed my forehead. Why was Laxus working against me on this? He had nothing to gain except to see me squirm.

"If that's what the queen wants," Harkura answered with a shrug. "Lord Gregory is just as accustomed to the queen's clumsiness as I am."

I was speechless. What happened to the nymph that was going to rain fire down on Greg? When I needed his fiery wrath, he'd let me down.

"It's true, I'm used to you stepping on my feet, and do I not always catch you when you fall, my lady?" Greg said, extending his hand to me.

I could feel my cheeks go red.

"So, Queen Mellissa, may I have this dance?"

I couldn't exactly say no now, but how I wished Victoria was here. She would have backed me up. I took his hand. "Just one dance. Then I get to sit the rest of the evening out."

A smile spread across his face. "If that is what you wish."

I wanted to smack that smile off his face. "Don't think this means I've forgiven you. You're just lucky Laxus enjoys putting me on the spot."

Greg led me onto the dance floor as Daniel frantically signalled the band to change songs to the one chosen for my first dance. Everyone moved aside as all eyes were on us. I dropped my head down and looked at the floor feeling extremely self-conscious. I knew how bad I was at this and everyone was staring. Greg placed one hand on the small of my back and held my hand with his other one. "Relax, you can do this."

"You know I can't," I whispered, "Everyone is going to see me fall flat on my face."

"Forget about everyone else. It's just you and me. And I promise I won't let you fall."

I prayed my cheeks didn't look as smoking hot as they felt. How was he always able to break through my defences with just a few words? It made it impossible to stay mad at him.

The music started up again. Greg gently pushed my hand back which indicated I was meant to step back, but on which foot? Daniel had gone over this so many times, but I couldn't remember. Taking a random guess, we began to move. I don't know how, but we seemed to be in sync. Everyone watched us for the first verse, then slowly others joined the dance floor. I let out a sigh of relief as we blended in with the crowd of people. Greg was just as good as Harkura at adjusting to my lack of dance skills. It was as if we were gliding.

"Did I mention how breathtaking you look in that dress?" whispered Greg in my ear.

"Flattery will get you nowhere," I replied.

"I know compliments won't mean you'll forgive me, but I'll find a way."

I bit my bottom lip to stop myself smiling. I couldn't give him the satisfaction. Even though he annoyed me, he always knew how to light a spark. I mean, the idiot had really let me down this time, and yet here I was dancing with him. It was extremely frustrating that I hadn't been able to say no and stick to it. Sometimes I wondered whether our friendship could ever flourish. Greg had been a big part of introducing me to magic – and the truth was, I wouldn't be here right now if it wasn't for him – but a lot had changed since then. In a short amount of time, he'd taken his father's place as elder and I'd become a queen. Maybe we both had to accept we could no longer be close – that we were both in positions of power with a lot of responsibilities. We had a duty to our people.

The music began to slow as the song came to an end. I looked up at Greg. He was likely going to try and talk me into forgiving him again, but there was no way it was going to happen that easily. Today had been a huge part of my life, being crowned Queen of the Elves, and once again he showed how unimportant I was to him. As Victoria had said, I kept setting myself up to get hurt. But even though I knew all this, it was hard to think of Greg as just another council member. The truth was, I just couldn't let him go.

An enormous explosion suddenly shook the room. I fell forward smacking my head on Greg's chest. My ears were ringing and dust fogged my view. Screams filled the room as people ran for the exits. As the dust cloud settled, I saw what everyone was running from. Piling in through a massive hole in the wall were glass creatures just like the ones from the beach.

My first instinct was to run away like everyone else, a perfectly normal response to danger, but I wasn't normal. This was exactly what Harkura was always going on about in training – expect the unexpected. I had to fight, protect my subjects. Pushing Greg away, I fired light energy at two nearby creatures shattering them in one shot as Harkura ran towards me with Daniel.

"We must get you to safety," cried Daniel.

"No, you two get my dad and Laxus out of here. I'll deal with our uninvited guests." I held my arm out to the side and the heart crystal glowed. In a blink of an eye, it transformed into the form of a staff, a long shimmering pole with the crystal embedded on top, that jumped into my hand.

Harkura nodded as he quickly disappeared off.

I ran towards the creatures twirling my staff and blasting them with luminous energy. As stunning as my ballgown was, the layers of fabric kept wrapping around my legs, restricting my movement as I rushed forward to fight. Luckily, I wasn't the only one fighting. Victoria had quickly taken charge of the castle guards and was holding the creatures back. Lady Gabrielle and the warlocks were also quick to defend everyone. Meanwhile, Samson along with a few staff members attempted to direct all the party-goers out in an orderly fashion.

I fired energy blasts at multiple creatures but they just kept coming. I tried to blast a creature behind me, but I got caught in my dress and tripped. Two creatures bounded towards me. I needed to move quickly, but I couldn't get up in time. Just as they were about to strike, a protective barrier made of light energy appeared in front of me. Greg ran over and helped me up and I struck both creatures with a flash of lightning.

"Your attack magic has improved but at the cost of your defensive skills," Greg said.

"Well, ballgowns aren't really made for fighting," I said sarcastically, gesturing to what I was wearing."

"What Harkura hasn't taught you how to fight in a dress yet?"

I might have found that funny if my castle wasn't under attack. We both ducked as glass shards flew at us. As the shards hit the floor they grew back into creatures. We split up, taking our own targets. Firing more lightening I sent glass flying across the ballroom. I ran after more of the creatures but fell face first hitting the ground with a smack. A creature had hold of the train of my dress until a barrier slammed down, cutting through the creature and my dress.

Greg pulled me to my feet. "Sorry about the dress, but you were right. It's not made for fighting."

"Don't worry about it. I should have thought of it

sooner." I tugged at what remained of my train, tearing it even more. Throwing the material to the floor, I kicked off my shoes. I was suddenly liberated and staff in hand, I sprinted towards the creatures. I kicked one with my foot engulfed in light energy and followed up by twirling my staff around, firing off multiple energy blasts. I kept smashing the creatures one by one, but there were too many of them to keep picking them off individually. If I could gather them all in one place, I could release one massive beam of light to destroy them all.

"Greg" I yelled, "can you use your barrier magic to push all the creatures into one location?"

"I can try," he replied. Greg placed energy barriers around the creatures, pushing them away from everyone and tunnelling them into one spot. Any strays were blasted back by Victoria and the guards. Once they were all trapped, I held my staff above my head and called for the heart crystal to 'release the light'. The crystal shone brightly and released a colossal pulse of light energy shattering all the remaining glass creatures. I returned the heart to crystal form as it appeared back around my neck, and scanned the room. All of Daniel's hard work had been ruined.

"What was that all about?" Greg asked from behind me.

"No idea," I said looking at all the splinters of glass at my feet.

There had to be a reason for this attack. And what exactly were those creatures? Emerson was meant to be looking into them but clearly, he'd failed. The way they were formed wasn't natural. These creatures had to have been created by someone and sent to attack – but surely their inventor knew they wouldn't be successful – we annihilated them easily the last time they attacked. I put my hand on my chest as I gasped … this was all a distraction. My heart raced. While I was fighting, I hadn't been paying attention to the one person who needed protection the most … Laxus! I ran off in the direction Daniel and Harkura had taken him, praying that I wasn't too late.

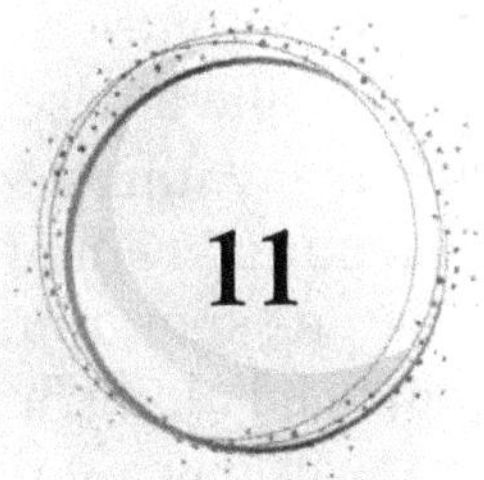

The Winged Woman

Mellissa

My chest felt tight. I should have realised it sooner. Of course, this attack was all about Laxus. He'd warned me he was in danger, but I kept telling myself he'd be fine, Thankfully, Harkura was with him. He was the one who'd taught me to fight and I was yet to beat him. My mind was whirling but it didn't matter what I told myself, dread filled me.

I sprinted down the corridor that lead to the kitchen staffs quarters, hoping I was heading in the right direction. Knowing Harkura, he would take Laxus out one of the less used entrances out the back of the castle. I heard a scream and shuddered. Rushing ahead, I pictured Harkura and teleported. As I materialised, I was knocked straight to the ground … Daniel had fallen on top of me. He appeared to be out cold.

Harkura was fighting off a woman with black feathered wings. She must be the bird-woman Laxus had warned me about, over six foot and slender with long curly, black hair. I carefully moved Daniel off me, checking there wasn't any sign of serious injury, and then clambered upright to see Harkura being blasted against a wall by shadows.

The woman turned towards Laxus as my father quickly jumped in front of him. "What do you want with the boy?"

"That has nothing to do with you, human," the woman

snarled as she threw two shadow balls at him, knocking him against a wall.

"Dad," I screamed as I leapt towards the woman blasting her with light energy. She blocked my attack with her wings and then flapped them, creating a violent gust of wind which threw me back. I teleported behind her and released a ray of light, and in response she spun round, blocking it with a shadow shield. Shadows danced along her russet brown skin.

"That power must mean you are the newly crowned queen I've heard so much about." She chuckled. "You're not exactly what I was expecting."

"So sorry to disappoint."

"I didn't think you'd be able to defeat my glass puppets so quickly without the Sea King's help. I'd planned to be long gone with the boy before you even knew what was happening." She sighed. "Oh well, I'll simply take him now."

"No, you won't," I screamed.

She rapidly fired three shadow balls at me but I quickly put up an energy shield that absorbed the attack. As I tried to storm after her, I was blown away by another gust of wind. She flew upwards at high speed and used her wings to create a stronger gust. These stupidly large corridors and high ceilings gave her enough room to reach full wingspan but were so narrow I had minimal leverage to her attack.

While I was fighting against the wind, she flew towards Laxus, reaching out her arms to grasp him. I teleported and snatched him away, dematerialising just before she could sink her talons into his skin. I paused momentarily to grab Victoria from the ballroom and then tucked them both away somewhere safe. Just in case I didn't come out of this fight alive, I knew Victoria would protect Laxus. I rematerialised back in front of the bird-woman. Only a few seconds had passed, but she was furious.

"Where have you taken him?" she yelled. She was surrounded by dark energy, her eyes bulging with rage.

"As if I would tell you that. Just who are you anyway?"

She swept her wing over her body as if to calm herself. Holding her head high, she curled her lips. "I guess it's only polite to let you know the name of the person who's about to kill you. I am Humarya the queen of darkness. Now bring the boy back or I will kill every person in this pathetic castle."

"I won't let you hurt anyone."

She gave me an eerie smile that sent shivers down my spine. "Don't worry, if you cooperate like a good little girl, your life will be the only one I extinguish."

"As nice as your offer is, I'm going to have to decline. Letting you have Laxus would doom the whole world." I transformed the crystal into staff form and held it in front of me prepared for attack.

"You have no idea what a huge mistake you're making." Her nostrils flared as her eyes widened. Humarya flew at me blasting me with a mix of air and dark magic. I blocked her attacks the best I could having never come across air magic before. It was a struggle to fight. She flew towards me, smacking me against the wall with her wing. I couldn't let her beat me that easily. There had to be a way to win this fight. While being crushed against the concrete surface, I remembered what Harkura had taught me: how to manoeuvre out of a stronghold attack. I shut my eyes and covered my body in rays of red-hot light. She screamed as she released me. I'd burned her wing. That's when I realised how important her wings were – they were extremely strong, creating all the powerful gusts. As I fell to the ground, I teleported around her and then struck her wings with lightning. She screeched as one of her wings had a singed burn, the feathers tearing apart towards the edge. I ran at her, spinning my staff around.

She jumped back, taking flight. "I may have underestimated your power." She was trying to create space between us. I could tell by her chaotic flying that I'd hurt her as she dipped up and down. I'm not sure what caught her eye, but her look of disgust turned into a smirk. "But I know your type. And you have the same weakness as all those so-called heroes."

"And what is that?" I asked, getting ready to attack again.

"You care about the lives of others."

She formed two shadow balls in her hands and turned

her head smiling. I followed her gaze and saw she was looking at Greg. I had no idea how long he'd been there but he was trying to help Harkura who was injured. She laughed and fired both shadow balls at him.

"Greg," I screamed. I instantly teleported in front of him to intercept the attack. I tried to put up an energy shield but I wasn't fast enough. I took both hits and fell backwards onto him. He shouted my name looking shocked. I wasn't sure if he'd even seen what happened.

"Now that I've seen what you can do, I'll be better prepared next time," shouted Humarya. She winced as she expanded her wings and flew away lopsided.

She was injured; I could catch her. As I got up to stand, I fell to my knees, clutching my side. I was hurt worse than I thought.

Greg grabbed hold of my arm. "Mellissa, you need medical attention."

"No, you need to help my dad and Harkura. I have to stop her." Pushing Greg away. With one hand on my blood-covered abdomen, I extended the other out to the side for balance, and stood. My stomach felt like it was on fire. As pain seared through my body I crumpled to my knees. I punched the floor with frustration. She'd used my humanity against me. She knew I would choose to save Greg allowing her time to get away. I gritted my teeth. There had to be a way for me to follow her.

Greg put his arm around my waist, pulling me towards him. "You're in no condition to go chasing after her."

"Let go of me, I'm fine. See to the others." I tried to pull away but ended up falling against him. The trouble I was having simply trying to stand upright didn't help my cause.

"I already checked them over while you were fighting," he replied. "They're fine for now, but they need more medical attention than I can give them here. I've called for help and your medical staff should be here soon."

Just as he finished his sentence the royal healers turned up. They headed straight to me first, but I ordered them to take my dad and Harkura to the infirmary before attending to my injuries.

"If you won't go to the infirmary, let me see to your wounds, Mellissa," Greg demanded.

I flinched. "How many times do I need to tell you, I'm fine. How's Daniel. He was also hurt?"

"I'm fine your majesty," Daniel answered, rubbing his head. He must have come round without me realising. "You really should let Lord Gregory look at your wounds if you insist on the royal medics treating your father and guardian first."

"Fine." I sat on the floor. It was so much easier than standing. "Will you please go to the infirmary and let me know what's happening."

"As you wish, Your Majesty" Daniel bowed and followed the healers and I reluctantly let Greg look at my injured stomach.

Greg placed his hands over my blood soaked wound. " Sanum quod fit." he muttered and his hands glowed green. My body tingled under the glow of his magic as my wounds began to heal.
"You should be more careful."

"Oh, I'm so sorry for saving you." I tilted my head sideways. "What do think you were doing anyway?"

"Well you had the bird-woman engaged in battle, so I thought I'd get your dad and Harkura out the way. Wouldn't want them getting caught in the crossfire."

"You almost made yourself another casualty."

"Sorry for believing in your fighting ability. You should have let her attack strike me, instead of getting yourself hurt."

I leant back on my arms and looked up at the ceiling. "Is it not better this way round? It's not as if I have the power to heal you."

"You have a whole team of royal healers. Elves are the creators of healing magic. I'm pretty sure you could learn."

"I've tried and it's hard. Look just because I'm mad at you, doesn't mean I want you dead."

"Well, I don't want you getting hurt, especially if it's to protect me. I'd have preferred it if her attack hit me."

"You know I could never allow that."

"Mellissa, you are the Queen," he yelled.

I shrugged. "And you're an elder."

He frowned. "You can be extremely vexing sometimes."

I rolled my eyes. This conversation was going nowhere, so I chose not to reply. He could at least be more grateful to me for saving his life. Instead, he took the opportunity to remind me how reckless I was. He didn't once acknowledge that he was just as reckless. As much as he liked to preach to me about having a plan of action, he was the one that followed me and then went to help Harkura without thinking. I sat pouting while he finished healing me. Luckily it didn't take too long.

Once all the bruising and torn skin were rejuvenated, I headed to the infirmary. Unfortunately, Greg followed, questioning me about Humarya. I'd only just met the woman, so clearly, I didn't know anything about her. Although, I might have lied about her motive for the attack.

Daniel was talking with the head of the infirmary when we arrived. He pointed me in the direction of Harkura and my dad. I was relieved to see both of them awake. The royal healers were amazing at what they did. I didn't know what I'd have done if they hadn't been okay. This was all my fault for being careless with Laxus. Instead of having him following me around all the time, I should have kept him hidden away. Now that I knew everyone was okay I needed to get back to Laxus. While Greg spoke with Harkura about the attack, I slipped away, to avoid anymore of his questions. As I walked out the infirmary Samson almost knocked me over as he rushed towards me.

"Samson, what's wrong?" I asked

"It's Victoria," he said, "She disappeared after the fight. I'm concerned something happened to her."

"There's no need to worry. Victoria is looking after my cousin for me."

"Thank you for letting me know, Your Majesty." He bowed, looking a little less stressed. Even in this chaos, he was still so formal. It was annoying.

"Daniel is currently overseeing the injured. I need you to check on the council members and do damage control, okay?"

He nodded. Giving him a task to focus on would hopefully stop him worrying. "Yes, Your Majesty. What about you?"

"I'm trying to figure out what our attacker wanted. Oh, and if Greg asks where I am, tell him you don't know."

"Well, I don't know where you're going."

"That's good." I teleported leaving him with a confused look on his face.

I rematerialised in my bedroom. As I opened the door to my laundry cupboard I was blasted by ice. "Hey, it's me," I shouted only just dodging the attack.

"Well, you could have said something sooner." Victoria stepped out smoothing down her dress. How she'd managed to fight and keep her gown in such impeccable condition was astonishing. "I can't believe you made us hide in a cupboard."

"I'm sorry. I was in a rush." The cupboard in my bedroom was the first place that popped into my head when teleporting them. If she tried to hunt him down, I figured Humarya would assume I'd hide Laxus somewhere much more secure.

The colour drained from Victoria's face. "What happened to your dress?" She grabbed the end of my skirt. "How could you ruin something so beautiful."

"It was restricting my movement."

Laxus came running out the cupboard and hugged me. "I'm so glad you're all right. I was worried about you."

Victoria shook her head. "I knew that dress was wasted on you."

"Forget about the ballgown, Victoria. We need to figure out what to do next. This is the second time those things have attacked."

"Fine, but shouldn't Harkura also be involved in the decision making?"

"I don't need Harkura to make a decision. Besides he's in the infirmary. We had the misfortune to come up against the woman who created the glass creatures."

Victoria slumped down on the sofa at the end of my bed.

"Very well what has the *queen* got to say?"

I didn't like the way she said queen, insinuating I was throwing my title around. I sat on the sofa at the end furthest away from her, deciding to ignore her snippy dig, and informed them both about my encounter with Humarya. She hadn't given anything away as to how she'd located Laxus. but then again, she knew he was with me and my coronation was big news in the magic world. And with the influx of people arriving, it would have been easy to grab a small boy in a panicked crowd.

Victoria crossed one leg over the other and folded her arms. "Clearly she knows he's with you so he can't stay at the castle anymore. He can't be with Harkura either. Somehow, she also knew he was who Laxus would be with when not with you."

She was right. Although, the stone was hidden in its box so it's dark aura couldn't be tracked, and Laxus was covered by my magic, he'd been attacked at two major events where it was common knowledge I would be in attendance. I tugged at my hair. "So where can we hide him? We need help," I said.

"You can't." Laxus jumped up from where he was sat on the edge of my bed and paced the room. "Don't you see that's how she found me. There is a spy on the council. Any help they give will be of no use as the spy will tell Humarya. I'll be in more danger."

"I think your jumping to conclusions." I said, "This was a high profile event. I shouldn't have had you following me around."

Laxus crossed his arms and glared at me. "I still say the council can't be trusted."

I rubbed the side of my forehead taking a deep breath. This pixie sure was paranoid. I looked at him with what I hoped was a stern face. "Look we need help. I never meant to involve everyone in the council, just one member."

Victoria smacked the armrest of the sofa. "You're not thinking of asking Greg for help after what he just pulled. I still can't believe you danced with him. You should have punched him right on the nose."

"I was put on the spot and you weren't around to save me. Laxus and Harkura completely failed to have my back." I waved my hands at her. "Anyway, we're going off-topic. After being unforgivably late to my coronation, Greg owes me. We can hide Laxus in Novosvillas, no questions asked."

Victoria's shoulders dropped. "You really think he won't ask questions?"

"He will undoubtedly ask questions, but I won't answer them. He asked what he could do to earn my forgiveness, and this is it." I put my hands behind my head. "You wanted me to punch him but violence isn't the answer. Besides he could easily heal any damage caused."

"Yes, but the scene would be priceless."

"Anyway, punching noses aside, not getting answers to his questions will eat away at him which will be a far better form of torture. You know how he hates not knowing. We then get a hiding place for Laxus with the added bonus of getting to mess with Greg's mind."

"Nicely played. I take my hat off to you." She removed an imaginary hat from her head.

Laxus huffed as he sat in-between us. "This is your idea of safety? Seriously, don't use me to get revenge on your boyfriend."

"He's not my boyfriend." I covered my face with my hands. The room suddenly felt like a sauna.

Victoria burst into hysterics. She was laughing so much, she was hanging over the arm of the chair.

"Whatever you say," Laxus said, "I don't like this plan. Greg is a member of the council and they have a traitor among them"

I groaned. He sounded like a conspiracy nut. Victoria wiped tears from her face. "It'll be fine. That freak Greg is too vanilla to be a traitor. Also, if Mellissa asks him to keep a secret, then he will. The idiot just can't be trusted to turn up on time."

Was Victoria backing my idea? I hadn't expected her to come round so easily.

"But Laxus will need more firepower on his side."

"I'm glad you think that," I said, "Because I'm sending you with Laxus.

"You're what?"

"Laxus needs someone in the know to protect him. We can simply tell everyone you're visiting your parents in the human world."

Laxus nodded. "Makes sense. So, are we all agreed on this course of action?"

Victoria curled her top lip in disgust. "I'm not going to Novosvillas to stay with that annoying know it all, Greg."

She was all for my plan until I suggested she go with Laxus. After arguing about it for an hour she agreed. Keeping Laxus safe was more important than her dislike of Greg. The only problem was that it meant I had to talk to Greg and I didn't want to. However, the fate of the world was also more important than our current disagreement. Whilst they were in hiding, I'd have to find a way to stop Humarya coming after Laxus again or getting revenge on me and my loved ones, which was easier said than done. I hoped Harkura had a way to fight air magic, otherwise, our next encounter with her was likely to end in bloodshed.

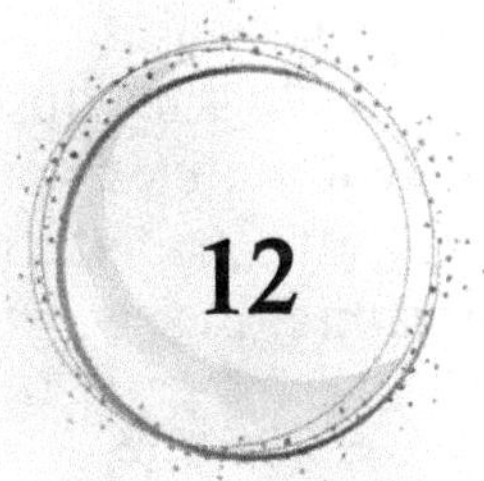

12

Secrets

Mellissa

I awoke to the sound of knocking. Sleepily, I clambered out of bed, pulled on my dressing gown and opened the door.

Daniel bowed. "Sorry to wake you, Your Highness, but an emergency council meeting has been called to discuss your coronation."

I rubbed my eyes. Of course a meeting would be called. Were the council really going to waste time talking about what happened, instead of doing something about it? "Don't they know we have a castle to rebuild.

"Yes, well, that's why I'm coming with you. I've already discussed it with Samson and filled out the correct forms to have the capital assist with our rebuild. May as well hand-deliver them while you are at the meeting."

He showed me a folder stuffed with papers. My eyes widened. "You and Samson have been busy."

"Yes, we have." He clapped his hands together. "Now chop, chop. You only have thirty minutes before the meeting starts."

"What! You could have led with that." I ran into my dressing room and began pulling out some clothes.

"Samson and Harkura are ready and waiting," shouted Daniel from outside the door. "Victoria says she will stay with the boy."

"Good," I shouted, "I'll be ready in five minutes."

I heard Daniel footsteps and the click of the door to my room open then close. and rushed around getting myself dressed. I was downstairs within ten minutes, gulping down a weird green milkshake, Harkura called breakfast. Luckily, I was able to teleport us to the capital in seconds, arriving just before the meeting started.

Daniel and the others went off to file the forms whilst I got interrogated, batting off endless questions. But I was proud of myself for answering succinctly, stating that Humarya claimed to be the queen of darkness and that she'd threatened to return, without revealing anything about Laxus and the stones.

"Are you sure you're not leaving anything out?" Lee asked.

"I'm sure," I answered, my cheeks flushed red.

"You really have no idea why this woman chose to attack so vehemently?" He didn't sound convinced.

"I am sorry my lack of knowledge displeases you. I wasn't aware that people with birdlike wings existed. What I do know is that my castle is ruined and the rampaging creature is still out there. I'd much rather be hunting down this Humarya, than answering silly questions from you." I clenched my fists as I tried to stay calm..

"Many who live on the land won't have seen entities like her before," said Greg, "I've done some research and she appears to be a hawk person – they're a race of winged beings that live high up in the mountains. They're rarely seen on low ground and tend to stay away from wooded areas as this restricts their wing movement. From what I've read the hawk race can manipulate the air around them using their wings."

I grimaced as I recalled my fight with Humarya. "Yes, I experienced that ability of hers and it wasn't pleasant." I bit my bottom lip. So Humarya was a hawk person. Surely, that couldn't be what her species were called. It wasn't any better than Laxus calling her a bird-woman.

"This Humarya seems to possess a great deal of magic

power and is clearly dangerous", said Lady Gabrielle. "However, we don't know what she wants. We need to discover more about her if we have any hopes of capturing her."

They all nodded in agreement and muttered amongst themselves as I gritted my teeth. This all felt like a big waste of time. No decisions were getting made. "Can't we just go to the mountains and search the area," I said speaking over everyone. "Even if we don't find her, the other hawk people might know something."

"You cannot just go to the mountains," said High Priestess Yuko. She looked at me like I was crazy. "The mountains are not part of the council's domain. We have no authority there."

"How else do you suggest we find Humarya?"

Yuko shook her head. "We must go through the proper channels. We can try and make contact with the hawk tribe to see what they know about this Humarya."

"How are we going to do that? It's not like we have a phone number for them. We don't even know where they live in the mountains."

Lady Gabrielle stood and everyone went silent. "Chancellor Den could you get your fast-flying fairies to search the mountains until they locate the hawk people. They are the best trackers. Once contact is made, we can then decide the best course of action."

Everyone agreed with her decision. I was the only one against it. I stood, shaking my head. "What is the difference between me going to the mountains and the fairies?"

Lady Gabrielle turned towards me. "I understand you are eager to catch the woman who attacked your castle, but this is a fact-finding mission. Once we have more information we can decide if your presence in the mountains is needed."

I sat back down with my arms folded. This was ridiculous. There was no chance anyone would side with me now that Lady Gabrielle had spoken. I spent the rest of the meeting scowling at all of them. Maybe I should have just told them about the dark stones. Then they'd understand how important it was to stop Humarya before she got her hands on any more. However, if Laxus wasn't just being paranoid and there was a spy on the council I couldn't risk them coming into contact with Him. I'd also lose his trust, which I couldn't let happen. I had to agree to do things through their annoying bureaucracy.

Once the meeting was over I swiftly left. I hated the decision that had been made but I had been out voted.

I leaned against the wall in the corridor waiting for Greg to leave the hall. Harkura stood beside me like a statue, and Daniel and Samson still hadn't returned. We'd been out here for what felt like forever. When the meeting ended, I'd stormed out, but Harkura reminded me that I had to speak with Greg. I sighed looking up at the ceiling. I didn't feel like talking to Greg, but it had been my idea to involve him.

Hakura tapped me on the shoulder. "I've been wondering how you'd feel about a blind date?"

"What?" I asked, turning around.

"A blind date. I've been looking at some potential suitors for you. I've based my decisions on your likes and dislikes, personal quirks and genetics. We only want good magical genes passed on to your heir."

I stood up straight, placing my hands in front of me like a barrier. "Wow, hold on a second. No and no! I already told you, I am not looking for a partner and I'm definitely not producing any heirs yet."

"But your majesty …"

"No buts, Harkura. This conversation is over."

Harkura crossed his arms. "Well at the very least could you and Lord Gregory sort things out."

"What are you on about?" I spotted Greg walking over to his guard Luke. "Never mind. Harkura, you and your crazy ideas can stay here. I'll talk to Greg on my own."

Harkura bowed. "As you wish, but while you're there, why don't you ask Gregory what his plans for an heir are?"

I narrowed my eyes at his smirk and then walked away.

"Greg," I said tapping him on the shoulder.

"Hey," he said, turning around. "I thought you'd be long gone. Emerson and Beatrice have decided the changelings still have business in the capital."

I tilted my head to one side and smiled sweetly. "I was hoping we could talk."

"Sure, what's up?"

I peered around him at Luke and bit my lip. "In private?"

Greg looked up and down the corridor. "Okay, come to my office." He turned to Luke. "If anyone needs me, you know where I am."

Luke nodded and bowed as we walked away.

I looked back at Harkura and he winked at me. I shook my head. I couldn't let Harkura's obsessions with heirs distract me.

Greg shut the door to his office and took a seat. I sat on the desk beside him, dangling my feet just above the wooden flooring.

"You do know there's more than one chair in here?" Greg said.

I shrugged, tilting my head back, letting my long curls fall onto the desk. "I know."

He rolled his eyes. "So, what is it you want to talk about that's so top secret, you don't want Luke to hear?"

I pushed my hair back. "Well you see, I came to ask for a favour."

Before Greg could respond there was a knock at the door. I instinctively jumped off the desk and spun around. A woman in her early twenties walked in. She had long black hair and was probably as tall as Victoria. Why was nearly everyone in this world taller than me? When she noticed me, the smile on her face dropped.

"Oh, I didn't realise you had company," she said whilst glaring at me.

"It's fine, do you have the paperwork I requested?" Greg asked, not paying much attention.

She nodded and handed him a large file, not taking her eyes off me. She made me feel uncomfortable the way she kept staring. It didn't help that she was nearly half a foot taller than me, making me feel like she could swat me like a fly.

Greg gave her some documents he had on his desk and asked her to make copies.

She took them and left, but not before giving me a dirty look.

"Is she new?" I asked, "I haven't seen her around before. You usually only travel with Luke."

"Oh, that's Julie, my new assistant."

He appeared to be oblivious to the unpleasant glare I'd received. Greg could be so rude sometimes with his indifference to situations and people.

"She started a few weeks ago. I thought about what you said, about how I expect too much from a newbie."

My eyes widened. "You mean you actually listened to me?"

He leant back in his chair and spun it round to face me. "Don't sound so surprised." He tilted his head. "Nice dress."

I looked down at my outfit. The top fitted snugly and the pleated skirt hung down to my knees. "Oh, it's just something I threw on this morning. All my clothes have been replaced with bespoke outfits."

"Suits you. Anyway, what was the favour you wanted?"

I fiddled with my fingers. I knew Victoria wasn't his favourite person and the feeling was mutual. They only managed to work together when it involved messing with me. At least Victoria knew why she'd have to tolerate him, but I couldn't tell him why. I figured I may as well just ask. And if he said no, I could persuade him otherwise. "Can Laxus and Victoria come and stay with you for a bit? I mean you have that nice big house all to yourself, so you'd hardly notice they were there." I gave him the biggest grin I could muster. "You're hardly there anyway and it would be a big help."

"Why would Victoria and Laxus want to stay with me?" he asked.

"They don't want to … it's more out of necessity.

Victoria's carrying out a social experiment and my cousin is one og her subjects." I clicked my fingers and pointed at him. "Oh and you have to keep it secret, cause it's part of her experiment."

He looked puzzled. "What?"

I smiled sweetly and batted my eyelids. "Please do this for me. It will be really helpful."

He looked up at the ceiling and sighed. "Fine. they can stay."

"Thanks, you're the best."

 Does this mean you've forgiven me?"

Of course, he had to bring that up, again. I hadn't forgiven him, but I couldn't let that stop me doing what was best for Laxus. "I don't know. I noticed you managed to get here early for that pointless meeting, but you couldn't make it to my coronation on time."

"Once again, I'm sorry. I don't know how many times I can apologise. How about I buy you some cake and we can discuss this favour a bit more," he said playing with his pen.

I thought about it for a moment. Cake sounded good. Then I shook my head. "You cannot buy my forgiveness with cake."

He stood up and took my hand. "Look, I know I messed you about, but you have to at least give me a chance to make it up to you."

"My coronation was pretty damn important. You should have been there on time. I was at your elder knighting ceremony thing."

"You teleported in ten minutes before it started."

I snatched my hand out of his. "Well then, I was early."

"I don't have your powers. No one has powers like yours, not even the sea king. I really am sorry, Mellissa."

I sighed, rubbing the side of my head. "Look, I didn't come here to argue. I just needed an answer to my request, so I can let Victoria know."

"Yes, they can stay." He sat back down and flicked his pen across his desk.

"Thank you. I'll leave you to your work then."

"Mellissa, wait." He quickly got up and grabbed my wrist. "Do the elves have any plans for summer solstice?"

I placed my finger on my lip. "Um, when's summer solstice?"

"Tomorrow." He shook his head slowly in disbelief. "How do you not know about summer solstice?"

I pouted. "Well you didn't know about Christmas when we met."

"They're not really the same thing." I narrowed my eyes at him. He waved his hand dismissively. "Never mind about that. Look I have the whole day free tomorrow. Come to Novosvillas. I promise I'll be on time and won't let you down."

"Hmm sounds like a nice idea, but Harkura has booked a meeting about the castle rebuild."

He raised an eyebrow. "Are you just making up meetings to avoid me?

I waved my hand in the air. "No, honest. Harkura offered to help Daniel with the rebuild. He only took on the role last night, but he'd already drawn up plans."

"If you have time after that then?"He gave me a dashing smile making me blush.

"I guess I could escort Laxus and Victoria to yours."

"There will be fireworks in the evening and I could get tickets to the special solstice performance at the circus "

I nodded and prodded his chest playfully. "You know what . I'm queen I can give myself the afternoon off. But after that, I'm done."

"Done with what?"

"Done with forgiving you. This is the last time. I mean it."

He pushed my hair behind my ear. "I will spend forever making it up to you if that's what it takes."

I jabbed his arm. "I also want that cake."

"If that's what you want." He took my hand. "Shall we teleport to the tearoom. I know how you like to avoid walking."

I glared at him, but he was right. I transported us to our destination. Samson and Daniel were already sat at a table, so we joined them. It didn't take Harkura long to appear and start lecturing me about how unhealthy cake was, but he respected my choices. It was progress for him.

It was annoying how rubbish I was at standing my ground. It was even more annoying that I actually had fun with Greg, but I meant what I said – this really was the last time I'd forgive him.

Victoria rolled her eyes at me. "So, after you said he couldn't buy your forgiveness with cake, you then let him buy your forgiveness with cake." She was laid across my bed flicking through a magazine.

I'd been preparing for tomorrow's meeting with the builders when she'd barged in demanding to know why we'd spent so long in the capital.

"It's not like that." I sat beside her. "He now knows he won't be fully let-off until he keeps to his word. Otherwise, this friendship is over." I slashed my arm down as if cutting something invisible.

"Oh, you're going on a date tomorrow. How nice." She rolled her eyes again.

"It's not a date. It's just two buddies hanging out. It's no different from when I spent time with Matt."

"That's almost laughable, Mellissa. The friendship you had with my brother is nothing like the relationship you have with Greg."

"That's because they're different people. Greg, like Matt, is just a mate."

"All right, you just keep telling yourself that. You may want to make sure he knows that too." She strolled off before I could say anything else, I assumed, to pack for her stay at Novosvillas. I hoped she wouldn't be gone long. Hopefully, we'd hear from the fast-flying fairies soon and I'd get the go-ahead to search the mountains. Humarya would definitely be on the hunt for Laxus … I just didn't know when.

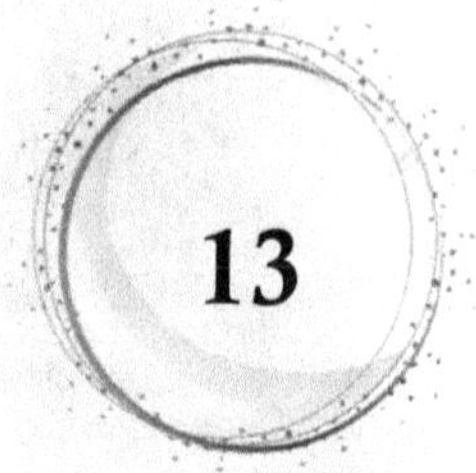

Questions and Answers

Gregory

After clearing books out of the second guest room, Greg was exhausted. He slumped down in the hallway next to the huge pile of titles on creatures, spells and healing. Why did he agree to this? He and Victoria didn't see eye to eye on many things and she'd made her opinion of him abundantly clear at the coronation ball. It wasn't going to be pleasant having her around, but he was sacrificing his privacy for one reason only – to make things up to Mellissa.

Being late to her coronation wasn't something he was going to be able to live down anytime soon. He had to do this otherwise he would lose her. It was never his intention to let her down but everyone had their limit, even Mellissa. Perhaps he should just tell Mellissa what happened. Why he was really late. She'd understand, wouldn't she? Perhaps, even Victoria would understand. Although he was certain her threat to freeze his limbs off would still stand.

He'd kept it all to himself because he didn't know what to do about his mother. It was a lot to process, something he still hadn't had time to do. He should have been happy to discover she was still alive – they could catch up on lost time – but the only thing he felt was anger. It didn't matter how she'd tried to justify her actions, whatever happened between her and his father, she'd made a choice, and she chose to fake her death leaving him abandoned and motherless. How could she walk back into his life now as if nothing had happened?

Greg ruffled his hair. Even with everything she had done she was still his mother Things were really messed up. So, for now, his mother's sudden appearance must remain a secret. Things were complicated enough between him and Mellissa so he didn't need other issues adding to the pile. Perhaps, in time, when he'd sorted his head out, he and Gwendolyn could rebuild their relationship.

Greg wandered to his room. He'd need some quality sleep if he had to put up with Victoria and Laxus staying for a while, and he had no idea how long they'd remain his uninvited guests. Laxus was still a complete mystery. Did Mellissa really think he'd believe they were cousins? Greg shook his head. It was too late to theorise who the boy was. But if Mellissa was going to so much trouble to hide him, it must be important.

He lay on his bed but shot straight back up. Living alone in such a big house amplified every sound, and he was certain he'd just heard a door close. Gwendolyn couldn't have broken in again? He tiptoed out of his room and listened. Someone was moving around downstairs. What would she be doing down there? Moving as quietly as he could, he snuck downstairs. Following the rummaging sound he tiptoed down the hall to the library. He opened the door and was greeted by a scream as Mellissa toppled backwards over a pile of books.

"What the hell, Greg?" she shouted scrambling onto her knees. "Why are you sneaking up on me like that?"

"I'm not the one sneaking about, you are. This is my house," he yelled.

"I … Well … You're meant to be asleep."

"I was clearing out stuff for your guests which kept me up late. What are you doing?"

She looked at the floor and twisted a loose curl around a finger. "I couldn't sleep so I thought I'd just …"

"You thought you'd break in and steal from me?"

She wagged her finger at him. "Hey, what I do cannot be counted as breaking in. I broke nothing upon entry."

He raised his eyebrow and folded his arms. "What exactly are you planning to steal?"

"I'm not planning to steal anything. I was simply looking for a book to borrow. I was going to bring it back."

"So, you came to see me this morning for a favour and now you're ..." He shook his head. "And let me guess, I'm still not allowed to ask why."

She nodded. "I'm so glad you understand. Anyway, you go back to bed and I'll see myself out once I've got what I need." She got up and started looking through the book shelves.

"Erm, I don't think so." He stepped closer, pulling her hand away from a book she was about to pick up. "You can't be trusted. These two shelves are off-limits to you. They are limited editions that can't be easily replaced."

"Geez, Greg I ruined one book. It was an accident. And you wonder why I prefer to secretly borrow stuff from you. "

"Why don't you just stop with all the secrets."

"Fine," she said pouting. "I was after books about the hawk people."

"Mellissa, we all voted on this. You can't go off fighting battles alone. You need to wait ..."

She waved her hands at him. "Yeah, yeah, I know, but it doesn't hurt to be prepared in case Humarya attacks again."

He wasn't sure if he should believe her. With her abilities, she could easily go against the council's orders. "The books you want are in my study downstairs."

"Thanks, I'll get them and be gone before you know it." She disappeared in a shimmer of light. Greg ran out the library shouting her name. He hurried across the hall to his study.

She sighed as he walked into the room. "What now? I thought you wanted me gone."

"They are the only books I have with any mention of the hawks. You can't just have them. I'll make you copies in the morning."

"But I want to read them now to help settle my mind. You're being so awkward."

"I'm awkward? Maybe if you came at a normal time of day!"

"Whatever." She rolled her eyes as she sat at his desk picking up a book on top of a huge pile.

"What are you doing?"

"I'm going to sit right here and read because you're stubborn and I can't be bothered to argue."

"You can't be bothered to argue? Well, that's a first."

"Hey, don't make me change my mind." She looked up at him her brown eyes sincere. "Go back to bed and get some rest. "

He went to leave but stopped. She could be trying to get rid of him so she could disappear without a fuss. "So, you won't just teleport the moment I leave the room?"

"Is my word not enough?" She placed her hand over her heart.

He still wasn't convinced but decided to trust her. If she couldn't sleep it was probably down to her castle being attacked. Better she was here safe and sound. Once the fairies made contact with the hawks she'd be off getting herself into all kinds of trouble, so researching the bird people was probably a good idea. He mouthed a goodnight and went to bed.

Greg got up bright and early as usual and headed downstairs to his study. The books were still there and so was Mellissa, slumped on top of them, fast asleep. Surely they must be uncomfortable to lay on. He walked around his desk and placed a hand on her shoulder. She stirred and mumbled something incoherent, but her eyes remained shut. Maybe he should leave her be; this might be the only decent sleep she got for a while. He also knew how grumpy she could be early in the morning, but he was going to need his desk back soonish. Just because he wasn't heading into the office didn't mean he couldn't work.

He gazed at her. She looked so peaceful, her long black lashes sweeping against her golden brown skin, her hair tousled as it hung in curls over her cheek. He'd leave her there for now.

Heading out of the study, he turned left down the

hallway towards his large kitchen on the right. Switching on the kettle, he put some wholemeal bread in the toaster. Thirty minutes later after finishing his breakfast and gulping the remainder of his milky coffee, he wandered back to his study and stood outside the open doorway. Mellissa was still asleep, and she wasn't going to wake up anytime soon unless he woke her, which he didn't plan on in case she bit his head off.

He paced up and down the hallway. All his research was on his desk. He'd taken it upon himself with a little help from Samson to investigate the glass creatures. So far, he'd learned they were created from complex air magic mixed with a sand spell.

Greg needed to continue his investigations, incognito. He didn't want to get Mellissa's hopes up when he hadn't found anything useful yet. Ideas were tumbling through his mind. Maybe he could move her without her waking?

Stepping softly, he headed back into the study. She was still sleeping soundly, her breathing slow and deep. He bent down and slid his arms underneath her legs, gently picking her up. She fidgeted slightly but didn't stir. Plodding slowly forwards, he carried her upstairs and placed her on his large double bed, gently pulling the duvet over her.

Walking back down to his study with a spring in his step, he felt like a weight had been lifted off his shoulders. Now he could get on with his fact-finding without any disturbance.

He pulled out the research, Samson had sent him to compare with his own when he heard a knock at the front door. What now? He tried to ignore it, but there was another loud knock. Whoever it was they were persistent.

A few minutes later he opened the door and a big box with a bow was thrust in his face. "Happy Birthday," exclaimed Gwendolyn.

Greg stepped back. "What are you doing here?"

She walked into the hallway, pushing the box into his arms. "It's your birthday. so I got you something. Don't worry, I won't stay long. I don't expect to be on the list of favoured people you'd want to see today. Not yet anyway." She put one hand over her heart and the other on his shoulder.

Greg looked down at the box she'd given him and then tilted his head back. "Look, now isn't …"

Ignoring him, she walked along the hallway and into the living room on the right. "I just wanted to apologise again to make up for my past mistakes." She ran her hand over the arm of the sofa as she sat down. For someone who wasn't staying long, she seemed to be making herself comfortable. "Well, aren't you going to open your present?"

He looked towards the door. Mellissa had been dead to the world, so it was unlikely she'd make an appearance anytime soon. He could humour Gwendolyn for a bit. He sat across from her as she leant forward eagerly and opened the box to a new telescope.

"I remember how you loved looking at the stars as a kid."

"Yeah, father got me one when I was nine."

"Oh," she said with a frown.

"But thank you, I've been in need of an upgrade."

A smile returned to her face.

Why was he trying to make her feel better? She'd done little to deserve his compassion.

"So, you like it?"

He placed his gift to the side. "It's nice, but just because you remember a few things about me as a kid, doesn't make everything all right."

"I know, I just want to show you that I'm serious about being part of your life."

"You know I'm an elder, right?"

"Of course, and I'm so proud."

"But you couldn't stand being the wife of an elder. Do you really think you could handle being the mother of one?"

"It won't be like before. I'm not the same person I was back then."

"I don't know if I believe you."

She reached a hand out towards him. "Please, just give me a chance to prove myself. I'll do anything to be part of your life again."

Greg jerked away from her and folded his arms. "First,

you'd have to declare that you're now very much alive, and second, you wouldn't be allowed to tarnish my father's name with your stories."

"I won't tell anyone anything." She cupped her hands under her chin, her eyes glistening with hope. "Does that mean I can stay?"

Greg ran his fingers through his hair. "Not today. I have guests coming later. I just need more time."

Her arms flopped down beside her. "I understand, but can I come back another day?"

"Not to the house. If you're serious, you'll need to come to my office where others can see you. Let the world know you lied. Then maybe we can talk."

She fiddled with a cushion beside her. Going to his office didn't seem to sit well with her. Gwendolyn looked like she wanted to say something when there was a loud thud from upstairs. She dove off the sofa and hid behind it.

Greg jumped to his feet. Mellissa must be awake. He needed to end this conversation.

Gwendolyn poked her head out from around the sofa. "What was that?"

"It's nothing." Greg walked towards her, stuck out his hand and helped her up. "Sorry, but you need to go. You know what you need to do if you want to talk again."

He walked her into the hallway. There was a crash and then a loud bang. What on earth was Mellissa doing up there?

Gwendolyn placed her hands over her head as if the ceiling was about to fall on top of her. "That didn't sound like nothing. You should leave with me before the house falls apart."

"It's just Mellissa. She's not a morning person."

Gwendolyn looked up at him with wide eyes. "So you have a girl upstairs?"

"Yes, and you were just leaving."

He tried to usher her out the door, but she dodged around him. She pointed at the stairs. "Can I meet her?"

"No." He guided her back towards the door.

"Meeting your girlfriend would be a good place to start

wouldn't it?"

"She's just a friend."

"Then why can't I meet her?"

" Look," he replied, looking into her eyes, "I'd rather you didn't meet anyone in my life for now." Greg opened the front door.

She rubbed her chin. "Mellissa! That's the name of the new elf queen. It wouldn't be that Mellissa upstairs. Doesn't she have a castle to sleep in?"

"Gwendolyn …" snapped Greg. He didn't want the two of them to meet. Not like this. It was a stroke of luck Mellissa hadn't come down yet.

"Don't worry, I'm leaving." Gwendolyn strutted past him. "I'll see you later this week then for that talk."

He nodded in response before shutting the door as he watched her walk past the fountain in the driveway. He needed to make sure she'd really gone. Then he ran upstairs and opened the door to his bedroom and spluttered out a cough, hit by the overwhelming stench of smoke. A grey cloud hovered over what used to be a wardrobe as Mellissa was on her hands and knees rummaging through a pile of shirts.

"Mellissa, what happened?"

She dropped some burnt fabric in her hands. "It was an accident."

"How did you accidentally destroy my house?"

"Not the house, just a wardrobe." She gave a wry smile. "And the contents … but who really needs that many shirts?"

He knelt in front of her. "So, tell me?"

"I had a bad dream and fell out of bed."

"So, you thought you'd take it out on the wardrobe?"

"No, I was disorientated and didn't know where I was. When I couldn't find the heart crystal, I freaked."

Greg stood up and walked over to the dresser. He picked up the heart crystal and handed it to her. He'd removed it worried that she'd strangle herself on the chain in her sleep. "So you didn't think to look for the crystal or come and ask where it might be? You just blasted away?"

"Well, it didn't help that I was dreaming about being

attacked. I'm sorry."

Crazy things like this only happened when Mellissa was around. Greg rubbed his forehead. "No wonder you don't sleep. I thought you were talking to someone to help with your dreams?"

She shrugged and sat up, laying her head against the end of the bed. "Well, when you consider that someone is Daniel. I mean, he's a great listener and doesn't judge me, but he isn't trained for my sort of crazy."

Greg sat on the floor beside her. "You're not crazy. We all deal with traumatic events differently. The stress of the recent attack probably hasn't helped either."

"No, it hasn't." She laid her head on his shoulder. "I don't even remember going to bed."

"You fell asleep at my desk. I needed to use it, so I carried you upstairs. Anyway, don't you have a meeting this morning or did you make one up to make a point?"

She groaned. "I wish I'd made it up. What time is it?"

Greg looked at his watch. "Nearly seven."

"I better get back, Harkura will go mad if he can't find me." She tapped his arm. "You know, I don't want to go to this meeting. Could you go in my place?"

He shook his head. "Nice try but no. Besides, it can't be any worse than a council meeting."

"Nothing is as bad as a council meeting."

Greg stood up, grabbed hold of Mellissa's hand and pulled her up from the floor. "Well off with you then, royal duties and whatnot."

"Hey, why aren't you working? It's your favourite pastime."

"I have the day off remember. I'll be seeing you later, won't I?"

"Yes, that sounds familiar." She scratched her head.

He wasn't sure if she'd actually forgotten or was just making a point. It was likely the latter, attempting to make him feel forgotten about. He could play along. "You're the worst, you know that. You better turn up as I got us those tickets for the circus."

"That's totally wicked." She cleared her throat and pushed her hair back. "I mean, yeah, I might go to that."

Greg laughed. Her act hadn't lasted long. "You don't have to do a fake formal response. I know what you're really like. It's not as if you didn't break into my house last night."

"Yet nothing was broken." She winked. "Anyway, better go."

"Wait a sec."

"What?" She looked at him with her large brown eyes.

Should he tell her about Gwendolyn? A second opinion would be useful. Mellissa was in a unique position to understand, yet the words wouldn't come. "Nothing. I'll see you later."

"Okay." She made a quick move towards him, kissed his cheek, and disappeared in a flash of light.

Greg touched his cheek and smiled. They'd definitely made progress. He could forget about his problems and spend the rest of the day enjoying some much-needed time with Mellissa.

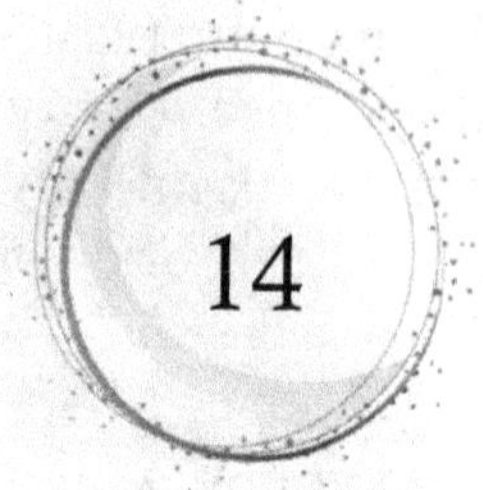

14

A distracted Heart

Mellissa

Something felt off when I left Greg as if he were keeping something to himself, but I didn't have time to dwell on it – the doors to my dressing room and bathroom were wide open. And Harkura was probably marching around the castle looking for me.

I quickly got changed into my running gear and went to find him. He grabbed my wrist when he saw me and dragged me back to my room saying there was no time for our morning run. He picked out a pretty dress and left me to get showered and dressed. The bodice had stardust beads lining the neckline complemented by a flowing mid-length skirt with black and white swirls. I didn't understand why this meeting called for this sort of fancy gown, but I did as I was told. He'd also chosen a pair of black and white sandals. Staring at myself in the mirror I ran my finger over the swirling pattern. Wearing dresses every day was something I was going to have to get used to.

There was a knock at the door. "Come in," I yelled.

One of the hairstylists from my coronation walked in and bowed. "Harkura, sent me to do your hair and makeup."

"Why does my hair need doing?"

She shrugged. "I just do what I'm told."

I sat down and let her get on with it. She gently brushed

my hair out, then pinned it up and round into a bun, leaving a few loose curls to frame my face. Green leaves were weaved around my bun and matching cuffs were slipped over my wrists. She blended green eyeshadow onto my lids and lined my eyes in black. Finally, she dabbed some pink colour on my lips and left.

I went downstairs feeling overdressed for a meeting with builders. I walked into the conference room to discover a room full of well-dressed young men. Not one of them appeared to be a builder or architect or anything to do with fixing the place. I should have known something was awry when Harkura had sent the stylist in.

"Harkura what's going on?" I asked, "Who are these people?"

"Potential suitors," Harkura replied.

"Suitors for what?"

"For you, of course. You came of age two years ago and now your coronation is over, it's high time you thought about marriage."

"Have you lost your mind?" I put my hands over my face feeling my cheeks grow hot. Marriage was the last thing on my mind, especially to some random person, Harkura, had found in the village. He knew I didn't want to date which was why he tricked me into thinking it was a meeting with builders. My hopeless love life was none of his business. "Harkura, this is not happening. You have to tell them to leave."

I turned to go, but Harkura blocked my path. "You must stay. I've invited all the single men from the city in your age range. It would be rude if you left straight away."

"You know what is rude? Letting me think this was a meeting about rebuilding the castle." I lowered my voice. "This is valuable time I could be figuring out how to neutralise the dark stones."

Harkura placed his hands on my shoulders and turned me around gently, pushing me back into the room. "As important as that is, it won't hurt for you to spend half an hour meeting a few potential suitors."

"I'm not interested in a relationship, especially don't

want a forced one."

"I am not forcing you. The final decision will be down to you. I'm just creating the opportunity for you to meet someone. If it makes you feel better rather than thinking of it as a relationship, think of it more like a business transaction to create a baby."

"That makes it worse," I shouted., then in a more hushed voice "What makes you think I want a baby? I'm happy as I am, thank you."

"I thought I explained this. You are currently without an heir. It is of great importance that we rectify that."

I threw my arms in the air. "Harkura, this is madness." Unfortunately, the option to leave was no longer available as my presence had now been noticed. I was trapped. Harkura paraded me around the room introducing me to everyone. I felt like a piece of meat on display. And with my new royal title, I wouldn't know whether someone liked me for me or because of the position I held. Harkura had hoped for me to meet someone but all he had done was depress me for any future prospects for when I may actually want to date. I was probably going to be single forever. I didn't get close to people easily. I was an overthinker with major anxiety issues not designed to be in a relationship.

The next two hours seemed to drag. The half an hour was clearly a lie, and my fake smile and laugh got put to good use. I practically ran out of the hall once it was over. Harkura must have lost his mind. I went upstairs to get changed but found Laxus and Victoria sat on my sofa. Victoria was giving Laxus a manicure. I guess even pixies liked to have nice nails. Once Victoria learned how Harkura had set me up, she burst out laughing. Laxus actually thought it was a great idea. I didn't find either of their reactions helpful.

"This isn't funny, Victoria." I frowned. "I didn't appreciate being blindsided like that."

"Well, you could have just told the nymph that you plan to have elf changeling babies with Greg," Victoria continued after she finally stopped laughing.

"I have no plans for any kind of babies," I snapped.

"Would they not be human elf changeling babies?" asked Laxus, "Mellissa is mixed race."

Victoria nodded. "I believe you are correct."

"Will you two stop it." I crossed my arms. "It's not like that."

"I believe she's still in denial," Laxus said.

"Big time." Victoria replied, "I don't think she realises that no one is buying the whole 'just friends' line."

"You know what, you two can make your own way to Novosvillas as I'm not talking to you."

"Changing the subject, a classic sign of denial," Victoria said.

"Seriously guys. Harkura is stressing me out enough, I don't need you two adding to it." I opened my dressing room door. "And I need to change out of this silly outfit."

Victoria walked over and put her arm around me. "Why? It shows off your figure nicely."

I sighed. "Never mind, let's just get out of here before Harkura sets me up again."

"Now, that's a good idea." Victoria smiled. " Besides if we don't arrive with you, we'll probably be turned away. We all know the only reason Greg agreed to let us stay was so he could see you." They both laughed.

"You are not funny!"

"We're sorry Mellissa. Shall we get going for real this time?" Laxus took my hand.

"As long as both of you stop talking."

They both agreed to keep quiet on the subject. Victoria still had her arm around me, and I teleported us to Novosvillas.

The sun shone down on us, it's heat warming my skin.

"Why didn't you teleport us straight inside?" asked Victoria. We were outside Greg's house on the driveway. I shrugged looking at the fountain in the centre and the flowers surrounding it. Victoria banged on the front door.

Greg answered within seconds. "Wow, you actually

used the front door."

"I don't know what's wrong with her," said Victoria. "Now, where are we staying?"

He pointed to the stairs. "Up there, last door on the left."

She breezed past him and sprinted up the stairs with her bags as Laxus followed behind, leaving me stood outside with Greg in the doorway.

"Are you going to stare at the fountain all day?" Greg asked.

I turned round to look at him. "I just wanted some fresh air after the stress of this morning's meeting?"

"What happened?"

I felt myself blush. I followed him inside and we sat in the living room as I told him about Harkura trying to set me up, and how Victoria and Laxus found this extremely amusing. I missed out the part about human elf changeling babies. Greg also burst out laughing. Why did no one understand my frustration?

I stood up, throwing my arms down by my side. "That's it, I've had enough of you lot. I'm going home."

Greg straightened his shirt as he stopped laughing. "I'm sorry, but I wish I could have seen your face when you realised what was going on. I guess Harkura is a little eccentric."

"Eccentric? I think the term you're looking for is completely insane. You know, I think I might spend time with someone who isn't going to be amused at my expense. You guys have let me down big time."

"Don't go, Mellissa, it's not often I get the whole day to myself. I'll be bored on my own."

"You have Victoria and Laxus to keep you company."

"I rather not spend the day being ridiculed by those two I also remember a certain someone being excited about the circus this morning." He produced two tickets from the inside of his jacket, waving them at me.

I sat beside him. "I guess you make a convincing argument. How did you manage to get the whole day off anyway? Ever since you became an elder you've been working 24/7."

"It's a changeling tradition to have your birthday off."

I gasped. "Today is your birthday and you're only just telling me. I didn't get you anything. I didn't even say happy birthday."

"That's exactly why I didn't tell you. Birthdays are a much bigger deal to humans. I didn't want you agreeing to come here out of some obligation to be nice. I'd rather know you came because you wanted to."

"I can't believe you lied to me about today."

"I didn't lie. I just withheld unimportant information."

"How is that not important? I guess I never asked when your birthday was, but I assumed it was something you'd tell me. Now I know, I'll be better prepared next year, when you'll be turning twenty-one. We'll definitely have to celebrate that."

"Why is turning twenty-one significant?" he asked.

"It's human tradition to signify the reaching of adulthood, and as my friend, you're going to have celebrate with me."

"I guess I can deal with that. Well, shall we get going?"

"But the show doesn't start for another few hours. What are we going to do till then?"

"I thought we could go to the magic musem. They have a great new exhibit for summer solstice."

" Why does everything we do have to be educational?"

"Because learning new stuff is fun."

"Fine, but this new exhibit better be amazing"

"Oh it is," he said with a smile.

I had to admit the solstice exhibit was fascinating. The different positions of the sun where painted across the ceiling in stunning colours. We trailed through the museum looking at all the different types of spells and potions that could only be cast during solstice. Victoria had been wrong about there being more to this day out. We were just two friends hanging out. I had to stop listening to her. She always made something out of nothing.

The circus was amazing. All the hype for once had been

correct. It was a completely different experience to what you see in the human world. The acrobats and fire tricks reminded me of Harkura. If he hadn't become my guardian, he would have been a great headliner. In fact, Harkura and Victoria would make the perfect double act with their fire and ice. If I completely messed up as queen maybe I could join the circus. It looked like it would be fun.

I could tell Greg hadn't had a day off in ages. He was trying to fit in everything he wanted to do in one day. He kept coming up with different places for us to go. We planned to finish our day by seeing the fireworks. Greg made me walk up to the top of the cliffside as he insisted, we'd get a much better view than down by the lake with everyone else. His father had discovered this spot and shown him it to him as a child.

I threw myself down on the grass as my feet were hurting. "We'd better have the best view ever after all that walking you made me do. You could have just pointed this place out and I could have teleported us up here." Even with all the training, Harkura had me doing, that walk still tired me out. It didn't help that it had been mostly uphill.

"We would have completely missed out on all the scenery. Besides teleporting is just lazy."

"Well then, I'm not letting you tag along on anymore teleports." I stuck my tongue out at him. It was pretty dark now and the fireworks would begin soon.

"This is also a great place to see the stars." Greg sat next to me and pointed out the different constellations. "You can see Scorpio and Virgo pretty clearly tonight. You can see even more when the sky is clearer."

I couldn't help but roll my eyes at him.

"I'm sorry, am I boring you?" he asked

"No, it's not that." I pointed to the stars. "There's Draco and the Ursa Major."

"Hey, you're getting good at this." He sounded surprised.

"That's because you're always pointing them out any chance you get."

" I can't help it. It's what my dad trained me to do."

"What know everything?"

"As much as possible."

"Well, if you know so much then why is it so hard to locate the hawk people?"

Greg ran his hand through his hair. "Mellissa, you know the mountains are outside the council's territory."

I lifted my legs and wrapped my arms around my knees. "I hate being restricted by silly things like territory issues. I feel like I shouldn't be sat here looking at the stars waiting for fireworks whilst Humarya is out there. She's dangerous and we need to stop her before she hurts someone else. Why are the fairies taking so long?"

"It's only been a few days, give them a chance. As a consolation, how about, I won't make you walk back down and you can use your powers."

I scowled at him.

He took hold of my hand. "Don't worry. The fairies will find the hawk people and we'll get permission to go to the mountains. Then Humarya will be captured and stand trial for her crimes."

"What do you mean we'll go to the mountains?" I asked.

"Do you think I'd let you leave me behind? You saw what was written in those books. We don't have a lot of information on the hawks and I can't trust you to document it all properly."

"Well while you're enjoying the educational trip, I'll be hunting down a crazy woman."

"I'll also be keeping an eye on you, ensuring you're not too reckless."

"I am not that reckless." I threw my arms down beside me.

He raised an eyebrow.

I hated it when he did that. It was like calling me a liar without any words. I folded my arms. "We'll probably only make it five minutes into the journey before you ditch me for work anyway."

"I've kept to my word, haven't I? You have had my undivided attention all day."

"Yeah, that's only because it's your birthday and changeling tradition dictates your staff don't disturb you unless the world is ending … which I wouldn't be able to fault you on as I'd also be called on."

Greg leant back and looked up at the sky, "I know I've been a major let down recently. When Victoria was laying into me after your coronation, I realised I needed to sort myself out. That's why I have more interviews scheduled to take on even more staff. It might allow me to finally have some free time."

"Wow, what did Victoria say to you?"

"She told me she'd freeze my fingers and then smash them one by one if I kept upsetting you. "

"I can't believe she said that. Hmm, actually I can."

"Yes, you have one scary, but dedicated guardian. You know, I'm the youngest elder ever? I mean the whole title of elder comes from the fact that they are generally someone older and wiser. I guess I've been trying to overcompensate and prove I'm just as capable as the other two."

"Well, you're certainly wiser than me. Trust me, I get how the whole age thing can be a problem. I'm pretty sure that's why Lees hates me so much. I'm at least half his age and I have all this power that he doesn't think I deserve."

"I think you've already proven how great you are and that your age is insignificant."

I tilted my head, so my hair covered my face as I felt myself blush. Today had been nice and I hoped that things could go back to normal between us. The last couple of months had been a strain. We sat and looked up at the stars while waiting for the fireworks to start.

"So, after you've hired new staff, what are you going to do with all this free time?" I asked.

"I was hoping to spend some time with you … to make up for being such a disappointment."

"You would have to check with Harkura. I have a very strict training regime. You see, he is also crazy, just not in the same way as Victoria. He might actually be worse as you never see his crazy coming."

Greg shook his head. "He can't be worse than Victoria."

"He's offered to cause all sorts of hell when you've upset me."

"But he is always so nice and polite."

"That's what I mean. You will see an angry Victoria coming, giving you time to prepare. Harkura can switch from sweet as a kitten to a deadly assassin in the blink of an eye."

"Well, it's a good thing I don't plan to upset you again."

"You say that, but I'll believe it when it happens. One day is not enough proof."

"So how long is good enough?"

I shrugged. "I don't know … a year, maybe two. Scratch that, let's say ten years."

"Ten years! Is that it?"

I laid my head on his shoulder. "Yeah, if you can manage that I think we'll be all right." There was a whizzing sound followed by a loud bang as the sky lit up with an eruption of colours. I looked up at the sky in awe. Greg was right. We had a great view from here. I jumped up and ran to the edge of the cliff. Pink and purple lights glistened in front of my eyes.

Greg walked up behind me. "Don't get too close to the edge."

"I'm not a child."

"Yeah, but you're terribly clumsy."

I took a step forward and dangled my arm over the edge. Taking another step, I dangled my leg over. Greg grabbed my arm pulling me towards him. "Will you stop that."

I laughed. "You need to chill." My heart raced as I looked up at him. I felt suddenly scared. I'd let my guard down and forgot to keep my distance. He grabbed hold of me, and then pushed my hair away from my face as he kissed me. I instinctively kissed him back. Why did I feel the urge to run? Maybe, because it was wrong to kiss your friends, and if we weren't friends, things would only get complicated. I forced my arms between us. "Wait."

He ran his hand through his hair. "I'm sorry if I overstepped …"

I looked at the ground not daring to make eye contact.

"No, it's fine." What was I doing? I needed space to think. Victoria was right. I had been in denial. Too scared to admit the truth to myself.

"Mellissa."

I looked up at Greg. A firework whizzed past us and explode above us, illuminating the green of his eyes. I could get lost in those eyes. Clutching his shirt, I pulled him down to my height and kissed him. Heat radiated through my body as he wrapped his arms around me. Things were never going back to how they were before, but that wasn't necessarily a bad thing.

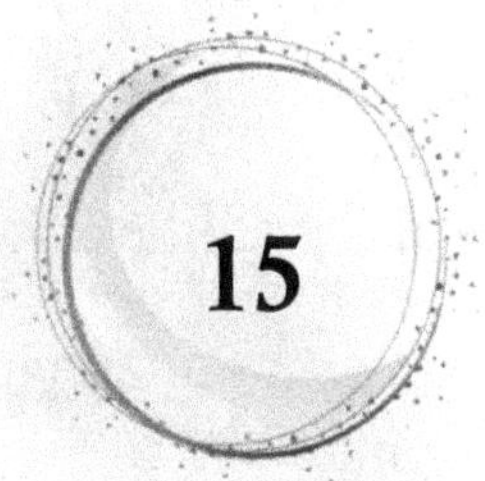

Missing

Mellissa

Thick fog clouded my vision. My skin prickled and I felt weightless as if I were floating. A cold chill ran down my spine.

"Mellissa," a voice yelled.

"Who's there?" I asked the empty grey fog. I held my arm up in front of me as I walked blindly through the haze. I heard my name again and headed towards the sound. I screamed as a person appeared in front of me. "Matt!" I gasped, "but how …?"

"You need to go to the mountains, Mellissa," said Matt.

"I can't, the council won't let me."

"You are the queen, not them."

I snickered. "Queen is just a fancy title that doesn't mean anything."

Matt grasped me by the shoulders. "You're the only one who can do this. I have seen it."

A strong gust whipped up my hair, blowing dust in my face. I covered my face with my hands and when I lowered them again, Matt was gone.

"Matt," I yelled. I ran through the fog calling his name. I skidded to a halt just before hitting some rocks, the atmosphere not as thick there. I was stood at the base of a mountain and looked up, unable to see the top of the rocks.

Someone was shaking me and saying my name. I opened my eyes, pushing the person away.

"Mellissa, I'm sorry to wake you like this," Harkura said. "Daniel is missing."

I sat up straight, dropping my blanket onto the floor. "What do you mean missing?"

"He didn't turn up for work this morning. He always arrives 5:00 a.m. sharp."

"Maybe he just slept in." I jumped out of bed and walked over to my dressing room. "I'll go to his house and check if he's at home with his family."

Harkura's brow creased into deep lines. He took a deep breath, placing a hand on my shoulder. "I've already gone to his house. His wife said he never came home. She thought he'd stayed at the castle. Mellissa, he hasn't been seen since yesterday afternoon."

"After I left for Novosvillas …" I suddenly found it hard to breathe. My chest tightened and I slid to the floor as the room began to spin. Maybe Daniel went away somewhere without telling anyone. But I knew he wouldn't do that. He took his job seriously and would always tell his wife where he was. "Humarya has taken him," I stuttered.

Harkura sat beside me. "We don't know that for sure."

"She said she'd be better prepared next time. That clearly involves kidnapping my chief of staff." I paused, my mind racing. "The knowledge he possesses about us."

"Daniel would never betray you."

"Not willingly." I jumped up. "I need to find him before she tortures him or worse." I shut my eyes and thought about Daniel, hoping he was safe. I teleported and then screamed as I was repelled back, hitting the floor with a thud.

Harkura was by my side in a flash. "What happened?"

"I tried to teleport to Daniel, but something blocked me."

Harkura grabbed my arms and helped me up. "I've already tried a tracking spell. I even tried blood magic with his son's help. Something powerful is obstructing our magic."

"Harkura," I yelled, "This is Humarya and you know it."

He rubbed his chin. "We could reach out to Chancellor Den and the fast-flying fairies. They are the best trackers in the magic world."

"Oh, yes, because Den and his fairies have been so efficient in finding the Hawk people." I took his hands in mine. "We need to go to the mountains ourselves. I don't care what the council decided. Their way isn't working."

Harkura 's jaw tensed, and his indigo eyes turned dark. "You're right, but we can't just go into this blindly. We need a plan."

I nodded, feeling numb inside. There had to be something more I could do to find Daniel. I lifted my hand and called for the heart crystal. It shimmered and shot from my bedside table into my hand. I wasn't sure how I could use it to locate Daniel – it wasn't something I'd tried before but I was prepared to give anything a go. I activated the heart and it shone brightly. "Please, heart crystal help to find my missing elf."

The crystal shone brighter and released an array of flickering lights that scattered all around. I could instantly sense thousands of tiny glowing lights flying across the land searching for Daniel. Shutting my eyes, I saw where the lights were inside my head; they covered the land, stopping short of the sea and sky, only able, it seemed, to cover the domain of the heart crystal. The golden flickers were still out searching when they came across a burst of darkness. I screamed in pain as they were suddenly snuffed out and opened my eyes gasping for breath. My heart was racing, and my body ached as if I'd been hit by that same darkness. I hadn't been able to find Daniel, but I was now certain of his location.

"He's in the mountains," I said.

Harkura put his arm around me. "We can leave tomorrow night. I'll put together a team of healers and guards."

I pushed away from him. "No, just the two of us are going. The more people involved, the higher the risks.

Somehow, Humarya knew I wasn't here protecting the city yesterday. Laxus is right. Someone is spying on us."

"Surely we can trust our people."

"We probably can, but I still don't know who we can trust."

"At the very least can we involve Samson? He has access to all the immense knowledge the changelings have."

That he did. Samson was extremely smart just like his cousin. His knowledge could be useful, but it wasn't fair to ask him to exploit his relationship with Greg. However, I could use mine. But there was something else I needed to do first. "Harkura, can you show me how to place a protection spell around the city. I can't leave this place vulnerable again, but I've never used magic this powerful before."

Harkura nodded. "You're right. With the two of us leaving and Victoria already gone, a protection spell is for the best. It's not my area of expertise, but I should be able to teach you."

"Then let's get started."

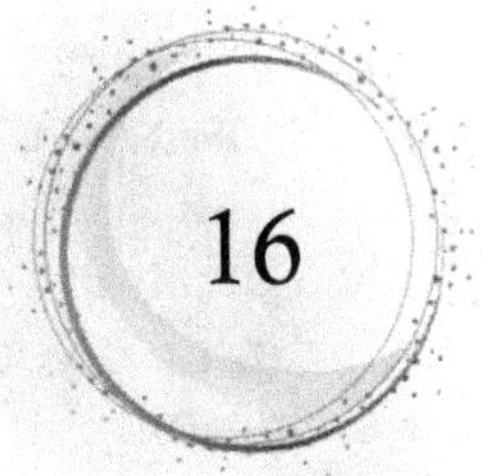

16

Split

Gregory

"**S**amson just tell her someone else is calling?" Greg asked tugging at his hair. He felt like pulling it out. All morning he'd been getting the run-around. Mellissa wasn't answering his calls and her staff were being extremely unhelpful. He'd hoped to have better luck with Samson but that didn't seem to be the case. Why wouldn't Mellissa talk to him? Their day together had gone well and ended even better. At least that's what he'd thought. Maybe she regretted their kiss.

"The queen isn't taking any calls. It's not just you," said Samson's voice coming from his communis device on his desk.

At least it wasn't only him, but he couldn't help taking it personally.

"Do you know why she's not taking calls?" he asked.

"She didn't give a reason. Just that she didn't want to be disturbed. Only emergency calls from Lady Gabrielle are to be put through."

"Tell her it's Lady Gabrielle calling."

"But you're not Lady Gabrielle."

"You really are rubbish." What was the point of having a family member on Mellissa's staff if he couldn't take advantage of it?

"Don't get annoyed with me for doing my job," said Samson

Greg laid his head on his desk. "I'm sorry. I just thought Mellissa and I were finally moving forward."

"Look, there's a lot going on here. Something has happened that's put Queen Mellissa on edge."

Greg sat up straight. "What's happened?"

"I don't know. I have a meeting with her and Harkura soon, but even if I find out, I can't tell you if I'm not permitted to." Samson let out a frustrated grunt. "If I'm being honest, I think she could use your help right now."

"How can I help her if I don't know what's going on?"

"Just come to Urbem Folium. Talk to her."

Greg pushed his fringe to the side. Something was troubling Mellissa, this much he already knew. She had to know she could talk to him about anything. She'd let herself into his house enough times. He ruffled his hair and groaned. Nothing was ever straightforward with her.

"Please wait," cried a female voice just outside his office. "You can't just go in there."

"Watch me," growled another female voice. The door to his office flew open and in marched Victoria, her eyes blazing.

Julie followed, gasping for breath. "I'm sorry, sir, I tried to stop her but she wouldn't listen."

Greg put his hand up. "It's okay. I'll deal with her. You can go."

Victoria glared at Julie. "Yeah, leave."

Julie looked Victoria up and down and then turned to Greg. "Are you sure? I can call the guards."

Victoria clenched her fist. "You'll call who?"

Greg leapt up, placing himself between the two of them. "Really, it's fine. She's Queen Mellissa's guardian."

"As in the elf queen?" Julie asked.

Greg nodded.

Julie looked over his shoulder at Victoria. "Very well." She bowed and then left, closing the door behind her.

"Do I even want to know what is going on there?" asked Samson. His communis was still active so he must have heard everything.

Greg leant over his desk. "I have an unexpected visitor, so I'll talk to you later."

"Is that Samson?" Victoria asked swiping his communis

off his desk. "Go get Mellissa now."

"Victoria, I can't, she isn't taking any calls."

"Get Mellissa now!" she shouted.

"I'm sorry but I have royal duties and stuff. Bye."

The device stopped glowing as it deactivated. Victoria slammed it on the desk and then spun around, jabbing her finger at Greg. "What did you do?"

Greg scowled at her. "I didn't do anything." That he knew of. He couldn't let her of all people see the doubt he was feeling. Greg walked back to his desk and sat down. He shuffled some papers to look like he had work to do.

"Cut the crap. Like me, you rang Mellissa this morning and got no answer. I called Harkura and got no answer again." She slammed her hand on his desk. "So, what did you do?"

"Why, does that mean I've done something?"

"Cause , you're always such a massive let down. She was fine before she went off with you." Victoria sat in the chair across from his desk. She folded her arms and tapped her chin. "I'd expected her to return with you last night, but she didn't. You didn't ditch her for work again?"

Greg shook his head. "No."

"Spent the whole time talking about work?"

"No."

"Not notice how adorably cute she looked in that dress?"

"She's always cute."

Victoria leant back in the chair and smirked. That last response had just slipped out.

Greg got up and flicked through the books on the shelf next to his desk. He understood why Mellissa didn't want to take her calls. All the questions she asked were making him feel uneasy and Mellissa was a lot more sensitive than him.

"Did you kiss her?" she asked.

Greg's hand froze over a book.

"I'll take that as a yes. Well, that explains it."

"How does that explain it?"

"This is Mellissa we're talking about. She's an overthinker. She'll spend the next few days freaking out about it because shes crazy"

Greg leant against the bookcase scratching his head. "I don't see what the big deal is. It's not like it's the first time we've kissed."

Victoria shot forward, leaning on his desk. "What?"

Greg looked away. Mellissa hadn't told Victoria? He thought she told her everything. She was going to kill him for sharing information she didn't want Victoria to know.

"How did I not know this?"

"Forget I said anything."

"Hey, spill now. When did this happen?"

Greg folded his arms. "I'm not saying anything else. I didn't realise she hadn't told you."

Victoria rolled her eyes. "Mellissa is rubbish when it comes to this stuff."

"Or she is just a private person and doesn't like the world knowing her business."

"I am not the world. Besides, it's my job to know everything about her. Just tell me. I might be able to help you figure out what the problem is."

A female perspective might help but Victoria was the last person he wanted to have this conversation with. But he felt cornered. "Fine." Greg sat back at his desk. "She kissed me back in December before everything went wrong with Kadon."

Victoria's eyes widened. "That long ago? Wait, she kissed you?"

Greg nodded.

Victoria whistled. "So, you two have been secretly hooking up all this time? No wonder she was so against Harkura's attempts to set her up."

Greg could feel his face turning red. "It's not like that. We never spoke about itLife got in the way and then I don't know." Greg laid his head on his hand.

"You mean you kept letting her down and standing her up?"

"I didn't mean to. Like I said life got in the way."

"Why do you think your job is more important than hers?"

Greg shook his head. "I don't, she's just better at hers."

"Stop making excuses. Mellissa is too good for you, but for whatever reason, you're the one she's chosen."

Greg's heart somersaulted at Victoria's words. "Did she say that?"

"Of course not." Victoria clenched her jaw. "She doesn't have to. It's obvious."

Greg raised an eyebrow. "Is it?"

Victoria clicked her fingers and pointed at him. "That's the problem. Neither of you can see what's right in front of your faces. You need to learn to talk about your feelings better."

"I've tried to make it up to her, but she doesn't make it easy."

"Why should she when you keep letting her down? You need to put everything on the line and make sure she knows without a doubt where you stand."

"Even if I don't know where she is on this?"

"You're such an idiot. The whole world knows where she stands except you."

Greg frowned. Everyone else seemed to know more about his relationship with Mellissa than he did.

Victoria shook her head and sighed. "She's coming to check on Laxus and my experiment tomorrow morning. I suggest you go into work late." Victoria got up and walked to the door. "Take some time to think about what you'll say to her."

"Since we're sharing, do you want to tell me what you and Laxus are really doing here?"

"Nice try." She walked out of his office with her chin raised as if she'd won a chess game.

He'd hated all her questions, but she'd given him a lot to think about. He'd hoped with time, Mellissa would open up to him. He'd been wrong about that. He'd have to be the one to bring it up and hope she didn't teleport if things got awkward. If he had to, he'd head to Urbem Folium. It wasn't just about his feelings for her, though. She was keeping secrets and he needed to find out why. Laxus was the key to figuring it out, but Greg still couldn't read the boy. All he could sense was Mellissa's magic whenever he tried,. For now, he'd make arrangements to work from home and catch Mellissa off guard when she came to check in with Victoria.

Greg stacked another pile of books by the fireplace, one of his favourite spots to read. The lighting here was just right. He'd cleared his day so he could spend the day at home on his own research project. There may not be many references to the Hawk people in his books but the little there had been written was by dwarfs. If he looked into the history of the dwarfs that used to mine the mountain area, he may be able to find some clue to any sightings. The fairies lack of progress was starting to concern him. If he could narrow down the area they needed to search, maybe they would yield some results.

"What's with all the books?" Laxus leant against the doorway.

"For research," Greg replied.

"What sort of research?"

"Nothing a twelve-year-old should be worrying about."

Laxus skipped into the room and peered at the pile of books. "I'm very well-read. If you tell me what you're researching, I could help."

"If you told me what your experiment was, I could help you."

A wide grin spread across Laxus' face. "I like you. You're smart."

"So are you." Way smarter than the average kid. Then again, he'd always been the smartest of his age group. Greg shut his eyes trying to read the boy's aura. Once again, all he sensed was Mellissa. She must have blanketed him with her aura, but why?

"Shouldn't you be at work?" Laxus asked

"I'm working from home."

"Hoping to catch Mellissa off guard when she checks in with us?"

Greg chuckled "Is it that obvious?"

"Yes." Laxuses smile fell as he looked at the ground. "I

think I misjudged you. Mellissa will need you."

"Tell me what's going on."

"There's nothing for me to tell. I'll be in the kitchen if you change your mind about wanting help." Laxus skipped out of the room.

Actions like that made Greg almost believe he was a normal twelve-year-old but the way he spoke showed that there was more to him. Why had he agreed to let him stay? He knew nothing about him. Mellissa had asked, that was why. If it had been anyone else, he would never have agreed without knowing more.

Greg sat in the armchair by the fire and opened the first book from his pile. If he managed to find something, it might break the ice with Mellissa when she showed up. He still had no idea what he was going to say to her.

A loud rat-ta-tat-tat sounded in the hallway. Someone was at the door. Greg put his book down and walked out to the hall. It wouldn't be Mellissa as she didn't use doors. Greg's stomach turned. What if his mother had returned? She'd threatened as much and had awful timing.

Greg opened the door. His jaw clenched. "Julie, what are you doing here? I told everyone I wouldn't be in today."

"I know," she said, "but you left all these applications behind and I thought you'd want them." She handed him a stack of papers.

"Thanks." He put his hand on the door to close it.

Julie poked her head round. "There's something else."

"What is it?"

"I wanted to talk to you about something. Can I come in?"

Greg looked at his watch. This was eating into his research time and he still had no idea what time Mellissa would be showing up. Hopefully whatever Julie wanted wouldn't take long. "Very well come in."

Greg led her into the living room and gestured for her to take a seat. She sat on the edge of the chair he'd pointed at fiddling with the hem of her skirt. Greg placed the papers on the coffee table and took a seat. "What seems to be the problem? Are you having any issues with the tasks assigned to you?"

"No, it's not that." She pointed at the pile on the coffee table. "I couldn't help noticing that along with the applications for chief of staff you also had some for a new assistant."

Ahh, so she was worried about her job. He could see why his search for a second assistant would make her think her job was at risk. "You don't have to worry about that. I'm not looking for a replacement, only an addition to the team. It is no secret we're understaffed."

"But why do you need another assistant? Am I not enough?"

Greg straightened his back. He thought his explanation would have been the end of it. "How I choose staff is none of your concern. You can leave reassured that it's not your position I'm advertising."

Greg got up to see her out, but she grabbed his wrist. "Wait. I understand now."

"Well good. I'll see you …"

Julie continued to hold onto him. "You want to free up more of my time so I can better assist you?"

"Sure." That wasn't what he'd meant but as long as this ended the conversation, he wouldn't contradict her.

"While I'm here, I could help you with whatever you're working on or I could make tea to help relax you."

"I can make my own tea, thanks."

She ran her finger up his arm. "Something else, perhaps, to help relieve stress."

Why did she suddenly think he was stressed and needed to relax? She leaned in towards him and Greg quickly stepped back almost falling over the coffee table. "What are you doing?"

"What you want." She advanced towards him.

Greg put his arm between them. "I want you to go back to city hall and do your job so I can be left alone to read my books."

"What do you mean? Is this a game? Like some sort of role-play. "

"What are you talking about?"

"I read all your signals." Julie tucked some hair behind her ear and smiled flirtatiously. Steve told me you were lonely and with all the late nights we've worked together, I know you want this." She pushed forward and tried to kiss him.

Greg ducked around her. "I don't know what Steve has been telling you, but he was wrong. And, for the record, I've not been sending you any signals."

She placed her hands over her heart. "The way you looked at me when you said you'd be working from home today."

He hadn't given her any particular look. She was obviously seeing what she wanted to see. He always aimed to keep things professional at work.

Julie took a step towards him. "When I saw the applications on your desk, I knew it was a sign. You'd arranged it all so we could be alone together."

Greg edged backwards aiming for the door. "No. I just meant I wouldn't be in the office today. Leaving the applications behind was a genuine accident."

Suddenly she threw herself at him, wrapping her arms around his waist.

Greg grabbed her hands and pushed them away. It was as if she refused to hear what he was saying. This was the last time he hired someone off a recommendation from an old classmate. She'd seemed so normal before. He'd shout for Victoria to help. She'd have no problem getting rid of her.

The door creaked open. It was as if he just had to think of her name and she'd appear. Maybe she was a demon after all. But as he turned to ask for help it wasn't Victoria he saw but Mellissa. She remained silent, her eyes flashing green before she walked away. Why did she have to pick now to show up? Greg pushed Julie out of the way and ran out of the room. "Mellissa wait ..."

"I didn't mean to interrupt," she said continuing to march down the hallway. "I was just looking for Victoria. Where is she?"

"It's not what you think. Let me explain."

"There is nothing to explain. It's not my concern as to

how you spend your free time." She stopped and turned to face him. "Now, Gregory, where is my guardian?" Her hands shook as she spoke.

He hated it when she used his full name and her wording had been so awfully formal. "Don't do that, Mellissa. If you want to scream at me, just do it. I can take whatever you have to say."

"It's not what I have to say you should be worried about," she shouted throwing her arms down causing the house to shake.

"Earthquake," squawked Julie, bracing herself in the living room doorway.

Mellissa clenched her fists. Her eyes turned green as the tremors slowed. "I should go."

"Don't." Greg grabbed her arm. She swiftly twisted around, releasing herself. Once upon a time, she'd have struggled to get out of a simple hold like that, but not anymore. And he knew there was no way he could force her to stay. She was going to disappear on him. If only she'd let him explain.

"What's going on?" Victoria shouted running out of the kitchen.

Mellissa shot out of the front door as Greg ran after her, thanking the gods she hadn't teleported yet. Hopefully, it meant she was willing to listen but just needed to get rid of some angry energy. He found her by the fountain. She was looking down at the water shaking, clenching her hands.

"Can we just talk?" Greg asked.

Her gaze didn't move from the water's surface. "What is there to talk about?"

"What happened just moments ago. Which was nothing by the way."

She wrapped her arms around her shoulders, hugging herself. "It doesn't matter."

"Of course, it does."

"No, it doesn't. Whatever this is." She gestured to both of them. "I'm so tired of it. I can't do this anymore."

"Why won't you listen to me?" No one seemed to be listening to him today, only hearing what they chose to.

"You're not listening," she yelled. "I'm done."

"You don't get to just decide that. Nothing happened. You're just using this as an excuse to run away, the same as when you wouldn't answer my calls yesterday."

"Oh sure," she snorted, "So me not answering your calls is an excuse to hook up with your assistant. You have no idea what is going on. I rang you back last night. You didn't answer." With every word she yelled at him a crack appeared in the fountain. She clenched her fists. "I'm not running. The problem is I was holding on so tight I was blind to the truth."

"What truth?" He regretted asking as soon as the words left his mouth. There was no way any response she had was a good one.

She finally looked at him, eyes full of tears. "We both know our friendship is a lie. I mean were we ever really friends?"

Greg swallowed a lump in his throat. "Of course we were. I mean are."

"Are we? We don't work together in any way. It's about time we both accept it."

"I won't accept something that isn't true," He took her hand. "Mellissa, you're right, we aren't just friend because I …"

Mellissa pushed him away. "Don't you dare finish that sentence. If you say it now, it's because you're trying to make me forgive you."

"But it's the truth."

She responded by instantly teleporting somewhere. This wasn't how the conversation was meant to go. Why did she have to arrive then? Why did Julie have to show up in the first place?

"What happened?" Victoria asked from behind him. She sounded genuinely concerned but he wasn't in the mood for a conversation. He walked past her back into the house. There were no words that could describe how he was feeling. It felt as if he'd been slapped in the face and punched in the gut at the same time.

"Sir, are you all right?" Julie asked as he walked down

the hallway towards his study.

What was she still doing here?

"Who was that? She was really rude."

She put her hand on his arm and he nudged her away. "Get out."

"What?"

"Leave now. I'll deal with you later."

Her jaw dropped and she froze on the spot.

She looked as if she was about to say something when Victoria marched in grabbing her. "You are not wanted." She grabbed Julie by the arm and yanked her out the house.

Greg should have called for Victoria straight away. She'd been surprisingly helpful recently. Then perhaps things wouldn't have escalated the way they had and Julie would have been gone before Mellissa arrived.

Why did nothing ever go the way he planned? Surely, this wasn't over. She couldn't dump him. They weren't even properly dating. He'd give her time to cool off, but he wasn't going to let her make this decision for both of them, especially when she didn't know all the facts. They needed to sit now together alone and then he'd tell her everything, including everything about his mother. It had been stupid to keep so much to himself. How could he expect her to tell him the truth when he was keeping his own secrets? He had to go to Urbem Folium and fix things.

Victoria walked back into the house brushing her hands together as if she'd just put out the rubbish. And Greg quickly rushed into the living room and shut the door, pushing one of the armchairs against it. If she really wanted to, Victoria could blast her way in, but he hoped his house guests would respect his need for privacy. For now, he'd focus on his research. Mellissa wanted to go to the mountains, and he was going to make it happen for her. If he could bring her some good news, it might give him five minutes before she disappeared on him again. One thing was certain: he wasn't about to give up on her. He never would.

Broken

Mellissa

I sat curled up under the tree of time, wiping tears from my face. There's no way I was going back to the castle – not like this. Greg was free to do what he wanted and so was I, yet, I still felt betrayed. It was my own fault, allowing myself to get sucked in. I was such an idiot. Of course, he didn't care about me as with everyone else here, I was just a convenient person to keep on side. Ever since I'd got here, I'd been used as a political device, a weapon of sorts to throw into battle when needed. I punched the tree. "You warned me, Matt. I let him play me."

I pulled my knees to my chest. "I don't know what to do anymore." I whispered to the tree. Matt was sealed inside it but I was sure he could hear me. At least that was what I believed. "I wish you were here Matt, you would know just the right thing to say to make me forget about Greg and get me to laugh." I looked up at the clear blue sky and sighed. This whole situation with Greg was ridiculous. I had let him distract me from what was important. I clenched my fists feeling a fire burn inside me. I was done with silly flirtations, I had more important missions to focus on. The council may have voted against me, but I was going after Humarya. She'd clearly taken Daniel as a hostage to goad me, and I couldn't leave him imprisoned any longer. Just because Harkura thought we needed help, didn't mean we did. I was the keeper of the heart crystal. It was entrusted to me for a reason, and I wasn't going to wait around to get permission to protect people.

I stood up placing my hand on the tree. "You know what Matt, I'm done feeling sorry for myself, and I don't care if the council get mad at me … I am going to find, Humarya, before she attacks again, and stop her getting her hands on another dark stone. Hopefully, I can also save my chief of staff in the process."

Matt may not be able to respond, but I was sure he was listening. Once this was over, I'd try once more to free him. The list of people I could trust was getting smaller. I could do with another ally like him. "Thanks for listening, Matt. "

With a clearer idea of what I had to do, I teleported myself back to the castle and found Samson in his office. He seemed relieved to see me. "Your Majesty where have you been? Harkura has been searching for you for hours. Also, Victoria and Greg have called at least a dozen times."

"I'm sorry, I needed some time to clear my head."

"Are you all right? You look pale."

"I'm fine. Could you get Harkura and tell him I'm ready to go."

Samson frowned. "Go where?"

"He'll know what I mean."

Samson bowed and hurried away whilst I ran upstairs to get changed. The silly dress I was wearing wouldn't be practical up in the mountains. I flicked through my clothes. My choice was limited as most of my old clothes had been thrown out and replaced with designer outfits, but I still had my training clothes. I was pulling my hair into a ponytail when Harkura walked in.

"Mellissa, you cannot just run off to the mountains."

"I don't need permission to do my duty as crystal keeper," I shouted

"There are rules and regulations for a reason."

Was he for real? He gave me such conflicting messages, I never knew where I stood. I shoved his hand off my shoulder.

"Lives are in danger. You can either help me or get out."

Harkura's mouth curled into a smile. "Of course, I'll help you. We can't just go in blind. How do you plan to get there?"

"I'll teleport."

"How? You've never been there before and have no reference arrival point."

"I don't know," I yelled, "but I have to do something."

"Okay, I have an idea. Follow me. Samson is waiting in your office."

I gritted my teeth. Every bone in my body wanted to teleport away, show him that I didn't need a plan. All this talking was just wasting time, but deep down I knew he was right. I had no notion of where I was going. I followed Harkura downstairs to my office where Samson was waiting. As we walked in, he bowed.

"Tell the queen what you told me," Harkura said.

Samson nodded. "You see when we were young, Greg and I used to play in the archives of city hall."

I clenched my fists at the mention of Greg's name. "That's nice but I don't have time for a stroll down memory lane."

He shook his head. "I have a point. In the archives, we'd go through the files sometimes, even though Uncle Steffen told us not to. I'm pretty sure there are old maps of the mountains down there."

My heart leapt for joy. I rushed over and hugged Samson. "That's brilliant. Could you get them?"

Samson turned bright red and scratched the back of his head. "I could talk to Greg."

I felt a rage wash over me. "No, we can't involve that lowlife."

Samson's mouth fell open as Harkura stepped towards me. "Are you okay?"

"Of course I'm not okay. Daniel is missing and I don't know who I can trust."

Harkura rubbed his chin. "As talking to Lord Gregory isn't an option. I suggest you secretly borrow the documents. "

I smirked. "Sounds good to me,"

Samson put his hand on his forehead. "This isn't necessary. Greg would help if you just asked."

"I went to him for help this morning, but things didn't go well." That was a massive understatement but it wasn't a story I wanted to regurgitate.

"Why don't you let me speak to him then?"

"Look, Samson, I understand Greg is your family and Novosvillas is your home, but you work for me now. If you want to be a part of this, you must promise not to speak a word to Greg."

Samson bowed. "I understand and I promise."

He left my office leaving me with Harkura who turned out to be the perfect partner in crime. Getting in and out of Novosvillas city hall wouldn't be a problem – finding the correct map in a huge pile was. We needed to strike in the middle of the night to reduce the risk of being caught.

Harkura left to pack for our trip while I rang Victoria to update her on what had happened. Before I could even mention our plan, she was demanding to know where I'd been.

"It shouldn't take this long to return my call," she said.

"I was out," I replied, "Anyway I called to ask you something."

"Don't *anyway* me," she yelled, "I won't be doing anything for you until you tell me what is going on between you and Greg."

Why was she being so difficult? Harkura hadn't pushed me about where I'd been. "There's nothing to tell."

"Like hell, there isn't. I know about the kiss and that it wasn't the first time. I can't believe you didn't tell me."

"He told you that?"

"To be fair to the idiot, I'm an expert at making people think I already know stuff. So, Mellissa, just come back and talk to him. He's moping about and depressing to look at."

Was she defending Greg? She was meant to be on my side.

"I didn't call you to talk about Greg. I am so over it," I said.

"Fine, then just listen. His assistant was the one trying it on, and he rejected her. Turns out she only wanted the job to climb up the social ladder. It was all her cousin's idea. I must say they are next level stupid to think she could pull that crap with someone as principled as Greg. Also, they must be the only people, besides you, that can't see he's madly in love with you."

My heart fluttered at her last few words. But I couldn't be dragged back towards Greg. "As I told him, he can do what he wants, and if that involves his stupid assistant, so be it. Nobody has ever committed to loving me."

"Oh, Mellissa, stop with the pity party, and tell me, how often do you teleport in on him unannounced? Have you ever caught him with someone?"

The answer was never, but I knew telling her that would only confirm the point she was trying to make. "I thought you hated, Greg. Why are you defending him?"

"Mellissa, you're my best friend and I want you to be happy. If it wasn't for you, I'd happily never interact with him. But for whatever reason, you've fallen for him, and I know you'll be just as mopey as he is right now. "

I sniffled. "I'm your best friend?"

"Yes, but if you tell anyone I admitted that, I'll freeze your toes off."

That was the Victoria I was used to. Unfortunately her threats were aimed at me and not the person I was upset with. I coughed, clearing my throat. "Anyway, can we get to what I actually rang you about?"

"Have it your way. You're only hurting yourself. So, what do you want?" Even though I couldn't see her, I could sense she was rolling her eyes.

"Daniel is missing. I'm convinced Humarya has him. Harkura and I are going to the mountains to find him."

"What!" she yelled, "Why are you only just telling me this?"

"I came to tell you this morning and ask for Greg's help, but you know how that went. Then this conversation got side-tracked."

"If you're going to the mountains, I'm coming too."

"No, Victoria, you need to stay with Laxus. Harkura and I can handle this, but there is something you can do to help."

"What?"

"I need you to find out when the last person at city hall finishes work."

Victoria responded with a long sigh. "Okay, I'm not happy about this, but I know how stubborn you are and that I won't change your mind. So, I'll ring you back with the information later."

"Thanks, I do appreciate it."

I deactivated my communis and went to find Harkura. Hopefully, it wouldn't take Victoria long to find the information and we could get moving later tonight.

As I walked down the corridor, the space in front of me suddenly became distorted and a powerful gust of wind filled the hallway pushing me back. In front of me seemed to be some sort of portal. I quickly transformed the heart crystal to staff form to prepare for what might emerge – and stopped dead in my tracks, my heart racing. Daniel was thrown through it, looking pale and dishevelled – and then the portal quickly closed.

I ran over to him and shouted for help hooping someone in the other offices would hear me.. Kneeling beside him, my stomach churned, and I began to tremble. There was so much blood. His fingernails had been ripped off and his back was covered in cuts. He was lying slumped on his side, so I gently rolled him over so I could see his face. His cheeks and forehead were covered in burns and deep red scratches as if he'd been clawed by a wild animal.

"Daniel, I'm so sorry. This is all my fault," I cried.

"My Queen, you cannot blame yourself," he stammered, his voice hoarse.

"Please, don't talk, the healers are on their way," I said taking his blood soaked hand. I didn't know what else to do. Panic bubbled up inside me. I needed to get him help, urgently.

"You must know, I didn't tell Humarya anything." He

tried to smile at me, but I could see it was a struggle as he could barely open his mouth. My eyes filled with tears as the healers arrived. Standing up, I quickly stepped back so they could work their magic. The team of four healers hovered their glowing hands over Daniels battered body muttering spells-but it was too late. I watched him close his eyes and let out a long groan as his battered body went limp. It was too late for them to save him. I felt numb. This was all my fault.

Daniel was declared dead and his body taken away. My heart felt as if it would burst with pain. I should have acted sooner. His poor family. This wasn't the news I'd wanted to give them. I was meant to save him.

"You cannot blame yourself," Harkura said taking my hand.

"How can I not?" I shoved his hand away. I didn't deserve to be comforted. "I knew he was in danger, and instead of doing what was necessary, I hesitated."

"This was the act of an evil, twisted person. This is what she wants. She purposely sent Daniel back in that state to get to you. You cannot let her win."

"I know what you're saying makes sense, Harkura, but-" I looked down at the blood on my hands, my tears flowing freely.

"I think you should go get yourself cleaned up. Have an early night to recover from the shock. I shall wait up for Victoria's call. Once we get all the information we need, then together we can stop this depraved, ungodly woman."

I nodded. Harkura guided me up to my room, hugging me gently before he left. I stood shivering in the shower, watching the blood being washed away. There was so much of it. I grabbed a sponge and scrubbed my skin raw. It wasn't enough. I couldn't get the blood off.

After climbing out and drying myself, I wrapped myself in my dressing gown and curled up in bed crying until I had nothing left in me.

I was bone-tired, but I couldn't sleep. Every time I shut my eyes, I saw Daniel's body lying there covered in blood. And the more I thought about it, the angrier I got. I should have followed my instincts instead of listening to the council. They knew Humarya was dangerous, but they'd been too concerned about bureaucracy to go after her, and I was stupid enough to obey. The list of stupid things I'd done was getting far too long. If I'd have had the bird woman on the run, she'd never have been able to kidnap Daniel. I spent the entire night tossing and turning, thinking about all the 'what if' scenarios.

When dawn broke, the sun shone through my window making me squint in the light. I clambered out of bed and walked through the doors leading to the balcony, and then stood there silently as a warm summer breeze blew through my hair. Harkura hadn't come back to tell me what Victoria had found. Perhaps he left me up here because he thought I was too fragile to handle things at the moment. I felt a surge of anger. Waiting on others was clearly pointless. It was time to take things into my own hands.

I untied the chain around my neck and held the heart crystal out in front of me. Harkura suggested I did this spell with the help of others as it needed to cover a large area. I pushed my will power into the crystal. It shined brightly, reassuring me that I could do this. Holding the heart out towards the city, I cast the barrier spell. Light shot straight up into the sky like a firework. It spread through the sky and domed down, covering the city. It then fizzled out, leaving behind a dome of protection so any dark magic would be repelled.

I got dressed and teleported to the city hall's archive room in Novosvillas. Unfortunately, the building wasn't as empty as I'd hoped. Of course, this lot would already be at work as they were employed by that overachiever Gregory. I found the sections where the maps were held and began searching through the cabinets for the one I wanted. The quicker I found what I needed the less likely I'd be caught.

"You," shouted a female voice, making me jump. Julie marched over to me yelling about something. I only made out half of what she said. Something about being transferred and it being my fault.

I shook my head. "I have no idea what you're on about."

I wasn't in the mood for her rubbish. Finding the right map was all I cared about.

"I don't even know what your job is here, but it can't be that important. You ruined my chances at promotion. I have been transferred out of city hall. I have no contact with our elder now." She flashed her hands in my face.

I stepped backwards feeling myself stiffen. I was struggling to remain calm. "How is it my fault? You obviously didn't do your job right. Now go away." I didn't understand how she'd come to this conclusion but it wasn't my problem. I flicked to the back of the cabinet and almost jumped for joy as I found what I was looking for.

"You know exactly what you did. Just as I was about to make my move, you walk in and steal his attention away. Then I get disciplined for inappropriate behaviour. I don't know what sort of hypnotising powers you have, but get me my job back!" She wagged her finger in my face. I smacked her hand away from me. She gasped and grabbed her hand as if I'd burned her.

"You are such an idiot. I don't know why Greg hired you in the first place. Be grateful you still have a job, if you'd worked for me, you would have been fired. You said yourself you were disciplined for inappropriate behaviour."

"I am not an idiot, and who do you think you are referring to our elder so casually?"

I put my hands on my hips. "You really have no idea who I am?" Even though I was livid, I couldn't help but laugh.

"Don't you dare laugh at me. That's it! I challenge you to a change off." she shouted

"A what?"

She jumped up, swiftly transforming into a large bird and flew at me. I suddenly understood what she meant. The idiot thought I was a changeling. After the night I had had, I really wasn't in the mood for this. As she came at me again, I fired a bolt of lightning her way. She screamed instantly transforming back and falling to the ground.

"What the hell was that?" she screeched.

"Lightning. I'm not a changeling, you dimwit. For someone who wants to climb the ladder, you really should know who's on it."

The anger I'd been holding back was seeping through. The ground shook as I stopped myself throwing an even stronger bolt at her. I stomped my foot opening the ground below her and with a flick of my wrist, up shot a giant vine which curled around her, encapsulating her in its leaves. I knew I shouldn't take my rage out on her, but she'd picked the wrong moment to run her mouth off. To my dismay, the emotional use of my powers had drawn the attention of others in the building. There was now a small crowd forming in the entrance and along with five guards'. My plan to slip in and out unnoticed was a shambles.

"Queen Mellissa what are you doing here?" asked one of the guards, bowing to me. "This woman didn't hurt you, did she?"

I flashed the guard a quick smile as I straightened my dress. "I'm fine. I was just borrowing some maps." I showed him the papers in my hand and then pointed at Julie. "As you can see, I trapped my assailant."

"Oh my god, you're the elf queen?" Julie cried. "I'm so sorry, I didn't know. You have to forgive me." She wriggled about in her leafy constraints. I should have hit her with the stronger bolt and knocked her out.

"You be quiet," snapped a guard. It was like he read my mind. He returned his attention to me. "Lord Gregory didn't tell us you were coming."

"That's because she didn't tell me," Greg answered as he walked into the room. The guards bowed to him just as they had to me. "You know, it would have been a lot easier if you'd just asked for whatever it is you want to steal."

"As you know, I prefer the term secret borrowing." I took a deep breath. This was all taking a lot longer than planned. If I didn't get out of here soon, this was going to turn into a council meeting with everyone moaning at me.

"Can't we just talk about what you're doing?" Greg asked. "Victoria told me that Daniel is missing. Maybe I can help."

I narrowed my eyes at him. "The whole point of secret

borrowing was to avoid talking to you. There are more important things going on right now, so get off your high horse, not everything is about you."

Greg turned to the guards and asked them to take Julie away and then ordered his staff to get back to work. We were now alone in the archive room. He walked over to the cabinet I had been looking through and flicked through the files inside.

"Maps, Mellissa. Are you planning a trip?"

"What if I am? It's none of your concern if I decide to take a trip."

"It is if that trip is to the mountains. I know you want to find Daniel, but there's a better way to go about this."

"I don't care anymore. I'm done waiting around. If I'd just acted sooner …" I spluttered out my words as my breathing became heavy. All the emotions I'd tried to push down began to overflow, causing the ground the shake.

Greg stepped closer. "Mellissa, I understand you're worried about Daniel, but could you please leave this building standing in one piece."

"No, you don't understand," I screamed. "Daniel's dead! And if I'd just followed my instincts, maybe I could have saved him."

The tremors got stronger as objects fell off shelves and cracks appeared in the walls. The guards came back in to check on us but Greg gestured for them to stay back.

"Mellissa, what happened?" Greg asked. He pulled some strands of hair away from my eyes as tears streamed down my face.

"Humarya sent him back to me just so I could watch him die."

Greg pulled me towards him, hugging me tightly. "Mellissa, I'm so sorry."

I buried my face in his shirt as he stroked my hair. I didn't want him to comfort me. There was so much anger I had towards him still, but I could barely breathe through my tears.

Greg tilted my head to look up at him and wiped my damp face with his hand. "You need to calm down."

"Don't tell me to calm down," I shouted, pushing him

away from me.

"Mellissa you could smash this whole building into a pile of rubble if you don't."

I looked around the room. Larger cracks had formed on the floor and walls and hardly anything was left on any shelves. I shut my eyes. This building was full of people. It was my job to protect not destroy. I had to get my emotions under control. Opening my eyes, I pushed my arms out and the quake stopped.

"Can we please talk about his now?" Greg asked.

"No, I don't need to talk. I need to take action." Before he could say anything else, I'd teleported.

Even if Greg tried to find me, he'd be out of luck. No one would expect me to be in this place. A wave of clarity had washed my anger away. It was something I couldn't see before but now the answer was clear. I'd teleported myself to the dwarf stronghold in the caves. I'd only been there once before and hoped I was in the right place to find Hogan. It was something I'd read in one of Greg's books. All the information about the hawk people was written by the dwarfs that used to mine in the mountains. Those dwarfs were Hogan's ancestors. He never said much in council meetings unless he made a joke. Hopefully, he'd help me get to where I needed to be as he wasn't like the others.

The cave settlement was actually quite beautiful and more like an underground city. Cables ran across the walls lighting the way and mimicking sunlight. In fact, it was just as bright down here as above ground. Small, mechanical, bugs flew around watering the plants and I followed the path until I found a group of people.

The dwarfs were surprised to find me wandering around, but they were very accommodating. They led me to Hogan and loaned me a cloak to wear as the caves, they informed me, were a lot colder than elves were used to. They also handed me something warm to drink as I sat and spoke with Hogan.

"So, what brings the queen of the elves to our caves?" Hogan asked, "It must be something important for you to come in person."

"I'm sorry for arriving without warning like this, but I could really use your help. I know this is not the proper way to do things but going through the proper channels is taking far too long. I want to go to the mountains to find the hawk people. They are the only ones who might know how to find Humarya. They may even know a way to stop her."

"The council has already voted on this. We are to wait until we hear from the fairies." Hogan said.

I was sick of being told to wait for the fairies. It had been ages since they were sent to the mountains and they hadn't achieved anything. Hopefully once I explained everything he would come round. "I know what was decided but that was before Humarya murdered my chief of staff. I don't want anyone else to lose their life while waiting for things to be done diplomatically. As long as you don't tell anyone you saw me today, I won't let anyone know you helped me. If there are any repercussions, they will be mine to take and mine alone."

Hogan scratched his head, wrinkles appearing on his face as he frowned. "Even if I wanted to, I don't understand how I could help you. My people don't know anything about the hawk race. I know we are the closest settlement to the mountains, but we haven't been there in over a hundred years."

"All I ask is that you point out the area that your ancestors used to mine on this map." I laid the map I'd taken out in front of him. "The changelings have books that refer to the hawk people and they were all written by dwarfs that mined the mountains. My theory is that the dwarfs may have interacted with them. They probably live somewhere above those old mines, much higher up. It would be a good starting point for my search. "

Hogan rubbed the stubble on his chin. With every tick of the clock, my chest tightened. I really needed him to say, yes, otherwise, I didn't know what I'd do.

After what felt like an hour of silence, when it was really just minutes, Hogan agreed to help.

"I will do better than point out areas on a map. I will take you to the mines myself," he said. "But that's a far as I go."

I grasped his hand tightly. "Thank you so much."

"And I won't tell anyone I saw you today.

I nodded with a smile. "And when everything is revealed, I won't let anyone know you've helped me."

Hogan jumped to his feet. "Okay, well, the fastest way to get there is by tunnelling. I understand you have the ability to manipulate the earth. This should allow you to travel through the tunnels alongside me easily."

"How do your tunnels work?" I asked.

"It's quite simple. All the tunnels are pre-dug so you just need to push away the earth around you. Stay close to me, as you could easily get lost."

Out of nowhere a hole in the ground suddenly appeared which he instantly jumped down and I eagerly followed behind. It was an odd way to travel. I'd never used my powers this way before but this was a speciality of the dwarfs. I remained close to Hogan as I didn't want to get stuck. Causing an earthquake was a piece of cake but this was something else and took a lot more concentration.

Ten minutes later we popped up in a mine. I was pleasantly surprised at how fast travelling underground had been. It could never be as fast as teleporting, but it was definitely something I'd try again.

"These are the old mines," Hogan said.

I curtsied. "Thank you, Hogan."

He bowed and kissed my hand. "I really hope you find what you're looking for."

He disappeared back underground as I walked around the mine and found my way out. Once outside, I was able to see the vastness of the mountains. I was at the bottom and the peak appeared to be well above the clouds. I wasn't sure how high they went but I teleported to the highest point I could see. It may not have been the best idea but I couldn't think of another way and I was determined. I ascended the mountains and as I got higher and higher, the temperature dropped. I wrapped the cloak I'd been given around me, wishing I'd dressed more appropriately. It was reaching nightfall and I'd lost count of how many teleporting trips I'd made. My eyelids felt heavy yet I couldn't let my tiredness get the better of me. Victoria and Harkura weren't going to be happy that I'd run off on my own like this but as long as I found the hawk people it would be worth them being angry with me.

It was now dark, and I could barely see where I was going. After teleporting so many times I'd worked through a lot of magic power but I couldn't give up. Humarya could attack again at any time, so I needed to find more out about her. I wasn't going to let her take anyone else from me. I beamed upwards again but this must have been one teleport too many. My vision blurred and I fell to the ground in exhaustion with everything around me spinning. I vaguely made out a bunch of people gathering around me, before I passed out.

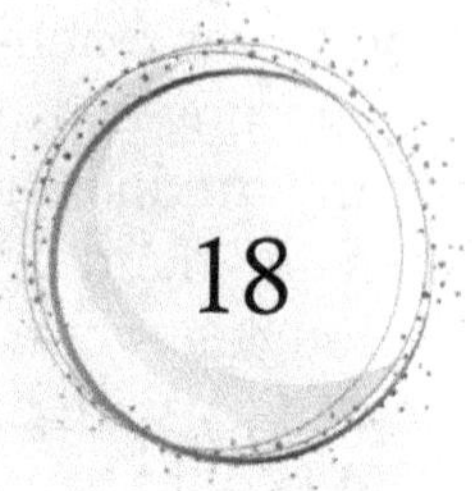

18

The Hawks

Mellissa

woke up inside a dome-shaped tent, laid on a soft mattress on the floor covered by thick blankets. My entire body ached, my mouth was dry, and my throat sore. I sat up and saw a winged woman knelt beside me. I jumped away from her and she jolted, startled by my reaction. I let out a sigh of relief when I realised, she wasn't Humarya. She had flawless terra-cotta skin and chestnut hair that fell in ringlets down her back. The biggest difference from Humarya was that her feathered wings were golden, not jet black. I quickly looked down at the ground as she caught me staring at her with my mouth wide open.

"It's good to see you're awake," said the woman. "My name is Faizah and I'm the healer here in our village. How are you feeling? When we found you, you'd collapsed from overusing your powers."

"I feel a lot better, thanks." I croaked. My throat felt like I had grains of sand lodged in it.

"Here, have this." Faizah handed me a small bowl of water.

I took it with both my hands and gulped it down. "I know this might be a silly question, but are you one of the hawk people?"

"Why of course, but we prefer to be called hawklings."

"Fantastic." I clapped my hands together. "I can't believe I've found you. I'm sorry I haven't introduced myself.

"We already know who you are, Queen Mellissa, ruler of the lands and keeper of the heart crystal."

"How do you know who I am? Hardly anyone on the land has heard of your people. It was down to an educated guess that I even knew where to start my search and pure dumb luck that I actually found you."

"It has been many years since we have ventured near the grounds. However, we were expecting your visit. It was foretold by our master … he said you would come. We also know what it is you seek."

"Then you know about Humarya?"

"Yes, we do." She stood holding her hand out to me. "The chief of our village will tell you everything you want to know. I'll take you to him now if you wish."

I nodded, taking her hand. She pulled me to my feet and guided me outside. I gasped at the sight. We were above cloud level up near the peak of the mountain and the sun was beating down. The sun looked so big and bright up here. Yet, I found myself shivering in the cold wind that was blowing my hair all over the place. I couldn't help wondering how we were able to breathe so easily this high up. Surely the air quality shouldn't be this good. I soon got my answer when I looked up and saw a giant dome barrier covering the village. It must be protecting this unusual race of people as well as keeping the air breathable.

It was a small settlement, and everyone stared at me as we walked through the village. The set up seemed similar to all the water nymph communities I'd seen. Except, instead of small stone houses, they had a mix of dome and traditional style tepees. Along the path were unusual yellow flowers, a type I'd never seen before. They must be a plant that only grew in the mountains.

We passed by a water fountain with a carving of a winged woman in its centre. Everything seemed to be set up in a circular shape with the biggest dome tent in the centre. This was where Faizah was leading me. She bowed when she entered and introduced me to their chief, Rowan. He was a butch man, who looked to be in his late twenties. He had dark brown skin and his hair shaved short. He also had golden wings and was dressed in formal robes of brown and yellow.

"It's an honour to meet you keeper of the heart." Rowan bowed his head. "It's my understanding that you've come for information. Our master has ordered us to answer any questions you have." He gestured to a small table to his right. "Come sit, so we can talk."

Faizah bowed and left as I sat down at the table. Rowan poured two glasses of water from a jug and placed one in front of me. He sat across from me resting his arms on the wooden surface. "What is it you would like to know?"

I scratched my head. "I don't really know where to start." I'd been so focused on finding the hawk people, I hadn't considered what I'd actually say when I found them. "I guess I was hoping you could tell me more about Humarya. She's a Hawkling like you, isn't she?"

He nodded.

"It's my understanding that you were peaceful people. So why did she abuse her position as protector? Maybe if I understood what put her on this path of destruction, I could find the answer to stopping any further attacks."

"We do know of Humarya, but she's not a Hawkling. Yes, she's a similar race to us but the differences between us are vast. She's a Valkyrie. They have much longer life spans then we do. There used to be a small village of Valkyries nearby and we lived in peace with them. That was until Humarya turned on her own people. You must understand, she wasn't always evil." He sighed, rubbing his chin. "She was once a good person, entrusted to protect the air stone from anyone who wished to use its power. And for a long time, she did her job well. That was until her husband was killed. We're not sure how he died, but she was overcome with grief. One day, she decided to take the power of the air stone for herself. She believed with its power she could bring her husband back to life."

My heart ached as I shook my head. "No matter how powerful the magic, you cannot bring the dead back to life."

"You are correct. She was unsuccessful in her attempt which caused her to fall even further. The other Valkyries tried to get the air stone away from her, knowing its power would end up causing destruction. But the stone had already corrupted, Humarya, and she destroyed her entire village, killing everyone."

It seemed that grief had turned a once good woman into a killer. She'd only wanted her loved one back, but ended up becoming a monster. It was tragic what had happened to her, but it didn't make what she was doing now acceptable.

Rowan continued his story. "Humarya then turned her attention to our master. She believed all she needed was a little more power and she'd succeed in reviving her lost love. Our master, however, wasn't easily defeated, so she turned her attention to finding the other dark stones. She managed to locate the protector of the land stone. Luckily he was able to escape and made his way to you."

I held my hand up gesturing for him to pause. "Wait, if your master was able to fight her off once before, surely, he's strong enough to stop her now."

"Unfortunately, our master's power doesn't respond well to the air stone as they are opposites. It was at great cost to him that he was able to oppose her. But, you shouldn't have that problem."

"Well, I've been unsuccessful in stopping her so far. How can I best deal with her? The power of the air stone is equal to the power of the heart crystal."

I was hoping they'd be able to tell me of her weaknesses.

"You didn't know who you were up against before, but now you do. Have faith, young queen, our master has foreseen that you will bring balance to this world."

"Your master sounds impressive. Does he have any idea where I can find her?"

"Humarya lives in a floating castle, residing above the clouds as we do. She There's an old rope bridge that connects her fortress to the furthest mountain from here."

"Thank you for your help. Before I go, is there any chance I could meet your master?" I really wanted to know who this guy was. He sounded pretty powerful. It was possible he was another crystal keeper, like me. No one knew anything about the keeper of the sun crystal.

"The day will come when you and my master will meet, but it won't be today. Now, please return to Faizah so she can check you're fit to travel. I also insist that you join us for lunch before you go. It isn't often we get visited by a queen who's the keeper of the heart."

I agreed to his request and went back to the medical tent with Faizah who'd been waiting outside for me. She gave me a quick medical check and insisted I stay overnight to ensure my magical powers were completely recovered. I didn't argue as I still felt exhausted. I really had overdone it, but thankfully, it hadn't been for nothing. I now had information I could use as well as a location for Humarya. This trip had been a success in my books.

They were wonderful hosts and looked after me well. By the end, I'd stayed for lunch, dinner and breakfast the following day, enjoying their tasty meals which were cooked outside over an open fire. The Hawklings spent most of their time outdoors in order to feel the changes in the wind. Most of the magic they used was air-based, as if the wind spoke to them, in the same way the trees did to me. I was glad I'd thrown caution aside and followed my instincts. I would never have found this place if I'd followed the council's procedures. They weren't going to be happy, but I didn't care.

Just before I was about to go, Rowan came to see me again. Taking hold of my hands, he looked at me intently, his eyes probing mine. "My master has warned of sharing what you've learned here. Humarya can use the power of the air stone to coerce people into doing her bidding."

My heart sank. His warning sounded similar to Laxus' concerns about spies in the council. I forced a smile. "I will keep your masters warning in mind."

He stepped back. Standing tall with his hands behind his back, he bowed to me. "I wish you well. I know you will succeed."

I bit my lip. I was desperate to return to the council with

this information. I may still be angry with them about Daniels death, but they still held a lot of power that could help me fight Humarya. With this warning, I wasn't sure I could. Instead of returning home, I'd ask Laxus for his opinion. After all, it was his life that was on the line.

I waved goodbye to Rowan and teleported to where I thought Laxus would be.

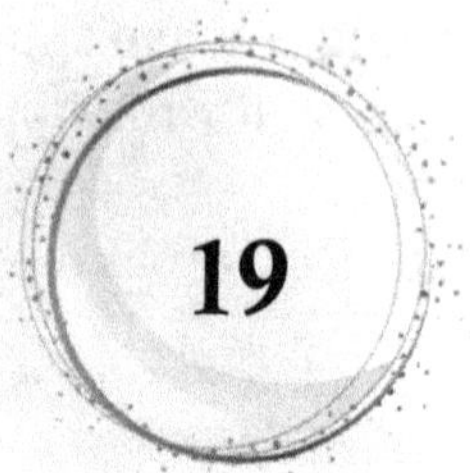

19

Return

Gregory

Greg deactivated his comunis. After spending two hours getting the run around from Mellissa's staff, he felt like throwing it at the wall. It had been three days since his run-in with Mellissa at city hall and no one had seen her since. They had to know more than they were telling him. Surely, if she'd just disappeared the way they claimed, they'd be more worried. And there seemed to be some more annoyance than concern in Harkura's voice when Greg spoke to him. Harkura would be in full assault mode if he didn't know where she was – which meant he did know but was unable to follow her. So, knowing her, she'd probably run off without a proper plan.

Victoria was also telling him nothing, and he was tired of being lied to. It was quite obvious they were hiding out here and not doing any experiments. They kept going through his books, but the topics they picked were all so random, he couldn't tell what they were looking for. Something was going on, but no one would tell him what, and he was done helping them if they weren't going to be honest. Greg looked at his watch. There was still some time before his next meeting – he could pop home and try to squeeze some information out of Laxus and Victoria again. But just as he was about to open the door to his office, it flew open.

Steve walked in, his jaw clenched. "Why did you fire my cousin?"

"She wasn't suitable for the position."

The vein on Steve's forehead pulsed. "How was she unsuitable? She was perfect for you. You ungrateful stuck-up snob."

Greg stepped backwards in shock. Steve had some nerve. Did he think he didn't know the part he'd played in trying to set him up? Julie's behaviour had all been because of info Steve had told her. Greg gritted his teeth. "No, I was perfect for your plan, to try and push your cousin onto me so your family could make better connections."

Steve's face turned bright red. "You can't fire someone for wanting to date you."

"That isn't what she got fired for. I was just going to transfer her. She really didn't tell you what she did?"

"She told me you fired her because your girlfriend wanted her gone." He pointed at him accusingly. "You said you were single."

"Whether I'm single or not is irrelevant. She challenged Queen Mellissa to a change off. Did you not think to brief Julie on who was who when making your plan?"

"Well, we all know about your close relationship with the queen. You can easily smooth it over. Julie shouldn't lose her job because of that."

"Get out Steve. I don't have time for this."

"Not until you give Julie her job back."

"If you don't like my decision, you can appeal through the proper channels to the other two elders. Although, I highly doubt they will overturn my decision. Keeping Julie on would be a political disaster."

Greg tried to walk around him, but Steve gripped his shirt, his fist clenched. Greg didn't flinch. "Think about what you're doing, Steve. I'm an elder. You will be arrested. Do you really want to tarnish your family's name, further?"

Steve grunted as he let go of him.

Greg straightened his shirt and walked away. It had taken everything he had not to hit him, but leaving after stating some blunt facts had a far greater impact on an imbecile like Steve.

Greg arrived home to an eerie silence. He couldn't remember the last time the house had been so quiet. Since Laxus and Victoria had been in residence, there was always some sort of loud bang or crash. It sounded as if they were destroying the place sometimes. He searched the house for them walking up the stairs, searching all the rooms and then heading back down. No one was about. As he entered the kitchen, he found a note on the side. It read:

> *Gone to the library. No, we can't answer any questions about Mellissa. We don't know what she's doing. Stop being so depressive already, you're getting on my nerves more than usual.*
>
> *Victoria*

Greg scrunched up the piece of paper and threw it into the kitchen bin across the other side of the room. Wasn't she lovely? The only thing missing off that note was a threat to harm him. There was no way she didn't know of Mellissa's whereabouts, she just didn't want to share what she knew. He felt like kicking them out, see if they started blabbing once they'd lost their hiding place. He leaned on the kitchen worktop. Was he really such a terrible a person that they wouldn't tell him where Mellissa was?

There was a tap on the glass. Greg looked at the back door to see his mother waving at him. He let her in. "What are you doing here?"

"I was hoping we could go for lunch." She tugged at his arm. "Right now."

"Why the rush?" he asked.

"I thought you had houseguests. It would be easier for us to talk elsewhere."

"How do you know about them?"

She bit her nails. "Umm, I came by the other day and saw them. I thought it best that I didn't disturb you. But you don't seem busy now so ...."

Greg didn't move. "I thought I told you to come by my office if you wanted to talk."

"I did, but you weren't there, so I came here."

She could be telling the truth. He hadn't been in his office much in the last few days. She could have tried more than once and just missed him. "We can have lunch here. My guests have gone to the library."

She raised her eyebrows. "They have. When will they be back?"

Greg shrugged. "I don't know. They don't tell me anything."

"Good good. We can have lunch here then. I'll just go make a call."

She stepped outside, shutting the door behind her. He thought she'd be happier he'd agreed to have lunch with her, but instead, she seemed distracted. But he guessed he shouldn't read too much into her actions. After all, she was the woman who thought faking her own death was the way to solve her marital problems.

A scream echoed from the hallway and Greg ran out of the kitchen. "Mellissa." She was sat on the stairs, grimacing in pain as she rubbed her side. He raced over to help her up. "Are you okay?"

She yanked her arm away. "I'm fine."

"Really, it looks like you just fell down the stairs."

"I tripped on the last two steps, it was hardly a fall. What are you doing here?"

"How many times do I need to tell you that this is my house."

"Well, I didn't come to see you. Where's Victoria?"

"I'll tell you after you say where you've been for the last three days."

Her jaw dropped. "Three days? I thought I was only gone two." She pushed her hair back. "Depleting my magical energy must have taken more out of me than I thought."

"What the hell were you doing to use up all your magic?" he yelled. How could she say that so casually? She had an abundance of magic. She had to have been doing something crazy to max it out.

She folded her arms and looked away from him. "I don't

appreciate your tone. You have no right to demand information from me."

"But it's all right for you to sneak into my offices, fire a lightning bolt at my ex-assistant and nearly destroy city hall, but I can't be annoyed at you for disappearing for three days!"

She cringed. "You're exaggerating."

"If you want proof, we're still fixing all the damage you caused."

"Well, it was an accident." She took a deep breath. "I can fix the damage, promise, but not now. Just tell me where Laxus is."

"I'm not inclined to share that information with you. Not until you start telling me what's going on. Why all the weird behaviour and where exactly you disappeared to?"

"Why should I tell you anything?" She jabbed her finger at him. "I don't need your help. I will find him myself."

Greg ran his fingers through his hair. He was losing her. She'd have no problem finding Laxus on her own. She'd never really needed his help.

She stood and walked towards the front door. "Mellissa wait." Greg took hold of her arm. She couldn't ditch him while he was holding her. "I was worried about you. Last time I saw you, you were pretty upset, and then you just teleported away, and no one seemed to know where you'd gone. You don't talk to me anymore."

She threw her arms out to the side. "And why do you think I don't talk to you? Because you're unreliable."

"I am not. I just have a lot of responsibility and things to take care of."

"And I don't." She stamped her foot. "At least you have a fully functioning and easily accessible city. I don't. My city is still under development. I can't even get a train line approved and I have to use my powers to bring in resources for my people. I have Lee constantly breathing down my neck just waiting for me to screw up, and it won't take long until he has something as I have no idea what I'm doing. On top of that my chief of staff was recently murdered. This is all before you add my responsibilities as keeper of the heart crystal. My time is valuable Greg. You should appreciate it more."

"I didn't mean it like that."

She shook her head as her top lip curled. "You never do. So what if I disappeared for three days. I got more done in those three days then the council has in weeks."

"You went to the mountains, didn't you?"

"What if I did? I'm done taking orders from you and the council. I got valuable information. If I had this information before then maybe I could of …" Tears filled her eyes as her words became disjointed. "Maybe, I could have saved Daniel, but like an idiot, I did as I was told."

Greg pulled her into a hug and she buried her face in his shirt. "I really hate you sometimes."

"I know, I'm sorry." This was his fault. Things never came out the way he intended but they couldn't seem to talk lately without it turning into an argument.

The kitchen door creaked open. "Gregory," called Gwendolyn. He'd forgotten his mother had popped out to make a call.

Mellissa pushed him away. "Another girl, huh. Tell me it's nothing again."

Greg tugged her back, stopping her from confronting his mother. "You really need to stop jumping to conclusions."

Gwendolyn walked out into the hall. "Oh, I thought you said your guests were out."

"They are," Greg said. "This is Mellissa. She's just arrived. As you might know, she's the elf Queen." He turned to Mellissa "This is Gwendolyn. She err … is"

"Your mum?" Mellissa said wide-eyed. "How … I mean … what? You said she was dead."

"Reports of my death were rather misleading." Gwendolyn shook Mellissa's hand. "It's lovely to meet you. Call me Gwen."

Mellissa narrowed her eyes. "So, you didn't die?"

"I just made it look that way. How about we take a rain check lunch. You can explain everything to your girlfriend." She patted Greg on the shoulder. "I'll bc in touch."

Greg watched as she strolled out of the front door. That

had been unplanned, but thankfully, it hadn't been a disaster.

Mellissa shook his arm. "When were you going to tell me about this?"

"Umm, now."

"How long have you known she wasn't dead?"

"She showed up the evening before your coronation."

"That's why you were late?"

"Yeah but …"

"You're such an idiot," she shouted. Taking his hand, she yanked him into the living room making his sit down. "Now tell me everything or I swear I'll stamp my foot and demolish this house."

"Victoria is starting to rub off on you."

She glared at him and over the next hour, he told her everything, starting with the weird letters up to their encounter moments ago. Mellissa listened intently and once he finished talking, she punched his arm.

"What was that for?" Greg yelled.

"For keeping everything to yourself for so long."

"You need to stop hanging out with Victoria."

"You need to stop shutting people out."

"You're one to talk."

She pouted. "I guess you have a point, but you know I can teleport. I could have been here in seconds if you'd told me what was going on."

"You had enough to worry about. It was your coronation."

Suddenly there was a massive boom and the ground shook. Mellissa fell forward, hitting her head on his arm. This was not her doing. They both ran outside. In the distance, a giant cloud of smoke drifted towards the sky. There was another bang and the cloud got bigger. A panicked Luke came running towards Greg.

"Lord Gregory and umm, Queen Mellissa." He panted as he bowed. "I've just received reports of an explosion at the library and glasslike creatures attacking the city." That was where Victoria and Laxus were. These attacks were definitely centred around Laxus.

Mellissa gasped. "She's found him again."
Greg shouted for her to wait but she was gone.

Attack on Novosvillas

Mellissa

I arrived at the library and was immediately engulfed in smoke. Flames danced along the shelves and a siren blared from every direction. The heat was unbearable as sweat dripped down my forehead. Laxus had to be nearby but I could barely see anything. I coughed as I inhaled smoke, making my lungs feel as if they were burning. A scream sounded close by. It was Victoria's voice. I ran towards the sound. Sliding on ice, I crashed into a bookcase. Books came crashing down on me, heat radiating from them and I quickly threw them off. I yelped as a frosty mist surrounded me. Small ice flakes flurried around me. The fire stifled, frozen in its tracks.

As the mist cleared, I saw Victoria running towards a huge gap in the wall. I chased after her. As I got outside, I saw Humarya drop to the ground, one of her wings covered in ice. Then Laxus thumped onto the floor. He kicked out a leg at Humarya and rolled away. Humarya lifted her hand and as she did shadows bound Laxus tightly so he couldn't move. Humarya flew up taking Laxus with her as Victoria hurled ice at Humarya, but her attack was intercepted by shadows.

I ran to a nearby tree, placing my hand on its trunk. Focusing on the magic within I whispered "Please help me. We need to save Laxus and banish the winged woman." The tree answered my call and rapidly began to grow far up into the sky. It reached out with its branches and grabbed hold of Humarya. Wrapping her up tightly it gently lifted Laxus, sliding him through its branches towards me. I caught him as he got to the bottom of the tree.

"Mellissa, I'm so glad you are here." He clung to me tightly.

"We need to get out of here." I took his hand and ran towards Victoria. Humarya screeched inside the clutches of the tree. Glass creatures materialised out of thin air. I fired off a row of light blasts destroying the creatures, but Humarya created more as she slowly blasted her way out of her constraints.

I couldn't just leave with Laxus and Victoria. The people of Novosvillas would then suffer her wrath. I told Laxus to remain with Victoria and put them in a protection bubble. My spell took hold just as Humarya managed to free herself, flying at high speed towards us. I braced myself. Humarya angrily threw a gust of wind my way, blowing me back towards the fire. She tried to break through my barrier only to be repelled by it. I teleported to her side and blasted her away.

"Well, it looks like my spell worked," I shouted.

"You are a thorn in my side. Instead of fighting, perhaps, we can come to some sort of agreement." She curled her lips. I think it was meant to be a smile. She held her talon out to me. "There must be something you want? Something that even your power can't grant, but maybe mine can."

"There is nothing you can give … nothing that would tempt me into helping you destroy this world."

"You don't understand. I'm not trying to destroy your world. I am trying to make it a better place for us all."

"How was torturing Daniel making the world a better place? Or killing everyone in your village and trying to steal the hawklings master's power? Everything you're doing is going to upset the balance and cause chaos."

"I see that you've visited the hawk village." She waved her hand as if swatting away a fly. "The hawklings are just as misguided as my own people were. I'm sure you'll see reason.

Just give me the boy and I will create a world where no one has to lose a loved one again. The elf I killed will come back to life. I will return anyone you have ever lost. All you have to do is stop fighting me."

"There is no magic that can bring back the dead. It hurts when you lose someone, but death is a natural part of life. Something we all have to learn to accept."

She tilted her head and smirked. "What about the boy in the tree?"

I gritted my teeth. "Leave Matt out of this."

"I could set him free. The dark stones are the opposite power to the life crystals." She took a step forward, her wings flapping gently in the breeze, her eyes blazing as her dark hair coiled around her face and body like a serpent. "It was I that kickstarted Kadon's release from the tree of time. I had high hopes for him but that didn't work out. With the added power of the land stone, I could completely break the seal this time. I could give you back your friend."

She held her hand out to me. My ears were ringing. I stepped back shaking my head. "No, you couldn't have."

"I've been working in the shadows for years, playing the long game, manipulating events to suit my purpose. If we connect our powers, we can reshape this world."

I'd been trying hopelessly for months to free Matt. And this was why I'd been unsuccessful. I needed a power that was the opposite of mine. I needed a dark stone. I held my arm to the side and the heart crystal shot into my hand in staff form. "I could never do that. I couldn't destroy the world for my own selfish reasons. Matt wouldn't want to pay that sort of price for his freedom."

Her nostrils flared as she threw her talons at me.

I jumped back.

"What would you know?" she shouted. "You're just a child. Once I have the land stone, I'll be able to see my beloved again. You obviously have never loved someone the way I love him."

"Even if you managed to gather all of the dark stones, it still wouldn't work. What you would bring back wouldn't be your husband." I hoped she would see reason and stop on her own, but I could tell that wasn't going to happen. She was far too gone to come back from the darkness. She truly believed in what she was doing and it didn't matter how many people she killed as once she succeeded. death would be no more. She wouldn't accept that you couldn't reverse death. I had to stop her, otherwise, she'd keep hurting people with no remorse.

"If you insist on getting in my way, I will destroy you," she screeched. The yellow stone around her neck was surrounded by a shadow. Humarya summoned a vast amount of dark energy and fired it at me. I quickly teleported out of the way and reappeared behind her. She swiftly turned, throwing a small glass bottle at me. I blasted it with light energy and the bottle smashed before it hit me, releasing a strange orange mist. It blew into my face causing me to cough.

"What the hell was that?" I shouted. I didn't get an answer as she launched at me. I ducked and rolled out of the way calling on the earth to protect me. Giant vines shot out of the ground tangling Humarya in them. She cut the vines with shadows and flapping her wings, she created a strong gust. As she flapped more, the winds picked up, and I could hardly move as the pressure became intense.

I covered my face with my arms. I couldn't let her beat me. What would Harkura do? He'd take the fight to her. I teleported myself into the sky and used the extra force from my fall to spin around and land a light energy kick on her. For some reason, my teleportation felt sluggish, but my plan had worked. I quickly followed up with a spiral of light energy knocking her to the ground. To stop my fall, I summoned a vine to catch me gently as I slid down it. Before she had time to recover, I used the branches of the tree to hold her but she cut through them with blasts of shadow. I created more binds and she broke them again. We kept repeating the same moves. I needed something stronger to hold her, but in the time it would take to create a stronger spell, she'd escape – unless I weakened her more.

As she broke out of the branches I'd placed around her, I ran at her, punching her in the nose. She stumbled backwards and I dropped to the ground spinning my leg around, taking her feet out from underneath her. As she fell, I launched a ball of earth upwards into her back. She screamed as she shot upwards and then back down again. Throwing my arms out, I lifted two rocks and slammed them onto her wings and then spun my arms, wrapping vines around her arms and legs. It wouldn't hold long but it would give me enough time to create a barrier.

"Humarya by order of our Lord elder knight, you are to be detained," boomed a voice from behind me. The Novosvillas authorities had turned up and surrounded her. But why now? They were in the way of my spell.

"I won't be defeated so easily," she screamed producing a massive ray of dark energy. Shadows burst from her body freeing her. She opened her wings wide, flapping them and creating a whirlwind, knocking everyone to the ground. Rubbing her hands together, she muttered something under her breath as glass creatures popped up around her. I tried to teleport beside her but screamed as something stopped me. It felt like I'd hit a brick wall and bounced back.

Humarya cackled. "It worked!"

My heart felt heavy and I gulped down a lump in my throat. "What are you talking about?"

A wide grin appeared on her face that sent shivers down my spine. "That orange mist has blocked your teleporting power."

"What!" I attempted to teleport again, but the same thing happened. I dropped to my knees. There was a ringing in my ears. Everything seemed to go into slow motion. This wasn't possible.

"Your Majesty," someone yelled, snapping me back to reality.

A creature towered over me as a guard knocked it back. Then a black wing slapped the guard away and Humarya grabbed me by the throat. "Poor little queen so lost without her ability to teleport," she said in a mocking tone.

I engulfed myself in light but it was snuffed out by her shadows. She threw me to the ground. Lifting her talons, shadows slashed out of them. I screamed as she swung the shadows towards me.

Victoria suddenly appeared, diving at Humarya, pushing me out of the way. She created a shield of ice, but the shadows shattered it and slashed through Victoria's side. Humarya cackled as Victoria flopped backwards into my arms.

I pushed Victoria's hair from her face. "Why did you do that? You were meant to stay in the protection bubble."

She shoved me away. "I'm your guardian, you idiot." She staggered to her feet and lunged at Humarya. Humarya flicked her wrist throwing her up in the air and Victoria hit the ground with a thud.

Rage bubbled through me and the ground began to shake. Lifting my hands, the ground shifted under Humarya's feet. She swiftly took flight as I clenched my fists radiating light from my body. Rays of light flew at Humarya, and she countered them with shadows. My heart thundered in my chest. I ran towards her, flicking my wrists as I lifted rocks and threw them at her. She narrowly dodged them. I followed up my attack with a wheel of light. It hit her head on and one of her wings twisted and she tumbled to earth. Stamping my feet, I increased the tremors causing the earth to roll. She scrambled back, eyes wide, barely blocking my blasts as I walked towards her.

She quickly muttered a spell in a panicked voice and glass creatures appeared between us. I yelled in anger as I produced a wave of light smashing the translucent beings. The misty glass cleared just in time for me to see Humarya run through a portal.

"No," I yelled as I ran towards it, but the portal closed before I could get through. I dropped to my knees and punched the ground in frustration stopping all the tremors. I took a moment to breathe. I'd been running on adrenaline and I was now coming down from the high. Screams echoed around me as people ran from the fire. Soldiers were trying to clear everyone out and get them to safety. The fire from the library had spread to nearby buildings and they were struggling to contain it. I could see Greg trying to organise his people and calm the situation. The place was in chaos and it was all my fault. I never meant for any of this to happen, but I was the one that brought Laxus here. They had no idea about who was hiding in their city, but I did. And now I didn't know what to do.

"Mellissa," Laxus shouted, "We need you." He'd left the protection bubble and was kneeled beside Victoria.

I ran to his side. "How is she?"

"I'm all right," she said attempting to get up.

Laxus shook his head. The look of dread on his face said it all. She was hurt badly.

I put my arm around her. "Don't get up. I'll get you two out of here."

"What about the fire? I can stop it."

"You can't, you're hurt. I'll take you to the healers back home and come back to …"

"To what? Throw some wood on it? I still have some fight left in me." She removed my arm from her and stood tall. "I got this." She rubbed her hands together and a cold mist formed around them. Throwing her hands out, the fire engulfing the library froze. She dropped to her knees.

"Victoria," I yelled running to her side. There was a loud rumble and a chorus of screams.

"Mellissa the building is crumbling," shouted Laxus.

I looked up. It was as if everything was moving in slow motion, the frozen part of the building sliding away from the rest. Those below were trying to run before it hit the ground. There was no way they'd make it. Without thinking, I threw my arms up, catching it mid air with my magic before it completely fell off. The building was made from brick making it something my powers could manipulate. Unfortunately, it was heavy and there was nowhere for me to let it fall safely.

"Amazing," Laxus said beside me, "but you can't hold it forever. "

"I know." I kicked my shoes off and wiggled my bare toes on the ground. That was better. Gliding my foot across, I sent a pulse of magic through the ground. Vines grew up either side of the library and wrapped themselves around the building holding it together. Pushing my foot out and lifting my arms, stone columns erupted from the ground. I forced them against the building creating extra support to keep the building from collapsing. The people of Novosvillas should be safe for now. I needed to get Laxus and Victoria out of here.

Running towards them, I put my arm around Victoria and took Laxus' hand. "We're leaving". I teleported and screamed as I hit the invisible wall, the three of us tumbling to the ground.

"What happened?" asked Victoria, her voice shaking.

"Humarya took away my teleporting ability. She's broken me." I laid on the soot-covered earth looking up at the sky motionless, my heart numb.

I'd never seen Harkura so angry. Initially, he'd hugged me with relief but that didn't last long. I sat in the middle of the sofa as he paced the length of Greg's living room. "How could you be so irresponsible? We had a plan. I was meant to go with you."

I hung my head. "I'm sorry, I wasn't thinking."

"It's obvious you weren't thinking. What if something happened to you?"

"But nothing ever happens to me. It happens to the people I care about." I yelled, "Victoria is upstairs injured because she was protecting me."

Harkura sat beside me and sighed. "Victoria will be fine."

I could feel tears building up. "I've never known Greg take so long to heal someone."

Harkura put his arm around me. "That's because you weren't awake when he healed you after you fought Kadon."

My chest tightened and I laid my head on Harkura's shoulder. My memory from that time was blurry. They must have been so worried about me, just as I was for Victoria right now.. I'd been selfish, too busy trying to stop Humarya that I hadn't thought about how my actions would affect those around me. "I'm sorry."

Harkura patted my shoulder. "It's all right. I just wish I knew how they'd found Laxus."

I sat up straight and looked Harkura straight in the eye. "Humarya has corrupted the council."

"Are you sure?" His eyes widened as he looked around the room. "They can't all have been compromised."

"No, not all of them. I have my suspicions, but we need proof."

The living room door opened and I was by Greg's side in a flash. "How is she?"

Greg stepped back. "Her injuries are all healed and she's currently asleep."

I let out a long breath.

"Laxus is sat with her at the moment."

I bit my thumb nail. I knew Laxus felt responsible for Victoria getting hurt, but it wasn't his fault. It was mine. This had all been my plan and it had gone terribly wrong.

Greg sat down and flicked through his tabular. He was straight back to work as usual. My stomach felt like it was in knots. Of course, he was straight back to work. His city had just been attacked. As the leader, he had a lot to sort out. I sat beside him. "If there is anything you need, the elves are happy to help. And if anyone needs a place to stay, they are welcome at Urbem Folium."

He gave me a weary smile. "I'm not sure what we need yet." His eyes narrowed as he looked at the screen. He gritted his teeth. "I think you should read this."

I took his tabular and read the message.

> *An emergency meeting has been called to decide on the ability to serve on the council of the following members: Gregory Ainsworth, Mellissa Hail.*

I rubbed my eyes and reread the message. "Can they do that?" I asked

Greg rubbed the sides of his head. "Apparently so."

"This is ridiculous. I was expecting them to call a meeting about the attack, not this rubbish. How is this even emergency criteria?"

"I'm, sure it's just Lee grasping at straws and the

motion will be thrown out."

"I don't have time for this." I pushed the tabular towards Harkura to read. "I'm not going to that meeting. Let them act like children whilst I figure out what to do about Humarya."

Harkura placed the tabular on the coffee table. "The subject matter may be stupid, but you can use this meeting to your advantage. Turn it towards your trip to the mountains. Tell them what you discovered and see who seems unsurprised by the information."

It was a good idea. I had no other plan of how to work out who the traitor was. As much as I didn't want there to be a snitch, it was the only explanation for how Humarya was able to track down Laxus. Who else but the council members knew my movements so well? I pushed my hair back. "I don't know Harkura. I'm so tired of their games. If they don't want me on the council then so be it."

"You don't mean that you're just angry."

Greg looked back and forth between me and Harkura. "Why would someone be unsurprised about what you learned in the mountains?"

I shrugged. "Don't know." I stood. "Anyway, we can't stay here any longer, not now we've been discovered."

Greg grabbed my wrist as I went to walk away. "Mellissa, what the hell is going on?"

"I'm sorry, I can't tell you yet, but I will explain next time I see you." I kissed his cheek and he let go of me.

"Victoria still needs to rest. She'll have to remain here."

I nodded. Harkura and I walked upstairs to collect Laxus. I hated to leave Victoria, but it had to be done. We went outside and got into the carriage Harkura arrived in, and then continued on our way to Urbem Folium.

"Why did I have to bring this carriage and why are we not just teleporting?" asked Harkura.

I looked out of the window. It felt like the weight of the world was pressing down on me. "I couldn't tell you before in case Greg heard. Humarya somehow blocked my ability to teleport."

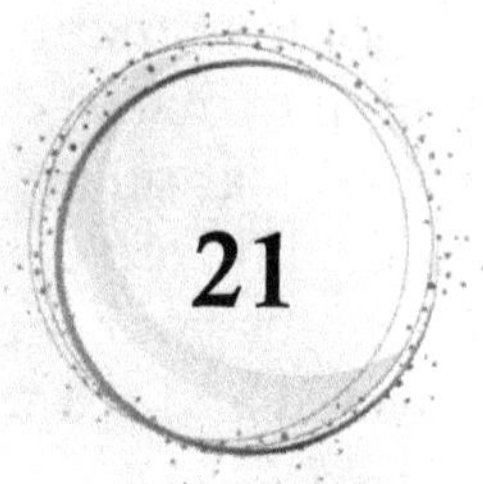

21

Guilt

Mellissa

There was a knock at the door. I looked up from the mass of papers I'd stuffed into a bag. Daniel's son, Josh, stood in the open doorway. I smoothed my dress down and smiled at him. "Come in,"

He stepped into my office and bowed. "I was told you wished to see me."

"That's right. " My chest hurt as I looked at him. Josh was a younger version of his dad with the same light brown skin, short curly hair and brown eyes. Just like his dad he looked younger than he was. Josh was at least ten years older than me but his youthful looks made him look as if he could have gone to school with me. I swallowed the lump forming in my throat. "I wanted to say, I'm sorry."

He frowned and tilted his head to one side. "Why are you sorry?"

I crossed my hands in front of my chest. "About your father. I'm sorry I didn't save him and I'm sorry I disappeared after what happened."

His eyes glistened as he stepped forward. "Your Majesty, you have nothing to apologise for. My father died at the hands of a mad woman. I know you and Harkura were planning to rescue him, but it all happened too fast.." He coughed as his voice wavered. "And I'm sure there's a reason you disappeared?"

"I went to the mountains to get information on Humarya's whereabouts, to try and stop her reign of terror. I now know I can't remain here if ..." I looked down at the floor. "I failed to save Daniel. I won't let that happen again."

"Is there anything I can do to help?" asked Josh

I forced myself to look at him. He stood tall, his hands clasped behind his back, his dark eyes full of determination. I straightened my back, imitating his stance. "There is something you can do. With your father gone, Samson will be promoted to chief of staff. This leaves me in need of another advisor. I'd like you to take on the role."

Joshes jaw dropped and he shook his head. "I don't have the political knowledge to be able to advise you."

"I don't need the kind of advisor I had before," I replied. "What I need is someone who knows all our traditions, the way Daniel did." I placed my hand on his shoulder. "You don't have to answer now, but I believe you're the right person for the job."

He looked at me, his eyes filling with tears. "Thank you, Your Majesty, I'd be happy to take on this role. It's what my father would have wanted."

I picked up the bag on my desk and hung it over my shoulder. "Wonderful. I'll leave you and Samson in charge while I'm gone."

His eyes widened. "What?

I smiled at him, my heart warming at the look of shock on his face. With all the decisions I've made recently, this was one that didn't worry me. I squeezed his hand. "I believe in you, Josh."

He squeezed my hand back. "And I believe in you, Queen Mellissa. I know that you'll bring my father's murderer to justice."

Every muscle in my body tensed as I looked him straight in the eye. "Yes, I will."

I walked out of my office with a new sense of purpose. I vowed to put an end to Humarya's bloodshed and pain, no matter what. Enough people had died on my watch and I couldn't let it happen again.

It was after 10 at night when my dad got home. His jaw had dropped in shock and he had been lost for words when he found his house wasn't empty. In the space of an afternoon, I'd already moved back into my old bedroom. Laxus was tucked away in the guest room and Harkura was in his tent. My dad never bothered taking it down. It had become a permanent feature after Harkura started living with us and refused to sleep in the house.

After promoting Samson and hiring Josh, I'd left Urbem Folium and crossed the veil. It hadn't felt right leaving again after only recently returning, but I was confident I'd left them protected. Once outside the city, Harkura helped me reinforce the barrier I'd erected before I'd travelled to the mountains. The elves would be much safer without Laxus in the city. Although, I still wasn't sure what to do next. While I figured out our next steps, staying with Dad seemed the best plan.

I made Dad a coffee and sat in the living room with him. "Not that it isn't good to see you, but what are you doing here?" he asked, "You didn't fall out with the entire magical world, did you?"

"Of course not. What do you take me for?"

"Antisocial and defiant."

"Hey, when I visit you're meant to jump for joy, not insult me."

Dad put his arm around me. "I'm sorry, sweetie, but the truth hurts sometimes."

"Dad!"

He chuckled as he took a sip of his drink. "Well, something happened. Where's Victoria, shouldn't she be with you?"

I fiddled with my fingers. "She's been injured and couldn't travel."

He almost dropped his coffee. "Is she all right?"

"She will be. That bird woman who launched an attack at my coronation, returned and she …" I gulped not wanting to think back to the horror, my words stunted.

"She attacked Urbem Foilum again?"

"No. Novosvillas."

"Isn't that where Greg's from?"

I nodded, looking down at my hands in my lap. "Yes"

"Is he okay?"

"Yes." I took a deep breath. "There were no serious injuries just property damage. Humarya was only after Laxus. I fought her and won, but I know she'll be back, and I'm running out of places to hide him."

"So you came back because Laxus remained undiscovered here?"

"Exactly." I put my head in my hands. "Dad, I don't know if I can stop her."

Dad grabbed my hands and squeezed them. "Don't think like that."

"But everything is falling apart. It's not just the attack on the citys. Humarya she..." I sniffled as I tried to hold back tears. "She murdered Daniel." Tears wet my cheeks as images of Daniels bruised and battered body flashed through my mind.

Dad pulled me into a hug, squeezing me tight. "Oh sweetie, you've been through so much."

I snorted wiping my tears with my sleeve. "It's hopeless."

My dad handed me a tissue from the box on the coffee table. "Things just look that way at the moment but I believe in you and so did Daniel. You'll find a way to stop this monster because you're a fighter. I've never seen you give up on anything, so don't start now."

I dabbed my eyes with the tissue. "Thanks, Dad."

"Now, go get some rest. I'm sure with a fresh mind, you'll figure out what to do." He kissed my forehead. "I'm here if you need to talk." I gave him a weary smile and nodded. I don't know how he had so much confidence in me, I'd already messed up so much.

Before heading to my bedroom, I checked in on Laxus. He was fast asleep curled up in the centre of the big double bed.. He looked so peaceful and innocent; laying on his side hugging the butterfly covered blanket, his curly hair flopping over his eyes. I needed to keep him safe, but I was out of ideas. Hopefully, Dad was right and some rest was all I needed.

That night, I snuggled under the duvet in my old room gazing at the shelf of well-thumbed books on the wall – fairy stories read to me as a child that now seemed more like fact than fiction. My desk still overflowing with art supplies. The pink cushions sat on my window seat and the handmade paper butterflies that hung from the curtain pole above it. I let out a long sigh. As nice as the castle was with all its gilded grandeur, servants, and a walk in closet it didn't ever feel like home. Not like this.

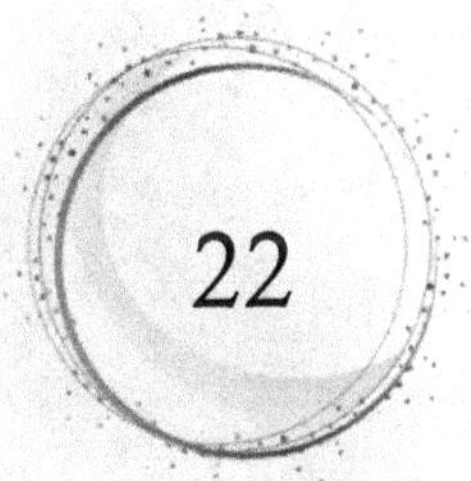

Confession

Gregory

Greg tugged at the collar of his robes. He was stood on the steps of the council building waiting for Mellissa. He needed to warn her about the forms he had taken upon himself to fill in without telling her, before the meeting started. The motion would be dismissed but not if Mellissa responded badly. Victoria had found it hilarious when he had told her about it. There was no doubt that she was fully healed. He couldn't wait for Victoria to go back with Mellissa today.

"Sir, the meeting will start soon. We should head in," said Mary.

"I need to talk to Mellissa first," answered Greg. "You go in and stall if needed."

She nodded and disappeared inside. Mary was his most recent recruit. After the attack yesterday, the applications for his chief of staff had dwindled to one, so he'd hired her this morning on a trial basis. And from the short time he'd spent with her, she appeared organised, professional and knowledgeable. He hoped she didn't turn out to be another mistake like Julie, and that being the only applicant still willing to do the job was a sign she wasn't afraid of a challenge.

A carriage pulled up in front of the building and Mellissa stumbled out. Greg's hunch had been right. He'd seen Mellissa leave in a carriage yesterday and now she was arriving in one again. Something was wrong. She also wasn't dressed up in one her new designer dresses. Instead she wore a long black top covered in stars and leggings, her long curls pulled tightly into two braids. Unfortunately, he didn't have time to question her about it before the meeting.

"Greg, why aren't you inside?" Mellissa asked.

"I was waiting for you."

"Okay, let's walk together."

He put his hand out to block her from walking in. "I need to tell you something first before the meeting starts, so you're not caught off guard."

She rolled her eyes. "I'm only at this ridiculous meeting because Harkura insisted I came. If it was up to me, I'd just quit."

Greg was taken back. She couldn't be serious. "You can't just quit."

"Why not? I was sold a lie when I became queen. I thought I'd be helping people, but I've done anything but."

"I know the council can seem restrictive, but do you think you can handle a crazed bird creature like Humarya on your own?"

"Yes." Mellissa threw her arms in the air. "If not for the council, I'd have headed to the mountains immediately. And, if I did, I might have prevented the attack on Novosvillas. The amount of pain caused simply because the council stopped me following my instincts."

Greg ran his hand through his hair. "You're right." He couldn't agree more. All these rules and regulations didn't help anyone, they just got in the way. They shouldn't be having a meeting to discuss his and Mellissa's ability to serve on the council, they should be discussing the attack that had just happened in his city and what they were going to do about Humarya. But this was how things worked and it wouldn't change overnight. The best way to affect change was to be part of the council." You were obviously more motivated to find the hawk people than the fairies. Once this motion about us is dismissed, you should tell everyone what you learned in the mountains."

"How can you be so sure it will be dismissed?" Mellissa asked.

Greg fiddled with his shirt collar. He may as well just tell her. He'd wanted to talk about it before they went off-topic. "Because Lady Gabrielle saw this coming and made sure I covered our backs."

"Cover us for what exactly? I still don't know what we did."

Greg locked eyes with her. "Our relationship is the problem."

Her eyes widened as her eyebrows shot up. "What! I didn't realise it was against council regulations to be friends with another member, especially when you hate the said member."

"Hate is a strong word and you know that's not how they see our relationship." He hoped his face wasn't as red as his hair. The last conversation about their relationship hadn't ended well.

Mellissa ruffled her hair and sat on the steps. "What does it matter to them?"

Greg sat beside her. "It's just Lee trying to gain more influence, but it's okay, I followed protocol."

"Protocol? What are you talking about?"

Greg clenched his hands together and looked down at the steps. "Lady Gabrielle came to me a few months ago and made me fill in a change of relationship form. I may have forged your signature."

"You what!" she yelled. Then taking a breath she said in a quieter voice. "Wait … a few months ago. That was pretty presumptuous."

"She was very insistent about it all."

"You didn't think to tell me."

"I didn't think you'd respond well. You haven't been responding well."

She folded her arms. "Well, there is no change of relationship to report."

"You really think that?"

She nodded. "Yes"

"Gee, thanks." He leaned back on his elbows and looked up at the sky. Had he misread the situation? He thought things *had* changed between them, but her words by the fountain repeating in his mind. *'We don't work together in any way. It's about time we both accept it.'*

Mellissa took his hand, pulling him to his feet. "I kissed you back in December before we were on the council." She circled her hands round between the two of them "So you see we joined the council as we are now."

Greg's eyes widened "but … I … you never said anything."

She shrugged. "You never asked."

"What are we then?"

"Well, you're a changeling and I'm a human-elf."

Greg pulled her towards him and cupped her face with his hands. "You know exactly what I mean. If I kissed you now, how would you respond?"

"We have a meeting to get to." She smiled, interlacing her fingers with his and leading the way inside.

Lady Gabrielle leaned on the table and steepled her fingers together. "Very well, shall we begin."

Lee rose to his feet. "I move that we dismiss Queen Mellissa from the council. Her blatant disregard of the councils ruling on going to the mountains proves that she is unfit to serve."

Lady Gabrielle lifted her hand. "Lee, we don't know why she did this … let her explain."

Mellissa cleared her throat." A crazy bird-woman is attacking innocent civilians. The fairies yielded no results. My chief of staff had just been murdered, so I took things into my own hands."

"Sounds reasonable enough to me. Her duty as crystal keeper comes first." Lady Gabrielle's steely eyes bored into Lee's and he scowled as he sat back down. Tapping her fingers on the table, she flashed a smile. "I have looked over the motion to remove Queen Mellissa Hail and Lord Gregory Ainsworth from the council. Four members have signed, meaning it must be discussed. I've reviewed the complaint and conclude that there's been no wrongdoing by either party."

Greg rubbed his nose to stop himself smiling. He didn't want to come across as smug, but he'd knew how Lady Gabrielle would rule.

"How can you say that?" shouted Lee, "Those two blatantly disregard council procedures all the time, especially that girl." He pointed at Mellissa with venom in his eyes.

Greg clenched his fists under the table.

Lady Gabrielle squared her shoulders. "That girl is queen of the elves and keeper of the heart crystal."

"So, just because she has a crystal, she shouldn't get special treatment?"

"If she got special treatment this meeting wouldn't be taking place. Now back to what I was saying …"

"Fine, then," shouted Lee. "Gregory, why don't you explain the nature of your relationship with Queen Mellissa?"

"How does that pertain to my ability to serve on the council?" Greg said

Lee wagged his finger at him. "Why are you avoiding the question? Is it because you know you've broken the rules with your inappropriate relationship."

"How is our relationship inappropriate?" snapped Mellissa.

"A relationship is deemed inappropriate if it gets in the way of a council member doing their duties effectively. The relationship must therefore cease or you risk being removed from your position."

"We all know the council definition, Lee," Greg said knowing full well that Mellissa didn't. "But Mellissa has never got in the way of me doing my job." Greg frowned and tilted his head. "However, now that I think about it, I have got in the way of hers. In fact, we all have."

"What are you talking about?" Lee demanded.

"When we voted against letting her go to the mountains,

we interfered with her duties as keeper of the heart. We gave Humarya too much time, and with that time, she murdered Daniel and attacked my city." Greg pointed to the notice on the table. "That list to determine our abilities to serve should be a lot longer."

Lee's nostrils flared as his face turned pink. "That's not the same thing."

Beatrice raised her hand. "You cannot compare a democratic vote to the two of you plotting between yourselves."

Greg grit his teeth. She had some nerve to accuse him of that. If anyone had an inappropriate relationship, it was her and Lee. There was no doubt they hadn't filled out the change of relationship forms. They wouldn't want their respective spouses accidentally finding out.

"Do you have any evidence to back up your claim?" Greg asked.

Beatrice's eyes widened. She glanced around the room as if trying to find someone to back her up. She nudged Emerson who looked away tugging at his robes nervously. "Um, yes, you two were seen at the circus together."

"I must have missed the rule that said you couldn't go to the circus on your day off."

"There are rumours about Mellissa teleporting in and out in all hours. How can she not be getting in the way of your work?"

"You base all this on rumours? And please, tell me, unless you have secret camera's in my house, how could anyone actually see this happening?" Greg took a deep breath. He couldn't let his annoyance show but his suspicion had been confirmed. Beatrice and Emerson were two of the four that signed the complaint. They'd been looking down their noses at him ever since he'd taken over the role as the elder of Novosvillas. He'd worked his butt off, sacrificed his personal life, and this was the thanks they gave him.

Beatrice reached a hand across the table to him. "We don't want to see you removed from your position. Just distance yourself from this girl and we'll remove our complaint against you."

"But you won't remove the complaint against Queen Mellissa," snapped Lee. "That still stands no matter what?"

Yuko raised her hand. "I object. Surely if you drop the complaint against Gregory then you must do the same for Mellissa. It's my understanding that your problem is their relationship. If it ceased, your problem is solved." She said exactly what Greg had been thinking.

Lee gave her a dismissive wave. "You wouldn't understand."

Yuko balled her hand into a fist. "No, you are the one that doesn't understand. According to you, their crime is the same, so their punishment must also be the same. Not that I think they've done anything wrong." She turned to Greg. "Although, I think you should fill in the change of relationship forms."

Greg went to reply but Hogan and Caleb burst into laughter capturing everyone's attention.

Lee scowled at them. "What's so funny?"

Hogan cleared his throat. "We don't think change of relationship forms are appropriate." Caleb continued to chuckle.

"Why not?" The vein on Lee's forehead looked like it was about to explode. "It's a council regulation for a reason. Our rules are no laughing matter."

"We only meant in this case." Hogan circled his finger on the surface of the table. "Maybe like hey just letting you know forms or something. They were already an item when they joined the council. So, no change to report. Man, you guys are slow."

Greg put his hand on his head. Mellissa looked like she wanted the ground to swallow her whole. Had his feelings towards her been that obvious? Mellissa had pretty much said what Hogan had. Was he the only one that hadn't realised what was going on between them?

Lee slammed his hand on the table. "That makes it even worse. You two should also be punished for keeping their secret." He pointed accusingly at Hogan and Caleb.

"That's enough Lee," said Lady Gabrielle. She didn't

yell but there was a firmness in her voice that silenced everyone. "There was no secret. The appropriate paperwork was filled out months ago."

"Why didn't you just say so?" Lee stuttered.

"You interrupted me. Your complaint has been heard per procedure but no wrongdoing has taken place. This discussion is over. Now, to move onto more important matters. This Humarya is a huge problem. What progress has been made? Den, have the fairies learned anything yet?"

"Not yet," said Den, "but they are still searching."

"How is it in all this time you've found nothing?" Mellissa asked. "I thought your team of fairies were the best trackers in the entire magic world."

"Well, the mountains are a vast area and it's not the sort of terrain we're used to."

Greg frowned. Something wasn't right.

Mellissa gripped the pen in front of her tightly. "Well, Den, I went to the mountains and found the Hawklings. It took me one day while your fairies have had weeks."

Den wiped sweat from his forehead. "They are doing their best."

"Well their best isn't good enough," she answered through gritted teeth, "I didn't see a single fairy the whole time I was in the mountains."

Lady Gabrielle put her hand on Mellissa's shoulder. "Never mind that. What did you learn?"

"Humarya is a Valkeryie, not a Hawkling. The best comparison is the similarity from a pixie to a fairy."

Hogan chuckled. "I'm impressed you know the difference between a fairy and a pixie."

Mellissa's eyes flashed green.

Greg grimaced. He'd thought the same as Hogan but hearing it aloud made him see how it could be taken badly – as an insult on her intelligence.

"There's more," Mellissa said, "Humarya is attempting to gain more power to resurrect her dead husband."

Greg's eyes widened. This was insane. He should have questioned Mellissa more when she was at his house instead of letting her leave.

"That woman is crazy," Yuko said shaking her head, "It doesn't matter how much power she seeks out, it's impossible to revive the dead."

"One last thing." Mellissa fiddled with her fingers. "Humarya is in possession of a dark stone."

"A what stone?" Lady Gabrielle asked.

"A dark stone. When the life crystals were created the dark stones were formed by the gods to create a balance."

"You're saying she has a stone full of dark energy as strong as the heart crystal." Lady Gabrielle rubbed her forehead. "No wonder she'd caused so much damage."

"How have we never heard of these stones before?" Kai asked.

"It was the wishes of the gods that the knowledge of theses stones were kept secret," Mellissa replied. "Only those chosen to act as protectors of the stones knew of their existence."

"How are we meant to fight a power like this?" Kai asked.

What had the gods been thinking? Greg understood that everything needed a balance. It just never occurred to him that this principle also applied to the life crystals. They couldn't fight these stones with power equal to the life crystals. Mellissa was the only one who could face Humarya. He watched Mellissa continue to play with her fingers. She knew more than she was saying. What else could there be on top of this revelation of dark stones? How did she know about them in the first place?

Emerson stood and pointed aggressively at Mellissa. "I have a new complaint against the queen."

"Are you serious?" Mellissa said.

Emerson pushed his shoulders back and took a wide stance. "I'm extremely serious. Is it not obvious this Humarya is after the heart crystal? You are the reason for these attacks. You're the only common factor in them all."

That wasn't true. Greg thought back to all the attacks that had occurred. Laxus was the common dominator. Mellissa had simply been there to defend him. But there was something special about him. That's why Mellissa had covered the boy in her aura, to hide the strange magic he had.

"I agree with Emerson." Beatrice pointed at Mellissa. "Our people would have never been attacked if Queen Mellissa hadn't been in the city. This also reveals how your inappropriate relationship has harmed people."

Mellissa rolled her eyes. "We already established mine and Greg's relationship isn't inappropriate."

"You are both making assumptions without evidence," Greg said. The lack of logic being used by these two was infuriating. It didn't take a genius to realise there was more to this situation.

Emerson snorted. "You would defend her."

"You weren't in Novosvillas when it got attacked. Mellissa was nowhere near where Humarya chose to strike."

"How do you know that?"

"I was with her. We're lucky she was in the city to defend our people."

"You're not helping your case."

"How do you know there isn't a power hidden in Novosvillas and the bay at Perluves that we don't know about. We didn't know these dark stones existed before."

Greg couldn't voice his suspicions about Laxus, but he could try and get them to engage their brains. There had to be a good reason Mellissa was hiding the young boy. All this sudden knowledge she had about pixies. Laxus could be one. That had to be why she'd learned about them. Pixies were rare but anything they could do, so could a fairy, except they had a longer life span – like a valkeryie.

Emerson stamped his foot. "What has Perluves to do with anything?"

"Those glass creatures were Humarya's creation. It's an ancient form of air magic. You would know this if you'd looked into it properly as you were meant to."

"You have no evidence it was Humarya. She wasn't seen. I'm sure there are others that use air magic."

"Those creatures accompanied her attack of Urbem Folium and Novosvillas."

Emerson folded his arm and lifted his chin in the air. "Coincidence does not count as evidence."

Why was he being so difficult? Moments ago, Emerson was happy to accept rumours as proof of something, yet this wasn't good enough for him.

Lady Gabrielle raised her hands in the air, gesturing to both of them. "Enough."

Emerson curled his top lip as he sat back down.

Greg gritted his teeth. It was like Emerson was being purposely argumentative.

Lady Gabrielle cleared her throat. "I think Gregory may be onto something. There are two other dark stones after all. What if that's the power she's searching for and not the heart crystal?"

Mellissa bit her bottom lip and frantically looked up and down the table. "So, she may have been after the heart crystal, but I can't help being a crystal keeper. Does this mean I can't go anywhere just in case someone wants to steal the crystal? I never asked for this power, but I will use it to stop her."

Greg narrowed his eyes at her and she met his stare with a steely look. He wouldn't say anything, but he was going to get an explanation out of her. He was done waiting around for her to come clean. This lie had gone on for too long.

"So, you admit the attack was your fault?" Emerson asked.

"No." She stared Emerson down. "The blame is with Humarya and no one else. I could come up with a way everyone in this room was responsible, but it would achieve nothing."

"Queen Mellissa is right," said Lady Gabrielle, "We must stop throwing blame around and deal with the real problem at hand."

And with that, Lady Gabrielle had taken back control of the meeting. Over the next few hours, they brainstormed ideas on how to handle Humarya, arguing over the best course of action. It was decided that the fairies and the northern changelings would search for Humarya's location. From what the Hawklings said to Mellissa, she had a floating castle on the far edge of the mountains. It should be easy to locate now they knew what to look for, although Greg didn't like this plan. Emerson and Den were in charge of the search and they'd both failed with the previous tasks they were given. It infuriated him that no one else shared his concerns. In the meantime, everyone else would prepare for battle as it was unknown when Humarya would strike again. Urbem Folium would act as a safe haven, already protected by Mellissa's magic.

Greg pushed his annoyance with the council down. Their plan didn't really matter, though. Greg was certain that Mellissa had her own that she wasn't divulging and was the reason she hadn't objected. Once the meeting was over, he headed straight over to her. "We need to talk."

"What's there to talk about," she said, "the meeting covered everything."

"It didn't cover Laxus," whispered Greg.

Her eyes grew wide and she flapped her hands at him. "Will you be quiet."

"The meeting is over, no one is paying any attention to us."

"How can you say that? Lee has obviously been spying."

"Only to try to discredit you and it backfired. So will you stop telling me half-truths? What is going on Mellissa? We both know Humarya wasn't after the heart crystal."

She placed her hand over his mouth and made a weird panicked squeak. The next thing Greg knew, she was pushing him down the corridor and into a cupboard. She closed the door and waved her arms about casting a spell. Greg's jaw dropped. This was a crazy reaction even for Mellissa. "Seriously, What is going on?" Greg's brow creased. Why are we in a cupboard and why have you cast a sound lock?"

"So no one can ease drop." She looked at him with her big round eyes like it was obvious why she was acting the way she was. She let out a frustrated groan. "Curse you and that brain of yours. You just have to know everything don't you."

"Well, no one can hear us now so just tell me what's going on?"

She put her hand up by the side of her mouth and

whispered. "There is a spy on the council."

"Mellissa, I know Lee can be challenging at times, but I don't think he's a spy."

"Oh, say it as it is Greg. Lee is an arse, but no, you're right, he's not the spy." She looked up at the ceiling as if to consider what to tell him.

"Just tell me what's going on? You've been lying for months. Mellissa, you don't have any cousins, yet you managed to magic one out of thin air."

She tugged at her hair. "What, you knew? Why didn't you say anything?"

"I thought you must have a reason for lying, and that you'd eventually tell me the truth when you were ready. I didn't think it would take you this long."

"Maybe you would know more if you hadn't been so unreliable all the time."

"Don't change the subject."

She raked her fingers roughly through her hair. It looked like she was going to pull it out. Greg took hold of her hands, untangling her hair from them. "He's a pixie, isn't he?"

She tilted her head to the side. "How do you know that?"

"It's a logical deduction."

"You don't think any of them figured it out?"

Greg shook his head. "I know you better than they do, and they were too busy with their own agendas."

Mellissa put her head in her hands taking slow breaths. She looked up at him, her eyes focused on is as her lips drew into a thin line. "Laxus is the protector of the land stone. That's what Humarya is after."

"Why did you keep that to yourself?"

"Because Humarya has someone on the council feeding her information."

"Well, it isn't me."

"I didn't say it was, but Laxus didn't like you until I made him stay with you. I needed him to trust me if I was going to protect him. He's currently at my dad's with Harkura. I need to get back there with Victoria, then we'll figure something out."

Greg shook his head "Your dad's isn't a safe place to stay either. The council all know where it is."

She bit her thumb nail. "We can't go back to Urbem Folium and the forest isn't safe."

"Why is the forest not safe?"

"Because it's home to the fairies."

"I know Lord Ping is kind of detached, but I don't think."

"Not Ping," interrupted Mellissa, "Chancellor Den."

"Den? Are you sure?"

"His fairies have failed on an epic scale." She rubbed her chin. "He may be able to help find Humarya's weakness though."

"No, Mellissa don't go confronting anyone yet. We don't know enough."

"Don't tell me what to do. The last time I waited, Daniel lost his life."

"It's not the same. First, we need to ensure Laxus is safe before doing anything else."

She put her hands on her hips. "Fine, but I'm out of ideas."

"Take him somewhere in the human world no one here knows about."

She opened her mouth, shook her head and pouted.

Greg put his hand under her chin, tilting her head upwards. "I'll come with you. We can figure this out together."

"You can't tell anyone anything and we can't risk being seen leaving together."

"I'll go home first, sort some things out and make my own way to the human world. Although it might not be easy getting past your guards."

"A pass from the queen should get you through easily." She swished her hand and produced a leaf. "The stone guards at the tear will recognise my magic and let you pass no questions asked."

Greg took the leaf. "Promise me, you won't do anything drastic in the meantime?"

"Fine."

Greg took her hand. "One more thing. Why didn't you teleport here today?"

Mellissa pulled her hand away and wrapped her arms around herself. "Humarya took away my teleporting powers."

"She what!" Greg exclaimed.

"She threw some potion at me, and now, whenever I try to teleport it's like I'm being repelled by a magic barrier."

"A power stripping potion shouldn't work on someone with your level of magic. I mean it shouldn't work on me, so it defiantly shouldn't affect you. This doesn't make any sense."

Mellissa's eyes filled with tears. Greg reached his hand out to her, but she shoved it away shaking her head. "It doesn't matter right now. I need to get Victoria and get Laxus ready to move again."

She tripped as she opened the cupboard door, grabbing his hand as they both stumbled out into the corridor startling Yuko. She raised an eyebrow and shook her head before she continued walking.

"You're really not helping maintain the appearance of our appropriate relationship," Greg said.

Mellissa's cheeks turned red. "Shut up."

She marched off down the corridor as Greg went to find Mary. Dread spread through him as he walked. Things were much worse than he'd originally thought.

Greg rummaged through his filing cabinet, pulling out files and handing them to Mary. His people were still shaken after the attack, so he'd had to ensure they were taken care of, but helping Mellissa was just as important. Hopefully, they'd be able to prevent any further attacks and stop Humarya in her tracks.

"Mary, I'm sorry to do this to you on your first day, but I need you to run things while I'm away for a few days."

Mary nodded to show she understood. "There's no need

to be sorry, it's what I'm here for."

Greg smiled. "We gained new information about the person who attacked our city and I'm going to help bring her to justice."

"No need to explain, sir. I know you wouldn't leave if it wasn't for a good reason."

"Good, good, well, everything you need to know is in those files I gave you."

"Don't worry you can count on me." She bowed and left the office with the files.

Greg sat at his desk. He was doing the right thing, wasn't he? Leaving someone he'd only just hired in charge may be unwise, but he didn't have many other options. Besides, she seemed eager and was more than qualified. Humarya was a much bigger threat than they'd realised. If Mary could handle the pressure of being chief of staff during this crisis, her trial was over, and the position was hers.

There was a knock on the door. "Come in," he shouted assuming Mary had returned with a question. The door clicked open and in walked a tall redhead. Greg stood up and walked around his desk.   "Mum what are you doing here?"

She took his hand. "I came to take you to safety."

"What are you talking about?"

"I heard about the attack. It's not safe for you here."

Greg pulled himself free of her grip. "I can't just leave. I need to make sure everything here is taken care of, then I'm going to help Mellissa."

"You can't," Gwendolyn exclaimed. She looked flushed.

"We are all in danger. I can't just run away and hide with you."

"Fine, don't come with me. Stay here and take care of the city, but you have to stay away from that girl."

"Why?"

"She's trouble. Danger follows her."

"Mellissa is the only one with the power to stop Humarya, but she can't do it alone."

Gwendolyn tugged at his arm. "She has her guardians. She doesn't need you."

"I am not running away."

His mother's eyes welled with tears. "Your girlfriend is going to get herself killed. I don't want that to happen to you as well."

"You are majorly underestimating her, Gwendolyn. Mellissa is stronger than she looks." Greg walked over to his office door and held it open to her. "Go and hide, but please, don't come back here again."

Gwendolyn placed her hands together as if she was praying. "Gregory, please."

Greg shook his head. "Just go."

Her arms flopped beside her as she slowly walked out of his office, her face solemn as she looked at the ground.

Greg slammed the door behind her. He should have known better than to expect anything different from her. As soon as things got tough, she did a runner. But he wasn't like his mother. He wouldn't run. He would stand and fight.

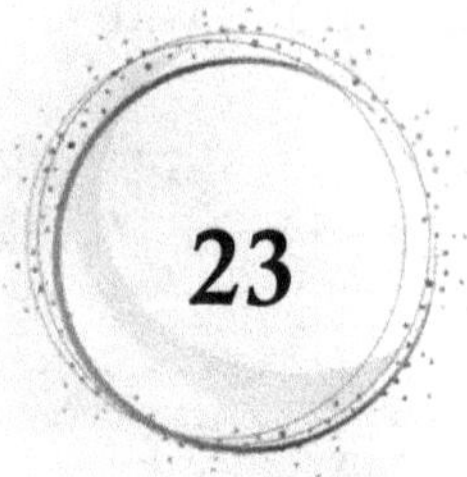

Stand-Off

Mellissa

"Victoria, we should tell Harkura about this," I said for what felt like the hundredth time. "This is crazy."

"But he might tell us to let him go." She pointed at the fairy trapped in a jar on the shelf in my dad's garage. I had promised Greg I wouldn't do anything insane but my guardians had made no such promise.

"Harkura is nothing but loyal," I said, "he could help us."

"What are you two doing in there?" Harkura shouted from the front door.

"Just putting something away," I shouted.

Victoria smirked.

I shouldn't lie. Harkura was always willing to bend the rules to protect me.

We headed into the house and down the hall to the kitchen. "Where's Dad and Laxus?"

"They went to bed," said Harkura. "Are you hungry? You missed dinner."

"Well, I could eat."

I sat at the table with Victoria as Harkura warmed up some pasta for both of us. He placed two full plates of food in front of us and we tucked in.

Harkura sat at the end of the table with a green smoothie in hand. "So, Your Highness, what do you think about me arranging another meet and greet for you?"

I almost choked on my food. "What? No!" With everything that had happened why was this on the forefront of Harkura's mind.

"Surely you want someone to carry on your family name. As queen, there must be someone to succeed you."

I slumped back into the chair. "Surely, there are more important things going on at the moment."

"Don't you see, Your Majesty, it's much more than that," Harkura said, peering at me. "If something were to happen to you, there'd be no one else to activate the heart crystal. Only someone from your bloodline can do that. And if the heart crystal were to deactivate, the balance of the world could be destroyed."

I pointed my fork at him. "There were hundreds and thousands of years between me receiving the heart crystal and the last elf queen, Freya dying. The world survived that."

Harkura squeezed my hand. "The crystal was never completely inactive before. It was constantly calling out to those of your bloodline. It was just unable to get to them from the other side of the veil. You are Freya's last living heir. The world needs you to reproduce."

I held back a giggle, but Victoria let loose, laughing so much she choked.

Harkura glared at her. "Now that you understand, shall I set up another meet and greet?"

"It's still a no" I pushed my plate to one side. "Look, I need to talk to you about something. I know who the traitor on the council is and I ..."

"You miniaturised chancellor Den and sealed him in a glass jar?" he interrupted.

My mouth fell open. "How did you know that?"

He wriggled his eyebrows. "It's my job to keep tabs on you."

"So, you don't think it was kind of drastic?"

"'Course not." Harkura took my plate over to the sink.

"Now, off to bed, you need to conserve your energy."

"Yes, sir." I did a mini mock bow. I got up to leave but paused by the door. "I almost forgot … Greg knows about Laxus."

"I see," replied Harkura his eyes widening. "Well then, I assume he'll step in and help us out."

I nodded, twirling a lock of hair with my finger.

"To be honest, I'm surprised you managed to keep it a secret for so long," he answered with a shrug. "But I'm glad he's onside. Goodnight, Your Majesty."

"Night, Harkura." I went upstairs and flopped down onto my double bed feeling drained, but ended up staring at the ceiling for hours. Victoria lay beside me, having come up only a few minutes ago was already snoring. I wished I could switch off as easily as her. What Harkura had said about my lack of an heir was bothering me and my mind was racing. I tugged the duvet over my face and tried to push the thoughts from my mind. I had to get some sleep. Tomorrow would be a busy day.

Over breakfast the next morning I explained everything that had happened at the council meeting to Laxus.

"How can you be sure he's the only traitor?" Laxus asked. As usual, the pixie was being his usual untrusting self. "And I can't believe you told Greg about me. You have such a big mouth."

I jabbed my finger at him. "I kept your secret for months. Besides he already had a big chunk of it figured out. Anyway, it doesn't matter. After breakfast, you need to pack as we're going into hiding."

"Do we have to? I like it here. Your dad is a really good cook. Much better than that chef at the castle."

"The chef is perfectly adequate at his job." I rolled my eyes. His safety was at risk and his only concern was food. "We have to leave. Greg was kind enough to point out that every council member knows where I live, and it won't be long before they look for me here when they realise I'm no longer in the magic world."

"So, there's another spy on the council then? Why else would you move me when you have the fairy captured."

"How do you know? I thought we'd been discreet."

Laxus shrugged. "Harkura told me. Anyway, back to the spy situation."

I pushed the seaweed wraps Harkura had made around my plate. "I don't know for certain if there's another spy, but it's better to be safe right?"

The windows and doors shook. "Wow," Laxus said, "The wind sure is strong."

"Hmm, too strong." I jumped to my feet. "We need Harkura." Just as I said his name a strong gust filled the room, the window shattered and Harkura was hurled across the kitchen. Pots and pans clanged and crashed as they fell to the floor, and the cupboard doors creaked as they flew open. The gale grew stronger, blowing the kitchen table over and throwing me and Laxus against the wall. Then the wind died down and everything fell quiet. We all glanced at each other, but none of us dared move. Then suddenly there was a loud boom as the entire house shook and the kitchen wall exploded. Rubble flew everywhere and silt-filled the room.

"Laxus," I shouted. My ears rang and dust clouded my vision. I crawled in the direction I thought he would be. Harkura shouted my name and dived on top of me flattening me on the floor. A shadow ball flew over us smashing the upturned table. Strong gusts pressed down on me and Harkura, restricting our movements. A small tornado appeared clearing the dust and Humarya stood in the huge gap that was once the kitchen wall. She turned to the left where Laxus was crouched over by the sink. I was on my feet in a flash but Humarya moved fast. I dove on Laxus as a shower of ice shot across the room encasing Humarya so she was in a see-through dome.

"That won't hold long," Victoria shouted, "Get Laxus out of here."

I grabbed Laxus' hand and tried to teleport but we fell to the floor as I hit an invisible wall.

Humarya shattered the ice surrounding her, firing shadows that lashed out in all directions. I shielded Laxus with my body as Harkura ran at Humarya flipping over the shadows she'd launched. With his feet engulfed in flames, he kicked her back towards the gap in the wall and then followed up by throwing a succession of fireballs. In retaliation, Humarya flapped her wings and summoned another strong wind that blew Harkura's fire back at us. Victoria protected us with a wall of ice.

Shadows slashed through the ice, wrapping around Victoria as they yanked her away. Her scream echoed through the house making my blood run cold as shadows snaked around me, twisting and turning as they grabbed at my throat. I turned to face Laxus. "Run!" I screamed as I surrounded my body in light, driving back the shadows.

Laxus shrank and flew towards the door but he wasn't fast enough as he got caught up in a spiralling vortex of air.

Humarya cackled. "I see you are lost without your teleporting abilities." With a flick of her wrist, she trapped Laxus in a shadow bubble and then walked through the gaping hole in the wall towards the garden.

Harkura and I sped after her, and together we took aim, firing at her, but she blocked our attacks. She opened her wings wide and flew upwards. I couldn't let her get away with Laxus. Jumping off the patio, I slammed my hands onto the lawn and rose-covered vines instantly sprouted through the earth and climbed high into the sky, grabbing hold of Humarya by the legs and smacking her into the ground. Laxus fell, bouncing in his fuzzy bubble as it hit the grass with a thud. Harkura tried to free him while I kept wrapping vines around Humarya's arms, legs and torso. However, she was destroying my plants quicker than I was making them grow and produced another massive gust, sending me flying backwards. I instinctively tried to teleport around her, but I was thrown back again.

"Still trying that old trick," she cackled.

I threw up a barrier as she released a flurry of shadows and in a blink of an eye, she closed the gap between us. Grabbing hold of my arms, she took flight, ascending higher and higher into the endless blue sky. Struggling against her, my hair blew around my face, my legs thrashing about as they dangled in the air. I gasped for breath as we almost reached cloud level.

"It's amazing how weak you seem now." She smirked letting go of me and I screamed as I hurtled towards the ground. Throwing my arms out, I summoned vines from the ground to catch me. While I attempted to save myself from fatal injury, Humarya swooped down and blasted Harkura away from Laxus in his bubble. Harkura slashed whips of fire at Humarya to stop her swooping off with Laxus as I slid down the vines to help him. Harkura launched a reel of fire balls at Humarya. With a mere flick of her wrist Humarya deflected the attack with a flurry of shadow. Fire and Shadow swirled around the garden as Harkura and Humarya both launched at each other their magic flowing freely.

I ran towards them summoning light into my hand. But before I could strike Humarya twirled round and blasted me back with a powerful gust as my legs buckled beneath me. I spun around mid-air, slamming into the garden fence. Harkura looked like he was about to land a punch when she swooped down, flapping her wings, and slammed him to the ground.

"Get off him," I shouted, hardly able to move under the wind pressure she'd created.

"Why would I do that?" She had a darkness in her eyes as she pushed her wings down onto Harkura's chest. He looked like he was struggling to breathe. There had to be a way around this endless vortex of air. She swiftly removed her wing and slammed the other one down onto him. I heard something crack. My chest tightened. I had to save them.

"He's been just as annoying as you. I should destroy the pest."

"No," I screamed.

"Then again, I may take him as well. He is your guardian; his knowledge could prove useful." With a flick of her wrist, she trapped Harkura inside a bubble of shadow. Her eyes narrowed as she looked at me. Pushing her hand to one side, the gust holding me down changed direction, flinging me upwards. She took flight lifting her arm, Harkura and Laxus in the balls of shadow floated up to her . They both kicked at punched at the dark sphere trapping them, their eyes wide with fear.

I hit the ground with a thud, my entire body screaming with pain, but that didn't matter. Scrambling to my feet, I ran after them. Jumping over the garden fence so I could keep her in sight, I pleaded with the heart crystal to show me how to fly again. I needed to save them, but the crystal wouldn't oblige.

I swiped my foot across the ground summoning vines. grabbing onto them I pushed my magic into them causing them to grow rapidly and thrust me into the air and reached out to grab Laxus in his bubble but Humarya hit me with a shadow whip causing me to plummet back towards the ground. She laughed as she disappeared through a portal with Harkura and Laxus. I cried out as I witnessed them vanish but somehow managed to soften my landing as I navigated into a flowerbed. I looked up to where they'd been; the sky was clear – they were gone. My eyes welled with tears as I got up and circled the area, looking up at the sky. They couldn't just disappear like that surely. There had to be something I could do.

I jumped back over the fence to my garden, but as I walked back to the house my legs gave way, and I fell onto all fours. Surely this wasn't happening. My heart felt like it weighed a tonne and I could hardly breathe. Punching the ground, I screamed at the top of my voice as the earth cracked beneath me. Laxus had been relying on me to keep him safe, to keep the land stone out of Humarya's reach. If she found out where the stone was hidden, it would all be over.

"Mellissa," Greg shouted. I looked up to see him running across the garden and tears streamed down my face. He dropped to his knees and embraced me. "I'm sorry I didn't get here sooner."

Why was he apologising? This was all my fault. He hadn't even known who Laxus really was until yesterday. He cupped my face in his hands. "What happened?"

I tightened my grip on him. "She took them. She took Laxus and Harkura." I gasped. "OMG Victoria!" I forced myself up and ran into the house as Greg closely followed. I stumbled on the rubble as I spotted her passed out in the kitchen doorway. Her pale blue top was soaked with blood. Greg kneeled beside her and lifted the fabric away from the wound. I gasped at the sight of her torn skin and the bone. Greg rested his hands on her stomach, his hands glowed as he began healing her.

"I've failed," I said.

"Don't say that, we can fix this," Greg said not taking his eyes off his patient.

"How Greg? She's won! Laxus and Harkura have been captured and Victoria is stomach has been slashed open" I waved my arms about in all directions. "In addition, she managed to infiltrate the council and have them feed her information. To top it off, I can't teleport. It's hopeless."

"It's not hopeless. Victoria's injury looks worse than it is." Victoria groaned as if in response. "See, she's fine." Her pale skin knit back together under the glow of his magic. Once finished the her blood soaked top was the only evidence she had ever been injured.

She slapped his hands away as she sat up. I dropped to my knees and hugged her. "I'm so glad you're okay."

She pushed me off her. "Get off. What happened?"

I looked at the floor. "She won."

"No, she hasn't," insisted Greg, "We just need to figure out where she is and bring them back. There's already a team of changelings and fairies tasked with finding her floating castle."

I frowned and wiped my wet eyes with my sleeve. "Fat chance of them finding her. I doubt the fairies were even given the order in the first place." I jumped up remembering what I had tucked away in my dad's garage. If anyone could tell us where Humarya was, it was that devious scumbag.

"Where are you going?" Greg asked.

"To the garage. There's a two-faced fairy in there that can tell me what I need to know."

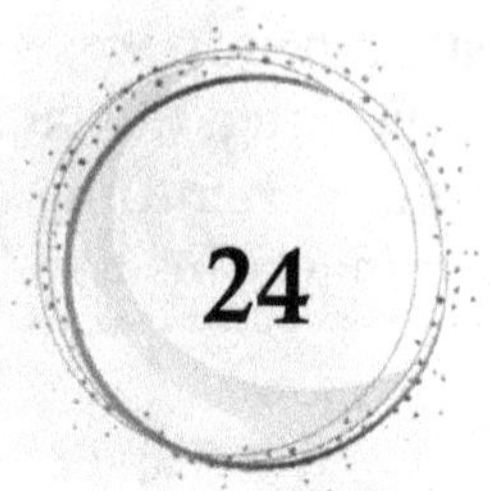

Council of Traitors

Mellissa

"I can't believe you kidnapped chancellor Den," shouted Greg.

"He was spying for Humarya." I folded my arms. "Anyway, I like to think of it as secretly detaining him." I was completely justified. He'd betrayed us all.

"You said you wouldn't do anything drastic," he said.

"I didn't. Victoria did."

Greg put his hand on his forehead. "Of course, she did. This is insane."

Victoria rolled her eyes and huffed as she walked past the two of us. The door to the garage slammed shut. Greg and I looked at each other wide-eyed and rushed after her.

Victoria was dangling the jar with Den inside it over a block of ice. "You better start talking, or things are about to get really cold."

"Victoria," I snapped.

Greg pushed past me, grabbing the jar from Victoria. She swirled around throwing ice at him and he swiftly pushed his hands out deflecting her attack with a barrier. Greg threw the jar onto the floor and it smashed as Den instantly grew back to full size.

"Oh, Gregory, thank the gods you're here, the queen and her guardians have lost their minds."

He dashed towards Greg but I flicked my wrist wrapping a vine around his feet. He fell flat on his face. "Not so fast," I said.

"Mellissa." Greg pulled at my arm.

I shoved him off. "He's a traitor. We can't just let him go."

Victoria towered over Den her hands glowing with magic, ready to strike. "If you answer my questions the queen may let you go."

Den wriggled into a seated position on the floor. "I swear I don't know anything."

"Don't lie to me," snarled Victoria, "We know you've had your fairies spying on Mellissa instead of sending them to search the mountains. You fed Humarya information on all of us. You're the reason we were attacked at the bay and the castle. Probably Novosvillas, too." Her eyes glowed with anger. The heat in the room was evaporating.

"I'm sorry. She didn't give me a choice," he whimpered.

I'd never seen Victoria so angry. My hand shook as I placed it on her arm. "Victoria this isn't right."

"He is the only way we have of finding Humarya. We have to save the others. Trust me, he'll tell me what he knows," she said forming an ice ball in her hand as Den shuffled back against the wall.

"That's it!" Greg grabbed hold of Victoria dragging her away from Den. She swung a punch at his face but he caught her fist, twisting her arm round. Grabbing her other arm, he tried to restrain her. She threw her head back and then headbutted him, stamping on his foot at the same time. He stumbled backwards. As they both went for each other again, I threw up a barrier in front of them both.

"That's enough," I yelled. "Both of you outside now."

Greg hung his head and Victoria glared at him, but they both walked out of the garage and then followed me into the living room, Leaving Den tied up.

"What the hell are you two doing?" I asked.

"I was getting Den to talk before *he* got in the way." Victoria made a rude gesture at Greg.

"She's completely lost it, Mellissa. You can't let her throw her powers about like that. Especially in your name."

"This has nothing to do with you." Victoria shoved Greg away. "I don't have time for this. Harkura and Laxuses lives are at risk." She went to walk out of the room, but Greg blocked her path. She clenched her fists.

I forced myself between them. "Don't start fighting again."

They stood glaring at each other and I didn't know what to do. Greg was right. Victoria was going too far, but I also understood her anger. Den had betrayed us and now Daniel was dead and Harkura and Laxus were captured. I couldn't let the same thing happen to them.

The front door slammed shut. "Mellissa," shouted my dad. He walked into the living room and rubbed his forehead, looking back and forth from Greg to Victoria. "What's going on?

I sighed. "It's a long story."

"Mr Hail," Greg said, "Your daughter kidnapped the fairy chancellor. He's currently tied up in your garage. Victoria was threatening him. I disagreed with her behaviour, so she attacked me."

My dad's jaw dropped. He looked at Greg than me. Shaking his head, he walked out of the room. I heard the front door bang open and shut. He returned a few seconds later. "I can't believe there's someone tied up in my garage. Mellissa, why are you kidnapping people?"

"I merely detained him," I shouted. "He's a traitor dad. He's done bad stuff. I need him to find Laxus and Harkura. They've both been captured."

His forehead creased into lines. "Oh, my goodness, I hope they're all right. You need to find them fast … but in the meantime, you shouldn't fight with your friends."

"I wasn't fighting, they were." I pointed at the other two.

"Right." Dad gave us a stern look, the kind where it bored into your brain. He didn't use it often, but I knew when he did, that I had to obey. "You three in the kitchen now." Dad put a hand on each of Greg and Victoria's shoulders and guided them out of the room and to the left . I followed behind dragging my feet. "Mellissa Hail," shouted Dad marching back into the living room. "What on earth did you do to the kitchen?"

I looked down at the ground. I'd forgotten about the wreck the kitchen had been left in after Humarya's attack. "It wasn't me. Humarya blew that hole in the wall when she took Laxus."

"Don't worry," said Greg, "Mellissa and I will fix this."

I bit my bottom lip. "We will."

Dad stood in the doorway watching Greg and I work. Victoria folded her arms and turned her head away, refusing to look at us. In about half an hour the kitchen was back to normal. The cream cupboards and black marble worktop were as good as new. The wooden kitchen table was no longer in pieces and had all four chairs perfectly placed round it. My powers came with their problems, but they were also pretty useful.

My dad clapped. "Nicely done. Now I'll put the kettle on. You three sit at the table."

Victoria and I nodded and sat on one side as Greg sat on the other. I stuck my tongue out at Greg as I wriggled into my seat. Victoria was the one taking things too far, but Greg had somehow made me out to be the bad guy to my dad.

"Oh, so mature," said Greg. I kicked him under the table as Greg narrowed his eyes at me.

Once we all had a cup of tea in hand, Dad joined us at the table. "So, what is the problem exactly?"

We all began talking at once as Dad put his hands up. "One at a time, please. Greg, you go first."

"Why does he get to go first?" Victoria and I said in unison.

"Because out of the three of you, he's the most honest."

I folded my arms and pouted. He was my dad. I should be getting favourable treatment.

We took turns explaining to Dad what happened, and that we couldn't agree on what to do next. Even though the fate of the world was in danger, two people had been taken hostage by a mad, winged woman and I'd lost one of my strongest powers – my teleportation. However, Dad seemed more hung up on the fact that I'd lied to Greg for so long. What was the world coming to? No one seemed to be able to get the point, not the council or my dad. That's why I'd let Victoria take things into her own hands. At least she was focused on the right problem.

Dad shook his head. "You do realise half of this could have been avoided if you'd all communicated better."

I swished my wrist in Greg's direction. "Well, he makes it hard to communicate with him."

"Really, I'm the one that makes it hard?" Greg said, "You disappear the moment a conversation goes in a direction you don't want it to."

"That's not true. "I crossed my arms. "You've kept things from me as well."

Greg pushed his fringe back. "You're right. I should have told you about my mum sooner. Maybe if I'd been more honest, you would have too."

I gritted my teeth. Why was he being so reasonable when I was mad at him? Dad cleared his throat. "I think we may have gone off-topic slightly." He interlaced his fingers. "Could you make a decision about the fairy in my garage? I don't like the idea of imprisoning people on my property." He looked at Victoria. "I know you're trying to protect Mellissa by being the bad guy in all this, but do you think this is what she needs?"

Victoria looked at the floor. "If I do the dirty work, Mellissa keeps her hands clean."

I placed my hand over hers. "You don't have to do that for me."

Victoria looked straight at me. My heart ached at how sad she looked. "I was useless in that fight and while I was unconscious, Humarya took Laxus and Harkura."

I shook my head. "Don't think like that. We'll figure this out."

Greg sighed. "Look, I agree that Den is our best source of information, but aggression isn't going to help. I've known

Den for years. He used to have a good relationship with my father. He isn't a bad person. There has to be a reason he's helping Humarya. "

"We don't have time to figure out how she managed to manipulate him," Victoria said. "You're just letting your personal feelings get in the way."

"No, that's exactly what you're doing," Greg replied coolly. "There's nothing wrong with taking time to think things through and come up with a proper plan."

Victoria slammed her hands onto the table. "Don't you remember what happened to Daniel? Humarya didn't have him long before she murdered him."

I looked down at my hands. It was as if Daniels blood was still there. "Daniel is dead because of me. I won't hesitate to put my life on the line if that means saving someone else. So, I don't want to waste any more time talking about this, when I could be out saving Harkura and Laxus."

Dad squeezed my hand. "Sweetie, you need to stop blaming yourself for things that are out of your control. You are not responsible for the actions of that mad woman."

I looked at my nails. "I don't know what to do anymore."

"None of what has happened is your fault." said Greg, "The council's plan could have worked but no one knew the fairies were corrupt. We need to think of a way to get through to Den. He's already terrified of Humarya, we don't need him further terrorised by Victoria."

Victoria clenched her fists but Greg was right. Den said he hadn't been given a choice, which means, she'd forced his hand.

"I think I might know why Den is helping her. He has a wife and kids, doesn't he?" I asked.

Greg nodded in response. I saw the expression on his face change as he understood what I was getting at. We all went out to the garage where Den was. I looked at his pale, drawn face feeling bad for what I'd done. I'd been so wrapped up in my own pain, I hadn't noticed that other people were hurting as well.

"I'm sorry, Den. You're free to go," I said unbinding him from the vines wrapped round him.

"Just like that? But I haven't told you anything," he said, looking wearily at Victoria behind me.

"I've come to realise that there are better ways to go about things," I said.

"Den, why didn't you tell us about your family?" Greg asked.

"How did you find out about that? She said if I told anyone, she'd kill them." I could hear the panic in Dens voice.

"We figured it out." I said, " I promise you, Den, I will get your family back along with Laxus and Harkura. I'm going after her no matter what. The question is, will you help me?"

He looked at me, then at Greg, and then back at me. He sighed. "She approached me some time ago but I initially refused to do what she asked. That's when she revealed that she'd taken my family. You see, I didn't have a choice. I wanted so bad to tell you after her first attack, but I was so scared about what she'd do to my loved ones."

"It's all right, Den we understand. You were put in an awful position." Greg put his hand on Den's shoulder. "I know Mellissa and her guardian haven't behaved in the best manner, but she has the power to stop Humarya. Could you tell us how you'd give her information?"

"Humarya blessed some fairy dust with the air stone. When I had information for her, I sprinkled some over myself, and it would take me to her castle. Here, this is what I have on me." Den produced a small pouch of yellow dust from inside his jacket pocket. "You only need to sprinkle a little for it to work, but if you want more, I have some back in my office."

"That's enough, thank you, Den." I took the bag from him.

"You promise me you'll bring my family back?" he asked.

"You have my word." I gave him a small smile. It was the least I could do after the way I'd treated him. "Now, Den, this is my dad. He's going to get you some food and show you where you can freshen up. It's my way of saying sorry for detaining you and my guardian going crazy. Then he'll show you the way back to the tear in the veil."

"What are you going to do now?" he asked

"I'm going Valkyrie hunting."

Den went inside the house with my father as I looked at the dust in the bag. All I had to do was sprinkle some over myself and I could track down Laxus and Harkura, but I wasn't sure that was the best plan.

"Mellissa, I hope you're not thinking of going after Humarya on your own?" Greg put his hand over the bag of fairy dust.

"Okay, I'll admit, I was thinking about it, but before you say anything else … I know, I need to make a plan. So, got any ideas?" I asked.

"Now, that you mention it, I do have one, but I'm not sure you're going to like it as it involves asking for even more help."

"It depends on who we're asking."

"It's quite simple really – a dark stone has the equivalent magical power of a life crystal. What we need to do is pit two life crystals against her one dark stone."

I blinked a few times trying to take it in. It seemed so obvious once he said it.

Victoria laughed. "Now, don't we just feel stupid."

I placed the pouch of dust in my pocket and then took both their hands and tried to teleport. We all hit the floor as I was blown back.

Greg pulled me up. "You should probably grab a coat as we have a long walk ahead of us and it'll be cold once the sun goes down."

I grunted as I walked back into the house dragging my feet. This not teleporting thing was the worst.

My legs ached from all the walking. I slumped down exhausted on the sofa in my bedroom back at the castle. I used to think my castle wasn't that far from the tear in the veil, but now I'd travelled the distance on foot, it felt like a million miles. Navigating through the forest hadn't been easy either. If it wasn't for Greg we'd never have made it back. He was the only one that new the way, as Victoria and I were too used to me teleporting us everywhere.

Greg was currently tapping away on his tabular. The walk didn't seem to have tied him out the way it had me. He'd spent the entire walk messaging King Radius explaining the situation. I hadn't realised how chummy they were.

As soon as we'd arrived Victoria marched off with Samson to prepare for the arrival of the council. Greg had decided to call an emergency meeting here. He seemed to think I was paranoid thinking there was another spy.

I threw a cushion at him, sick of being ignored. He pushed it away. "Hey, what was that for?"

"What exactly have you and King Radius been talking about?" I asked.

"Humarya. What else?

I shrugged. "I just feel useless sat here waiting when Laxus and Harkura are held captive."

Greg took my hand placing his tabular down. "I understand but we need to wait for King Radius with the moon crystal, but in the meantime, lets brainstorm some ideas for when he arrives. Humarya's smart. She probably knows you found Den out and will expect you to come after her."

"You think I don't know that. I'm not stupid."

"Why do you always take what I say the wrong way?"

"I don't know, because I'm freaking out not having Harkura here, and I don't know what to do. It is easier to pick a fight with you then admit all this."

Greg pulled me towards him. "Your dad was right when he said we need to communicate better. We need to be honest with each other, even if it's just to say you're freaked out. Okay."

I'd only been half-listening to him, my mind elsewhere. Images from the recent fight ran through my mind. I shot to my feet. "How did she know we were at my dad's?"

Greg looked confused. "The whole council knows where

your dad lives."

I paced back and forth. Humarya finding us so soon in the human world didn't add up. "Victoria captured Den pretty quickly after the last council meeting. He didn't have time to tell Humarya that I was in the human world. I know you think I'm paranoid."

"No, what you're saying makes sense." He ran his fingers through his hair. "I didn't want to believe it but you're right, the council has another traitor, and I just called them all here to your home."

"That you did, but maybe we can make that work in our favour." I smiled, glad I hadn't agreed to Greg's line about honesty. Humarya had more than just Den doing her bidding, and with some careful planning, I was going to find out who, but Greg wouldn't like what I had in mind.

I sat across the table from Lord Ping in my office. He'd been the first to arrive as the fairies shared the forest with us. Samson had warned me he wasn't happy, but that had been an understatement. His eyes looked like they were about to pop out of his head. His jaw was clenched and he kept wagging his finger at me. "Where on earth is Chancellor Den? He's missing and the last time he was seen he was arguing with your guardian."

"As I have already said, Den will not be attending this meeting." I resisted the urge to slap his chubby fingers away from my face.

"You have no right to ban him from this meeting."

"I didn't ban him. Den didn't think it was appropriate."

"Not appropriate," he yelled, "Yes, he's right, this meeting isn't appropriate. Any council meeting should be held in proper chambers in the capital."

"Due to extreme circumstances, we can't do that. Some things are more important than silly rules."

"You can teleport to the capital in seconds. I don't see

what's so important that we had to make the inconvenient journey to you."

I lowered my gaze "I can't."

"Can't what?"

"I can't teleport anymore!"

His face froze in a confused expression.

Lady Gabriele marched over and stood between me and Ping, "What do you mean you can't teleport?"

"When did you get here?"

She waved her hand dismissively. "That isn't important. What happened to your powers?"

I shrugged. "Humarya did something to me and now there's a barrier constantly around me keeping me grounded."

Lady Gabriele put her arm round me and looked over at Ping. "Could you give us a moment?"

He nodded leaving the two of us alone.

She sat across the table from me and cleared her throat giving me a stern look. "Now, tell me everything from the beginning and don't leave anything out this time."

I told her the full story from the moment I met Laxus; up to that moment – how Laxus and Harkura had been taken captive, about Den spying on Humarya's behalf, and most importantly, that Humarya was now extremely close to getting her hands on a second dark stone. I had no idea how long Laxus could hold out. For all I knew, he'd already revealed the land stone's location to her. But I couldn't think like that. Laxus was strong-willed, he wouldn't give in so easily.

Lady Gabrielle rubbed her forehead. "This isn't good."

I scanned the room, checking we were still alone. I leaned in closer to her and whispered. "There's another traitor on the council."

She arched an eyebrow. "I suppose you want to go after Humarya alone?"

It was uncanny the way she knew what I was thinking. I bit my thumb nail. "Yes … no … well, sort of."

"You never wanted this meeting. Gregory made you. May I ask why you haven't already gone?"

"Because I have a plan and I can't do this alone. I need

King Radius and the moon crystal. He's on his way but I don't have time to wait. That's where you come in."

Her eyes widened. "What do you need me to do?"

"You're the only person I'll reveal my plan to. Promise you won't tell any of the others until absolutely necessary."

" I understand not wanting to wait around for Radius but must you head out alone? Surely your guardian ...?"

"No, I have a different task for her."

"What about Gregory? You know he'd help you."

"I can't." I wrapped my arms around myself rubbing my shoulder. "There's something else. You've knew Steffen a long time, right?"

She nodded.

I shifted my weight from one side to the other. "What about Gwendolyn?"

She frowned. "Gregory's mother?"

"Yes, what do you know about her death?"

She crossed one leg over the other as her lips pursed. "Maybe I should be asking what you know."

She knew. I don't know why Greg hadn't thought to ask her. Maybe he didn't want to know but I needed to. "She faked her death and you helped Steffen hide the fact she was still alive."

Lady Gabrielle stood and turned away from me. "Does Gregory know?"

"That she's alive, yes. Your involvement I can't say. I figured it out and we both know he's smarter than me. However, he's more emotionally involved, even if he won't admit it, his judgment is impaired."

"How did you find out?"

"I met her."

She spun round almost knocking over her chair. "You mean, she's back?"

"She came to Greg and fed him some story about Steffen forcing her to disappear."

"That's nonsense. You cannot believe a word that woman says. She's a liar."

"I don't. If Steffen really was the reason she'd stayed

away, why did it take so long for her to reappear?"

Lady Gabrielle paced the length of my office. "She left for her own selfish reasons. Steffen was madly in love with her, but she only married him for his money and title, and then had a son to cement her position, but when things got challenging, she abandoned him. She's only returned because she wants something from Gregory."

It was safe to say Lady Gabrielle was not a fan of Gwendolyn's. "I think you're right. She returned right after Humarya first showed up. I think she only wanted to use him for information."

Lady Gabrielle froze on the spot. "You think she's working for Humarya?"

I nodded. "That's why I have to do this myself. Information can't be leaked if no one knows what I'm doing … even by accident."

"Why tell me then?"

"I need someone to ensure King Radius arrives in time to bail me out."

She shook her head. "I don't like the sound of that. What exactly have you got planned?"

I scratched the back of my head. "Well, as we speak Humarya has probably sent orders to her minion to prevent us going forward with our plan, but she still needs me. I used a blood lock on the land stone."

"You used blood magic." She rubbed her forehead. "I knew you were extreme, but I never thought you would gamble with your life."

"It's only a gamble if you're not sure of the outcome."

"I'd never have expected a line like that to come from the nervous girl I met last winter."

A lot had changed since then, not all good. I handed her four pieces of paper and the pouch of yellow fairy dust from Den. "That piece of paper tells you when and where I need you to be. When the time is right, you need to give those letters to Greg, Victoria and Samson."

Lady Gabrielle frowned as she looked at the piece of paper I'd scribbled all this information on. "Are you sure about these timings?"

"As long as I'm correct about who the traitor is, yes," I replied. "Now Samson will knock on the door and tell us everyone is ready and waiting in 3,2,1 …"

Knock, Knock

Lady Gabrielle raised an eyebrow as I stood up and opened the door to Samson. "Everyone is ready and waiting for you in the main hall," he said.

"We're just on our way," I answered with a smile.

Samson led us to the main hall. I dug my nails into my leg as I walked, trying to keep my head high. I needed to show my confidence in all of this. So far everything had gone the way I'd thought, but people could be unpredictable. Harkura was enough proof of that. It didn't help that I wasn't a hundred per cent sure who the other spy was. I pushed my hair behind my ear. This was going to work. Once Greg had fallen asleep on my sofa, I'd plotted my strategy throughout the night, covering all the possibilities for who the other traitor could be, and this was the only person who made sense.

Victoria intercepted me just before we got to the hall as Lady Gabrielle and Samson walked ahead without me.

"I'm coming with you," Victoria said.

"You know you can't, right."

"Damn it, Mellissa, I'm your guardian. You can't expect me to let you fight without me."

I placed my hand on her forearm. "I know this is hard for you, but I'm not the one who needs your protection."

"I don't appreciate you two hiding that thing in my office without my permission."

"You're the only one I could trust."

She stomped her foot. "Fine, but you better come back alive or I swear I'd find a way to hunt you down in the afterlife and slap you silly."

I winked at her. "No need to worry. I have a plan. "

Victoria ran her fingers through her long fringe. "That makes me worry even more." The corner of her mouth curled into a small smile and she grabbed my hand and walked with me to the hall. A cold chill ran over me and I froze on the spot.

Everyone was passed out on the floor. I searched the room. We'd just been outside. There had been no cries or shouting … so what had happened? I gasped as I spotted Greg slumped on the floor, his red hair covering his face. I ran to his side dropping to my knees. There were no signs of injury. I checked his pulse and let out a long jittery sigh. He was still alive.

"Sleeping powder," said Victoria standing over Samson. "It had to be pretty strong to take out the whole room."

"Someone's missing." I stood up as I tried to account for everyone. My hunches were right about who the traitor was as my top suspect was the only one missing.

"Seems I released the sleeping powder too soon," snarled a hoarse, gravelly voice.

I spun around. Where was he? This hall was an open space with nowhere to hide. A small bird dropped from the ceiling transforming into Emerson. "I'd hoped to avoid a direct confrontation."

"I knew you didn't like me, but this is a bit much," I said.

"It's not that I don't like you. In fact, I envy you. It must be nice to be the sole ruler of your people."

I narrowed my eyes at him. "You sold us out because you don't like sharing rulership with Beatrice and Greg."

"Exactly." Emerson lifted his arm and formed a shadow ball. Dark magic. How had he got through my barrier? The dark magic should have bounced back. "Once I deliver you to my queen, she will reward me by getting rid of those two fools." He threw the shadow ball at me. I stepped back, put up a barrier, but the blast disappeared on contact. What was going on? A blast of ice shot through him and he disappeared.

"A mirror image," Victoria said. waving her arm around where Emerson had just stood. She jerked towards me throwing an ice blast. I spun around to see her attack go through another mirror image of Emerson. Victoria pulled me towards her. "Stay close. He has to be nearby. Illusion magic hasn't got a wide range."

Of course, It wasn't real dark magic.. Emerson specialised in illusion magic. I screamed as a lion ran at me. I threw a bolt of lightning towards it and it disappeared. Another illusion. A pack of wolves appeared out of nowhere and surrounded us as they panted, saliva dribbling from their open jaws.

Victoria took my hand, standing with her back to mine. "Don't worry, it's just a mirage."

The pack charged us, baring their teeth. Instinctively I put my arm over my head and screamed as one of the wolves sunk its fangs into my arm. I dropped onto one knee. With my free hand, I blasted the wolf away with an energy ball. The wolf flipped over mid-air shifting into Emerson. Victoria ran towards him throwing ice shards whilst I rose to my feet to find myself no longer in my castle.

Waves crashed against the shore and the sun's rays blazed down on me. A gentle breeze brushed over my skin. It was another one of Emerson's illusions, but it felt so real – the smell and taste of the salty air, the sound of seagulls squawking in the sky. There was no one here but me. No Victoria. No council. This mirage was more powerful than his others. He must have cast a spell when he made contact with me, making a stronger spell. Just because I couldn't see them, the council members were still dotted about on the floor, so I had to be careful where I stepped. While I was blind to the real world, Victoria was fighting Emerson alone. She could need help and I wouldn't know. My inability to see if an attack was being directed at me would also make her job harder. I had to break this spell, I just didn't know how.

All the fighting techniques Harkura had taught me were useless. This sort of magic messed with the senses. And it wasn't something I could punch my way out of, but I could punch the person performing the magic. The illusionist himself was the weakest part of this technique. He may have messed with my senses, but I still had a few tricks up my sleeve. I crouched down and placed my hand on the sand. Annoyingly the grains felt real, but I could also feel vibrations from the movement of people I couldn't see. I kicked my shoes off and planted myself firmly on the ground. I shut my eyes and focused on the vibrations my feet could feel. The heavy but quick movements I recognised as Victoria which meant the slower less agile ones were Emerson. I pointed with two fingers and aimed, firing a small burst of light energy. A man's yell echoed off the high ceilings. I opened my eyes to see that I was back in the main hall.

"I have to admit you're good." Emerson clutched his shoulder. "Your guardian put up a good fight too. She almost had me beat."

I gasped as I spotted Victoria frozen like a statue. She had her arm up as if to defend herself and her mouth was wide open as if she was about to shout something.

"What did you do to her?" I shouted.

Emerson smirked as he transformed into a bird. Suddenly a flock of birds flew at me. I spun around releasing a pulse of light, hoping to hit the real one. A sharp pain shot through my side. I dropped to my knees. Emerson appeared beside me and pushed my hair behind my ear. I tried to shove him away, but my arms wouldn't move.

"Don't fight it," he whispered, "it will only hurt more."

I tried to speak but no words came. My lips wouldn't move. He stroked my head. "Don't worry, I'm not going to kill you. That honour belongs to my queen. Like your guardian, you'll end up frozen." He walked over to Victoria and ran his fingers down her face. "The best part is, she's completely conscious in there. She'll see me take her beloved keeper, the person she was meant to protect, and yet, be unable to do anything about it." He dug his nails into her cheek drawing blood. A rage stormed through me. This was not part of my plan. Victoria wasn't meant to get hurt. No one was. How could Emerson do this? He was so cold. I understood why Den had betrayed us, his family's lives were at stake. Emerson was doing this all for purely selfish reasons. But he was going to pay.

He casually strolled back towards me. "Now to disarm you. The heart crystal will be a great addition to Queen Humarya's power."

He reached for the crystal around my neck but pulled his hand back swiftly as it blasted him. I would have laughed had I been able to. Taking a life crystal wasn't that simple when it was where it desired to be. He would have to kill me if he wanted it, which I wouldn't make easy, and neither would the crystal. For some reason, it liked me, even if it didn't always listen. He should have put me to sleep like the rest of the council. As long as I was conscious, I knew I was in danger and the heart would protect me.

Emerson swished his arms around and lifted me off the ground. I couldn't feel the movement, but my range of sight had changed. My body was numb, and my blood felt like ice. This must be exactly what Victoria was feeling, except she didn't know my strategy. She didn't know that I was going to kick his butt as soon as these spells wore off. I watched Victoria's statue like figure became more distant as a tear ran down her frozen face.

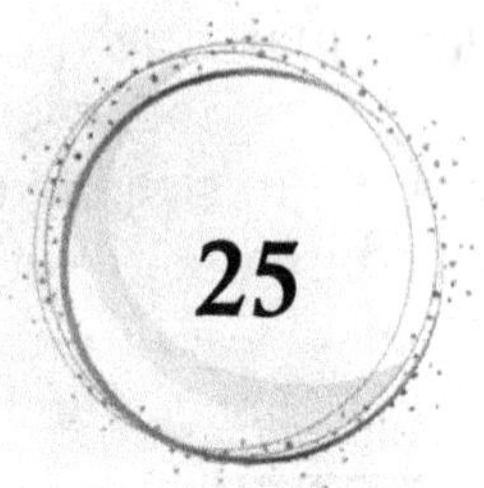

25

Lies

Gregory

reg woke up feeling groggy. He was on a camp bed with a bright light shining down on him. He sat up rubbing his head. Across from him were several brooms and shelves full of cleaning products. It appeared he'd slept in a store cupboard. How had he got here? The last thing he remembered was Lady Gabrielle and Samson coming into the main hall, then nothing. He got up and opened the door to a startled woman on the other side. She seemed to be about to open it.

"You're awake," she said, "that's good, but you should have someone check you over before you go walking about."

"Who are you?" Greg asked.

"I'm Carter one of the royal healers."

"I don't need a healer. I need to know what's going on."

She clasped her hands together. "We don't exactly know. Most of the council members were found unconscious and brought to the infirmary. We believe you were all doused with sleeping powder."

"Sleeping powder." Greg's eyebrows raised. It must have been a strong dose to put them all to sleep. Who'd do something like that? "Where's Mellissa?"

"We don't know."

"What do you mean you don't know?"

"We've been unable to locate the queen. Lord Emerson is

also missing."

"Emerson?" Why would Mellissa disappear with Emerson? They didn't exactly get along. "What about Victoria?"

"She was brought to us as well, but we don't know what's wrong with her."

"Where is she?"

"In the intensive care ward in the infirmary. There were too many of you, so we had to put those that didn't need monitoring in makeshift beds."

Greg walked out of the room. "Which way?"

"But I haven't checked you over."

"I'm fine, now take me to Victoria."

"As you wish."

Carter led him down the corridor and into a large room on the right. Most of the council were still in bed asleep. Carter pulled back a curtain to her right revealing a rigid Victoria standing upright, her eyes and mouth wide open and her arms frozen upright, hands balled into fists as if she were in combat. Greg recognised the toxin used straight away.

"I've never seen anything like it," Carter said.

Greg rummaged through a cabinet on the left in the cubicle. "I have." Hopefully, they'd have all the right ingredients. He pulled a few veils of different elixirs and mixed them together in a bowl.

"What are you doing?" Carter asked.

"Making an antidote. The toxin will wear off eventually, but we don't have time for that. She'll have seen everything that happened."

"How? She was paralysed."

"Yes, the toxin does that, but the person is still aware of everything around them."

Carter clamped her hand over her mouth.

He understood her shock. It was a nasty potion that not many knew about, but Emerson did. They were the only two council members that had studied deadly toxins, clearly for different reasons. This was his doing, which meant Mellissa didn't disappear with him out of choice. Either he disarmed and kidnapped her, or she'd gone after him alone. Neither sat well with him, but he prayed for the second option.

Greg tipped the bowl slightly to check the consistency was right and then handed it to Carter. "Inject her with this. It should only take a few seconds to work."

Carter filled a syringe with the mixture, pulled up Victoria's shirt sleeve to expose her arm and jabbed her with the needle. Within seconds, a rosy colour slowly returned to her face and she gasped for air. Staggering about, she grabbed onto a chair to steady herself. "What the hell," she spluttered. "Where is he? I swear I'm going to rip him to shreds if he's hurt, Mellissa …"

"Victoria what happened?" Greg asked.

She stared at him as if she'd only just realised he was there. "Emerson took Mellissa."

Greg's blood ran cold. So Emerson had betrayed them. It didn't make sense. What could Humarya give him that he didn't already have? And there'd been no signs he was under distress or being manipulated in any way – surely, he couldn't have done this of his own free will. He'd always seemed slightly detached as if he had firm boundaries, but not evil. Greg rubbed his chin. "How did he manage to overpower her?"

"He gave her the same toxin as me, and then took her while I stood helpless. Now she's being delivered to Humarya, completely defenceless."

"Oh God," stammered Greg as he took a step back, overwhelmed with unexpected emotion. Images flashed through his mind as he pictured what Humarya might do when she got her talons into Mellissa, torturing her, no doubt, for mere pleasure. He shuddered, worried that he might never see her precious face again.

"Greg, are you still with us?" said Victoria, leaning forward. "The clock is ticking."

"Oh, yes, sorry, I'm just so worried." He had to be strong, pull himself together. "But this is at least some good news … Emerson hasn't put her to sleep. But we need to locate them, preferably before they reach their destination." He rubbed his eyes trying to think of a way forward. And then he remembered: the castle was full of Mellissa's personal belongings. They could be used to cast a tracking spell.

Victoria waved her hand in his face. "Hello, hello, can't read your mind."

"As long as she's aware of the danger the heart crystal will protect her."

"So, they can't just kill her to break the curse?"

"Wait, what curse? He thought Mellissa had finally told him everything, but clearly not.

"I'm not authorised to say."

"Now is not the time for this, Victoria. You do realise I outrank you, right?"

"But not Mellissa, and it's her orders I'm following." Victoria flashed her hand in his face. "This is all your fault, so you don't get to complain."

"How is it my fault?"

"You're the one that called everyone here."

Greg massaged the sides of his forehead with his fingers feeling a headache coming on. "How was I supposed to know this would happen? We need to gather the splinters of information she gave each of us, so we can figure out what to do next."

"Fine," Victoria said through gritted teeth. "Mellissa cast a blood lock on the land stone so if it fell into Humarya's hands, she wouldn't be able to access it without her."

"She what?" He shouldn't be surprised at the extremes Mellissa went to anymore. But the only way to break a blood lock was to kill the spellcaster if they wouldn't do it willingly. Her life didn't seem to matter to her as long as she thought she was saving others. What other details had she conveniently left out? "Is there anything else I should know?"

Victoria shrugged. "You should already know that she doesn't tell me everything either."

"There's something else you should both know," said Lady Gabrielle.

She was leant against a post behind him. How long had she been standing there?

"Mellissa always intended to be taken captive."

"What?" Greg and Victoria said in unison.

"It was the only way to have the traitor reveal themselves. It would also give Humarya a false sense of security now she thinks Mellissa is a helpless prisoner."

"Why didn't she tell us about this?" Victoria asked.

It was the same question Greg desperately wanted an answer to.

"Because you'd have tried to stop her. But now we must urgently meet with King Radius and stick to the plan Mellissa gave me. It's very particular. "

Lady Gabrielle handed them each a letter Mellissa had written them. Greg took it and read through it. "How did she come up with these timings?"

Lady Gabrielle shrugged. "I have no idea how her crazy little mind works but she is brilliant and she hasn't been wrong yet."

It was good to know he wasn't the only one that couldn't figure out what made Mellissa tick. But how could Lady Gabrielle let her go ahead with this risky strategy? It was insanely detailed, but also dangerous. Greg pushed his fringe to the side. There was no point dwelling on it. Getting to King Radius was the best course of action to take. As the King was the only one that could back Mellissa up.

"Shall we go?" Lady Gabrielle asked.

Both Greg and Victoria nodded and she escorted them out through the castle.

"Wait," yelled Yuko. She ran up to them alongside Hogan. "Where are you going? We need to come up with a new agenda now that Mellissa has disappeared."

"Mellissa already had a contingency put in place," Lady Gabrielle replied, "Time is against us so we must go."

"If that's the case, I'm coming with you."

"If you're both going, does that mean I get to be in charge?" Hogan asked.

Lady Gabrielle raised an eyebrow. "Very well. Yuko your assistance would be appreciated and yes, I'll leave you in charge in my absence, Hogan."

"I'll ensure to oversee everything here." Hogan bowed then skipped off with a smug smile on his face.

"Are you sure you should leave Hogan in charge?" Yuko asked.

"Better Hogan than Lee. Now let's go."

Yuko nodded and followed Lady Gabrielle's lead.

They were on the edge of Urbem Folium when Victoria

suddenly stopped walking. She was looking down at the note Mellissa had left for her. "I can't."

"You can't what?" Greg asked.

"I'm not authorised to say."

Not again. What else could she be hiding on Mellissa's behalf? "Victoria, we don't have time for this."

"I know, but I really can't tell you this time and I can't come with you. That's literally all my letter says." She clenched her fist. "I really want to, but it wouldn't help the situation."

Lady Gabrielle put her hand on Victoria's shoulder. "If this is part of Mellissa's plan, I'm sure you have good reason."

Yuko and Lady Gabrielle walked off into the forest. Greg went to follow but Victoria grabbed his arm. "I'm trusting you to come back with her. If you don't, I will find the most terrifying ways to make you suffer."

"Don't worry, I understand," he said as he removed her hand from his arm and then waved Victoria goodbye. How could she even suggest that? There was no way he'd return without Mellissa. His letter had also detailed Mellissa's agenda which also requested he didn't get involved, but there was no way he was going to oblige. He didn't like this risky game she'd devised and isolating herself from anyone that could help was madness, but he couldn't change what she'd already done.

He ran after the other two. He wasn't being left behind again.

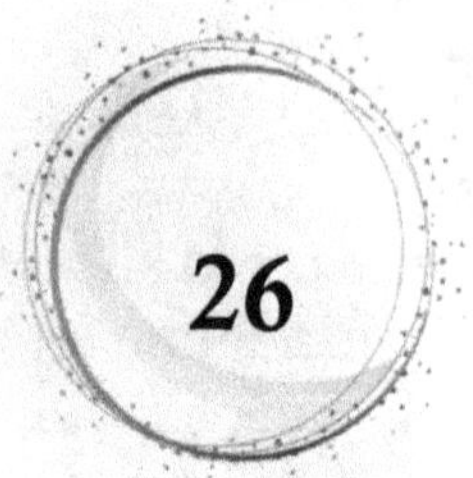

Captured

Mellissa

Emerson had his own pouch of yellow fairy dust to transport us to this strange place within minutes, but I now lay on a cold, hard floor still unable to move. All I could see ahead was a brick wall, giving me no clues as to where we were, but I knew I was where I wanted to be.

Emerson had announced that his queen would be back soon and I so needed this poison to wear off before that happened. Being paralysed wasn't part of the plan. Then again, being kidnapped by your enemy wasn't an exact science. Hopefully, this wouldn't throw everything else off.

A thud of footsteps approached me. Then a click of a lock and a creak of hinges.

"Oh my," gasped a female voice. It sounded familiar, but I couldn't place it. "I can't believe you really got her."

"Of course, I did." snapped Emerson. "What do you take me for?"

"How did you manage it?" the woman asked, "I witnessed her fight with our queen in Novosvillas. She's tougher than she looks."

"Having the trust of the council helped. I took all those idiots out in one strike."

The pitch of her voice rose. "You didn't hurt him? You promised."

"I just put them to sleep. As long as he stays out of my

way, there'll be no need to kill him."

I heard footsteps as someone walked away, but the door didn't close. then a hand gently patted my head. "It's a shame to get rid of someone with such incredible potential." The woman was still here. "Maybe when I change his fate, it will also change yours. You may never get dragged into this world of magic."

Gwendolyn? She really was working for Humarya. Her tone wasn't as cheery as when we'd previously met, but her voice … it had to be her. What did she mean by change his fate? She must be referring to Greg, but no amount of sorcery could change what had already occurred. Was she just as delusional as Humarya? Trying to achieve magic that didn't exist. The door suddenly slammed shut. I wanted to chase after her and get some answers. Being unable to move was beyond frustrating.

I had no idea how much time passed, but the room that had been filled with sunlight was now pitch black. How dare Humarya keep me waiting this long. Didn't she know I was royalty? A loud bang echoed behind me and a hand grabbed me, turning me over. It was Emerson. He had a long needle in his hand. Was he going to top up this toxin? I suddenly felt all tingly as if I had pins and needles all over my body. Movement in my arms and legs was returning.

Emerson pulled me up by the front of my dress. "The queen will see you now." He went to jab me with the needle, but I grabbed his wrist, twisting it around, forcing him to drop it. I quickly followed with a punch, hitting him right on the nose and watched as he staggered backwards.

"You little …"

I kneed him in the gut and then elbowed his back, dropping him to the floor. Before he had time to draw breath, I slammed my hand onto the floor cracking it. Instantaneously vines sprouted up and wound their way around him, creating a cage.

"I'll make my own way there, thanks." I walked away with my head held high.

Once I was at a distance, I leant against a wall to catch

my breath. I was in a dark corridor. Taking on Emerson was a piece of cake in comparison to what would come next. I stretched out my arms and legs making sure I had full movement back. This was all part of the plan. Lady Gabrielle would be doing her part, so I would have back up when needed. Hopefully.

Holding my hand out I summoned a ball of light, illuminating the area. The walls were bare grey stone. I walked along the corridor until I came to a stone staircase. I could sense dark magic above. I ascended the stairs and arrived to what looked like a throne room. It wasn't warm and welcoming like my castle but cold grey empty space. Humarya had dubbed herself the Queen of Darkness. And every queen needed a throne. I hated mine. She obviously didn't feel the same. And there she was sat in it with a smug look on her face. I straightened my back and strode across the room. "I heard you wanted to see me?"

Her nostrils flared and she slammed her hand down on the arm of her throne. "Where's Emerson?"

"He's a little tied up at the moment."

She stood up, expanding her wings to their full width. "That doesn't change anything, I still have the upper hand. I don't care what Emerson's fate is, but I know you care what happens to your guardian."

I clenched my fists as I stepped towards her.

Humarya wagged her finger at me. "Now, now, we don't want him to end up like your last idiot staff member, do we?"

I gritted my teeth. How dare she refer to Daniel like that? I had to keep my cool or my strategy would be ruined.

Humarya sank back down into her throne. "Now, if you're a good little girl, I may let him live."

"What about the others?" I asked.

"What others?"

"Laxus and Den's family."

"Ahh, well, I was going to dispose of them. They serve no purpose anymore."

I flung my arm out to the side. "You can't."

"I guess, I would be willing to make a trade. You remove that stupid lock on the land stone without a fuss and all my captives go free. Oh, although, I still intend on killing you."

"Deal."

She tilted her head to the side. "You would willingly trade your life for the family of the man that betrayed you?"

"You didn't give him much choice. They are all innocent in this."

"Remove the spell then." She swished her hand producing Laxus' wooden box. She reached down and placed it on the floor beside her, and then pointed at me. "No funny business or everyone in my dungeon dies."

"I will need Laxus to remove the lock. We cast it together."

She narrowed her eyes at me as she flicked her wrist. The area beside her became distorted and Laxus fell out. He ran towards me and wrapped his arms around my waist. "What are you doing here?"

I knelt to look him in the eyes. "We need to remove the blood lock."

"Are you sure about this?"

"It's the only way."

He glanced at Humarya. "What about the effect on the rest of the world?"

"Trust me, I know what I'm doing."

Humarya had a big smile on her face as she slit mine and Laxus' hands with her talons. We circled the box, letting our blood drip onto it – and together we chanted: "What once was locked away by blood can now be released." After repeating it several times a bright light shimmered around the box.

Humarya shoved us out of the way, scooping it up as I pulled Laxus behind me. As she opened the lid, her look of glee turned to anger and shadows formed around her. "Where is the stone?"

"Not what you were expecting?" I released a burst of light and dove behind the throne with Laxus.

Humarya opened her mouth wide and let out a birdlike

screech that filled the room.

"Now what?" Laxus asked.

"Don't worry, I have it all figured out."

The throne shattered and Humarya's body was completely covered by shadows. I took Laxus' hand and shouted, "Run."

I threw up a barrier as we fled the shadows until a gust of wind swept us off our feet. I tried to keep hold of Laxus but he slipped through my fingers. Instead of fighting the wind, I let it lift me up and I twisted around mid air. Once I had Humarya in sight, I fired a bolt of lightning at her, and she screamed as she dropped to her knees. Laxus and I face planted the hard stone floor, as the wind ceased. I jumped up and ran at Laxus, pushing my arms out to create a protection circle round him. "Stay put," I shouted as I ran past him, whilst I dodged shadow balls being hurled at me. I pulled my arm back, shifting the ground as Humarya stumbled and took the opportunity to throw a kick at her. She dived back, throwing her wing at me. As I ducked I shot lightning through her wings. Her screech echoed off the high ceilings. I grabbed her torn wing and stamped my foot cracking the stone floor, I lifted my arms wedging, her between two rocks made from the stony floor.

"Where is the dungeon?"

Humarya's head dropped. "I won't be beaten by the likes of you." Shadows shot from the air stone around her neck, knocking me backwards, and a sharp pain shot through my shoulder. Humarya blasted herself free sending bits of rock flying. I put my hand up and stopped the pieces in mid-air before they hit me. She opened her arms and wings wide and then slammed them together blowing me clean across the room. Her body was surrounded by darkness. "Give me the land stone or I will smash this entire place to smithereens with everyone in it."

"Not if I bring it down first." Waving my arm, I pulled the ceiling down on top of her. Dark beams shot out from the rubble as Humarya emerged with pieces of grit in her tangled hair. She flew up to the ceiling, flapping her wings at high speed, creating a strong wind so powerful that I was forced against the back wall. My ability to teleport would have been perfect right now. Where was Lady Gabrielle? This was the part of the plan where King Radius was meant to bail me out. I needed to make a note for future rescues not to anger my enemy this much when trying to buy time. Humarya screeched and her attack ceased. I hit the floor with a thud.

"Another crystal keeper," said Humarya. She threw up a wind barrier as a gush of water came her way. Radius had arrived. His broad shoulders were tight as he lifted his golden trident in the air. His brown eyes shone cerulean, and the moon crystal gleamed with power in the centre of the fork. Light spiralled out of the crystal and slithered its way around Humarya. Someone grabbed my arm. I filled my hand with light energy spinning round, ready to attack. I quickly stopped in my tracks. "Greg."

"Are you insane?" he shouted.

"You're still asking that question?"

"You seem to be outdoing yourself recently."

I threw up a rock to protect us as a gush of water was deflected our way. "I know what I'm doing. I told you not to follow me here."

Lady Gabrielle skidded to a halt beside us. "Can you two settle your differences later?"

"You weren't meant to bring him along," I said.

"I thought you may need a healer."

Out of all the healers in my castle, she decided to bring Greg. The whole point of me not telling him what I was doing until after was for his own safety. At least she half-listened to me.

"Where's Yuko?" Greg asked.

"She's with the boy." Lady Gabrielle said.

"Yuko's here?" I said.

They both nodded.

Great another person that wasn't meant to be here. I couldn't concentrate on fighting with this many people to worry about getting caught in the crossfire. Although they could be useful, as I still had no idea where Harkura and Den's family were. "I need you guys to take Laxus, find the dungeons, and free Harkura."

"What about you?" Greg asked.

"I'm going to back King Radius up and kick some butt."

"Just be careful."

I winked. "Aren't I always."

"You did not just say that?" said Greg.

Lady Gabrielle grabbed his arm. "You can tell her about her poor choice of wording later. We have a job to do." She pulled him away as he reluctantly left with her.

I took off the heart crystal from around my neck and transformed it into staff form, releasing the protection circle around Laxus. With nothing on my feet, I could feel the vibrations of everyone's movements, sensing four people leave the throne room and two locked in battle. Twirling my staff, I joined the fight, firing bolts of lightning. My attacks were deflected.

Humarya threw a wheel of shadows at Radius and me. He cut through her shadows with a water whip while Humarya scurried back. She opened her wings and blasted Radius back with a powerful gust of wind and fired off large amounts of energy. King Radius and I easily blocked her attacks. I could see she was panicking, and it made her attacks weaker. Throwing her arm up, she scattered shards of glass which rapidly grew into glass creatures.

I sent out a beam of light energy smashing half of them as King radius used a hydro blast taking out the rest. As she tried to run, Radius wrapped her legs with a water whip and she fell to the ground, but not before pushing a button on the wall that was camouflaged to merge with the stone. Suddenly the whole room began to shake.

"What did you do?" shouted King Radius.

"Initiated self-destruct." She narrowed her eyes at him and curled her top lip. "This entire place is about to fall out of the sky with all of us in it. I would rather die than let you take me captive."

I gasped. "We need to get everyone out of here."

Humarya launched a wave of shadows at us both. As we deflected her attack, she smashed a window and dove out it. It appeared she wasn't as prepared to die as she'd made out. Panic spread through me. She was getting away, but this place was about to drop thousands of feet and plummet to the ground. I needed to find the others.

"Queen Mellissa," Radius said, "go get your people, I will chase Humarya." He jumped up and flew out of the window.

My jaw dropped. I was impressed and irritated at the same time. How was it that the moon crystal allowed him to fly at will? I'd been in possession of the heart crystal for longer, yet it was still being so awkward with me. Shaking my head, I returned the heart to crystal form and placed it back around my neck.

Running from the throne room, I tried to sense my friend's auras. Laxus would be the easiest to locate as he was still covered in my magic. Hopefully, they were all still together, otherwise, it was going to make escape difficult.

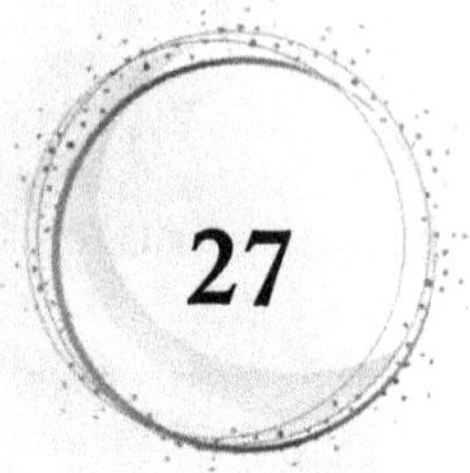

Betrayed

Gregory

ady Gabrielle led the way through the maze of Humarya's castle. Greg knew this was the best idea, yet it still didn't feel right. He had come here to find Mellissa and he'd already lost sight of her. They paused as the corridor split off in two different directions. Lady Gabrielle closed her eyes and held her hand up. "I can't tell which way to go."

Greg tried to sense Harkura's magic. It wasn't the strong aura he usually felt, but it was there. He couldn't be too far down one of these hallways, but he couldn't tell which. "We'll have to split up," Greg said. "Laxus and I will go this way, and you two the other. Let's meet back here in twenty minutes."

"Fifteen." Lady Gabrielle said, "Regardless of what we find, we regroup in fifteen minutes."

Greg nodded as Lady Gabrielle and Yuko ran down the left corridor.

"I think you should have your wings ready just in case." Greg said.

Laxus rolled his shoulders, releasing his wings. His olive skin shimmered and his hair transformed from brown to blue. Greg had known he was really a pixie, but it was odd seeing him in his true form for the first time. They ran down the right corridor. Just around a corner was a double-panelled wooden door. But there was some sort of barrier around the room. That had to be the dungeon. If it was Humarya's magic protecting the room, he'd have trouble getting round it. Greg skidded to a halt as the area began to distort and birds flocked down the corridor towards them.

"Emerson." Greg created a barrier. Pushing it up, he crushed the birds against the ceiling and they disappeared.

Laxus stared upwards open-mouthed. "An illusion?"

"It's a speciality of Emerson's." Greg swivelled round. The corridor was empty, but Emerson could be right in front of them hidden by a mirage. They both jolted as a pack of wolves materialised out of nowhere. They were surrounded. Greg narrowed his eyes at one of them. It looked different from the rest. Then the wolves all pounced at once. Greg spun Laxus round, swapping places with him, and then flicked his arm up creating a barrier. As the wolf hit it, he shouted, "Discutio." The shield burst outwards causing the pack to disappear, except one that hit the wall.

The wolf shifted back to human form and Emerson dragged himself up using the wall. "You really are annoying."

Greg pushed Laxus behind his back. "You should have known that trick wouldn't work on me."

Emerson smirked. "It worked on that girlfriend of yours."

Greg clenched his fists. Mellissa wasn't used to illusion magic, but he was well versed on Emerson's tricks. The devious scoundrel was just trying to get under his skin. He had to remain focused. "Laxus shrink," Greg said.

Laxus immediately obeyed, shrinking down to the size of a butterfly and then flying up to the ceiling. Emerson transformed into an eagle and flew at him. Greg met his transformation with a bird form of his own until they both skidded back to the ground in human form.

Anything Emerson could shift into, so could he. This fight would be decided by their other abilities. The walls began to close in around Greg. Another illusion. The weakness of this magic was the spellcaster themselves. Greg sliced through the phantom vision and quickly surrounded Emerson with energy shields. "Displodo," he shouted. This time the shield imploded. Emerson was hit from all directions and fell backwards. Greg rushed forward, locking him into a magic bubble when he was knocked sideways. The whole building began to shake. This was not Mellissa's doing. There was no way she would make a quake this strong while they were all still in the building.

Emerson brushed some dirt from his face. "Looks like Queen Humarya has pushed the self-destruct button."

"How can you call her queen when she is willing to bring this place down with you still in it?" Greg asked.

"We are changelings, Gregory, we can survive this sort of thing. Besides I don't need her to care about me, merely grant my wish. Although there is something I may be able to do about that myself." Emerson produced a blade and threw it at him. Greg dove to the side narrowly dodging it.

"No," cried a woman's voice. A small lizard dropped from the ceiling and shifted. A flock of red hair dove at Emerson. "You promised."

Everything seemed to be in slow motion as Greg rubbed his forehead. "Mum."

She struggled with Emerson but he overpowered her, throwing her to the floor. "Stupid woman. I told you I'd dispose of anyone that gets in my way."

Greg ran at Emerson punching him in the nose.

Emerson clutched his face staggering backwards. "Not again. You little …"

Greg ducked down grabbing Emerson at the same time, slamming him into the ground. As he stood up, he locked Emerson in a magic bubble.

Greg turned to his mother. "What are you doing here, Gwendolyn?"

She scrambled to her feet and tugged at his arm. "We have to get out of here before the castle falls apart."

The tremors were getting stronger as cracks appeared along the walls. Greg's experience with Mellissa's powers was the only reason he was able to keep his balance. Gwendolyn, on the other hand, was stumbling around.

"Greg," shouted Laxus now back to full size. "We have

to get away."

"See the boy agrees," Gwendolyn said.

Laxuses eyes widened. He looked terrified. "Get away from her … that woman … that voice. She was with Humarya when she attacked my village."

Greg peered at his mother, her sudden return began to make sense. It had nothing to do with wanting to be a part of his life now. It had all been about taking advantage of his connections. He pulled away from her. "You used me to get information on Mellissa and Laxus."

"You don't understand," she said.

"I understand just fine. You're the reason my people were attacked. You put Mellissa's life in danger."

"No, she did that herself." Gwendolyn held her hand to her heart. "It's all right, once Humarya sends me back, it will be like none of this ever happened. You won't remember having ever loved her."

Greg took a step back to create more distance between them. "What are you talking about?"

"Humarya promised to send me back in time," she continued. "This time, when I leave, I'll take you with me."

Greg felt a rage rise within him. She was insane. How had he not seen her deceit sooner? She reached out to him with her hands but a plasma blast hit the ground by her feet forcing her back.

"Get away from him," shouted Lady Gabrielle. She ran down the corridor placing herself in front of Greg as Yuko followed, pulling Laxus to her. They both looked prepared to fight.

The pleading look on Gwendolyn's faced turned to one of loathing. "Gabrielle, it has been a while. I bet you were just itching to take my place when I left."

"I don't have time for your rubbish." Lady Gabrielle threw a plasma ball at Gwendolyn, but she shifted into a bird, flying away. Lady Gabrielle turned towards Greg. "Are you all right?"

"I'm fine." His head was spinning. He never should have let Gwendolyn in. Deep down he'd known she was lying about wanting to be part of his life, but he'd wanted it to be real.

"Is that the dungeon?" asked Yuko

"Yes," said Laxus.

Yuko took a wide stance and flashed her arms about. Creating two water whips she sliced the door open. Luckily the damage to the building had weakened the barrier on it.

Greg ran into the dungeon. It was a cold dark room with no windows. Harkura was slouched over in a corner with gashes all over his arms. A fair haired woman and two children were huddled together behind him. Their pale faces were gaunt and covered in dirt. "Harkura." Greg grabbed his arm to help him up. He didn't look in good shape. His lean body was covered in purplish bruises. He had a deep cut above his left eye, which was swollen and puffy. Greg pulled Harkura closer to him supporting the nymphs weight. They needed to get out quick.

Lady Gabrielle supported the woman by putting her arms around her and Yuko lifted the two small children. Just as they were about to walk back out, the corridor ceiling caved in blocking filling the exit with rubble. Greg chocked on dust almost losing his grip on Harkura. Luckily no one was hurt, but they were now trapped. It wouldn't be long before this room caved in and with no way out, they'd be under a pile of rocks like the ones in front of them.

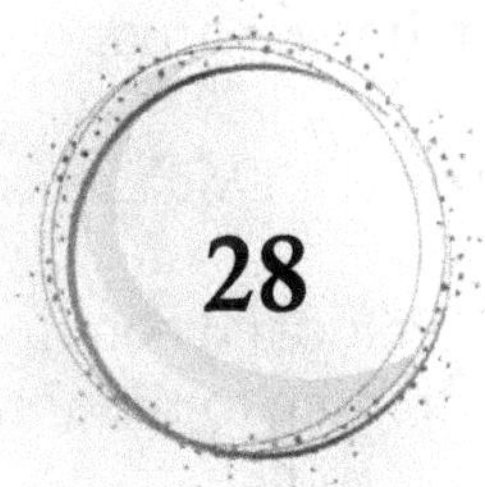

Confrontation

Mellissa

I ran at full speed trying to keep the building upright and in one piece. All those morning runs I'd moaned about under Harkura's strict tuition were now coming in handy. I may not be able to teleport, but I had locked onto Laxus' aura. I rounded a corner. A bird flew at me knocking me off balance and I tripped over losing my concentration. There was a loud crack and the corridor ceiling fell apart. Large parts of grey stone crashed down towards me. . With a quick wave of my arm, I redirected the rubble that was a bout to flatten me, but my path was blocked where the rest of the ceiling had caved in. I placed my hand on the pile of rubble. I could sense Laxus and Greg. They must be behind this. I'd been so close to reaching them. This may be the air domain, but this was still an earth product so I could manipulate it. Taking a wide stance, I punched the rubble blasting a hole through it. Then I ran through as fast as I could down what remained of the corridor, skidding at the end and falling flat on my face through what I assumed used to be a doorway.

"Mellissa," exclaimed Harkura.

"Harkura." I jumped up and hugged him. "I'm so glad you're all right." My heart felt like it could burst with joy. His pale blue skin was splattered with purple bruises and his left eye was red and swollen. He didn't look good, but he was alive.

"We're not going to be all right for long," Greg said. He was full of doom and gloom, but he had a point. There's no way I could hold the building up anymore, but I'd make sure I got us out.

I flicked my hair back. "Don't worry, I've got this under control."

No one in the room looked convinced. Walking around, I knocked on the walls listening to the sound they made.

"What is she doing?" Yuko asked.

"No idea," Greg said.

The back wall was the one I wanted. It would lead us outside. I punched the brick, cracking it, and then gave it a huge kick, bringing it down. A cold chill blew through the room. We were above cloud level and all I could see was endless sapphire-blue sky. I squinted. In the distance, I could see the top of a mountain. That's what I was aiming for.

"Are you trying to kill us?" Yuko asked her voice shrill.

"Have a little faith." Slamming my hand on the floor I grew several vines. Intertwining them together, I shot them across to the mountain top. It wasn't my best work, but it would serve as a reasonably stable bridge. "I suggest those of you who can fly do so. The rest of us need to move as quickly as possible whilst holding on tight. I have no idea how far a drop we'll suffer if we fall."

"What about him?" Yuko pointed at Emerson trapped in a bubble.

I shrugged. "He's smart, so I'm sure he'll figure his way out."

"Mellissa," Greg said, peering at me.

I rolled my eyes. "Fine." I hadn't been serious anyway. Spinning my arm, I wrapped a vine around the bubble Emerson was in and shot him across to the mountain top.

"Couldn't you do that with all of us?" asked Yuko.

"Probably, but I'm sure it will hurt. He'll likely bounce pretty hard when he lands and will probably end up with at least a broken arm."

"Across the vine bridge it is," Yuko said.

Laxus, Den's wife and two children, with their delicate

mother of pearl wings and Greg in bird form all flew outside. The rest of us clambered onto the vines. Lady Gabrielle led the way while I stayed at the back ready to manipulate the vines if the castle fell apart before we finished crossing. We were almost all the way across when I felt the vines being pulled down. I tried to keep them up, but the weight of the castle was too much. I shouted for everyone to hold on tight as I cut the vines attached to the castle and swung us all towards the mountain.

We smacked into the side of the mountain hard. Everyone climbed up towards a nearby ledge except Yuko who was struggling to catch her breath. I grabbed her hand but she tripped and fell onto a rock below. She cried out, her hand slipping out of mine as I gripped onto the rocks with one hand and held onto her with the other. Soon I lost my grip causing us both to fall. I could hear Yuko scream as we were freefalling through the sky. In desperation, I shut my eyes and pleaded with the heart crystal to save us. The crystal started to glow and I felt someone grab hold of me. I opened my eyes to see Laxus and the fairies. They'd come to our rescue. Fluttering their wings at high speed they flew us up to the ledge where the others were.

"Thank goodness you're still in one piece," Harkura said hugging me.

Relief washed over me and I held onto him tightly.

"What about me?" yelled Emerson from above us. My aim appeared to have been spot on with him. "That crazy cow broke my arm."

Lady Gabrielle waved her hand at him. "Oh, shut up and be grateful we didn't leave you behind." She turned to me. "What happened to Humarya?"

"She jumped out of a window and flew off like a bird-witch on a broomstick," I said.

The expression on their faces ranged from wide-eyed wonder to deeply etched frowns. I put my hands up in front of me, "but it's all good, King Radius went after her."

It was so unfair how good he was at flying. I couldn't help being jealous of his ability. He had being a crystal keeper figured out a lot better than I did.

"Well, what are you doing standing around with us?" Laxus asked. "We've all been saved. Go help the king"

He was right, it was going to take both of us to take her down. However, I had no idea where they'd gone. And if the fight was airborne, I was going to be at a disadvantage.

"You all need to get off this ledge first. Then I'll find where they went." Just as I finished my statement there was a loud crash to the right of us and a big dust cloud appeared from a nearby mountain.

Yuko pointed at the dust cloud. "I think they're somewhere over there."

I didn't need to be told the obvious. I turned and placed my hands onto the craggy mountainside. Tree branches instantly grew out of the rocky surface and I produced as many as I could going down the jagged cliffside.

"Use the branches to get to safety. I'm going to help Radius," I said. Everyone obliged except of course Harkura, Laxus and Greg. They never seemed to do as I asked.

"How exactly do you plan to get over to that other mountain?" Laxus asked.

I put my hands on my hips. "I'm going to fly."

"You've never been able to float more than a foot off the ground in our training sessions," Harkura said.

He had a point, but there hadn't been any real danger in training. Now it was a life or death scenario, I'd have to take a leap of faith. "I think if Laxus hadn't saved me from my fall, the heart crystal would have rescued me." I clutched the crystal around my neck. "So, I'm going to give it a stern talking to."

Laxus put his hand over his face. "Oh, no, she has officially gone crazy."

Greg sighed, running his hand through his hair. "Trust me, this isn't the craziest thing she's done recently."

"Hey, everything has worked out according to schedule," I said. "Will you guys just go with the others. It'll be easier to concentrate without you."

There was another crash and a bang as the sound got louder and I could see Humarya in the distance. She was flying towards us, but where was Radius? As Humarya zoomed in on our mountain, I ran in her direction and jumped off the ledge. I heard them all shout my name in shock. Their lack of faith didn't help. I shot a vine up out of the ground and launched myself at Humarya. She was taken by surprise as I hurtled towards her, grabbing one of her wings as we both fell into the side of another mountain.

"Not you again," Humarya screamed. "I thought you went down with my castle." She tried to hurl me off her wing, but I clung on for dear life. I needed to stop her becoming airborne again. She blasted me with shadow balls forcing me to let go. I hit the hard ground with a thump. As she attempted to take flight, I swiftly rolled to my feet and fired bolts of lightning at her wings. She screamed and fell to the ground, her wings gone limp.

"Where's Radius?" I asked.

She peered over her shoulder. Her feathers were singed and black smoke billowed from them. "You little shit. My wings." Her nostrils flared as she gasped heavily, and the stone around her neck pulsated with dark energy. She ran at me firing shadow balls. I blocked each one with ease, but she kept firing more. She grabbed hold of me and heaved us off the side of the mountain. As we fell, she scratched and kicked me. I blasted her away as she spread her wings. They may have been torn and scorched, but she still easily glided to the nearby mountain, whilst I plummeted towards the earth – and Laxus wasn't around to rescue me this time.

"Crystal heart, please," I yelled. The heart crystal shone brightly and transformed into staff form as I caught it in my hand. The crystal at the top kept shinning. It was like the crystal was telling me I was an idiot, but it also showed me what I needed. I flipped around mid-air and flew back up the side of the mountain. As I got to where Humarya had landed, I was greeted by a wave of shadows and swept up in a gust of wind. But, her gust wasn't as powerful as usual. I put up a light barrier and ploughed my way through, landing awkwardly on the mountainside. Humarya ran at me again trying to scratch me with her talons but I dodged her attacks. As I went to retaliate, she swiftly lifted her wing and threw me against the craggy surface.

"Why won't you die already!" she shouted firing a beam of dark energy at me.

I flung myself to the ground to dodge her attack, lifted my staff into the air and released a blinding ray of light. Swinging my staff around I smacked her feet out from beneath her.

She pushed me back with a spiral of shadows. "I've had just about enough of you. I was so close to being able to see my husband again. The power was just within my reach and you ripped it away from me. Once I am done with you, I will hunt down every one of your friends, so they will also suffer for your sins."

She fired shadow ball after shadow ball and each time I blocked, making her angrier. Running at me, she created two shadow whips, hitting me with both at the same time. I yelled out as she ripped skin away from my ribs. With my staff still in hand, I released a beam of light destroying the shadows and blasting her back. In one swift movement I bound her with some vines I'd produced from the ground and formed a cage of light around her. I couldn't believe it. I'd done it! I had her trapped, but now I needed answers.

"Where is Radius?" I shouted.

"If you're referring to the other crystal keeper, I left him in a ditch on another mountain. He was still alive when I left him, but you won't be when I'm finally finished with you." She swung her hair over her wings and squared her shoulders, standing tall. "The other royals were nowhere near as hard to kill as you."

I pointed my staff at her. "What are you talking about?"

"I'm sure you've heard about the darkness that hunted the elvish royals." She smiled from inside her cage. "Well, that was me. That last one put up quite a fight. I tortured her for weeks, but she never gave up the last royal.. She died protecting their identity … to protect you, her daughter."

I gasped, my legs almost buckling beneath me as her words hit home. "You killed my mum." My voice sounded small and high pitched like a child's. I shook my head slowly from side to side as I tried to understand what I had just heard. "But why? All the elves were living peacefully in the human world. I would never have got in the way of your plan if you'd left them alone."

"Because of the lizard's prophecy." Her eyes flashed with rage. "It's why I freed Kadon. It's why you have to die. It has been foreseen that the keeper of the heart will defeat the darkness and bring back balance to the world. I can't have you doing that."

"So, you thought you'd kill us all before we could be reunited with the heart."

"Exactly, but you eluded me. That's where Kadon came in. He was the threat needed to push that stupid council into finding you for me. Unfortunately killing you wasn't as simple as the others."

I crumpled to my knees. "You're a monster." The words slowly sank in … she'd killed my mother. My mother hadn't simply disappeared– she'd died protecting me. That entire side of my family had been murdered by her. She was deranged. All these deaths because of revelations from a lizard.

She cackled. "And you're a fool." Her body was covered in shadows, the entire cage filled with darkness, so much so, I could barely see her. Cracks began to appear in the cage. I held my staff up to try and reinforce the barrier, but her shadows were pushing against me. The barrier shattered and I was smothered by shadows. I huddled close to the ground, clutching my staff, channelling all my energy into the crystal. I produced a giant burst of light, cutting through it, just in time to see Humarya jump into the air and throw a kick at me. I blocked her with my staff and pushed her back, but she stormed towards me in a rage. I fought her off as best I could, but she was out for blood. In her mind she'd been so close to achieving her goal, and I'd ruined it all.

Her wing slammed into me crushing me against the side of the mountain. As she pulled it back, I crumpled to the floor, spitting blood from my mouth. Clasping my ribs, I took slow breaths, trying to remain calm. Shadows wrapped themselves around my body and everything turned black. I was done.

She'd beaten me. Finally, she'd be able to kill the last royal. Her hunt would be over and the lizard's prophecy would never come true.

"No," I screamed. Too many people had died because of this woman. She thought making me witness Daniels death would scare me off. The only reason she'd revealed the murder of my mother was to crush my spirit. I dug my fingers into the rock and the ground began to shake. Everything she'd disclosed only made me more determined. I wasn't about to give up. I wasn't going to die today.

I sent a shock wave through the ground. Humarya was knocked off her feet. Light shot from my staff surrounding the mountain disintegrating all of Humarya's shadows. I screamed as she bit into my arm. I fell to the ground as she let go of me, my arm bleeding. As she ran at me, I jumped up and smashed my fist to the ground. Everything shook, knocking her off balance. I was going to bring this entire mountain down if I had to. Rocks fell towards us as the mountain began to fall apart. Humarya struggled to regain her balance, trapping her wing. Here was my chance. She started randomly tossing shadow balls trying to hit me. I dug my hands into the ground and lifted the rock firing it at Humarya. With her shadows she turned the rock to dust. She spread her wings. She looked as if she was going to try take flight even with her injured wings. I swiped my foot across the ground. Two rocks shot up clamping onto Humarya's wing. She let out a shrill scream.

Magic surged through my body bubbling up along with my rage. I lifted my arms and hovered the massive boulder over Humarya. She frantically tried to free her trapped wing, her dark eyes full of fear. My heart ached with pain. I shook my head, dropping the stone behind her and the tremors stopped.

Humarya let out a high-pitched cackle. "You really are so weak. I murdered your mother and her entire bloodline, and you spare my life?"

"We do not all have a twisted soul like you, Humarya. You will be arrested, and a trial will be held. I have no right to play judge, jury and executioner. It's wrong."

"No, you just don't have the guts." She flapped her free

wing, creating a gust.

It whipped my hair around as I staggered backwards. I crossed my arm over my face as she blasted her trapped wing free. Humarya lifted her hand with a shadow ball but she didn't throw it. Instead, she fell to the ground and was tugged backwards. Water swirled around her legs and wings, creeping up towards her chest.

Then King Radius stepped out from behind a boulder with his arm stretched out manipulating a funnel of water.

Humarya thrashed about slashing through the water binds

Sweat dripped down his brow. He pursed his lips and his brown eyes flashed with power as he as he tightened his grip on the funnel of water. Humarya pushed a gust of wind at him. Sweeping his arms round in the air, he kept forming and tightening water binds around her. Radius gritted his teeth and planted his feet on the ground taking a wide stance. "We need to remove the stone around her neck,"

She jerked about, mouthing obscenities as she tried to escape the water surrounding her.

I ran towards her as she snapped at me, attempting to bite my hands. I crouched down, placing my palms on the ground. With a flick of my wrist, I wrapped Humarya in vines like a parcel, and then muzzled her with the dark green stems, to stop her biting me again. I took a deep breath and finally removed the stone from her neck.

I looked at the air stone in my hand, it glowed yellow and shadows danced with init. I could feel the darkness within it calling to me. It didn't want to be hidden away again. Covering it with my hands, I surrounded it in light to dampen its demonic presence. Without the air stone, Humarya's powers were weakened. Now, she could no longer break out of mine and King Radiuses spells. It was finally over. We had her beat.

29

Falling Wings

Mellissa

King Radius and I saw in the distance that the others were still back on the mountain where I'd left them. As I went to land, I realised I was coming down too fast. I hit the craggy surface and rolled into a rock. As if my body wasn't already aching this just topped it off. Radius landed gracefully behind me bringing Humarya with him trapped inside a water barrier. He was such a show-off. Harkura came to assist me, but I quickly got myself up. I didn't need any help. Radius didn't have any of his guardians running around after him. This wasn't the first time I'd fallen out the sky and it probably wouldn't be the last.

"Queen Mellissa you really need to work on your landing technique," Radius said.

I forced a smile. I didn't want to admit this was only the second time I'd managed to take flight. I attempted to dust off my clothes, but it wasn't easy. Humarya had ripped the side of my dress exposing my ribs literally as the bones stuck through the skin. A chunk of flesh had also been taken out of my arm and I was covered in my own blood.

"Are you both okay?" Lady Gabrielle asked. "I see you succeeded in capturing the target."

"Only a few scratches, but we're both fine."

Greg lifted my arm and stared at my ribs. "Mellissa, these are not scratches. You're seriously injured."

"Well, we had a bit of a tussle and she whipped and bit me, but it's all good."

Laxus peered closely. "They look nasty. You need healing."

"I'm fine. We should concentrate on getting out of here."

"I think you should let Gregory heal you first." Lady Gabrielle said. "I realise you're eager to get Humarya imprisoned, but it shouldn't take long. It didn't take him long to heal Harkura and the fairies."

I looked at Harkura and saw his wounds had disappeared. It seems Greg was a wise choice after all.

"It really won't take long to heal your wounds," Greg said touching my arm. I winced as pain shot through me.

I narrowed my eyes at Radius. It was a miracle he didn't have a scratch on him. I was so grateful to him. If he hadn't turned up when he did, Humarya could have finished me off and that would have been the end of the royal lineage. I sat on a rock and let Greg heal me. It seemed a tad indulgent. We had two prisoners with us. The more we hung around here the more we risked them escaping.

"How exactly are we getting back from here?" Harkura asked, "I don't mean to complain, but I don't fancy walking all the way back to Urbem Folium."

I frowned and leaned against a rock. I hadn't thought past defeating Humarya. Urbem Folium was the furthest place from here, but if we headed to the closest city by train, we could then hire a carriage for the rest of the journey. I sighed. Being unable to teleport made everything more challenging.

"It's my understanding that King Radius can create portals to any pool of water," Yuko said. "Wouldn't that be more convenient. We can all go to the lake near the capital and get Humarya jailed quicker."

"A perfect idea," I answered, relieved.

Yuko smiled at the sea king while batting her eyelashes at him. She was clearly in awe.

"We would need a body of water here to travel through, though," Radius said.

I looked around. There were plenty of rocks for me to play with, but no water for Radius to manipulate. He'd been able to produce water attacks inside Humarya's castle. There hadn't been any flowing water there. He'd created it himself.

"What if I made like a big hole and you filled it with water?" I asked, "So we make our own lake."

"Unfortunately, I can't create portals in water I've created myself," he said. "It must be natural not magically made.

There I was thinking water was water. I guess there were limits to what even he could do.

"What if I used my powers to funnel water from the clouds?" Yuko asked.

Radius rubbed the stubble on his chin. "That might work."

Yuko bowed her head and gestured to the ground with her arm. "If you wouldn't mind, Queen Mellissa."

I took a wide stance, stretching my arms out in front of me. I then crouched down and punched the mountain, cracking it open, and swept my feet across the craggy stone, making more cracks. As I lifted my arms, slabs of stone rose upwards. I stacked the rocks along the side creating a good-sized hole. Yuko spun her arms around pulling moisture from the clouds around us. Within a few minutes, the hole was full of water. I peered over the edge. It looked big enough to me.

Yuko placed her hands on her hips. "Does that work for you?"

"Yes, it was the perfect distraction," Humarya shouted.

She had somehow managed to escape the water barrier and partially removed her ties. With her arms still bound, she spun them around at speed creating a whirlwind, sweeping us all up in it. She ran at me, knocking me out with the spiral of wind. I hit the ground with a thud with her on top of me scratching at my face, and I felt her teeth bite into my neck.

Gritting my teeth, I kicked her off me and fired lightning at her. It was a direct hit. She went flying into some rocks, but it was too late. When she bit me, she'd managed to free the air stone and it had landed on the rocks between us. We both ran at it, but I skidded sending a ripple through the rocky surface and throwing her up into the air. I quickly grabbed the dark stone. As she came running at me again, she was hit by a funnel of fire and screamed as she went up in flames. Kicking her legs in pain, her face a mask of agonised horror, she tumbled off the side of the mountain until the sound of her shrieking slowly disappeared. I ran over to the edge. She wasn't anywhere to be seen. And there was no way she could survive that fall, burnt to a cinder with her wings still bound.

Harkura pulled me back from the edge. "Mellissa, are you okay?"

"I'm fine," I said rubbing my shoulder, it was bleeding. "Why am I the one that always gets bitten?"

Harkura shrugged. "Maybe you're more edible than the king."

I laughed, that was one way to look at it.

"Should we go after her?" Radius asked.

"There's no way she could have survived that fall with her wings still bound." Lady Gabrielle said. "but to be safe we should head back and have the army search the area for a body. In any case, at least Mellissa was able to keep hold of the air stone and we still have Emerson."

I wanted to search for Humarya myself, but everyone was insistent we leave. Even if Humarya had survived that fall and her burns, she'd no longer be a threat. Now, I urgently needed to get the air stone locked away until a new protector could be found.

King Radius dipped his hand into the pool of water. There was a ripple effect as a portal opened. One by one everyone jumped in. I shut my eyes and taking a deep breath I followed them.

I was back in my house. Stood on the landing trapped in a bubble filling with water. Kadon laughed at me with Matt's face. I couldn't breathe. My heart raced and my lungs burned.

This wasn't real. It was all in my head. I opened my eyes. Everything was dark and I was sinking down somewhere. I thrashed my arms about, but it just made me sink further. Suddenly, I felt someone's arms hold onto me as I was being pulled up. As we emerged from the water, I gasped for air and wrapped my arms around, Greg, clinging to him for dear life. He pushed my hair out of my face. "It's okay. I've got you."

Greg swam us to shore. We were on the edge of the capital. The portal had worked just as it should. This must have been how Humarya's power worked but in mid-air rather than water. Harkura helped pull me out of the lake. "I'm sorry, I should have remembered about your fear of this. It's just you've been doing so well."

I gave him a weary smile. "It's okay. I'm fine."

Soaking wet, we made our way to the council building. Harkura ended up giving me a piggyback after I sliced my foot open on a stray shard of glass. All that fighting I'd done in the mountains barefoot and it was walking in the capital that finally got me.

"Mellissa," shouted Victoria as we entered the building. She was sat on one of the benches in the foyer. Harkura lifted me down as she ran over and hugged me. My body went rigid. Victoria was actually hugging me. She held me at arm's length. "I'm glad you're okay." With narrowed eyes, she pursed her lips as she slapped me on the arm. "If you ever do something like that again, I'll kill you myself."

"Good to see you too," I replied. "What are you doing here?"

"Lee insisted on the remaining members meeting here to come up with a plan for when you failed. I had to cosy up to Hogan to get them to let me come."

I rose an eyebrow. "For when I failed?" Lee had some nerve. I didn't mind them coming up with a backup strategy, but his cynicism was typical.

"Can we talk about this in the infirmary. Mellissa requires a healer again," said Harkura.

Victoria linked arms with Harkura. "As you wish. I missed you, fellow guardian, nearly as much as I missed queenie.

I stepped backwards, shocked at her compliment. She must have gone through some kind of transformation.

"Oh, and before I forget." Victoria said, "here's your stone back. I much prefer being a guardian then a protector of a dark stone." She handed Laxus back the real box containing the land stone. We thought it would be safer with Victoria in case something happened.

The whole group were ushered off to the infirmary for a check-up, and everyone was quickly given the all-clear, except me. Greg had already healed everyone in the group who'd been injured. I was the only one who'd got hurt again. My shoulder still had a bite mark in it, and I had scratches down the side of my face. I'd also managed to fracture my hand without noticing. I thought it was just hurting from punching one too many things. Unfortunately, as it was a bone injury it was going to take longer to heal.

I placed a stronger seal round the air stone and handed it over to Lady Gabrielle to lock away. King Radius and the rest of the council went off to have a meeting about what had happened in the mountains. As boring as sitting in the infirmary was, unable to move my hand off the healing stones, it was still more enjoyable than going to that meeting.

Luckily, I had my guardians and Laxus to keep me company. Although, Victoria spent most of the time complaining about Lee being a snob and moaning about Hogan drooling over her legs. Harkura lectured me about my poor diet when a well-meaning member of staff brought me some cake, and Laxus teased me about my crazy plan. I could have cried from joy.

After two hours, I was given the all-clear. I couldn't wait to get home but to my dismay, we'd missed the last train. Luckily, I had my own quarters across the road in the council building. I'd just never used them before.

We left the infirmary and as we entered the council block, I was greeted by King Radius. . "It's good to see that you're strong and healthy again."

"What can I say, I'm accident prone," I said with a grin.

"You're also very skilled. It was an honour to fight by your side, but I must be getting back to the ocean."

"Thank you for your help. I couldn't have done it without you."

I put my hand out to shake his. Instead, he kissed it as he bowed. "Till we meet again."

I blushed as he walked away. Even if he did put me to shame as a crystal keeper, I was deeply thankful he'd come to help. We wouldn't have defeated Humarya without him.

I spotted Greg at the end of the corridor. I'd barely made eye contact when he lowered his gaze and walked away. I suppose I deserved that. He hadn't spoken to me since we'd got back. I guess now that everyone was safe, he didn't have to force himself to talk to me. It appeared everyone was stuck here for the night. Except for the dwarves who had tunnels to use. I needed to learn how to use them too, as this no teleporting thing might end up permanent.

We made our way upstairs to my sleeping quarters which was just as grand as the rest of the building, with its high ceilings and ornate furniture. There was a small sitting area with two bedrooms adjoined to it. One room was mine with a grand four poster bed and the other with two single beds for my guardians. Victoria volunteered to share my bed and let Laxus take hers. It wasn't the first time I'd been forced to share with Victoria. After spending 30 minutes convincing Harkura I would be fine as Victorira would be by my side all night, he went bed. Laxus had already gone to sleep. After what the two of them had been through they deserved a good night's rest.

As Victoria soaked in the bath, I found myself wandering the halls of the council. I didn't know what to do with myself now everything was over. We'd put a stop to Humarya's destructive agenda and had the air stone locked away. Harkura and Laxus were okay. I'd also rescued Den's family as promised. I should be happy. Yet for some reason, I was filled with anxiety. Humarya was still out there and despite a fate that should have ended in death, she was far too resilient for my liking. Lady Gabriele had dispatched her personal guard to search the area, but something still didn't sit right. Gwendolyn had also vanished. There was no doubt she'd find another way to cause trouble.

I made my way up up the winding stairs that lead to the balcony on the roof. As I opened the wooden door I was hit by a cool breeze that felt refreshing on my face. The flat white stone beneath my feet shone in the moonlight. There was about two feet of space up here. I leant on the metal railing surrounding the edge of the building. Looking out over the city my worries didn't feel as big. Everyone here was safe because of what we'd achieved today. I needed to stop focusing on the what-ifs and fully appreciate the now.

"I thought I might find you up here," said Greg walking out onto the roof.

I wrapped my arms around myself. "What are you doing up here?"

"I came to check on you."

"I thought you were mad at me."

He leaned on the railing beside me. "I was for a short while, but then I realised you were just trying to protect me. You figured out my mum was working for Humarya, didn't you?"

I looked at my feet. "I'm sorry I didn't tell you. If my mum had returned from the dead, it would break my heart to learn she was using me like that. I couldn't do that to you."

"Mellissa, stop," Greg gently tilted my chin upwards, so I was looking at him. "I understand, I really do, but I wish you had told me. Not just about my mum, but everything. I don't need you to protect me, I need you to be honest with me."

"What like you were honest with me? Would I have ever found out about your mother if I hadn't stumbled across her?"

He pushed his fringe to the side. "Fair enough. We both need to improve our communication skills."

I nudged him. "Why are you being so reasonable? It makes it hard to come up with a good argument."

"Because I don't want to fight." He sighed as he looked

out over the city. "I just need to know if you meant what you said that day by the fountain? You know about us not working in any form."

I looked up at the night sky. Stars shimmered above us. "Not really. I was angry when I said that, but you have to admit things have been strained between us."

"That's because we haven't been honest with each other." Greg took my hands, pulling me towards him. "All those months ago when I told you I was returning here to become an elder, you told me we were better as friends. Is that what you really think?"

"I don't know," I stammered. I hung my head, letting my hair cover my face. "I only said that so you wouldn't reject me."

"You are silly. I was in love with you even back then and my feelings have only gotten stronger."

My face felt hot like it was on fire. "What?"

He pushed my hair behind my ear. "You're the most gorgeous but confusing person I've ever met. You drive me crazy, but I love you."

I stood on my tiptoes and kissed him. And then he lifted me off my feet and I wrapped my legs around him. I'd told myself I was going to appreciate the now, so I let myself get lost in the moment. Just because I hadn't said 'I love you' aloud, didn't mean I didn't feel the same way as him.

Home

Gregory

Greg awoke to a knock on his door. He threw on a shirt and opened it ajar knowing he was still half-undressed in only his boxers.

"Did I wake you?" asked Lady Gabrielle, She was neat and tidy as usual, in a black suit and her hair pulled tightly in a bun. "It's not like you to sleep in this late. Is everything all right?"

Greg rubbed his eyes. "What time is it?"

"Half seven." Lady Gabrielle frowned. "Are you sure you're okay? It is all right not to be, considering everything that happened with your mother."

"Gwendolyn has always been a disappointment, so why would she change now."

Lady Gabrielle's gaze lowered as she interlaced her fingers.

Greg shook his head. "Honestly, I'm fine."

"If you want to talk about any of it. I will answer any questions you have."

"I know all I need, thanks. I understand why you and my father hid it from me."

"So, Mellissa told you?"

"No, I figured it out once I started thinking clearly. Anyway, I'm sure you didn't come to talk about Gwendolyn."

"I'm just making the rounds, letting everyone know

there'll be another meeting in two hours."

"Was last night's meeting not enough?"

"Certain members have complained about Mellissa not being present. She must explain her actions. It's a waste of time if you ask me, but it's in the rules."

"Are these certain members, Lee and Beatrice?"

She nodded. "And Ping. I have contacted Den and he's also agreed to come in and explain what happened. It should help shut the doubters up."

"Hopefully, it won't take long. I'd like to get home. My new chief of staff is good, but it's a bit much of an ask to have her running things this long."

"Don't worry, I highly doubt this meeting will run late. Anyway, I shall finish informing the others and talk to Mellissa about getting Laxus to convey his side to everyone."

Greg ran his hands through his hair. "I'll talk to Mellissa."

"You sure? I thought you'd both fallen out again?"

Greg shrugged. "That's all water under the bridge, but you know how grumpy she can be in the morning."

"I can never keep up with you two, but it's true, she is a late riser. Better she blames you for waking her than me."

Lady Gabrielle waved goodbye as she walked down the corridor, turning right towards Yuko's quarters.

Greg shut the door quietly. He walked back over to the bed where Mellissa was sound asleep. How she'd managed to sleep through that conversation amazed him. He leaned over the mattress and stroked her forehead gently. "Morning, Mellissa," he whispered.

She rolled over, pulling the covers over her head. "Go away, Harkura, I'm not running today." She was still half asleep.

"Hey, you, I'm not Harkura."

She popped her head out, her hair messily hanging over one eye. "No, you're not, but my response still stands, I'm not running today." She disappeared under the covers again.

"No one said anything about running." Greg sat down on the edge of the mattress. Maybe he should have just confessed to Lady Gabrielle where Mellissa was and let her deal with her. "Wake up and I'll buy you breakfast."

She immediately sat up and tugged him towards her by his shirt. "Or you can come back to bed and we can spend our morning here."

"As nice as that sounds, Lady Gabrielle just informed me that there's a meeting to attend and she wants you to bring Laxus."

"Hmm, think I'll pass." She laid back down wrapping herself up in the blankets.

"You can't pass on the meeting."

"Watch me. I'm not going to spend hours with that lot when all they'll do is have a go at me."

"How do you know that?"

"Everyone was debriefed last night. Emerson has been imprisoned and the air stone locked away. This meeting has been called because I wasn't at that the last one, so Lee will have a go at me for not following protocol."

She was spot on. "Okay, so Lee will probably still have a bit of a moan, but you can handle him. No one else is going to dispute what you did once they've heard all the facts. Which is why you have to bring Laxus with you."

She resisted as he tried to pull the covers off her, but she grabbed him, pushing him on the bed as she straddled him, pinning him down. "You know you could skip this meeting with me."

"You're such a bad influence." He smiled as she kissed him. The suggestion to spend their morning in his room was pretty appealing.

There was a knock on the door and before either of them could respond, Victoria strode in. "Mellissa put the changeling down, we have things to do."

Mellissa sat up in a flash. "Victoria what are you doing?"

"You and Laxus need briefing before this meeting. So, let's go."

Mellissa barcly had time to get dressed properly before Victoria marched her out of the room. Greg shook his head in disbelief. Her guardians really were as intrusive as Mellissa said.

Mellissa had been right. This meeting was taking hours. Laxus had joined them and explained everything, starting with his first encounter with Humarya and went on to explain how he contacted Mellissa for help, insisting she hid him. His story ended with Mellissa saving him and capturing Humarya.

Den also stated his version of things, confessing everything – how he'd had his fairies spying on everyone who had contact with Laxus and how he fed that information back to Humarya. He also explained that if Mellissa hadn't gone to the mountains on her own, contact with the Hawklings would never have been made. He'd refused to let his fairies search the area out of fear of what Humarya would do to his family.

Yet, none of this appeared to matter. Lee and Ping complained about Mellissa not following proper procedure. All Ping really cared about was that Victoria's abduction of Den made his security look weak. Lee, on the other hand, demanded she and Den were both removed from the council. Considering the meeting was going just as she'd told him it would, Mellissa was taking it pretty well. They'd spent three hours moaning about her and she'd sat there and said nothing. There hadn't even been a change in her facial expression.

"Queen Mellissa cannot be struck off the council," Lady Gabrielle said, "She's the keeper of the heart crystal, so we need her."

Lee folded his arms and scowled at her. "I don't understand why you defend her. She's been a menace since she got here."

"How can you say that? She's saved us all multiple times," Greg stated.

"You would be on her side," snapped Lee. "I don't see why she's awarded such leniency just because she wears some shiny crystal round her neck. She broke the rules. Therefore, she should be punished."

"I don't think that punishing Queen Mellissa will

achieve anything," said Yuko. "Can any of us really say we'd react any differently when faced with the knowledge there was a spy on the council. How would you know who to trust?"

"Not you as well." Lee moaned.

Lee was being ridiculous. Everyone else seemed to be able to accept the rules hadn't been followed for good reason. Why couldn't he let this go? He was clearly letting his dislike for Mellissa get in the way of his reasoning skills. Not that Lee ever had reasoning skills.

"Lee, why do you hate me so much?" Mellissa asked.

"Because you are a silly little child that suddenly arrived and was given all this power. You haven't earned your position. It was all down to luck," he shouted.

The entire room fell silent but Mellissa didn't flinch. All Lee had done was confirm something she already knew – that deep down, they all knew.

She clenched her hands together. "How exactly did you earn your position, Lee?"

"What has that got to do with anything?"

"You say I haven't earned my position. So, I'm trying to understand how one earns their position here."

"This is what I was raised to do. I am not some commoner pretending to be royalty."

"So, you earned your position by being born into a royal witch family. Sounds like luck to me. No different than what made me the leader of my people really."

Lee's face turned pink and the vein on his forehead bulged.

Lady Gabrielle clapped her hands together. "I think we should end the discussion there before you dig yourself into any more ditches, Lee. Any other issues to discuss?"

"We still have to vote on the matter," yelled Lee.

Greg put his head in his hands. What exactly was there to vote on? He thought he'd finally be getting out of here.

Lady Gabrielle narrowed her eyes at Lee. "Meeting adjourned." She picked up her books off the table and marched out of the room.

Lee stood opened mouthed starring at where Lady

Gabrielle had just sat. Seemingly, she didn't think there was much to vote on either. Everyone began talking amongst themselves until they slowly walked out into the hall.

Greg got up and wandered out of the room but was swiftly tugged away from the group. "Lord Gregory, how was the meeting?" Harkura asked with a way too sweet smile.

"Fine. Don't you usually talk with Mellissa about this stuff?"

"I just need to have a quick word." Harkura narrowed his eyes and leaned in. "Just to say, that if you become a problem, I will rain all sorts of hell down on you."

Greg tugged at his collar. He was starting to see what Mellissa meant about Harkura being a bipolar demon. Harkura was still smiling sweetly, but there was a fire in his eyes and a darkness in his tone. "I will protect her from anything and everything, including you, and if I fail in my duty, I will get revenge."

"That's good to know. Thanks for sharing," said Greg, feeling droplets of sweat trickle down his back.

Harkura's smile grew into a toothy grin.

Greg wanted to walk away but wasn't sure if he should.

Laxus skipped over to him and tugged at his arm, looking up at him wide-eyed. "So, where's my cake?"

"What cake?" Greg asked.

"Mellissa said if I came to the meeting and answered all my questions truthfully, you'd buy me cake."

"Oh, did she now." No wonder Laxus and Mellissa got along, they both only ever thought about food.

Harkura placed his hand firmly on Greg's forearm. "You should get the boy his cake."

A shiver shot up Greg's spine. Harkura was definitely scarier than Victoria. "Okay, let's get some cake, Laxus."

"There's no time for that," said Victoria marching over to them as she dragged Mellissa behind her. "We have a train to catch."

Greg looked at his watch. "Well, we better get running if we want to catch it."

Victoria looked him up and down. "That didn't include

you."

"The quickest way for you to get home is to go through Novosvillas."

"Whatever." Victoria pulled Laxus by the hand and pushed Harkura towards the door. She seemed eager to leave.

Mellissa dragged her feet. "This is all so long-winded."

"Get your lazy butt moving, Mellissa, or I'll freeze it off," shouted Victoria.

Greg took Mellissa's hand and pulled her along. "Hurry up, we don't want to anger Victoria."

"Victoria's always angry." Mellissa complained the whole way to the train station. Having to run for the train was probably a shock to her system. They arrived just as the train pulled into the station. There was a slight hitch as none of them had any money. Not being able to teleport was something Mellissa's guardians would need to adjust to. Greg scowled as he paid for all five tickets. He didn't actually mind, but he decided to make a point of it as Victoria had complained about him coming.

They spent the rest of the journey in silence. When they got to Novosvillas. Greg ended up buying them all dinner, at a local restaurant.

He was unable to get to city hall to relieve Mary of her duty as planned but it wouldn't hurt to leave her in charge a little longer. First thing in the morning he'd go into work and let her know the trial period was over and the position was hers. He couldn't ask for a better chief of staff.

Mellissa walked the entire way back to Gregs house holding Laxuses hand pointing out the different constellations to him. She'd gotten really good at knowing which star was which. And after the pressure the two of them had been under the last few months, Greg could see why such simple things excited them. Hopefully, life would stay like this for them for a while at least.

Greg woke bright and early like always. The sun shone through the curtains spreading colourful lines across the carpet. Mellissa lay beside him sound asleep. She looked so peaceful. There had been some benefit to getting stuck in Novosvillas; he'd got to spend an extra night with Mellissa even if he'd had to put up a few snarky remarks from her guardians.

Suddenly, there was a clattering sound from downstairs. Greg sat up straight. It could just be Harkura wandering about, he always seemed to be up early. There was another clanking sound. Something was wrong. He sensed an uninvited aura that shouldn't be here. Jumping out of bed, he threw on his robe and was downstairs in a flash. Standing in the kitchen doorway he snapped out his words: "Show yourself."

Gwendolyn stepped out from behind the kitchen counter. "How did you know I was here?"

Greg folded his arms. "You're not as good at masking your aura as you think. What are you doing here?"

"Don't be like that son."

She walked towards him and touched his cheek. He shrugged her off. "I stopped being your son the day you faked your own death."

"I don't know what Gabrielle has been telling you, but it's all lies."

"She hasn't said a word on the subject, but you have some nerve accusing her of being a liar."

"Gregory, please, I just want to talk."

"Talk about what exactly? How you're the perfect example of a bad mother."

She put her hand over her heart. "Just let me explain and you'll understand."

There wasn't anything to explain. He now knew exactly what sort of person she was. She'd helped the enemy. That made her a criminal.

"You should go."

What was he saying? He couldn't just let her go. He should keep her here, shout for assistance, have her arrested. She and Emerson could share a cell. Anything, but let her go free.

"Things weren't meant to turn out like this," she said. "I really wanted to make up for my past mistakes."

"Then maybe, you shouldn't have returned under false pretences."

She grabbed his hand. "It was the only way. Humarya promised to send me back in time so we could have a second chance as a family. All I had to do was help her find the pixie. If you didn't have such a close relationship with that girl, none of this would have happened."

He pulled himself free of her grip. She'd somehow made her betrayal his fault. So many excuses, yet no real apology. The facts were she'd put the lives of the people he cared about in danger for some crazed fantasy. Yet, for some reason, he couldn't bring himself to turn her in.

"Even if that sort of time travel was possible, given a second chance you'd still be a rubbish mother."

"You don't mean that."

"Yes, I do." Greg draped his arm around her and nudged her towards the front door. "You have to leave."

She waved her arms around trying to grab on to something so she could stay. "No, you don't understand the power of Humarya. Come with me and you'll see how she can transform our lives."

"I won't be going anywhere with you, Gwendolyn. Haven't you heard Humarya is dead."

Gwendolyn gasped, clutching her chest. "How can that be?"

"Mellissa and King Radius defeated her. She fell off a mountain in a blaze of flames."

"What!" She stepped backwards in shock, her face drained of colour. "This is all that elf girl's fault."

"No, Gwendolyn. This is all your own doing. You have no one to blame but yourself. Now get out."

"But Gregory, Humarya could still be out there. You have no proof that she's dead. If we find her, I'm sure she'll reward us."

"You have five seconds to leave or I'm turning you in."

"This isn't over."

"Yes, it is, *mother*," he said, his voice dripping with sarcasm at the word. "If I ever see you again, I'll have you arrested on the spot."

Her mouth dropped open as Greg began counting down from five. He opened the door and she ran out and shifted into a bird disappearing into the sky. Had he done the right thing letting her leave? Mellissa had been right to keep some of her plans from him. He was too emotionally involved.

Greg shut the door and turned to see Harkura glaring at him. "What are you doing?"

"Nothing," Greg said. How long had he been standing there?

"How could you let her go like that after what she did?"

So, he had seen what happened. "I don't know. I just couldn't do it."

Harkura grabbed his arm. "I meant what I said before … that if you become a problem … The same goes for your mother. I will not stand by and let you make the same mistake again."

"I wouldn't expect you to." Greg looked Harkura straight in the eyes. "You know, I'm glad Mellissa has you to protect her, especially in situations where my judgment is skewed, but know this, if it ever came to a choice between my mother and her, I would pick Mellissa in a heartbeat."

Harkura let go of him. "As long as she produces an heir before I have to kill you, everything will be fine."

"Wait, what?" Greg shook his head wondering if he'd misheard him.

Harkura flashed his hand at him and wandered off.

Mellissa appeared in the doorway of the kitchen rubbing her eyes. "What were you and Harkura doing? It sounded like you were slamming doors."

Greg pushed some strands of hair away from her face. "Harkura was just being overprotective, reminding me how he'd rain hellfire down on me if I upset you."

She poked his chest. "Too right and don't forget once he's done with you, I'll wrap you up in a vine squeezing the last breath out of you."

Greg chuckled. "Good to know you won't stand helplessly by."

Her lips briefly met his. "It's all right because it won't come to that, will it?"

He wrapped his arms around her waist. "No, it won't." Now that he had her in his arms, he was never letting go. She really was the best thing that ever happened to him.

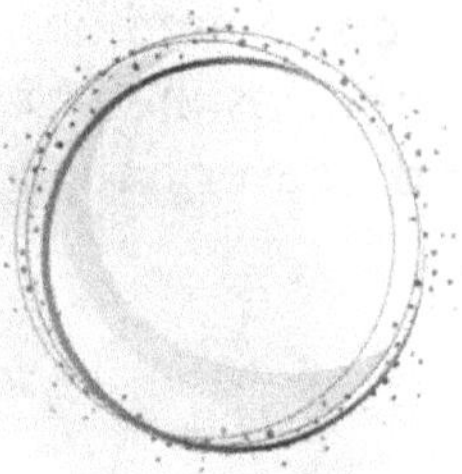

Epilogue

Humarya

Humarya clutched her side as she staggered into a cave, leaving a trail of blood behind her. Her wings were burnt and torn, her right leg broken and her abdomen ripped open. The mountainside was crawling with the council's army, searching for a body they were never going to find. Did they really think they'd finish her that easily? She may be injured and her power seriously depleted, but she would rise again. And that girl would not get away with destroying her dream. She'd been so close to getting the power she needed – to seeing her husband again.

She wedged herself between two rocks wrapping her broken wings around herself. This wasn't over. She would get her power back and when she did the elf queen would fall. She would make sure of it. It didn't matter how long it took she would have her revenge. She'd make that girl suffer the way she had and ensure all those she loved would be taken from her.

A cold breeze entered the cave. Humarya shuddered as she sensed a dark presence. She was no longer alone.

"Who's there?" she called. She may be injured but she could fight her way out. She poked her head forwards and in response, a powerful gust blew dirt into her face.

"Humarya," whispered an eerie voice.

"Who's there? Show yourself," she shouted, her talons

extending.

"Do not worry, I mean you no harm." said the voice

"What are you?" she asked.

"Thanks to the elf queen, I have no form."

"And what has that got to do with me? I don't have time for spirit creatures." She turned away stumbling into a dark corner.

"I can help you. I know how you can retrieve the air stone. And I also know where to find the sea stone."

Humarya spun round with a new fire burning inside her. "How do you know this?" This was too good to be true. If she had both the air and sea stones she would be unstoppable. She could have her revenge and her husband returned to her.

"Without physical form, it is easy to travel this world unnoticed. I know many secrets."

"Why would you help me? What's in it for you?" She had learnt you never got something for nothing.

"All I want is for you to use the power you gain to give me a new body. Once I am whole again, I would like the pleasure of choking the life out of the elf queen."

A devilish smile spread across Humarya's face. "I believe this could be the start of a deadly partnership."

ABOUT THE AUTHOR

Whitney Morris has always had a passion for storytelling. Growing up she loved to escape to into the fantasy worlds of magic from her stories. She is a cat lover with one of her own, is crazy about owls, and is addicted to chocolate.

Whitney loves books, and she and her husband are raising their four children to be fellow bookworms in South Yorkshire, England.

Whitney has a degree in psychology and uses it to make her characters feel authentic. Glowing Heart is the second book in The Life Crystal Chronicles.

Find Whitney on social media

Instagram	@wrlmorris_author
Facebook, BookBub, Twitter & Pinterest	@wrlmorris

Other books in the series:
Crystal Heart
Glowing Heart
Final Heart

www.ingramcontent.com/pod-product-compliance
Lightning Source LLC
Chambersburg PA
CBHW060544310726

48982CB00009B/1369/J